BOOK TWO: RIVER WOMEN SERIES

THE
Broken
STATUE

MARGARET LUKAS

BQB

North Carolina

The Broken Statue: Book 2 in the River Women series
© 2021 Margaret Lukas. All rights reserved.

This is a work of fiction. All of the characters, names, incidents, organizations, and dialogue in this novel are either the products of the author's imagination or are used fictitiously.

Published in the United States by BQB Publishing
(an imprint of Boutique of Quality Books Publishing Company)
www.bqbpublishing.com

978-1-952782-23-7 (p)
978-1-952782-24-4 (e)

Library of Congress Control Number: 2021941928

Book design by Robin Krauss, www.bookformatters.com
Cover design by Rebecca Lown, www.rebeccalowndesign.com
First editor: Olivia Swenson
Second editor: Andrea Vande Vorde

Praise for *The Broken Statue* and Margaret Lukas

"More than a tale of murder and vengeance, *The Broken Statue* is one visionary woman's quest for justice that leads her on a harrowing journey to darker truths, and ultimately to love. A wild read."

— Debra Magpie Earling, author of *Perma Red*

"Margaret Lukas's *The Broken Statue* is a crime story and romance wrapped in a gritty portrayal of early 20th-century Omaha's darker side. Lukas's historical sensibilities are finely tuned, her characters individually etched, her sense of dialogue pitch-perfect. She captures the banter that both disguises and conveys deep feeling as well as any writer I know. I loved her complex and sorrowful portrayal of Plum Cake, a brothel madam, whose journey down a simple set of steps toward redemption is a marvel of harrowing tension and suspense. At all its multiple levels, this is an intriguing and serious novel that makes us re-think our history and our prejudices.

— Kent Meyers, author of *Twisted Tree*

"A skillfully written novel, *The Broken Statue*, is a swift-moving thoroughly enjoyable tale that offers insights into the often-overlooked lives of the women of the frontier. Lukas's characters, many marginalized by race or circumstance, fairly get up and walk off the page into your heart."

— Karen Gettert Shoemaker, author, *The Meaning of Names*, Winner One Book One Nebraska Award.

"In *The Broken Statue*, Margaret Lukas continues the story of Bridget Wright-Leonard of *River People*, now eighteen and with her heart set on medical school. Instead, Bridget wakes up one morning to a murdered father and a stolen horse. Determined to get to the bottom of the crime, Bridget pursues the murderer to Omaha and quickly finds herself caught up in the complex world of an upscale brothel. With evocative prose, an engaging plot, and well-drawn characters, Lukas celebrates the resiliency and sisterhood of early 20th century mid-Western women, while casting an insightful and feminist eye on historic—and timely—issues of domestic violence, disenfranchisement, and racial injustice towards indigenous people."

— Erica C. Witsell, author of *Give*

"In *The Broken Statue* Margaret Lukas gives us a spellbinding look into the lawless gilded age; a world full of suspense, murder, prostitution, and redemption.

— Jeff Kurrus, editor, *Nebraskaland Magazine*, author of *Can You Dance Like John*

To Jackson, Sofia, Lukas, Molly, Stefan, Colin, and Owen

One
1905

The world drifted.

Beyond the old farmhouse window light crested in the east, spreading a glittering sheen over the foot of new snow. Tall grasses lay blown over and buried, trees hung laden, and the fence posts running down the lane looked as if each held a round, fat hen.

Bridget clutched her cup. At eighteen, she'd already lived in Nebraska for several years, had seen many quiet and beautiful January mornings. So why was her stomach jittery and the coffee she held quivering?

Behind her, logs burned in the stove and Papa Henry sat at the table finishing his breakfast, his third coffee refill. He pushed back his plate and rose. Wire, on his three legs, came from beneath the table, his tail wagging.

"It looks cold out there," Bridget said. "Shall I run and grab you an extra shirt?"

Papa took his coat from a peg by the back door, palmed his floppy leather hat, and pushed it low, covering the tops of his brown ears. He was a giant of a man to Bridget, though with his gently sloping shoulders and back, she'd grown nearly as tall.

"Nebraska's always freezing," he said. His eyes, surrounded by crinkled and leathered skin, smiled. "Least when it ain't hotter than Hades."

"The roads will be closed. Dr. Potter won't be taking his buggy out. I could help you in the barn and walk into town an hour or two late."

He nodded at her books on the table. "You got your work right there. Take my chores and I'm staring at a day of boredom."

"I could help hang the new barn door."

"Nah. Facing's rotted, need to tear that off. We'll wait for a warmer day."

She moved from the front-facing window to the back, watched dog and man trek through the snow. At seventy-four, Papa Henry was stubborn and content to remain so. He didn't have much time for the bother of people, white or red, and he saw no need to change his ways. He loved her fiercely, though sometimes that love scared him, and Bridget could feel the tightness in his chest clutch in her own. He'd loved his wife and son, but he'd lost them both. Now she, the daughter he'd adopted and loved, was all he had left. How could he not fear losing her too?

She continued watching the pair, Papa Henry with his long white braids hanging down the back of his dark coat, scuffling in tracks for Wire's use. She dismissed a sudden tugging at the back of her throat. He was aging, but he could still steady a plow behind a team of workhorses, pull fence, chop wood, muck the cattle barn, harvest.

Man and loping dog rounded the corner of the barn and disappeared, but in Bridget's mind, she saw Papa Henry stop at the double-wide doors, check that the long two-by-four he used as a buttress was tight, keeping the old door with its rotting hinges secure. He'd open the smaller side door only wide enough for them to slide through, and then pull it shut again, conserving as much heat as possible for the animals inside. He believed himself the brother of his horses. His four-horse team, their large, thick bodies and muscular legs, bred for labor rather than speed; and his two spotted horses, Smoke and a mare named Luna-Blue. In the spring, there'd be a spotted foal.

For Papa Henry, his horses, his dog, and his land sufficed for all the "churching" he needed.

Bridget sipped her cooling coffee. The breakfast dishes needed washing, and she planned to study before heading into town, but she couldn't pull herself from the blue-gray luminous light and the shadows the farm buildings threw over the snow. There were two barns. The second, three stories tall, Papa Henry used for carpentry. He'd built an ark there, a project he'd toiled on for years. Now he worked around the great vessel making coffins for grieving families who couldn't afford newfangled, factory-produced boxes. Or families who believed those caskets disrespected their dead. Folks preferring simple wood.

She looked past the barns and through a thin growth of trees several yards beyond to the silver band of the Missouri River. A stag appeared, having walked out of the water, or from between trees, she wasn't certain. She smiled. A second animal surprised her more. A third and then a fourth splashed coffee over her cup rim. A single male deer in mid-January, running across a pasture or along the road with a still-unshed rack, was rare. Though even then, she'd never seen a deer with such a large crown of antlers. Never seen one approach so close to the buildings. And never had she seen four seemingly conjured out of thin air.

She set her trembling cup on the sill.

The first animal reached the side of the carpentry barn and stopped. One by one, the others joined him, and then waited for the one behind. When they stood four abreast, they started for her. Their eyes fixed, aiming.

She sucked in a breath, held it burning in her lungs.

High stepping through the snow, they crossed the wide yard for the house, keeping their precise formation. Shoulder to shoulder, they might have been harnessed to an unseen sleigh. Guided by reins under supernatural control.

She dared not move. She wished for Papa Henry, even Wire to bark and prove he saw the impossible too.

She'd believed the animals fully formed, but as they continued coming, their bodies thickened, chests expanded, copper coats deepened, antlers swelled and swept to the height of elk crests.

Breathing was hard, backing away from the window, impossible. Her knees trembled against the insides of her worn dungarees. The animals held her as if they'd thrown out a line, roped, and tethered her soul. What otherworld prompting had sent them?

The closer the deer came, the more quartered she felt. Each stag taking his acre. They continued, hoofs punching through the snow, not stopping until they reached the window. The pools of their eyes locked on her. Eyes deeper than human eyes. Containers of deeper stories.

She found herself nodding, sure they'd come to be seen, recognized. "Yes. I see you," she whispered, though she had no idea what they meant her to take from the encounter.

The stags blinked, their legs stiffened, and their tails shot up. Startled as if from deer dreams, they turned, the white undersides of their tails flashing. In a series of leaps and bird-like swoops, they half-flew back toward the trees and river. Vanished.

Bridget's mouth felt full of dust, her bones brittle. The animals had wrung the moisture from her, leaving her suddenly ancient. They'd also left behind darkness that made her turn and look over her shoulder. A gloom waited for her somewhere close: on the stoop just outside, under the table where Wire slept, in the next cupboard she opened.

With unsteady hands, she began stacking the breakfast dishes, coaxing her heart to settle. "Nera, Nera." The words she'd so often used as a child. Wanting to summon the will of young Nera, who in Irish legend gathered the courage to save her people by facing the most frightful thing in her world: a red-eyed skeleton hanging in a tree. And doing the most frightful thing: stealing a fingerbone from the fiend.

"Stop," Bridget scolded herself. She wouldn't let a few deer scare her. She was grown now and would start medical school in the fall. That good fortune was incredible enough to warrant a visit from stags. They'd probably come to tell her not to worry, that she could easily make the grade and measure up to the males in her class. She knew that already.

She forced her mind off the deer and onto the day, weeks earlier, when Papa Henry returned from town with the letter from the board of admissions. As she'd torn open the envelope, he'd taken a chair at the table. Staying so close, she imagined that if she crumbled on reading a rejection, he meant to be there to catch her.

The interview with the board had not gone smoothly. The requirements for entry were a high school diploma, a command of the English language, and a strong moral character with a reference confirming the fact. She had the diploma and her six-page essay proved both her intelligence and command of the language. It was the third requirement—despite a glowing letter from Dr. Potter—that made the committee frown. She lived with an Indian.

"A savage," the board president had said, his eyes nearly rolling back to white.

"A young female," this from the jowled, paunchy man farther down the table, "with a *female temperament*." The last two words haughty with accusation.

"Unchaperoned," another said.

She'd kept her tongue, not fired back in Papa Henry's defense. Even now, weeks later, that silence continued to shame her. Afraid of rebuttal, she'd let the wind of their hate speech blow and what they assumed was Papa Henry's low morality go unchallenged. She'd taken her cues from two men who sat quietly but for their gentle reminders that since opening in 1880, the school had kept with the progressive model of admitting a few qualified women each year. Should such individuals present themselves. If they were to admit her, that would raise the number of females in the freshmen class to an impressive three among the nearly fifty males.

"Accepted on a probationary basis," the formal letter read, going on to say she must throughout the course of study "prove herself exceptional and above moral reproach."

She'd described the interview to Papa Henry in detail but not mentioned the board's disapproval of her living arrangements. She felt certain he believed all acceptance letters contained probationary conditions.

"I'm in," she'd cried, wrapping her arms around his neck. "I'm in."

Neither of them felt threatened by the restrictions. Of course, she'd act above moral reproach. And without question, she would excel academically. She would fulfill her dream of becoming a doctor.

When Papa Henry stepped back into the house two hours later, Bridget had not yet washed the dishes. She closed her book and waited as Wire tried to shake snow off his back and landed on his legless hip, then worked himself back onto his three legs. She waited as Papa Henry removed his coat and hung the thick wool on its peg. She waited as he palmed his large hat from his head onto hers, something he'd done affectionately every day for the six years he'd been her father.

"You'll never believe what happened." She hugged his hat as she crossed to hang it with his coat.

She told him about the deer and watched his white brows lift. "They were larger than deer," she stressed. "I'm sure they were tricksters."

He poured himself a cup of coffee and sat. "Some folks can walk into a thin stand of trees and get lost. Others walk into forests and find themselves."

That sort of talk—a hundred things implied in the subtext—

usually made her smile, but the volume in the animals' eyes and how they'd left her hollowed out haunted her. "The deer?"

He shrugged. "They didn't come to me. What do you think?"

"You interpret things all the time." She cut a slice of bread from a loaf on the table, used it like a rag to wipe grease from the frying pan. "A beetle turns around twice, and you're changing all your plans for the day." She leaned down to Wire, and when he'd licked her cheek, she rewarded him with the bread.

"Beetles visit me. The deer visited you." Though he seemed to refuse her, his eyes held an uneasy concern. "What do you feel they said?"

"I'm not sure."

He waited.

"I don't know."

He leaned back in his chair, his cup swallowed in his brown hands. "Nature acting different than it does: fish in trees, rain falling up, stags in foursomes. They are messengers."

A chill clawed across her shoulders. "Messengers?" Even though she'd felt the same, coming from Papa Henry the word increased her foreboding. "Can that be a good thing?"

"Could."

She thought of the animals' march forward, the winter sun striking their endless antler points, the fur on their pole legs, each foreleg lifting from the snow and striking down again, soundless. Even through the window she'd smelled their musk and the trees and the river they'd just left. The closer they'd come, the deeper that coming pierced.

Picking up her anatomy book, she hesitated, set it down again. What if she'd been wrong? Imagined the whole event or fallen asleep on her feet and had some kind of weird, waking dream. She wasn't getting enough sleep, studying into the late hours, and only two days previously, she'd spent dawn to dawn with Dr. Potter at the bedside of a baby dying from pertussis, the horrid sound of the toddler gasping for air after each coughing spell, sending the mother into a new fit of weeping.

She didn't have to get all mystical over deer, digging into her Irish heritage full of fairies and harpies, or into Papa Henry's Omaha Indian culture full of tricksters and animal spirit-guides. Deer were deer, and that was that.

She hoped.

Two

The walk into Bleaksville took Bridget longer than usual. Even in places where the wind had cleared the road, she refused to hurry. The first flush of mystery and disquiet from her sighting had eased, and she walked through a world lit with beauty. Snow and ice thickened even the smallest nibs on trees, grasses waved icy seed heads, and the fields lay in sprays of crystal.

Dr. Potter, in his mid-eighties, sat behind his desk. He'd been in and out of retirement a couple of times as younger doctors came to Bleaksville but left after a year or two, seeking larger practices in larger towns.

"Top of the morning." He added something of a nod and a pleasant enough grunt and returned to his task—comparing her ledger notes to those he'd written on a patient's card. A practice he enjoyed on slow days when no appointments pressed for his time and he'd caught up with his medical journals. He jotted corrections to her observations or expanded on her details in the margins she kept clean for him. More than once, she'd seen him add a notation to his records after reading hers.

She'd come to him the summer before with a stack of her anatomy drawings, hoping to so impress him with her knowledge and determination to get into medical school that he'd take her under his wing. If she proved herself, wouldn't he then write a recommendation? She'd arrived just as he was crawling into his buggy to visit a family with four little ones and the mother in labor again. He settled on the buggy seat as if every bone in his body protested.

"I'm too old for this," he said, looking down at her youth. "Get in. We'll talk on the way."

Now these months later, she'd yet to miss a day, and he'd come to rely on her. And slowly, so had the town, happy for her willing hands and the aid she gave Dr. Potter.

She hung her coat and hat, remembering Dr. Potter's reaction when she told him of her probationary acceptance to medical school. His bushy gray brows came together as he took the letter with a frown and rapped the sheet with a thick finger. Then he picked up his pen and circled the word *acceptance* so many times the ink marked through the word *probationary*. "Congratulations. This town is going to have a fine doctor."

The office door burst open. "Doctor!" Timmy Fester smelled of cold and fear. He wore a coat he'd not wasted time buttoning and was hatless. His nose and ears were red, tears streamed down his face. "It's Ma. She's hurt bad."

Dr. Potter rose with a catch in his hip. "Tell her we're coming."

Bridget grabbed one of his old gray sweaters from the coat rack, draped it over Timmy's head, and tied the sleeves under his chin. She reached for her own coat, Dr. Potter's bag, and hurried after the boy.

"Tell her don't move," Dr. Potter called after them. Bridget paused for any further instructions, but he shooed her. "Go on, hurry."

Catching up to Timmy, she knew her assignment: cover the four blocks to the Fester house as quickly as possible. She could run, keep up with ten-year-old Timmy, stand over Mrs. Fester, and make sure she received no additional injuries before Dr. Potter arrived. When they were called to farmsteads outside of town, she went to his barn, hitched his old nag to his even older buggy, and brought the trap around to the office. The Festers lived close. A distance covered faster on foot.

Mrs. Fester sat slumped on a chair by the stove. She moaned, cradling her arm and rocking in pain.

Bridget knew something of the Festers' story. Years of failed crops, a tornado that finally sucked away their last bit of hope, taking the house, barn, and windmill. Forcing them into Bleaksville, carrying only the few salvaged items they'd dug out of the mud, and into an abandoned house on the edge of town.

Mr. Fester, a man Bridget had met on another occasion when Timmy came crying for help, hovered close to his wife. His eyes were glassy. "She fell down the stairs. The woman can't stay on her feet."

Bridget dropped to Mrs. Fester's side—a young woman not a full decade older than herself. "Dr. Potter is on his way. He'll be here soon. I'm not leaving you." She lifted glowering eyes to Mr. Fester. "I'm not going anywhere."

Nearly three hours later, Bridget and Dr. Potter made their slow way back over unshoveled streets. Mrs. Fester's arm had been broken. After being sure the bone lined up correctly, Bridget had helped Dr. Potter wind on strips of plaster-soaked gauze. All the while, Mr. Fester paced.

When they'd finished, they helped her into Timmy's room and left her in a well-sedated sleep. With Dr. Potter repacking his bag in the kitchen, Bridget stayed in the bedroom to pull the boy from beneath his bed, hold him a moment, and promise his mother would be all right. She helped him make a pallet on the floor where he was to sleep the next week and gave him two grownup jobs. The first was keeping the secret he could only share with his mother: the bottle of pain medicine Dr. Potter was leaving. And the second, very grownup responsibility was to run back to the office if his mother's arm began to hurt too much. This was his assignment, Bridget told him, because his mother would not think her pain was worth bothering Dr. Potter.

Now as they walked through the snow, Bridget fought down her anger. "It's awful. That man's a monster." Dr. Potter hadn't asked Mrs. Fester what happened, nor had he threatened Mr. Fester. "He's got to be stopped." There were no laws against a man's treatment of his wife, no matter how callous. And neither the sheriff—absent from town for a month or more—nor the acting sheriff, Mr. Thayer, would involve themselves in the matter. But Dr. Potter? "Someone has to speak up, make that man stop."

Dr. Potter's cane left a trail of pecked holes in the crusty surface. "It isn't time."

"Last time wasn't 'the time' either. When will it be 'the time'?"

"I brung that man into the world. Watched him grow up. A good boy."

When Dr. Potter agreed to let Bridget work as his assistant, she'd made a solemn promise to him: She would not offer any medical opinion in the presence of a patient. However, they were alone now.

"You're the most respected man in Bleaksville. If you aren't going to speak up, who will?"

He watched his footing for slick patches. "If I had accused him, what of the next time? Suppose she suffers another broken bone, or worse, and he refuses my help? She needs to know I'll always come."

He was scolding her, she felt it, but the tragedy she'd witnessed gripped her. He was a compassionate man. That, she'd never doubt. Still. "You could do something."

"What do you suggest?"

They covered a full block in silence.

"Anger won't serve your patients," he said. "Judging neither. Nearly every case you'll see is the result of human folly. Diseases because of overindulgence, accidents because of carelessness. Hatred, anger, drunkenness. Take your pick. You plan to curse every patient? Or you plan to try and help?"

The question was rhetorical, and the only answer, silence.

They'd reached Main Street again. Bleaksville looked as idyllic as a snowy-roofed Currier and Ives Christmas card. For the Festers, the reality was vastly different.

Dr. Potter lifted his gaze from the snowy scene to Bridget. "Keep your eye on your medicine."

A brilliant doctor, he'd never been subtle with her. She admired him and owed him for his strong letter of recommendation and the invaluable medical training she received working with him. That didn't help Mrs. Fester. The woman needed more than a kindly old doctor. She needed laws. Dr. Potter was aging, growing weak physically and in spirit. When she had her license and the authority that came with it, she'd call out wrongs.

Bridget took the steps to the hayloft. The temperature outside had dropped further with the setting sun and even inside the barn she could see her breath and that of the animals. Still, the solid walls kept out the wind that ripped and tore the air outside. Though she rarely helped with the morning chores, she only missed the evening ones when she worked late with Dr. Potter. After a day of tending wounds and putting mustard packs on wheezing children's chests, feeding horses and running a hand over their powerful shoulders and haunches was her own hour of church. She pitched hay down into the long trough for Papa Henry's team, then crossed the mow to use the fork again and throw down for Luna-Blue and Smoke. Chaff fluttered in the lantern light like flakes of gold, but the sight didn't brighten her mood.

Finishing her task, she came out of the loft and took up the iron curry brush. She couldn't bathe Smoke—or any horse—in winter, but she brushed him in firm circular motions to loosen dead hair, and then used long strokes to rid it from the coat.

Across the barn, Papa Henry sat perched on his milking stool, his two braids swaying as he worked. He gave her sidelong glances but left her to her fretting. He knew she'd returned from Dr. Potter's troubled, and he knew she was sworn never to discuss patients outside of the office.

Mrs. Fester is in so much pain, Bridget wanted to say. *It's wrong.* She finished Smoke's grooming and laid the brush along the top railing of his stall. She held his cheeks and stared into his large, dark eyes. He blinked, his long lashes going down and up. His breath was rhythmic, wheaty, and warm. Deepening and steadying her own.

"There was a woman today," she told him, loud enough for Papa Henry to hear. Even omitting Mrs. Fester's name, she knew she crossed a line. "A broken arm. Her pain was awful. Her husband was at least partially responsible. She did everything she could to keep from screaming. Her little boy was there, watching."

With the cow securely in its stanchion, Papa Henry's hands worked two teats, a rhythmic spurt-spurt as milk gushed into his pail, froth rising. A line of cats stood close, waiting for the moment he'd turn a cow's nipple and squirt warm milk into each mouth.

"Once again, nothing will be done." Bridget choked back emotion. "Her eyes were empty. Like she looked into the future and saw only more hopelessness."

"Dr. Potter?" he asked.

"He thinks I'm too emotional. Too impatient."

"A warrior must learn patience. He must grow the power to let an enemy he cannot defeat pass. He must learn to wait, let the buffalo come close and the hunters get in place before he shoots."

"Oh, Papa." She gave Smoke a final pat and stepped out of the horse's stall. "You should have been raised on the prairie with Indian chiefs instead of on this farm."

"I read books, and my mother taught me about her people. I know a young warrior without patience must stay in camp until he is wise.

Until he does not desire fame but that his people eat through the winter."

"You and Dr. Potter. When I'm a doctor ..."

When I'm a doctor had become her mantra, the final thought on any discussion that ended without resolution. The phrase pleased Papa Henry as much as it did her, and pride passed over his eyes every time she said it.

Later, Papa Henry closed his journal and readied for bed, adding logs to the kitchen stove and to the hearth in their sitting room where Bridget studied. He dropped a hand on her shoulder, kept it there, brown and strong. "You get a good night's sleep. No need to push yourself so hard."

She patted his hand. "You worry too much. Only a couple of hours more."

She watched him climb the stairs, Wire on his heels. Having Papa Henry for a father made her rich. The farmhouse was old, and their clothes were rough—shirts and dungarees with patched elbows and knees—but thick and warm. Their table had plenty of good food, planted and harvested by them. They had stories and dreams and love for each other. Though only seven years had passed since she'd said goodbye to dying Grandma Teegan and boarded a train with other orphans, or half-orphans, those younger years of starving in New York felt a lifetime ago.

She returned to her reading and note taking. This ledger Dr. Potter would never see. She consulted a diagram in the anatomy book he'd loaned her and copied it, changing the drawing to match how she imagined the bone in Mrs. Fester's arm had looked. A thin arm, blotches of purple bruising, and a break across the humerus. She finished by writing detailed notes on Dr. Potter's process for setting the break.

She dipped her pen, touched the rim of her inkbottle to remove the excess. In the morning, she'd go, with or without Dr. Potter, and check on Mrs. Fester. Give her a woman's company. Until then, she and Timmy would hopefully have a comfortable night. Dr. Potter had left enough laudanum for pain.

An hour passed, two. Her head sagged, and she woke with a jerk. She turned out the kerosene lamp and climbed the stairs. When Papa Henry walked past her bedroom door a few minutes later, she'd changed into her nightclothes and crawled into bed with her eyes already closing.

"Where are you going?" she managed.

He stopped, looked into the dark room. "Horses are pacing."

"In the barn?" Even speaking took effort. Wire stood at his side, and she was glad to see the dog there. "You sure?"

"Old men are light sleepers. I'll see you in the morning."

Her eyes closed. She thought to say, "Dress warm, be sure to grab your hat," but she lacked the energy.

Three

Bridget woke the following morning with the sun not yet risen, but her window more charcoal than black. Her room frigid. She hesitated before leaving the warmth of her bed, then rushed to touch the stovepipe running up from the kitchen, through her floor, and venting out her ceiling. Cold. Mornings normally called Papa Henry, and he went down in the predawn to build up the fires. As the stove warmed the kitchen, the rising heat warmed her room. But not today.

She pulled on britches—a pair with only a single patched knee—and two flannel shirts. The now-empty hangers swung beside her only skirt. She'd need a few more for attending classes in the fall. Pants might be seen as unseemly attire for a female student and threaten her probationary status.

Before stepping into the hall, she stopped at her dresser and ran her hand down the sleeve of hanging red calico. Grandma Teegan's braid was tucked carefully inside, and touching the talisman a morning ritual. She gave her own hair a couple of brushstrokes, twisted it into a sloppy braid, and pinned that to cover the narrow scar running over the crown of her head.

From her end of the hall, she couldn't see inside Papa Henry's room, only that his door was open, proving he still slept. Given his late-night tramp to the barn and his age, he'd earned a morning of sleeping in. She headed downstairs.

They had a system for conserving heat in the house. At night, they both left their bedroom doors open, Papa Henry to receive warmth rising from the living room hearth, and she to share the warmth from the stovepipe in her room. During the day, Papa Henry kept his door closed to keep as much warmth as possible from being drawn into his north-facing room and out the old windows. Of the three upstairs bedrooms, his was the coldest. Still, he preferred that room. From there, with the soft glow of the moon lighting the yard, he could peer out over the paddock, checking periodically for the yellow eyes of circling wolves.

Alone in the dark kitchen, Bridget shivered again, struck a match, touched it to the cord wick of a lantern, and replaced the glass shade. She couldn't see more than a couple of feet past the window, but she knew yesterday's snowdrifts still whorled across the yard and the country roads. Too high for buggy passage. For the second day, Dr. Potter would remain in town. Only an emergency would make him saddle his horse, use a stool, hoist himself into that saddle, and ride out to give assistance. Thankfully, no women were scheduled to deliver for a few weeks and no old men wheezed alone and needed a tonic or the touch of a supportive hand. However, illnesses and accidents—even so-called *accidents* like Mrs. Fester's—didn't stay away because of snow.

Kindling filled a box by the back door. A second box held the short logs Papa Henry had measured and cut to fit the stove's firebox. Using the iron poker, she lifted the metal plate, added sticks, laying them crosshatched to allow for draw, then logs.

With the fire burning, she pumped water for the kettle and set it on the heat. Rubbing her chilly hands together, she eyed the eggs sitting on the counter. When Papa Henry walked into the kitchen, felt the stove's warmth, saw eggs cooking, and smelled coffee boiling, his kind eyes would twinkle and a smile would spread across his wizened face.

Folks in town likely thought them an odd family—elderly Papa Henry with his dark skin, white hair, and half-Indian blood, and she with her poppy-colored hair, pale skin, and Irish blood. But a twelve-year-old girl with no one else, and a kind man with no one else also constituted a family. A judge believed so too, and put his signature on adoption papers. Henry Leonard became her legal father, though for the year previous, he'd already been the father by every measure. She'd always call him Papa Henry, not just Papa, the single word too close to Pappy, the man who'd abandoned her to Grandma Teegan in Ireland and taken away Mum.

Lifting eggs from the basket, Bridget hesitated at how cold and heavy they felt. She didn't usually handle them first thing in the morning and never in a kitchen so cold. She shuddered suddenly, remembering the deer she'd seen the previous morning.

"Don't be silly," she whispered to herself. "Those deer didn't mean a thing."

From a can of lard, mostly bacon drippings, she spooned out a small dollop and dropped it into her frying pan. When the grease popped, she cracked in two eggs, the whites bubbling around the edges and turning golden. Tipping the pan to pool the hot grease in the lower curve, she spooned it over the tops of the yolks. The skin whitened just the way Papa Henry liked.

She took a long look through the door into the living room and to the stairs she'd used half an hour earlier. Though she tried to deny her growing unease, the knot tightened in her stomach. She slid the eggs onto a plate and dropped two slices of bread into the pan for grilling.

With everything done and the morning light brighter, she listened. No sound came from overhead, no weight creaked boards there or strained the stairs. She approached the barn-facing window, this time looking over the backyard. Only muffled tracks. Footprints half erased by the night's wind and a dusting of new snow. Papa Henry had not risen before her and gone to the barn.

Her heart kicked. Wire? Even if the cold and a late night caused Papa Henry to sleep in, where was Wire? He ought to be sitting at her feet, his tail rapping the floor, his eyes begging for food.

She forced herself to walk, not run, through the sitting room and past the cold ashes in the fireplace. The absence of a single red ember meant Papa Henry had not woken even once in the night to add logs.

The staircase, full of a new day's promise when she'd come down, looked shadowed. "Papa Henry? Wire?"

The blankets on his bed were thrown back. His shoes gone. Wire too. Trying to wrestle her mind around what it might mean, she half stumbled back down the stairs. Her coat hung by the kitchen door; the hook where he hung his empty. She forced herself to slow and take deep breaths. Papa Henry would laugh at her fright, or possibly be saddened by the fact that even after six years under his roof, she still felt so insecure. For how many months after moving into his house had he needed to come into her room at night, wake her from the same sobbing nightmare, dry her tears, and assure her she was no longer alone?

"I'm here," he said night after night. "Right down the hall."

She stepped out, winter's cold grabbing her. The barn looked half a mile away, not just across the yard. She followed the tracks she'd help carve deeper the night before. Crossing the windswept hoof prints of four deer, she nearly cried out remembering how they'd come to her.

She went on, running now. Just because she couldn't think why Papa Henry might have spent the night in the barn didn't mean there weren't a dozen reasons. Had a skunk or coyote wedged its nose in somewhere, gained entrance to the barn, and upset the horses? The night had been so cold, Papa Henry would have come to the house periodically to warm himself, leaving evidence that he'd been there: melted snow inside the door from his galoshes, a cold coffee cup, and the fires built up.

Meeting a set of horse tracks made Bridget stop and look carefully. They'd been made hours earlier. One horse coming down the lane to the barn and two leaving. She breathed easier; someone must have come for Papa Henry, an emergency requiring his help. Though why would he not leave a note on the table or wake her to say he was going? And Wire?

The sight of the broken barn door, the gaping maw of it hanging on one hinge, and the lumber buttress on the ground, threatened to sink her to her knees. No emergency would cause Papa Henry to leave the door so carelessly open to wolves and winter.

Wire bounded out of the building's shadows and jumped at Bridget's chest. She caught him in a momentary flood of relief, but he squirmed away, whining and scuttling back inside. She followed at a slower pace. "Papa Henry?" In the dim light, they passed Smoke's stall, the gate open and the horse gone. Farther on, Papa Henry's hat lay on the floor. Bridget's heart hammered. Wire whined for her to hurry.

Deeper still, the four-horse team huddled, their ears high, their tails tight against their rumps. She patted flanks, coaxed them to separate and let her through. Papa Henry lay facedown on the floor, two blood-soaked patches soiling the back of his coat. The hilt of his own knife sticking up from one.

Wire howled.

She dropped to the floor at Papa Henry's side, leaned over him, disbelief and shock wracking her with uncertainty, her lips an inch from his cheek. Barely visible puffs of his breath lifted in the cold air. She thought to run for Dr. Potter but couldn't make herself stand again. She needed to think, do the right thing, and do it immediately. Ought she pull out the knife, end the horror of seeing the blade in his back? Or would that open the wound more, cause more bleeding? Indecision screamed through her. Going for Dr. Potter and returning would take at least a half hour. Maybe twice as long by the time he dressed and saddled his horse. Suppose he wasn't home but called off to treat a patient? For all those long minutes, she'd be away while Papa Henry needed her.

"I have to go for help." Yes, she had to. "I'm going for Dr. Potter. Please, please don't die." She gripped his hand and cried out in anguish.

At the sound, Wire pushed into her lap, stood on his back leg, braced his front paws on her chest, and forced his head under her chin.

Papa Henry's hand, which only the night before had lovingly grasped her shoulder, was ice cold.

She lowered the dead weight onto the floor and let Wire push her over. Lying beside her father's body, she knew she'd not seen his breath. She'd seen her own breath bounce off his frozen cheek.

Papa Henry was gone.

Four

Sheriff Thayer dropped Papa Henry's prized knife onto the kitchen table. Accusation in the sound of the weapon's cold clang. Bridget flinched at the clatter, the knife still stained with traces of blood, though the smearing showed an effort had been made to wipe it clean in the snow.

Thayer tipped his head toward the knife. "That his?"

Wire sat on his haunches beside Bridget, his head against her thigh. She kept one hand on the dog's neck, dug her fingers into the dog's cowl, and managed to nod.

"You sure it's his? It's from wigwam days. Could belong to another redskin. You seen one of 'em hanging around? The law ain't got no concern with what red does to red."

She wanted the man gone. The entire morning—could it still be only morning?—was a murky swill. She'd ridden Gus, one of the horses in Papa Henry's team, into town. She'd burst into Dr. Potter's house screaming, found him struggling to get out of bed and pull on his pants before she reached his room. "Papa Henry's been murdered!"

For a moment, disbelief had clouded the old man's eyes. "Get the sheriff," he'd said. "I'll be along."

In Thayer's office, she'd screamed the same news but hadn't waited to see him rise from his desk. Running out the door, she'd heard him call in the direction of the office's two cells. "You boys slept off your drink? Looks like I need you."

She'd left them to locate horses. She ran on, slipping in the snow to the rear of the mercantile and to her friend Cora living in the back with her husband.

"My God," Cora had cried. "I'll get my coat."

She'd not sent her husband to the livery for her horse but climbed on the back of Gus. Bridget wondered now if Cora had done so not just to save time but so she could wrap her arms around Bridget and hold her through the ride back.

Now, Sheriff Thayer stood in the kitchen, glaring down, and Cora stood behind her, close as a hen ready to stretch out a wing. Dr. Potter, along with Thayer's two men, hadn't yet returned from the barn.

"You listening to me?" Sheriff Thayer's voice a near shout. "You suppose that's what happened? Another redskin knifed him?"

No, Bridget thought, *and you don't suppose it either.* Thayer, who'd been acting sheriff for only two weeks, didn't want to investigate. He likely had no idea where to begin, and the way he kept fiddling with the ends of his weak mustache bespoke his nervousness. Was it his fear of trying to arrest a murderer, or his fear of never finding him?

"It wasn't an Indian," Bridget said. "And it wasn't just a knife. He was shot in the back too."

Thayer pulled again on the end of his straggly mustache. "If this here is a redskin problem," with a gloved finger, he pushed the knife an inch closer to Bridget, "then it ain't mine. I'm beholden only to white. How you know this ain't red?"

Bridget's eyes burned. The horror of Papa Henry's murder and the loss of him came at her like bursts of wind. She was rocked, raked, pushed back, then minutes later it subsided enough for her to scrub her face and gasp for steadying breaths. Before the horror gusted again.

She swallowed hard. Thayer's badge, pinned to the front of his coat, looked dull as a flattened tin can. "It wasn't an Indian. No Indian is stupid enough to leave behind such a valuable knife."

He sucked at his top lip, exposing a gap in his front teeth. One tooth chipped, the remaining stub jutting at an angle. "The law's got nothing to say about a dead redskin off the res."

"Mr. Thayer," Cora interrupted. "I think you've made that point abundantly clear, but a man has been killed. One of our own. It's your job to find out who did it."

Bridget couldn't lift her eyes from the bloody knife hilt. She'd cried and screamed at seeing it in Papa Henry's back, but at the moment, she felt empty, the knife's lying there impossible. The first years of her life, she'd listened to Grandma Teegan's admonishment to "fight death." Papa Henry had not fought hard enough. He'd drawn a knife rather than a gun.

"As you well know," Cora seemed to place each word as though carefully stacking a shelf at the mercantile, the better for Thayer to examine, "Henry was not off a reservation. He was born right here in this house. You went to school with his son."

Thayer sniffed. "Ain't any of those matters. We got us a sit-u-ashun here. There's laws for whites. Chief being—"

"Henry," Bridget cried. "If you can't say Mr. Leonard, at least say Henry."

"Was." Thayer chuckled in Cora's direction. "Was his name. Dead now."

Bridget gripped harder at Wire's cowl. "Whoever killed Papa Henry took Smoke."

"Smoke?" His eyes narrowed.

She wanted to push him out the door, refuse to answer another question. "Our black-and-white-spotted stallion. You've seen him a thousand times."

"Horse thieving? Redskins love horse thieving."

"Mr. Thayer," Cora said. "Please. Show some respect."

He looked down at Bridget. "You got any proof a horse was stolen?"

A gale struck her. Wire whined at her clutching, and she moved her hand to his shoulder. "Smoke is gone. That's your proof."

"A feisty horse will run off given a chance. A barn door left open."

Acting sheriff, Papa Henry had said of Thayer, *only until there's a proper election*. Papa Henry hadn't minded the man though, had thought someone interested only in his monthly pay was healthier for the town than someone walking the streets looking to make trouble.

"Smoke didn't run off," Bridget said. "Papa Henry was killed, his horse stolen." Her voice broke. "The tracks. One set led to the barn. Then two sets came out. Side by side. Evenly spaced as train rails, the distance of a lead rope apart." She watched the shadow pass over his expression. "You didn't see them, did you? You and the two you brought out rode in right over the top of them." So had she, kicking at Gus's flanks, desperate to get help and return to the body.

"Oh, Bridget," Cora said. "We rode over them too. We aren't any of us experienced in crime scenes."

Thayer shuffled, a wet, slushy sound coming from the floor where snow melted off his boots. "Hoof prints ain't like a boot or a lady's shoe. They don't tell you a dang thing. You know anyone had an eye on that horse?"

Bridget shook her head.

He glanced again at Cora, his lip giving a single, determined twitch. "I'll get to the bottom of Chief's murder."

Chief. Most of Bleaksville referred to Papa Henry as Chief. Even Bridget had before her adoption, before he explained all men have names to which they're partial. Now, hearing others use the term hurt, reminding her of her own insensitivity and thoughtlessness. And making her think of Sheriff Cripe. The man Thayer replaced hadn't much liked anyone in town, thought them all country hicks, but he'd hated Papa Henry most. His list of racist monikers had been long: half-breed, braid, blanket. And the name Bridget hated most: buck. Said with a gyration of his hips, intended to suggest an animal rutting.

"If Papa Henry were white," she said, "you'd care about his death."

He looked at her as if she'd suggested *if dogs were kangaroos.*

"It's our country." His gaze lifted to her red hair. "White race."

The words cold and cutting. She'd heard the whispers, read the papers, and seen the cartoons. Negros, Jews, Chinese, Irish, Indians—all depicted in caricatures with features more animal than human.

"Cripe." The name flew from her mouth. "Your boss. He'd do it. Cripe hated Papa Henry."

Cora had gone to stare out the back window at the barn. She turned on hearing the name. "Mr. Thayer," she said, "please. Bridget doesn't know what she's saying. A father's death is a terrible thing."

A bubble sputtered from the gap in Thayer's teeth. "It ain't lawmen need looking into."

Cora squatted beside Bridget's chair. "You don't want to start accusing a man who could make trouble for you."

"Cripe would do it."

A man stuck his head just inside the door. "Freezing our balls out here."

"I know Sheriff Cripe disliked Henry," Cora tried again. "And I've never cared for the man, but he was elected. We need to respect that. Why, when he no longer has any contact with Henry, would he do something so awful? And Smoke is, what," she tried to keep her voice soothing, "eight or nine years old? If Cripe wanted that horse, he'd have stolen him long ago. Sheriff Thayer has a point, this does look like someone traveling through, happening on your place. Though," Cora looked pointedly at Thayer, "it's highly unlikely that it was an Indian."

Thayer touched his hat in Cora's direction and started for the door. "I had the boys put Chief in one of 'em coffin boxes. Law says redskins can't no longer hang their dead in trees or put 'em up on scaffolds. Civilized folks need them in the ground."

Bridget watched Thayer's wet tracks crossing the floor, the heels of his rundown boots, and the dirty hems of his trousers. The town's *acting* sheriff. "Wait." When he turned, she eyed him squarely. "Isn't all murder against the law?"

He sucked his crooked tooth. "A trial's needed to decide a man's guilt. And that'd be a jury of white men, all of 'em remembering Custer and his fine soldiers." He threw open the kitchen door to winter. "You best forget this here happened and study 'em there books. Cora done bragged to half the town how you figure on being a doctor."

"You're not leaving us alone?" Cora asked.

"Ain't nothing else to be done here."

"There's a murderer out there." She crossed her arms over her chest. "And tonight?"

He considered. "If I ain't settled nothing, I'll be back. Stay the night so you women can sleep. Keep 'em barn doors closed. Wolves'll catch a scent. Ground thaws in the spring, you can hire yourself a grave digger." He stepped out. "Body's froze up good. It'll keep."

Five

For several long minutes, while wood crackled in the stove and a slow block of sunlight spread over the kitchen table, Bridget sat with Cora, her head on Cora's shoulder. When she felt able, they pulled on their coats and walked arm in arm through the trampled snow back to the barn. They carried warm water and towels. Cora thought to grab a comb.

The body lay in a box Papa Henry had built himself. Seeing it there, Bridget couldn't immediately cross the barn floor. She went to Luna-Blue milling nervously in her stall, the horse's eyes showing too much white. The mare had heard the shots fired. She'd smelled the gunpowder, seen the stabbing, and watched Smoke being led away. She smelled Papa Henry's blood even now and knew the body was there.

"It's all right, girl." Bridget stroked the long face, pushed back the white mane from Luna-Blue's eyes. "Sherriff Thayer will find Smoke." Would he?

She left the horse and dropped to her knees on the straw-littered floor beside the pine box. Thayer's men hadn't bothered to fit on a top, and Papa Henry's gray eyes stared.

Cora knelt beside her.

"You've done this before?" Bridget asked. "Washed the dead?"

"It can be nice. The last moments with a person. When you are serving them."

Bridget dipped a washcloth in the water and wiped Papa Henry's cheeks. She'd kissed them countless times, but she'd never run an intimate hand over the wrinkled, leathered skin. She stopped and sank back on her heels. He was beautiful. The etchings on his face like the fine grains in wood or the ridges and veins in leaves. Only the sight of his staring eyes tore at her.

"His eyes," she sobbed.

Cora reached to touch them closed, but the frozen lids remained open. She patted her coat pockets, then the pockets on her trouser skirt. "I haven't a coin on me." She sighed, held out a handkerchief. "Is this all right?"

Bridget nodded.

Carefully, solemnly, Cora draped the starched and pressed hankie with its lace trim over the dark and frozen face.

Bridget's lungs heaved. The act felt like a burial. She reached behind Papa Henry's neck to pull his braids forward and lay them over his chest. Only stubble.

"Cora," she cried. "His braids are gone!"

"God save us! Why would someone?"

For trophies? Grief coursed through Bridget. With fresh horror, she noticed his hands were open, palms up. He'd frozen facedown, his fingers splayed. Turned over, his hands looked as if he wanted them held. His shoulders had been crammed into the box, and dirty boot prints soiled his coat front.

Wire leapt up at her gasp, stood on his hind leg just as he'd done earlier, and leaned into her. Luna-Blue whickered in her stall. At the edge of the haymow, two peering cats scurried off, knocking down loose bits of straw.

After Dr. Potter had finished his examination and returned to the house, Thayer's men, Bridget knew, had put the body in a coffin. One that was too narrow. Rather than look for a larger box, they'd stomped on Papa Henry's chest, breaking frozen joints.

"Don't weep over it," Cora said of Bridget's furious brushing at the mud. "He's at peace. Whoever did that hasn't disrespected Henry, only himself."

The minutes dragged into an hour. Bridget hated leaving the body again despite Cora's coaxing. She relented only when they both shivered and even their gloved fingertips stung with cold.

Papa Henry's knife still lay on the table. Afraid Cora meant to somehow dispose of it, or that Thayer might realize evidence should be secured and return for it, Bridget slid the blade into a drawer.

Cora added wood to the stove and in the rising warmth rubbed her cold hands together. "I'm afraid Thayer's in over his head."

"It's not just that." Bridget drew in a tight breath. "He doesn't care. And he's not going to question Cripe."

"An investigation doesn't need to begin and end with Thayer. A state marshal can be brought in."

"How? Who decides that? Do we write the governor, and how long will that take? And when he hears Papa Henry was half Omaha Indian?"

"I don't know." Cora stopped rubbing her hands. "I'm only saying justice doesn't begin and end with what Thayer decides."

The eggs Bridget cooked earlier sat cold and rubbery on a plate. She picked one up by its crusty edge and held it out for Wire. Then the second, letting the dog lick the grease from her fingers. Papa Henry had saved Wire, fishing him out of the river after someone cruelly wrapped him in barbed wire and threw him in to drown.

"Did you know Papa Henry thought Cripe caused this?" She patted the stub off Wire's hip.

Cora shuddered. "Cripe likely isn't the only man around who'd toss a dog into the river."

The morning before, Bridget had been in the Fester house. Though she hadn't cursed Mr. Fester, her looks hadn't been sweet. Had she so angered him? He'd suffered a host of hardships that were turning him into a mean and desperate man, but he wouldn't steal and murder. Would he?

"Many men around here," Cora went on, "could use the money a beautiful horse brought. Let's see what Thayer does. If his investigation goes nowhere, or he does nothing, we'll go over his head. I'll do as you say and write to the governor."

"And wait weeks for an answer."

"Justice is more important than speed."

"What if justice depends on speed? If even a few days pass, Smoke will be long gone. He needs to be found now, see who has him before he's sold. Sold again and again, passing through a number of hands."

Cora carried the plate Bridget had emptied to the sink and began to pump water. "I don't like that look in your eyes. Let men handle it."

"Even if they don't care? Papa Henry would want Smoke brought home. And Cripe—"

"Henry would not want you running off looking for a horse and a murderer," Cora said. "Think about your future."

"I am." She'd shamed herself by standing silently in front of the admissions board. She wouldn't disrespect Papa Henry a second time. "I can't live with myself if I do nothing."

"Writing to higher authorities, insisting on a full investigation, isn't nothing."

Bridget held her tongue. Cora and her letters. Before Papa Henry adopted Bridget, Cora had written to newspapers in states west of Nebraska seeking any information on Bridget's parents. A letter arrived from a stranger stating Kathleen and Darcy Wright had passed on. Died in Butte, Montana, of camp sickness. That information, Bridget knew—though Cora believed it like a Biblical truth—might easily be false. The letter writer may have heard about the camp's sicknesses second-or third-hand, the story mangled with each retelling, names added, others only assumed dead. Or a case of mistaken identity, another couple from Ireland having died that harsh winter. Or the letter could have been an outright hoax. Bridget hadn't seen a body or even a grave marker. With almost no memories of Pappy, it was easier to believe him dead. Believing it of Mum was another matter.

A letter could not confirm her parents' death, and a letter would not find Papa Henry's murderer.

Six

Dressed in her heaviest dungarees, Bridget paced in her cold room.

Thayer still snored on the sofa though the sun was nearly up. She didn't want to go down and possibly wake him trying to sneak by. Didn't want to see him at all, but she had work to do and a barn door to check. Yesterday morning, before Thayer arrived with the other two, Cora had helped Bridget work the large stone back underneath the sagging door, then wedge the two-by-four buttress into place. After a long, windy night, the door may have shivered off the stone, the cows needed milking, and the horses waited for feed and water.

From the bed, Wire let out an impatient sigh that sounded more like a whine.

"You didn't sleep either. Did you?" She scratched behind his ear. "I miss him too. If I'd only gone with him, I could have grabbed a pitchfork, jumped the murderer's back. The two of you would be out there now."

Seeing Grandma Teegan's braid hanging from the frame of her mirror made her think of the death space. Even as a very young girl, she'd seen the death space. The cloying shadow attached to the backs of the dying and swelled like a blooming black rose. People who rode by on horses or called out *hello* in the mercantile with no idea the horse would throw them just down the road, or the drunken neighbor would accidentally shoot them that afternoon while hunting a turkey. The curse—how else to view it—seized her only a time or two a year. Some years not at all. When she saw the maw, it took her breath, left her staggering. Why in Papa Henry's case, when she'd needed to see it most, hadn't she? She would have gone to the barn, stood over him like an archangel, fought off his leaving this realm and his entrance into the Otherworld. She hadn't, and the failing felt double. This even after the deer visited. If she'd understood nothing else of their coming, she should have known to stay aware, to heed the world.

Wire stared at her, and she tried to read his eyes. "You were there. If only you could talk."

She'd spent the night trying to imagine who would steal a horse and murder a man. She and Papa Henry both rode Smoke into town when the errand was simple and the bother of hitching the wagon unnecessary. Everyone in Bleaksville had seen the spotted horse dozens of times. His markings made him striking but not famous. He'd won no big prize monies, wasn't sought even for stud fees. No one outside of a twenty-mile radius likely even knew of him, so it made no sense to suppose he'd attracted a big-time thief. And locals? The whole county consisted of hard-working people, mostly farmers. Feeding, shoeing, and stabling a horse that couldn't be ridden in the open and was of no use in the field was too costly. Unless Smoke was sold and quickly, before he was seen. The nearest place to sell a horse was likely Omaha. There were other small towns, but in Omaha, Smoke could be led onto a train car and sent to Kansas City, Chicago, Denver. Once that happened he'd be gone for good, and so would the only evidence pointing to Papa Henry's killer.

Sheriff Cripe. The name, like a blistered heel, wouldn't leave her alone. He thought himself a dandy, a modern-day Wild Bill Hickok. Strutting with his wide mustache, his thumbs in his belt, and wearing a showman's costume years out of fashion, but an identity to grab and model when you lacked another.

Cora, still asleep in the bedroom across the hall, had made legitimate points. Cripe hadn't been around the village for at least a fortnight. Rumor said he was enjoying the pleasures of Omaha. A woman who'd taken the train in for a day's shopping claimed she'd seen him on the street with a girl "overly rouged."

"Busy there," Cora had asked, "why would he do something so horrific in Bleaksville now?" Still, who but Cripe carried such hatred for Papa Henry?

Bridget rolled onto her back, pulled Wire close, and remembered a day a full two months ago. The weather already cold, Cripe shouting at her and Papa Henry as they were leaving the mercantile. He eyed them, his chest out and puffing against his thick vest with its tooling of bucking broncos and border of silver studs. The tassels on his buckskin coat dangling. "Them's against the law," he said of Papa Henry's braids. His hairy mustache, waxed and flaring, like miniature horns on a miniature steer. "The commissioner of Indian affairs says you bucks got to cut them."

Bridget's hands had itched with wanting to reach up, break the wax of his facial hair, and watch the droop. He thought them a symbol of his masculinity while Papa Henry's braids were somehow an affront to white, Christian sensibilities.

That day, Papa Henry ushered her away.

"You want to live amongst decent folks," Cripe yelled after them, "you oughta try and look like us. No telling what might happen to a buck around here."

There was no such law concerning his braids, Papa Henry explained later, though a sad proclamation had been aimed at reservation Indians who seemed less than eager to convert to the ways of their conquerors. He owned his two hundred acres and would keep his braids.

She'd begged him not to be dismissive of the sheriff. Cripe could deputize any man, any number of men, a posse of dozens, to come and assist in an arrest. Like the murder of Sitting Bull only a decade and a half earlier, Papa Henry could be shot in a botched, or fake, arrest. He wasn't well known like Sitting Bull, but the story could be whipped up. Keeping the country afraid of Indians was a fire needing constant attention. Nothing else sold as many papers or riled as many citizens at campaign rallies. Shouting out over the heads of a nodding crowd how Indians threatened to cross reservation borders and overrun the country ignited voters. Politicians knew to find what frightened the blood out of people, add details that titillated, and turn the line into a catchy slogan.

The truth didn't sell papers; fear did. In addition, fear needed big, splashy stories like how Henry Leonard was a braid-wearing, thus lawbreaking, Indian living off the reservation. Fashion the story, tell how good Christian men exterminated a murderous renegade.

And Thayer? Would he put as much effort into the case as he did into his snoring?

The bang of the back door made Bridget ease out a breath she felt she'd held all night. *Finally.* The man was leaving.

Cora stepped into the doorway. "He's gone. Did you sleep at all?"

"Did you?"

"People fuss too much over sleep." Cora shrugged. She'd let her hair down for bed and now scooped it up whole, twisted it a couple of times, and began putting in her pins. "I need to fix my husband's breakfast. He can run a mercantile, but he can't fry an egg or pour himself a cup of coffee." She gave Bridget a second smile, this one sad. "Will you be all right for a few hours?"

I'll never be all right. She knew what she had to do. "I've got the chores. I'll be busy. You don't need to rush back."

"I'll hurry and help you."

"Please don't. Take my chores, and I'm staring at a day of boredom. I need the extra work to fill the hours." Did she sound convincing? "You'll be back tonight, though? You'll sleep here again?"

"As many nights as you'll let me."

From Papa Henry's bedroom window, Bridget watched Cora in her winter clothes walk to the barn. The track was wide now and well trampled, but either side and to the river and beyond, the world looked crisp. So clean it had to be make-believe. She felt she could poke a finger through the chimera and have it all tinkle down like thin, broken glass.

In this world, even in its beauty, Death could snap fingers and pluck a soul.

Late the evening before, Cora's husband had brought out her horse, but Bridget imagined her first kneeling a moment at Papa Henry's box, dirtying the knees of her wide-legged skirt again. Then she'd go to Luna-Blue and stroke the horse's muzzle before throwing a saddle over her own horse.

When Cora rode down the lane, Bridget forced herself from the window. It was time.

She took the stairs slowly, sliding her hand along the railing. Papa Henry had gripped the same wood from the time he'd been tall enough to reach it. His father had built the house in 1818, hewn the mantle, fashioned the windows looking out on the river. Here the elder Mr. Leonard had brought his wife, an Omaha Indian. At the time, white women were scarce in the territory, and men's needs for helpmates gave Indian women a modicum of acceptance. As more and more white females arrived, or came of marriageable age, darker skinned women were pushed aside. Seen as having served their purpose.

Papa Henry's father had not done so. He loved his wife, and they remained married until he died. They raised their son in the house. After Henry grew, he married and lived there with his own wife and son. Until tragedy struck. The boy drowning and the wife lifting off and away like weightless thistle in the wind of heartache.

Now Papa Henry's desk, the chairs, the kitchen table with its lantern—all seemed only props on an abandoned stage.

She'd let Papa Henry down when she'd stood in front of the medical school's admission's board. Stood there placid, mute. She'd let Papa Henry down, allowing him to go alone to the barn, even though she'd known some ruckus mattered enough to drag an elderly man out of bed and into a winter night.

She let Wire out to do his business, her mind flipping through tasks to complete before leaving. At some point in the night, it had become obvious to her: she had to find Smoke.

Seven

In the barn, Bridget sank again to the dirt floor beside Papa Henry's body. She tried to imagine him only asleep beneath the handkerchief. Or his wizened face smiling at her and saying, "Daughter."

She laced her fingers through his. His frozen, upturned hands, so like the picture she'd seen of Spotted Elk's hands. The Lakota Chief murdered at Wounded Knee. And when she could speak again, she promised him, "I'll bring Smoke home."

She used a dozen nails more than necessary, making sure each went in straight despite how tears blurred her vision. Any nail hit at an angle and protruding irregularly, she pulled out and drove in again.

"Nothing to be done until spring," Thayer had said.

She gathered the eggs, brought in the two milk cows, relieved them of their bulging bags, poured milk in pans for the cats, mucked Luna-Blue's stall, put a measured amount of oats in her trough, pitched down fresh hay, dumped out the frozen block of water in her bucket, and refilled it at the pump in the yard. The water would freeze again, but Cora would return before nightfall. She'd find a note on the table and know to feed and water the horses.

"I won't be long," she told Luna-Blue. "Only a day, maybe two." Did a horse know truth from hope?

She stepped out.

"Top of the morning."

She jumped. Dr. Potter had come down the lane, ridden past the house and on to the barn.

"Top of the morning to you too," she said.

He wore a long wool scarf wrapped around his neck and up to his nose and ears. He peered at her over the top. "You all right?"

"I'm fine." He'd not dismounted and, seeing her in the paddock and working, not curled up somewhere sobbing, she knew he wouldn't. He'd need a chair brought out again in order to get back in the saddle.

"Roads are pretty bad," he said.

"Have you seen Mrs. Fester this morning?" she asked.

"Can't make a woman in this town stay in bed." His horse shifted one front leg then the other. "Whoa now." He gave the reins a quick tug to get the nag's attention. He turned stiffly, as though his head, neck, and shoulders were one fused block, and looked back at the house. The empty yard and lane made his eyes narrow. "Folks will be along to pay their respects. I imagine they're finishing up their own chores, making you casseroles, baking you pies."

He thought he offered reassurances, but his words increased her urgency; she needed to get on the road. She wouldn't lose a day, stopped by well-wishers.

"Thanks for riding out. If I can expect visitors, then I'd better finish these chores. You're welcome to wait at the house." *Please don't accept the offer.*

"What you planning for the body?"

The question struck hard. Her heart rocked and sought balance.

"You don't want to move it inside," Dr. Potter said. "You're not thinking that?" Even through the layers of wool, she heard how he hated having to ask. "He doesn't need a change of clothes. Henry would tell you himself. Ain't a man ever shit in the woods who cares about that nonsense." He paused, sat his horse. Studied her. "Now, if you ain't listening and think something more needs done, I'll stop by and see the undertaker. He'd do the fussing and put in some of that embalming fluid."

Bridget shuddered. Papa Henry had loathed the idea of embalming: "Filling a body full of poison, keeping a spirit from finding the red road."

"The body is fine," Bridget said. She couldn't have the undertaker coming for it when she was gone.

"It ain't a pleasant thing to think about."

"My chores." She lifted the bucket high. "If you say well-wishers are on their way."

"All right then." His rheumy eyes blinked against the cold. "You need anything, you know where to find me."

She watched him ride half the distance of the lane before she pulled herself away, emptied her bucket, walked among Papa Henry's team, and stroked their flanks. Which horse ought she ride into Omaha? She couldn't take Luna-Blue. The distance might be too much, the risk too great for her and her foal. On top of that, Luna-Blue was also a beauty, as striking as Smoke. Her black spots outlined sharply on her linen-white coat. A temptation to horse thieves; a complication Bridget couldn't hazard.

The sun tipped past midday. A well-wisher might arrive at any time, keeping her.

Hurrying back to the house, she put on a second pair of socks and trousers. Papa Henry had shown her a strongbox in the back of his closet. Additional money was hidden in tin cans under the floorboards beneath his bed. She'd need just a couple of nights lodging for herself and stable fees. If she couldn't find Smoke by then, she'd know she'd lost him.

Please take care of the animals and Wire. She scribbled a note to Cora. *I'll be back in . . .* She hesitated. *Three days.* Better to over-estimate so Cora wouldn't be watching the lane.

Grabbing Papa Henry's knife from the drawer, Bridget's heart sank again. When going out to work for the day, he'd often worn the knife on his hip. A tool for pulling out burrs, cutting leather or rope, slicing an apple for a horse, prying open walnuts, even digging slivers out of his thumb.

Using the tip of the blade, she made a slit in her coat lining and buried the steel in the thick batting. Only the hilt was left exposed— chest high and easy to grab. The thought of using the weapon to defend herself was scary, but that scenario was unlikely. She'd never held a gun, and though Papa Henry had one in the barn and one upstairs, she knew nothing about handling them. Holding a knife at least felt familiar; she cleaned chickens and chopped vegetables. This knife, as much as anything, was a talisman.

The need to hurry rode heavier on her shoulders and shouted in her ears, reminding her that if Smoke were sold or shipped off before she found him, her only link to the killer would be lost. She rarely went to Omaha, and she always rode the train. Not this time. The evening train was hours away and going to the station meant any number of people could see and stop her.

"Nera, Nera," she coached herself. Nera, the mythic heroine of Grandma Teegan's story, had faced her skeleton, faced the red eyes in their sockets and the bones that came alive, clambered out of the branches, and followed her. The story was meant to inspire bravery and warned that all actions had consequences; a person needed the courage to survive the chase of skeletal bones.

Inaction, Bridget knew, also had consequences.

At Papa Henry's desk, she reached for his current ledger. Several more lined the shelf behind the desk, and decades more were wrapped in oilcloth and boxed in the cellar. They contained everything from how to prevent worms from climbing the apple trees to treating calves for scours and checking a horse's teeth and shoes. Unlike her journals, his had figures running in rows and columns. Like her journals, his also had sketches: the cut and spread of the Missouri River as it snaked back and forth; the orchard with the fruit trees labeled; detailed drawings of Luna-Blue and Smoke.

Keeping the farm and making it flourish had been Papa Henry's stand against the land theft and genocide inflicted on the Omaha and all the tribes. Keeping the land, he'd believed, kept open a door for other Natives: past and future generations. He'd not seen time as linear, but cyclical, and he'd believed his ancestors were pleased by his farm. Future generations too, though they'd never walk his acres, would profit from the stand he'd maintained. The spiritual space his land kept open.

"I'm going to be a doctor," she'd told him each time he opened a ledger to explain some accounting or method and set it over the top of one of her books. She hadn't wanted to know about wheat crops; she wanted to be more than a farmer, to prove to her parents—or was it only to herself?—that they'd erred in leaving her behind.

Though she had no idea how she'd manage the farm, the daughter wouldn't become the wife, wouldn't succumb to sorrow and drift away. Nor would she give up her medical school dreams.

Opening the ledger, she thumbed and found an exact drawing of Smoke. Down to the number, size, and placement of his spots. She'd recognize him anywhere, but here was a picture a newspaper could print, or the police could use for identification. It wouldn't take long for cops to ride up and down the streets of the lower ward and check the half dozen or so liveries there. If they found nothing, she'd go to the newspapers, have a drawing printed, and get so many people informed that if the murderer was in Omaha, he couldn't escape.

She tucked the book inside the front waist of her britches, pulled her coat over the top, and hurried back to the paddock.

She'd seen Papa Henry work the team, holding two sets of reins in each large hand, threading the leather through his strong fingers, controlling each of the four horses separately, but she could hardly handle one. She eyed Gus, the off horse in the lead pair. The previous morning she'd ridden him to town and sounded the alarm. He'd been deplorably slow, and they'd gone only a quarter mile when she'd cursed herself for not having taken off on foot. But panic had locked her knees, and she'd trusted him more than herself. Despite his lack of speed, he'd been gentle and easy to handle. Gus's partner was a horse of the same height and build. "Temperament and intelligence need to be matched in a pair," Papa Henry had said of the twosome. "Same as the length of their strides and the heights of their withers."

Choosing Gus for the second time didn't seem fair to him, but he'd acted gallantly the morning before. Going the mile alone was one thing. The nearly twenty miles into Omaha without his normal harness and the structure of his companions was entirely different.

She ran a hand down his long muzzle, saw tension in his eyes. He too had witnessed the scene in the barn, and he remembered how frantic and upset she'd been the last time on his back. "Easy. Easy, boy."

Gus tossed his head, refusing to accept the bit. No saddle fit him, but she needed reins. Yesterday, she'd been so distracted, she could scarcely remember sliding iron between his teeth. She must have. Had Gus also been so distracted he'd not noticed her doing so?

She tried again. "Gus, please." His teeth clamped. "Gus," she cried, and let the bit drop and hang at her side. "Help me."

With his next refusal, he added a second toss of his massive head.

She stepped back, her frustration threatening to bring tears. There was no choice. She had to go. Gus had to take her.

She took a deep breath. She'd seen Papa Henry handle the horses enough times. He stood directly in front of them, not at a cheek, and not coaxing or demanding obedience. He commanded respect.

"Gus." She stepped in front of him and pulled back her shoulders.

He planted his front legs and stared down at her with large eyes.

She lifted the bit and, pretending more confidence than she felt, pushed the snaffle against his lips. "Take it," she said. He set his lips, and she pushed firmer, not backing down, not accepting less of herself. "This isn't about what either of us wants. This is what has to be." She pressed again.

His lips parted, his teeth opened, and the iron was in. She sighed and dropped her forehead onto his nose. "Thank you."

Eight

Riding down the lane, Bridget yelled for Wire to stay, but the dog loped stubbornly alongside. She'd knelt to him. "I'm not leaving you. I'll be back in two or three days." He hadn't understood, and with Papa Henry gone too, she wanted to dismount and pull him into her lap for her comfort as well as his. She wouldn't give into the weakness. Wouldn't risk him to the long, cold ride.

They reached the end of the lane, Wire panting. "Stay!" She raised her arm, pointed at him. "Stay!"

He whined but dropped back on his haunches with sorrowful looking eyes.

"Stay with Papa Henry," she said. *Don't let anyone open his box and take pictures.* "Stay with him."

The road was empty. The shortest route into Omaha meant crossing Nettle Creek—frozen solid this time of year—and going through Bleaksville. She couldn't risk riding past the sheriff's office with Thayer twiddling his thumbs behind his desk, staring out. Or past the mercantile's big windows, with the possibility of Cora or her husband glancing up.

"This way." She turned Gus the other direction, where the road's lazy curve swung out and around, adding an hour of riding. She guessed the killer took the same route with Smoke. She'd scan pastures and barnyards along the route, look every stranger she met in the eye.

Wire still whined, but each time she looked back he'd grown smaller. Behind him, the aging house and barns lay like receding treasures.

She rode with the company of trees lining the road. Giants against the winter sky, their arms outstretched, the Missouri River blinking in bright snatches through the gaps of their trunks. She passed the cut leading off the road. A deer trail. A girl trail. Down there, Old Mag was always waiting in a small clearing. The cove where the massive felled oak lay, made a resting, hiding, dreaming place. Since working with Dr. Potter, she spent fewer afternoons there than she had as a child, but she still found time to visit her friend. After this trip to Omaha, she'd spend an afternoon telling Old Mag about Papa Henry's death.

Farther on, the incline down to the Missiouri River grown steeper, lay the huddled remains of the burned-out cabin. Half covered by snow, the still ashy-looking shell made her lift her heels and urge Gus to hurry on. Before Papa Henry's rescue, she'd lived there a year, labeled one of the "river people." How she'd struggled, all but abandoned on the spit of bottom ground by Rev. Jackdaw, the preacher who'd signed papers on her when she first stepped off the orphan train from New York. Rev. Jackdaw, the self-ordained preacher who'd made her and her adopted mother's lives a hell on earth.

The two-mile stretch of trees ended, the land turning to flat, snow-covered pastures and stubbled fields. She rode on. Twice over the next hours, she needed to dismount, pull and plead Gus through knee-high drifts. She feared leaving the roads and going around the obstacles, possibly not finding her way back, dying lost and wandering in a field. Feared leading Gus into a deceptive ditch, his bulk sinking chest high. Impossible to dig out.

Hours of an empty, white world, cold seeping into her bones.

She knew exactly where to go. Omaha's famous sporting district. Everyone in the state, and many in surrounding states, had heard of the place. Cripe wouldn't be up along the Gold Coast in the rich neighborhoods, he'd be in the thick of the city's growth, downtown with the big banks, posh restaurants, stores, hotels. The nightlife with its myriad gambling houses and brothels. She'd shopped in the stores with Cora, visited the library, even the courthouse where she'd watched Papa Henry sign adoption papers. She estimated the hub was no more than ten blocks by ten blocks.

By the time the sun finished its slow track across the sky and sank, she'd gone through shivering into shaking. She'd not given enough attention to what surviving the cold would take. She ought to have worn more layers, grabbed a long sheet of oilcloth to tent over her shoulders and legs, even drape over Gus's back to help him. Instead, she'd been distracted by the need to hurry the chores, blinded by loss and anger and the dread of going.

Estimating the time it would take, she'd imagined about five hours of Gus's steady walking. Surely, they'd already been exposed for longer. She was exhausted and fought to keep upright, keep her eyes open. Time was a trickster, the hours looping and spiraling in long tails, avoiding capture and measure. Every hour she'd been in the cold, her body had expended large amounts of energy trying to keep warm. She leaned down, so cold even patting Gus's neck took effort. "Good boy." She wanted to say *I'm sorry*, but the darkness and a deepening fear kept her still. Suppose Gus heard the panic in her voice, started acting up?

Papa Henry had schooled her: A horse loitering in the paddock, drawing in slow, casual breaths suffered no harm in cold temperatures. He never strained his horses in severe weather though, forcing them to draw quick, frigid breaths. He would never have taken Gus on such a trek in the bitter cold.

She passed landmarks recognizable even in the dark, the Florence Mill and Lake Nakoma. They were nearly there, but she needed to find warmth now.

She swayed over Gus's shoulder, nearly fell, and jerked awake with her heart pounding. She couldn't fall asleep again. If she lost her seating, she wouldn't have the strength to climb back up; she and Gus would both freeze. At times, the possibility sounded like promise. She tried to force herself out of her slouch. Could not. Her lungs burned. Her limbs were numb and at the same time on fire.

The size of the large, dark buildings—some as high as ten stories— told her they'd reached east Omaha. Windows were dark though, and the painted signs impossible to read in the pitch. She thought to ask Papa Henry which direction for a hotel, but her lips were swollen. Her brain the same. She was near passing out, once again hanging over Gus's shoulder. Through the ice on her lashes, she sought a stable, a haystack, even a sewer grate.

Through the afternoon and evening, Gus had obeyed her feeble working of the reins, her weak commands, but now he was agitated. At this late hour, no pedestrians, wagons, or streetcars irritated him. Were the buildings, something he'd never seen, affecting him? "Whoa. Gus, Whoa." Was it the streetlights illuminating intersections, though not down the blocks to help her read painted signs?

Gus walked on, passing more hovering buildings, more shut doors.

She lost her grip again, slipped, nearly fell. Her legs weak, not able to clutch. She wrestled to get her shoulders centered back over Gus's neck. Her rattling teeth drummed in her ears.

Dr. Potter walked alongside. She told him she had something for his medical journals: Freezing is easy. Only close your eyes, give into sleep.

Gus's steps quickened. He whinnied, and she imagined she clutched the reins, though she couldn't feel her hands. "Whoa." Her voice not carrying past her cracked lips. Gus ignored her commands, ignored her efforts to pull back on the reins. Through the slits of fainting eyes, she struggled to focus, saw a flash of light as two men in bowlers stepped through a door and into heat.

Fear pounded in her chest. They'd arrived in the district, but she'd lost control of Gus. He controlled his own reins, and she was helpless to stop him. What if he walked on, past all the hotels, back onto residential streets and out the city's other side? They would not survive the miles to South Omaha.

She bent closer to his cheek, tried to yell, but stopped on seeing a phantom half a block ahead. A ghost horse. Only a moonlight vision and it disappeared. Papa Henry spoke in her ear. "Deer spirits," he said. "Nature acting different than it does, fish in trees, rain falling up, stags in foursomes." A ghost horse was nature acting different than it does.

She would die now, or had died; proof lay in the horse from the spirit realm. Her body would be found, but she'd ride the horse, let the chariot of it take her to Papa Henry.

Gus kept to his quickened stride. He'd seen the phantom too, had even been following it. Was he also dead? She was too groggy to hold the thought. Reaching the place where the horse had disappeared, Gus turned, entering an alley, brick-floored, brick-walled.

Bridget smelled fresh horse manure, saw steam rising from a new dropping. She thought to slide off, plunge her hands in the warmth, but she was too weak. Gus walked past a line of empty buggies and wagons harnessed to sleepy-eyed horses. Ten yards. Fifty yards. He stopped.

A door. Red lanterns hanging on either side. *Warmth.* She had to reach it; she couldn't help Gus now. She was sorry for bringing him, sorry for everything, but she couldn't do any more. Even getting off him and making the few steps to the door seemed impossible.

Gus made a snorting sound, his ears alert.

A row of horses stood crowded and hitched to a long rail. She blinked, closed her eyes, and opened them. Again. She was sleeping or hallucinating, still possibly dead. Nothing else explained the horse. No longer a ghost. He stood bunched with others, packed too tightly, watching her with ears up, and eyes wide. Her thoughts seem to loop, trail off, and need marshalling back. How could Smoke be there? On the dark street, moving through the outer swell of a corner lamp's glow, the black markings on the white coat had looked like holes, eerie voids. She fought to make sound. "Smoke."

She fell more than slid from Gus's back. Her knees buckled and struck the snowy alley floor. She worked to her feet, pushing herself up the wall of Gus's leg, then his shoulder. A niggling question wobbled again at the edge of her mind: How was finding Smoke possible? She couldn't reason, only thought to set him free so that the two horses could be together.

She slid between the flanks of Smoke and the roan to his right, the two horses packed so tightly she had to make them part. On a far periphery of her blurry attention, a door opened behind her. Two men, their voices raised in argument, stepped out, but their concerns were somewhere in the distance, ten yards or ten years away.

She dropped her head against Smoke's neck, stumbled on liquid knees, and fumbled with gloved and frozen fingers to untie the reins. Impossible. The thief had used a hitch knot, and then added half hitches.

The roan shuffled with her stumbling, the odor of her upset, and on hearing raised male voices. Shuffled again, pulled at its lines, its hoofs knocking. Smoke's eyes remained white-rimmed. Tense. The roan's flank pushed the next horse, sent unease tracking down the row. Horses jockeyed, huffed, their ears pricked higher.

Bridget moaned at the knot that would not give, the small spate of energy she'd felt on finding Smoke falling away. She pulled at her coat, gripped Papa Henry's knife. She'd cut the reins.

"The hell you doing?" The voice roared at her shoulder, a man between the horses with her. Rough hands grabbed her collar, twisted her around, and pushed her into the rail. "Stay away from my horse."

Cripe! Seeing his face, his eyes wide with recognition, the wet lips under his mustache parting just wide enough for a coin to slide through, felt like the collision of two dreams.

"Well, if it ain't the buck's little bitch."

The ugly moniker. She couldn't take any more. Not from this man. She turned the knife out, poked the air, fell.

Cripe sidestepped the clumsy attempt, the fringe on his coat swinging. "Hell!"

On her knees again, nearly under Smoke, the horse shifted, yanked on his reins. The roan shied, its forelegs punching the ground. Once more, the horses responded in kind, a swell moving out in both directions. Snorting, grunting breaths puffing rosy in the red light.

Bridget struggled to stay focused on Cripe's sneering face.

"Go home!" he shouted.

Dismissive. She was nothing to him. Murdering Papa Henry was nothing to him. She staggered to her feet, the ground rolling. She willed herself, pointed the knife, fell a second time when the roan slammed into her. Losing consciousness, she was aware only of the sound of the knife clattering on the bricks and thousand-pound horses trampling nervous hoofs inches away. In the darkness, pain seared through her shoulder. Then through her stomach. She floated, the warmth spreading across her stomach delicious.

Nine

Bridget's eyes fluttered. Someone tugged on her arms, dragged her, stopped, tugged again, breathed heavily with the effort. A few inches at a time, her body endured scraping over snowy bricks and ice chunks. Her shoulder and stomach screaming.

Darkness.

Her mind rose to a foggy awareness, her shoulder ripping, her body dropping with a thud, pain, dropping. Thudding down a sharp-edged staircase.

Darkness.

Voices made her struggle to wake, fight heavy eyes that refused to do more than flutter. A woman held a lantern over her, the light distorting her face. A second shape at her other side. Icy fingers. A man drawing a threaded needle up from her stomach. The instrument catching a glint of the lantern light and falling through the air like a tear. A prick of pain, cruel probing fingers, her own muffled attempts to scream.

Darkness.

Fever filled her mind with half-remembered, distorted images. A foursome of stags circling her. Shaking with cold at twelve years old, nearly drowning, clutching at a branch in the Missouri River to keep from washing away, and her scalp burning from lye. A supposed cure for lice she didn't have.

Another day. Another night in which infection stewed in her veins, thickened her tongue.

Papa Henry sat on a chair, whittled wood only a few feet away. She cried out to him. He knew soul cures, communed with the stars, and climbed hillocks where buffalo still trembled the ground beneath his feet.

She was running, branches of trees slapping, cutting her arms, her face. The forest was alive with women and children screaming and fleeing through the trees with her. Behind them mounted Roman soldiers torched the sacred grove, swung forged swords at the men of the clan who'd stayed to fight, facing certain death but hoping to give their mothers, wives, sisters, and daughters minutes more to escape. The dying wore moccasins, hide robes, failed to outrun the revolving barrels on each of the four Hotchkiss guns. Horses trampled, broke bones with their hoofs. Soldiers carved out hearts, sliced off breasts, held up the bleeding, glistening trophies like rubies. *Pagans, redskins. Kill them.*

She wept. Over and over through the centuries, races brought to such a frenzy they acted without humanity. The genocide in Grandma Teegan's story repeated in Papa Henry's. She wanted Papa Henry to help her understand. His knife continued peeling off curled wood rinds, the slow motion of the white chips sailing down to his feet.

She woke. The room cold and so dark she couldn't see. She stiffened. Her heart kicked against her ribs. Someone was there. Sitting, unmoving in the dark. Not close to the bed like a caregiver, but across the room, watching her. A presence, silent but for the smallest sounds of unquiet breathing.

She tried to cry out, scurry up. Her heart kicked with more force. She was bound and gagged. There'd been fevered nightmares with an unearthly, sinister thing entering the room like a cloying vapor, but she was awake this time, not dreaming. Which meant the previous nightmares had also been real. Then as now, she lay helpless, staked out like an animal waiting to be gutted. She struggled to breathe. Only evil held another prisoner.

Darkness.

Wind blew and rattled a window. Bridget opened her eyes. Years seemed to have passed, but her fever was gone. At the foot of the bed, a woman tugged at the blankets, slid in the welcome warmth of heated bricks, and tucked the bedding tight again.

"You're awake," she said. A pretty woman, she came to the side of the bed, lifted a small towel from Bridget's forehead, dipped it in a bowl of water, wrung out the excess, and draped the wet cloth back across. "Your fever has broken. I'll untie you if you're done thrashing. We couldn't have you screaming or rolling around and reopening your wound."

Bridget shuddered. Her feet and one hand were tied to the bed. The woman promised release, but waiting even moments felt too long.

"I'm Tate." She pulled the gag from Bridget's mouth. Tall and slim with light-brown hair, high cheekbones, and porcelain skin. *Pretty,* Bridget thought again, though Tate's eyes held a keen intensity that bordered on disapproval and looked ready to accuse.

Bridget struggled with her dry mouth to form words. "Where am I?"

Tate untied the wrist binding and reached for a glass of water sitting on a bedside table. "You ran into a bit of trouble."

Bridget winced with the effort of lifting her shoulders and drinking from the glass Tate held. She swallowed and remembered the man standing over her with a needle. "I was cut."

The nearly bare room had brick walls, a steeply pitched roof with a thick ridgepole, rafters, and trusses hung with old cobwebs flaring down. A single window. An attic.

"Lily wouldn't risk letting us take you to the hospital." Tate lifted the blankets from Bridget's feet again and worked off the ankle bindings. Then rubbed Bridget's feet and toes as if scrubbing life back into them, and repositioned the warm bricks. "Doc sewed you up, though convincing that man to put down his whiskey took some work.

He couldn't see the use in wasting the time. Turns out you received only a long surface cut. More a slice than a stab."

"You held the lantern."

"And here you are," Tate said. "I'd just as soon let a girl die as bring her through the doors of this house, but Lily has her own ideas."

Cold moaned through a loose window, sounding like river reeds weeping.

With her head clearer, Bridget thought of Gus and Smoke. She realized what must have happened. She hadn't found Smoke; Gus had. For years, the two horses had shared a barn, water tanks, feed troughs, pastures, and on the coldest nights huddled together for warmth. Gus was in the habit of following the stallion. He must have caught a scent, heard a familiar whicker, or seen the flash of a white coat. Away from everything he knew, with no pull on the reins telling him left or right, Gus had simply done what he was accustomed to doing. Follow Smoke.

"My horses? One gray, the other pretty, spotted. I need to contact the police. Papa Henry's stolen horse is here. In Omaha. I know who has him."

"Well, we are not going to the police over a horse." Tate frowned. "Things are more serious than that." She gave Bridget a quizzical look. "So what was it? You dressed like a man, alone in the alley late at night. Were you there to steal horses or steal our clients?" One perfect brow lifted. "Or were you seeking company of one of our girls?"

Bridget could only stare.

"There was so much blood everywhere," Tate said. "We couldn't tell how much you'd bled and how much came from the ghost."

"The ghost?"

"There was nothing to do for that one. You'd killed him."

Bridget sucked breath into startled lungs. "I killed . . . him?" She pleaded with Tate's eyes to say it wasn't true. "Cripe's dead? I killed him?"

Tate's hand rose as if to block Bridget from saying more. "Save the vaudeville, honey."

"He's dead?"

"Whatever you were doing out there, thieving or whoring, your actions won't bring you any sympathy. A jury won't waste five minutes deciding you need to hang for murder."

Bridget's stomach clenched. She thought she'd be sick. Everything had changed; she was a murderer. The word echoed in her brain. *Murderer.*

"Lily was right to hide you and keep you away from the law." Tate went around the bed and untied the sling at Bridget's neck. "Your shoulder will be fine. It's black and blue, but not dislocated. You're one lucky person."

"Lily? The law?"

"Leave the police to me," Tate said. "Now, you'll go by Hannah."

Hannah? To hide my identity? Tate was agreeing to hide her even knowing that she'd murdered. For how long? Why?

Tate dropped the bindings on the table, went to the window, and leaned against the frame. "The police spent over an hour questioning everyone in the house. The girls don't know you are here. Stay hidden." She nodded at the strips of rags. "No screaming or stumbling around, or those go back on. Rest another day or two. Then we'll talk about your future."

"I have no future."

"We can't always undo our mistakes." Tate's voice softened, and she returned to the bed. "The best we can do is try and help those we've harmed."

"He's dead. Not harmed." Her eyes stung. "Dead."

"What I mean is, you're young. You still have time to do good. Your life can still matter."

"I'll hang."

"As I said, the police questioned everyone in the house. Asked all the girls what man might have been in the alley at the time. The cops assume it was a man who did the killing. They aren't looking for a girl." She gave a soft *harrumph.* "Actually, they likely only want the incident covered up or forgotten. Every time something like this happens, there's renewed shouting about the need to close the houses."

"If he's dead?" Believing it was still impossible. "Why are you hiding me, lying for me?"

"I suppose for Lily." Her smile said there was more. "Though not even I wish to see someone hang."

"They'll find me. How many know I'm here?" Besides Tate, there was Doc and this Lily. "Someone will talk." The ache in her gut felt as though it seared back to her spine. "There was another man. I heard arguing. What if he saw?"

"No one has come forward yet, and so no one will. Ghosts don't admit to being here. He won't want to get involved and possibly have his name in the paper."

Bridget couldn't relax. Cripe was dead.

"Here." Tate lifted a half-empty brown bottle and a spoon. She frowned at Bridget's refusal. "Doc's orders, not mine."

Over the last few days, spoonfuls of liquid had burned down Bridget's throat, and she'd slept with heavy dreams. She wanted sleep now, even the nightmare to transport her far away, but she had so many questions.

"The police," Tate went on, "said the ghost was stabbed in the throat. Lily pulled you away before they arrived, and Goose carried you up from the basement using the back staircase so you weren't seen."

"Goose?" Another person who knew. Number four. "What is this place? Where am I?"

"Plum Cake's."

"A bakery?"

"Some days I think so. No, this is a brothel."

"A brothel?" She remembered the red lights over the door. The line of horses tethered in the alley.

"In case you're wondering, there won't be any ghosts coming up here expecting you to spread your legs."

"Ghosts?" Tate kept using the word. It described exactly how Bridget felt: no longer a part of this world.

"They are all ghosts, to me," Tate said. "Wisps." She batted a hand in the air as if brushing away a puff of smoke.

Bridget glanced at the elixir she'd refused. Ghosts and a murder. She didn't need sleep; she needed to flee. But where would she go? The police might be looking for a man, but they'd figure everything out soon enough.

By now, the town of Bleaksville knew Cripe was dead and that she was responsible. Thayer would have ridden out to the farm with more questions, or to sleep again on the sofa, and found her gone. Cora would have shared the note and told him another horse had disappeared. As had Papa Henry's knife.

"The knife?" Bridget cried.

"I've no knowledge of any knife."

Cora, Dr. Potter, Thayer, they could all link the knife to her. "The cops aren't looking for a man. They're looking for me."

"Then we'll be careful."

"Papa Henry's ledger? Who has that?"

"I do. The book saved your life, blocked most of the cut."

"I can't ever go home." She rolled her swimming eyes to the bottle. "I'll take it now."

"Girls come and go." Tate poured and held the spoon of liquid to Bridget's lips. "Once you're healed, if you keep your mouth shut, you'll just be another new face to them." She poured a second tablespoon. "They'll have no reason to connect you to an event that happened in the alley days earlier. They've likely already forgotten the incident.

In this neighborhood, men fight and kill each other all the time. I'm certain it's God's way of taking pity on women by keeping the numbers down."

Bridget closed her eyes, let the liquid warm her throat. "I don't understand. Why did someone named Lily want to help me? Why would a prostitute care?"

Tate's eyes flashed, and the empty spoon she'd been laying down hit the table. "Never use that word again. Ever." She took a moment, drew in a long, settling breath. "Every one of us is a victim of greed and lust and lies about male superiority."

Asking felt intrusive, but the potion already caused a slight buzz in Bridget's brain, and for her own safety, didn't she need to know everything she could? "You do that work too?"

"On occasion. Long-standing ghosts." Tate's anger left as quickly as it had come. "A few have convinced themselves we are in a monogamous relationship." She gave a wry smile. "With that bit of self-delusion, they can imagine themselves better than the rest. They tell themselves they aren't players, that I'm something of a second wife. Mostly, I run the bar, keep the books, and manage the girls. Rest now." She started out, pulling the chair she'd used from the bedside and leaving it a few yards from the door.

An odd thing to do. The breathing specter of Bridget's nightmares had sat there. "I'm sorry he's dead," Bridget blurted to Tate's retreating back.

"Don't weep for any ghost. It hasn't earned that. You don't deserve to hang for killing something already dead."

"I'm not sorry for him. I'm sorry I'm the one who did it."

"Nothing easier in the world." Tate's eyes drifted off Bridget to the staircase leading down. "Being sorry after we've ruined lives."

Alone again, Bridget's eyes grew heavy. The life she'd dreamed was over. As over for her as it was for Papa Henry in his box. She'd never be a doctor now. With every loss she'd suffered, with every person who thought she wasn't good enough or smart enough, the dream of being a doctor had remained her North Star. She'd followed its brightness through the worst times, gone through the fray and out. Now, she'd shot her own star out of the sky. Condemned her own life. Doing so, she hadn't made Cripe pay. Dying, he'd slipped from his human skin as easily as a selkie in one of Grandma Teegan's stories.

Bridget wept softly, waiting for the tonic to finish working its magic. The buzz was increasing, her mind feeling loose, scraps of pictures appearing and disappearing. The alley had been dark but for the lantern lights bleeding through red cloths; her body so cold and exhausted she could scarcely stand. She'd lunged with the knife and fell. Cripe must have been knocked by the horses, rumps shoving him off his feet, the blade catching his throat before it went clattering out of her hand. Wounded and dying, he'd grabbed the knife but had the strength for only one cut, striking mostly ledger, as though Papa Henry's hand had reached down and saved her. Why had he bothered?

Ten

When next Bridget's eyes opened, night had returned, and the room once again lay shrouded in darkness. The just-audible plinking of a piano sounded far below, but something much closer had awakened her. The touch of slow treading on the stairs, something creeping up toward her.

She froze, watched weak gray light reach the landing just outside her room. The light continued to swell and waver. A candle, its small flame still several steps down but coming closer.

No! Her heart bounced in her chest. This wasn't Tate, who climbed boldly. It wasn't the heavier footfalls of a policeman or any man, not even one Tate would label a ghost. This was the quiet, breathing apparition from Bridget's nightmares.

She thought to scream for Tate but feared doing so. What if Tate didn't hear over the piano music or had left the house? What if screaming only enraged the intruder? In the past, the figure had sat and watched her, not approached the bed. The thought gave little comfort but enough to help her lie still.

The landing swelled with growing light, the empty space expectant. The treading on the stairs grew closer.

Nera. Nera. Even her thoughts were shaking. *Only a nightmare, only a nightmare.*

A black-robed figure stepped into view.

Bridget's fear pitched, shrieked in the pit of her stomach.

Thin, shapeless, a form masked by a robe. Hidden eyes peering out through black veiling. A puff of breath and the only light blinked away. In the quick void, the darkness sank deeper. Whispered footsteps entered the room.

Bridget clamped her eyes closed, tried to shut out the hush of rustling cloth.

The hour, the sneaking, the covered face. Only unwanted things, the frightful and evil, prowled night's deepest hours. A banshee? Cripe's ghost? Could a ghost hear a human heart exploding in a human chest?

A muffled bump, a scrape of chair legs, and the faint brush of a body lowering onto the seat. Tate had deliberately placed the chair just there. Was it her? Was she two-spirited, one by day and one by night? She spoke of ghosts as though the entire house was haunted.

Bridget forced herself to think rationally. The stairs, the candle, the chair. Otherworldly things did not need to climb or require light to see. They didn't bang into furniture and need to sit. They weren't hesitant or afraid of being discovered.

Smells of rose oils and a more strident medicinal odor lifted, wafted. The breathing, barely heard, came in short inhales, short exhales: Weak lungs, winded just with the effort of the climb.

Bridget continued to feign sleep. Given her stomach wound, she couldn't fight off a large attacker if it came to that, but something weak and ill? Still, safest was to do nothing, say nothing. Even speaking might cause the eruption of a violent reaction.

The minutes folded in Bridget's mind, then stretched. She dared not peek with even one eye.

"Hannah," a whisper. A woman's voice. "Now we can be together again."

Tate had also said Bridget would go by Hannah; the use of the name wasn't startling. The other words banged through Bridget. What woman would think of them as being together again? She could think of only one. The chances though of this dark-night presence being Mum after eight years were zero. Impossible.

Except ... Bridget's mind whirled, tried to outrun the threat of her situation. Rev. Jackdaw had always insisted Omaha's brothels festered with "Irish whores." If Pappy had died as the letter from Butte said . . . if it had been only Pappy who died, then Mum might have been reduced to a life of prostitution. She might have worked her way east, gotten as far as Omaha. Perhaps she'd found out Bridget was in Nebraska. If that were so, what kept her from stepping forward and identifying herself? Shame?

Beneath her blankets, Bridget's hands clenched. This wasn't Mum. Imagining so could only be the lingering ill effects of her last dose of medication, traces of laudanum, maybe cocaine tracking through veins. Yet Gus found Smoke. Deer walked up and stared at her through a kitchen window. She was wanted for having killed a man. And Papa Henry was dead. What was more impossible than all of that?

The minutes dragged on. Half an hour. An hour as Bridget wrestled her fear of what could be sitting there. And the hope she and Mum had found each other. She battled against calling out. Suppose it was Mum and she ran? Lost again.

Scariest of all? Suppose a cry proved it wasn't Mum?

Finally, weight lifted off the chair, fabric rustled, the air stirred again with odors. Feet shuffled as much as walked back to the door. The tiny sigh of a wood match being struck.

Bridget opened her eyes. The snatch of a black shape stepping off the small landing, disappearing, candlelight fading down the stairs.

In the alley, sounds echoed off the buildings opposite of Plum Cake's as though the clatter of hoofs, rolling wheels, squeaking axles, and drunken talk were living things slithering up the bricks. Bridget tried to imagine herself back at the farm and the sounds only trees cracking in the cold, ice shuffling in the Missouri River, coyotes howling and marking the night.

In the morning, Bridget winced as she worked herself into a sitting position. Day two of returned awareness. She'd fought fever and infection and won. She was alive. Her stitches burned, spreading a tight pain out six inches either side of the wound, but they were less sore than yesterday. Tomorrow would be even better. In a couple of days, she'd be well enough to walk out of the brothel, though where could she go?

She inched her feet over the side of the bed and rested, the pain needing a moment to rear down. She raised her right arm gingerly and found it ached less too. The floor chilled her feet, but she gripped the iron bedstead and pulled herself into a standing position. Soreness made her suck in another sharp breath. How far could she get setting out across Omaha on foot? Wounded? In the dead of winter? How far did she need to go to escape the law? Back to Ireland?

The wish was fantasy. Sheer self-delusion that threatened to toss her back into bed. What of Papa Henry's farm and his funeral? Leaving America would also mean betraying Grandma Teegan, who'd given everything to bring her across. And, a small voice in her mind wouldn't let go, suppose Mum did live in the house, sick and needing her?

She reached for the brown bottle sitting on the small table. Not bothering with the spoon, she took off the cap and swigged. The sweet syrup would ease her physical pain, but she needed it most for the pain of being in her own skin.

With emotions as unsteady as her legs, she took the three steps to the window and sank against the frame. Where last night there'd been noise, now there was only a wide and empty alley. She'd arrived there with Gus, half frozen and seen Smoke. There she'd aimed her knife at a man without a weapon. He'd died. There was no middle ground. She couldn't call it an accident. She'd wanted to kill him.

The long hitching rail stood empty. Inches of fresh snow along with days of horses trampling had erased both her and Cripe's blood. It worried her to think about her horses. Smoke, still tied to the railing, had likely been confiscated by the police. Thayer or Cora would be asked to identify him when they identified the knife. Gus? Had he headed out of the alley in the confusion, the stabbing, and smelling blood yet again? Could he have made the trek back to his barn, so many miles away? Impossible, yet she'd try to believe in magic for him. Even when she couldn't believe in it for herself.

To her right, the end of the alley was gray. To her left, the end of the alley held more light. East. The Missouri River bordered Omaha's eastern edge, running down from the north alongside Bleaksville, reaching the city, and continuing on south. She had her bearings, but it hardly mattered. She took another swig of Doc's elixir and dropped her forehead against the frosty glass. She was *hunted*. The word closed doors in her, sucked air from her lungs.

Clopping horses and the rumble of a large dray with iron wheels echoed through the alley's canyon of buildings. She'd heard the wagon the day before and maybe the day before that. It came into view, long, low, and drawn by two broad-backed draft horses. The driver yelled a command and the horses stopped. The foot-high sides of the wagon bore gold lettering she could read even from three stories above: Storz Brewing Co. Five barrels of beer on each side leaned in, braced against a center ridge.

A black-and-white-spotted dog sat on the front seat with the driver. Coloring like Wire, Luna-Blue, and Smoke. She knocked hard on the glass, and when the Dalmatian looked up and barked, she waved both hands, the left more vigorously than the sore right. The dog barked harder, its tail swinging back and forth. The moment of connection felt blessed, even as it filled her with pangs of regret for all she'd lost.

The driver stepped down, reached back, and patted the dog's head. The Dalmatian quieted and jumped off the seat to join him on the ground.

A good man, Bridget thought. There was much to see in how a man treated his dog.

She rapped again on the glass, wanting to meet the dog's eyes a final time. It barked and the man looked up to see her waving. He squinted in surprise. She waved at him though a part of her insisted she ought to stay out of sight. Was it Doc's potion making her bold? The man looked harmless. He delivered beer, wasn't a cop, wasn't someone who would link her to Cripe's death.

He lifted a hand and smiled. Then turned to his wagon and began unstrapping a wheelbarrow. She felt dismissed. He had a job to do, and his glance and wave had been only a polite acknowledgement, a "how do." She kept watching. He was young, in his early twenties, she guessed. Handsome, though she'd seen his face for only a moment. Tall, his shiny black boots rising to the knees of his long legs. Broad shouldered in his heavy coat, had to be in order to heft full barrels of beer.

He pulled one off the wagon, lowered it into his wheelbarrow, and steered his load into the brothel.

Turning for her bed, Bridget crawled in gingerly. She ought to have jumped back before the man saw her. Tate, who tried to keep Bridget's presence a secret, would be angry.

Estimating time by staring at weak winter light spreading over brick proved hard, but she guessed a full hour had passed before the wagon rolled out of the alley. She didn't need to wonder why a delivery to a brothel took so long.

Tate's heels on the steps echoed up the stairwell. "Good morning." She looked happy and carried Bridget's washed and folded clothes. "I had the laundry patch the cuts in your shirts and coat." She held Papa Henry's hat too, the leather looking as wonderfully battered as before and thankfully unscrubbed. She laid the items on the foot of the bed, and Bridget snatched up the hat, breathing in the scent.

"You must know that driver," she said. She instantly regretted the comment. She had no business prying.

"Kid?" The name easy in Tate's mouth.

So the two of them? "That's a strange name for a grown man. Can he be trusted? He saw me in the window."

"His mother called him 'the kid,' and it stuck. Trusted? I'd trust him with my life."

What about my life?

"A woman came looking for you. A Cora."

"Cora?" Bridget grabbed the sudden stab of ache running over her wound. "How did she look? What did she say?"

"There's no reason for tears. Plum Cake's was just one more door to her. I didn't tell her a thing. I'm not letting anyone take you yet."

Bridget hugged the hat. "I'm not afraid of Cora. I miss her."

"Is she a relative?"

"A dear friend. More than that, more a surrogate mother these last years. And now she'll see to the tending of my horses." How long before she'd give up and sell the stock? Even Luna-Blue. Wire, she'd take into her home.

Tate crossed her arms, hugged herself. "Horses? Livestock? You own land too?" Her dark brows pinched. "You have money. Girls who end up here have nothing."

Bridget thought of Papa Henry, facedown with two bloody holes in his back. "Poverty isn't the only thing that can ruin us."

"Money means freedom." Tate walked to the window, leaned close, and tipped her face up to the meager sunlight. "There is nothing more important than freedom."

We're the same, Bridget thought. *Both trapped in these walls.*

"Cora was here before," Tate said. "She admitted visiting every hospital, hotel, and rooming house she could find. Any place she thought you could possibly be. She seemed satisfied this time that you weren't here." Tate gave a slight *harrumph.* "She didn't say so, but it was obvious she never really believed you'd be at a brothel. I'm sure she won't be back a third time. She only came again because the newspaper mentioned this place." Tate's lips pressed.

"What?" Bridget asked. "What else?"

"I'm afraid she and your local sheriff identified the murder weapon as belonging to your late father. I'm sorry to hear he was murdered."

Bridget's throat tightened. She'd suspected the knife would link her to the murder and now she knew for certain. Cora might not believe she was living in a brothel, but she knew who had murdered Cripe.

"She said you were from Bleaksville. What a horrid name for a town."

Bridget needed a minute to put aside her ache for Cora and focus on Tate. "Soldiers returning from the Civil War changed the name." She didn't have the will to explain how some of them, including Papa Henry, had survived Andersonville. Their bodies wasted to skeletons, their spirits dead.

"Are you able to make it downstairs?" Tate asked. "Plum Cake wants to hear your pledge of loyalty. Hannah."

Bridget didn't want to meet the madam; she wanted to be left alone. She'd take enough potion to sleep and dream of spotted dogs and horses. She sighed. What she wanted didn't matter. She needed their protection, and thus she lived at their mercy.

"Stand," Tate said. "I best change your bandages."

With the wrappings off, six inches of ugly stitching looked like chicken scratch across Bridget's stomach. Unevenly spaced, spreading knots, and each with varied tails of black thread ranging from an eighth inch to a full inch. Not the meticulous work of Dr. Potter's hand. These looked as if she'd put them in herself, bleeding, in the dark, and half out of her mind with pain. No matter: she was alive, and the man Tate referred to simply as Doc deserved credit. He hadn't done fancy work, but it had been fancy enough.

Tate wrapped fresh gauze around Bridget's middle. "I think I could grow to like Cora. She's talkative and friendly. Pleasant even to me."

"She doesn't judge people. Though she'll never again think positively of me."

"She made a second trip to Omaha in search of you. You're lucky to have such a friend."

With new dressing and back in her own clothes, Bridget pushed her cold feet into her cold boots. "Am I lucky even if I never see her again?"

"Even if."

The narrow stairwell had no lights, only a small window several steps down. Bridget followed Tate, pressing her hands against the brick walls for stability. She thought of the strange figure from the night before. Now that day had returned, she wouldn't let herself fall victim to the idea Mum could be in the house.

"You said a woman named Plum Cake owns the place. Do you think she visits my room at night?"

"Ha!" A chuckle full of irony. "No, Plum Cake does not visit your room at night or anytime. Can you read? I could bring you books."

"I'd love that." The thought of a book was a sunbeam piercing her cell. "Is the library close? Could you find an anatomy text?" She was being greedy and yet she dared. "Could you bring paper and a pen? I can pay you." Her coat lay back on the bed, though she'd not thought to check for her money.

"An anatomy text?" Tate continued down. Her erect shoulders, the stiff collar of her shirtwaist high on the back of her neck, and her hair carefully styled, made her look more schoolmarm than lady of the night. "That's a strange request."

Tate's remark sounded easy, agreeable, and the sunbeam in Bridget's imagination became a shaft of light.

"We're a sinking ship here," Tate said. "So many of us are only just hanging on."

Bridget tried to keep up, but with each descending stair her stitches pulled and burned.

"You'll fit right in," Tate added.

Fit because she too was only hanging on? Why would a sinking ship need, or want, the weight of her? She thought of the ark Papa Henry had built in the second of his barns. The massive thing was never intended to see water. It was an ark symbolizing endurance, holding on through hard times with the faith in better ones in the future. For Papa Henry, building the ark had given him the will to live, even after the loss of his son, his wife's leaving, and the weight in his blood of ancestors who'd suffered genocide.

Plum Cake's brothel will be my ark, Bridget vowed. *Where I weather the worst possible storm.*

They reached the second story landing and the window no larger than a dinner plate. Tate opened a door, but Bridget hesitated, looked down the stairs and on into the sinking darkness. From below, she heard the faint sound of a woman crying.

Shivers pricked across her shoulders.

"This way," Tate said.

Eleven

They'd left the stairwell and headed down a dim, windowless corridor. Wallpaper in deep purple, swelling with thick swirls of flocking like long, reaching fingers made Bridget draw her arms in close. Brass sconces coiled upward every dozen feet, their bulbs dark as empty eyes. The smell of cigarettes, cigars, and pipes lingering in the air attested to the number of men who'd gone in and out of the rooms only hours earlier.

They passed three quiet, closed doors on each side of the hall before reaching a wide center staircase. Six more doors lay beyond. *A brothel with a dozen rooms: Twelve working women.*

Though Tate seemed to float down the staircase, Bridget stopped at the top, stunned by the grandeur. A four-foot-wide runner of Persian carpeting poured over the entire length. Cora had a small Persian rug in her sitting room, but she'd be amazed to see this and to imagine how many weavers worked on the intricate pattern. Polished redwood shone a foot wider on each side. Equally striking was the architectural design of the staircase itself, a sweeping serpentine shape that swung far out to the left, then back to the right. Requiring three times the number of stairs necessary to reach the bottom.

Tate stood at the turn of the first wing. "Come along."

Bridget hurried to catch up. In the room below, drapes in plum-colored velvet and tied back with gold tassels hung from the top of tall windows and pooled on the floor. Over two dozen tables had accompanying Victorian chairs upholstered in rich, burgundy hide. A long row of stools lined a polished redwood bar. Shiny brass trimming ran end to end and matched gleaming spittoons. Mirrors and a chandelier the size of a water tank made bottles of liquor lining shelves look twice their numbers, and the whole twinkled like a carnival midway.

"Hannah. Are you always this slow?" Tate asked. She reached the bottom and waited.

"I didn't expect a palace," Bridget said. She hurried to catch up, going down the last few steps, the only ones making a straight descent, and where the carpeting lay over rich marble.

"Opulence allows ghosts to tell themselves they aren't stepping down. They can tell themselves this is a gentleman's club, not a whore house."

"And that works?"

Tate didn't bother to turn. "They aren't known for their deep thinking."

Bridget held her stomach and the flaring ache. She meant to keep up with Tate, but a portrait slowed her again. The life-size picture of a woman painted against a dark background made her ivory skin stand out in striking relief. She lay on her side, naked and Rubenesque with large, exposed breasts and thighs, and a pubis disguised by cloudy washes. Most arresting were her burning blue eyes, haunting in their light and haunting in their depth.

"Come on." Tate coaxed again. She'd already passed through the bar and entered a wide hallway.

Bridget moved on, feeling the eyes of the painting follow her.

At the far end of the hallway, a door with a large window led to the alley and across that a wall of bricks. She'd ridden down the passageway on Gus. There she'd seen Smoke and killed Cripe. She preferred thinking of the door simply as the one used by the deliveryman, Kid.

Halfway down, Tate stopped, knocked.

As they waited for an answer, Bridget continued her cataloging, trying to remember every detail of the house's layout—escape routes should the police come. Across the hall a lavatory with a toilet and sink—no exit to freedom. A bit farther on, an open door onto what appeared to be a kitchen. She could see part of a stove, a sink. Did the room have an escape to the alley or street?

A door opened. "Goose," Tate addressed a huge man.

He filled the frame. Towering in greasy, baggy pants with suspenders hanging at his sides. He wore a union suit without a shirt, the top of which had yellowed and needed washing. The worn cotton stretched wide between the buttons running down his hairy chest, stretched still wider over his stomach where flesh bulged between the gaps and looked to Bridget like a stringer of pale fish. He leaned down, peered through thick glasses. A cloud of stale breath hit her face. "Morning."

He'd carried her up from the basement to the third floor, playing a role in saving her life. He was also part of the group willing to hide her from the police.

"I assume Plum Cake is in." Tate waved a hand at something across the room.

A fire roared in the hearth, though it didn't entirely mask the thick sour musk of sweat and urine. A table with two chairs sat in the middle of the over-stuffed room and a narrow bed along a wall. Bridget tried not to see the snarled gray sheets. A plum-colored sofa stood on three legs with a short stack of red bricks substituting for the fourth. Everywhere a clutter of newspapers, books, and clothes.

Tate met Bridget's surprised look. As if to say, *I know. It's shocking.* "Stay right here," she said aloud. "I'll talk with Plum Cake."

Tate's mood had changed. Gone was the enjoyment she'd derived from Kid's visit. Plum Cake was the employer, but the tightness in Tate's brows and the set of her mouth said that relationship didn't include friendship.

"Tate?" a voice called. "Is that you?"

"I brought Hannah." Tate crossed the room and stepped behind a purple curtain of the same fabric as the drapes in the bar and the broken-down sofa. The purple swung closed.

Goose stepped in front of Bridget as though warning against any interest she might have in following. The thought of his carrying her up to the attic, three flights while being pressed against his dirty body, made her fingertips sweat. Though he'd made it up through the narrow passage once, she knew he wasn't the one sneaking quietly up at night. A tread so light the climber might be weightless. Not a clumsy, half-blind giant.

Satisfied Bridget wasn't going to follow Tate, Goose nodded with a pleasant enough expression and sank onto the couch. The springs moaned.

The house was a quilt of mix-matched patches. Sparseness in the attic, lavishness in the bar and likely the bedrooms where clients were entertained, and here the madam lived in windowless, cramped quarters. Where nothing new had been purchased in years.

Goose picked up a cookbook and held it so close to his face he could lick it. Did staying at the brothel offer safety or did it mean captivity? There was Tate and her ghosts, now Goose, and Plum Cake concealed behind a curtain. There was also the specter at night who believed the two of them were together again.

"Yes," Tate said, "Hannah's right outside."

Every time Bridget heard the name Hannah, she felt as if a pinch of flesh were being pulled off. In a deal with the devil, she was letting those who hid her fashion her into what they needed. Using her pain, fear, and loss to their advantage.

She pressed her lips together. She was being overly dramatic. They hadn't asked anything serious of her. Was there so much soul in one's name that losing it harmed you?

"Lily believes this one is her Hannah?" Plum Cake asked.

Bridget had her proof. The one who crept up the stairs, sat silently in the chair, and watched in the dark, was Lily.

"The numbers promised," Tate said. "At least the year. In Lily's mind, everything lined up. Even the hair color, red like her own. She's convinced."

Red hair? Bridget nearly gasped. She and the woman who went by the name Lily had the same hair color? Trying to remember time spent with Mum back in Ireland was as hard as trying to remember last year's sleeping dreams. Bridget did remember, however, the afternoon the two of them lay in clover, their heads touching, and their poppy-colored tresses a perfect match. And Mum promising they'd never be separated. Had she been fighting with Pappy at the time, insisting moving to America could not include leaving Bridget behind?

"Believing she's found her daughter," Tate said, "she's resting better at night."

She recognizes me! Isn't that proof enough? Bridget thought. *Mothers know their children.*

"Though last night," Tate went on, "Lily left. I'm sure she went to the river again."

The river? How many times during Bridget's first winter in Nebraska had she stood on the banks of the Missouri? A twelve-year-old screaming again and again for Mum. Believing that all water in the world was connected and Mum was a selkie. Believing that one day Mum would hear the calling and come. Was it possible that Mum had stood twenty miles downriver, screaming for her?

"The girl has agreed?" Plum Cake asked.

"Being wanted for the murder will keep her here."

Bridget glanced in Goose's direction. He'd lowered his book to watch her, but his round face showed no judgment over the crime she'd committed. One lens of his glasses caught the lamp light at his shoulder and seemed to wink. He nodded pleasantly, as though the two of them had reached an agreement. Entering the room, she'd wanted to turn from the sight of him, but he was offering friendship, understanding. She nodded in return. He hadn't become suddenly handsome, but friends were never ugly.

"Lily didn't visit me again last night." Hurt in Plum Cake's voice. "She saw Hannah?"

"Lily loves you," Tate said. "She's failing fast, though. We have to allow for whatever she does."

"Lily loves me," Plum Cake repeated Tate's words like a promise.

"Yes, she does, but she's busy with dying. You have to let her go."

A loud, breathy sigh. "Then I'll be dying too." The words sounded as though Plum Cake's mouth was suddenly full of food. "My poor Lily. This house is killing her."

"This house," Tate answered, "is killing us all."

In the silence that followed, Bridget imagined the two women glaring at one another.

"Don't forget who you work for," Plum Cake said.

"I haven't forgotten." Tate's voice was even again, but a degree or two short of apologetic. "My cleaning woman is home with a dying husband. Hannah can help me tremendously."

"Fire that maid and hire a dependable woman."

"She is dependable. And loyal. I won't replace her. Hannah can also help Goose in the kitchen."

"You heard that?" Goose asked from the sofa.

Bridget nodded, hoping surprise wasn't registering on her face. He was the cook? In those germ-ridden, greasy clothes? She thought of the broths spooned down her throat as she'd tossed with fever. Her stomach churned. She'd killed a man, though. How could she judge another for anything?

"Hannah will earn her keep only by housekeeping," Tate said.

"She's not to entertain ghosts. For Lily's sake. And when this is over, she leaves. If she goes to another house, I can't stop her, but she's not to see ghosts here. For Lily's sake."

"Hannah?" Plum Cake's voice called through the curtain.

How easily the name slipped off everyone's tongue.

"Do you agree to the terms?"

"Yes." Though Bridget wasn't exactly sure what all those terms were. Or how many more would be added.

"You are to stay away from Lily. If you don't, I'll call the law, tell them I have the murderer they're looking for hiding right here under my roof. You understand? Lily's terribly disfigured from a fire and wants her privacy."

Bridget felt struck. Was there anything more painful than severe burns? Extensive scarring explained the full body covering.

"Hannah, there's always jail for you," Plum Cake yelled. "A rope."

Bridget followed Tate back into the hall. "I need to lie down." She'd been on her feet for what felt like hours, but hearing about Lily's burns hurt worse than the soreness in her gut.

"Of course," Tate answered. "Rest another day, then tomorrow you'll help with the cleaning. You heard Plum Cake, and I'll say it again. Stay away from Lily. Don't get too close." She started off, urgent steps pulling her a yard ahead of Bridget. "Let her die believing her daughter has returned."

"Is that what you fear? If I get too close, she'll see I'm not who she thinks I am? Why do you doubt her so much? If she recognizes me, maybe I am her daughter."

Tate drew up. "Don't be ridiculous. Lily is not your mother." Her eyes narrowed. "Not you too? Not another one out of her mind."

"Is Lily?"

"Life can be cruel to women."

"She's mad?" That could explain her seeing a dead daughter in a stranger's face? *I'm mad too*, Bridget thought, *to still hope Mum is alive somewhere. To suppose that could be under this roof.*

"Take those stairs back up." Tate pointed to a narrow door between the lavatory and kitchen. "Can you make it?"

"I'll take my time."

"I don't know what Lily expects of you," Tate said. "Doc believes she won't live much longer. Just knowing you're in the house may be all she wants."

"Let her watch me? Let her sit in the chair while I sleep? And answer to Hannah?"

Tate met Bridget's gaze. "A small thing in return for your life."

Niggling thoughts crept around the edge of Bridget's mind. Burn victims who had recovered enough to be up out of their beds did not then die weeks or months later. "How long ago was the fire?"

A combination of emotions plied Tate's face. "She is not your mother."

"How out of her . . ." Asking was hard. "Her madness?"

"Who knows? Pain, depression, Doc's little brown bottles of cocaine, whiskey, laudanum. Take a guess. Maybe she sent her mind off because that's a whole lot easier way to live. There are days I envy her."

No more of Doc's cure, Bridget promised herself. She needed to keep her mind.

"Stay out of Plum Cake's room too. She also demands her privacy. Disobeying that commandment guarantees she'll have Goose cart you back to the alley." Tate stepped away, called over her shoulder. "She'll have your stitches picked out one by one."

"You seem normal."

Tate stopped a second time, turned back, her expression quizzical.

"Plum Cake and Lily live in hiding, but you in your tailored waist and skirt, well-groomed. You're not the sort of woman I supposed worked in a brothel. Why do you live here?"

Tate's eyes darkened. "If you have to ask, your life's been too lucky for you to understand."

Bridget watched her walk off. *Lucky?* Tate had no idea.

Twelve

Bridget had no comb or mirror, and she wouldn't bother asking Tate for the items. It would be a long time, if ever, before she wanted to see her reflection again. She gathered her hair and pushed in pins. She only cared that it covered the scarring and didn't hang to interfere with her work. She didn't care about looking as coiffured as Tate.

Dressed, Bridget sat on the side of the bed and waited for Tate to come with the all clear. This was day three of consciousness, and she felt quick, sharp stabbing only when she forgot her wound and made careless movements. Doc had climbed the stairs late the afternoon before, the whiskey on his breath as cloying as the floral scent of Lily's midnight visits. Bridget tried to engage him in conversation as she had Dr. Potter, but he'd only looked at her wound in the poor light. "Stitches should come out in a week, maybe ten days or so."

Before leaving, he'd lifted the bottle of elixir from the table and, checking to see how much remained, wobbled it in the air. Finding little left, he pulled a full one from his bag. A bit of sticky-looking shine on the front, a drip of concoction not wiped away, proved the bottle hadn't come from a chemist's shop but Doc's own laboratory.

"Please don't leave that," Bridget said. "I don't need it."

He frowned. "You suppose you know best?"

She hadn't meant to challenge him. "It's just that—"

He'd already snapped his bag closed, turned for the door. He might still be mad at her, but she could take her own stitches out, if it came to that.

Footsteps sounded on the stairs. The confident heel strikes Bridget had come to recognize as Tate's.

"I'm glad to see you're up." Tate carried a small parcel and textbook. She laid them on the table.

"Thank you." Bridget hurried to touch the book. Dr. Potter had the same medical volume in his library: the tome was current and invaluable. "Last night, I nearly went crazy with boredom. Tonight, I can read."

"Did Lily visit you?"

"I didn't wake until she was leaving."

"Then you weren't frightened."

"It scared me more to think I slept through someone coming in and spending an hour staring at me. Did she go to the river afterwards?"

"When I checked her room at two, she was gone. By three, she was back. It worries me every night."

"Isn't there a way to stop her?"

"I hoped visiting you would do the trick. The thought of locking her in breaks my heart, and Plum Cake forbids it. Suppose she starts screaming, wailing while the house is open?"

"You wouldn't gag her?"

"Never. Not Lily." Tate pulled the merchant's string from around the package, her fingers graceful. She laid back the brown paper to reveal a pen, a small bottle of ink, and a thick journal.

"Thank you," Bridget said. "Oh, I'm so grateful." She blinked against the emotions rising in her. Books were hopeful. They said not all was lost. Papa Henry would smile to see the hefty journal. He'd press his palm to the cover four times. "What do I owe you?"

"Being here for Lily and helping with the housekeeping more than pays."

She wore another white waist, this one with even lacier but still tasteful flourishes. She could walk into any shop, Bridget imagined, and the proprietor would see no hint of her occupation. Though perhaps everyone in Omaha knew of her. She stepped away from the table and went to the window just as she had done the previous morning. "It feels nice up here. Away from everything."

Bridget opened the journal cover and ran a finger down the first page. Tate had known where to buy and to choose a sewn rather than a glued binding. "Do you keep diaries?"

"Only the records for the house." She rocked nearly imperceptibly, a slight motion along the hem of her serge skirt giving her away. "There's nothing about this place I'd want to write down and remember."

"The journal I had in my pants?"

"I've been enjoying it. I dream of a life where I've the leisure to write about things like fruit tree yields and rainfall totals."

"I suppose keeping Plum Cake's books isn't the same."

She let out a wistful sigh. "I thought I'd teach school."

"What stopped you?"

"That was a long time ago." The hem of her skirt went still. "A woman's education—any she's lucky enough to receive—is designed only to make her a better wife. Not support herself."

"Women do teach."

"Allowed until they marry." She turned and faced Bridget, but her gaze went through and back in time. "What stopped me from that? Being a fool."

Bridget wouldn't share her own dream of being a doctor. She'd keep it close, a small, still hopeful seed she'd protect.

"Men are allowed to recover from their worst mistakes," Tate said. "Women are not."

Bridget wouldn't ask about Tate's mistake. She didn't want to know. Carrying the weight of her own was hard enough. "I'm ready to work . . . if it's safe to be seen."

"Men, ghosts, build this town," Tate said. She'd not moved from the window. "Women feed them, do their laundry, and spread legs for them."

What to say?

"I watch the ghosts," Tate went on. "The timing is a science. Too much liquor makes them slow in bed, takes up valuable time. If they can't perform, they can become belligerent, blame the girl." Her eyes locked on Bridget. "Girls learn the art of making thirty minutes seem like two hours. Learn to tell a ghost 'slow, slow' even as they maneuver to rush him."

Was it the excitement of having the book and journal? Bridget felt like laughing. "You're trying to shock me."

"When the ghost returns to the bar, that's the time to pour whiskey more generously, and from a more expensive bottle. Pencil up his bill."

Bridget smiled.

"Well," Tate crossed her arms over her chest. "I think you have the grit to survive here."

"I passed the test?" Tate's brash talk, for all its challenge or banter, seemed to come from a deeper space of heartache.

Tate roused and headed for the door, deliberately slowing to touch the journal on the table. "So, you're ready to do some cleaning? That will help with your boredom."

Bridget swept the barroom floor. The work pleased her. Stretching, using muscles after so long flat on her back, felt good. When she finished with the cleaning, the textbook and journal waited in the attic. She'd begin filling the creamy pages with thoughts and drawings, remembering when her life was ordered and safe.

Moving forward, another patch of stickiness stopped her. She scoured the broom's bristles over the spot. The floor looked and smelled as though the men paid no attention to splashed drinks, flicked ashes, even occasionally spat where they pleased despite the shiny spittoons.

"Who do they think cleans up after them? A bunch of elves?"

"Women." Tate sat at the bar, a pen over her ledger. "Underlings."

Walking through the room the day before, Bridget's worry over whether Plum Cake would accept her had consumed much of her attention. Today, she had more time to study the gleaming staircase, the double-wide doors with stained-glass windows featuring a modestly posed nude on each panel, and the life-size painting of the nude on the wall. She'd seen the full, round breasts, the generous hips, and the blush of healthy-looking flesh. As they did yesterday, the eyes held her. Bluer than the crown on a jay and full of a blend of magnetism and pain.

"This place changes men," Tate said. She rose from her barstool, walked to the center of the room, and looked down the hall to the back door. "It peels away their skin, bloats their minds. It's a contagion. They forget who they were before they started coming, satisfying themselves with purchased human flesh." She turned to point at the floor in front of the doors where sunlight bleeding through the stained glass pooled in a wash of colors. "Right there. Every time they step through, they shed skin. It's stacked up like cord wood."

The back door opened and boots stomped on the rug just inside. Bridget glanced around, wanting to disappear into the first closet she could find.

"You stay right there," Tate said. "I need that sweeping finished. The tables washed." She closed her ledger, went behind the bar and set out two cups, saucers, and a plate of pastries.

"Good morning, Tate." The man she'd called Kid pushed his wheelbarrow, his cap tucked under his arm and his dog trotting at his side.

"You're late." Tate smiled. "Did you decide to sleep in this morning?"

"Gear's cold, hard to handle. The horses are worse." He bent to his load and with a soft grunt hoisted a wooden barrel into the air and onto his shoulder. The drum's size required him to tilt his head to one side, his jaw and neck straining. He caught sight of Bridget, an easy grin breaking his look of exertion. "Morning, ma'am."

"That's Hannah." Tate spoke before Bridget could. "She's only here for a few days and she'll be moving on."

The Dalmatian, eyes bright, sank onto his belly in front of the bar, kept his head high.

"Passing through town?" Kid asked. "Where you headed?"

"Just headed."

She swept dirt into a tin receptacle. Her first impressions from the attic window had been correct: handsome, even with a nose that had seen roughhousing and now looked a bit like Papa Henry's noble nose. Wide-shouldered, slim-hipped. Older than herself by a couple of years, but as much as a couple of decades younger than Tate. What did years matter to lovers? With his height advantage and build, he was very much a man.

Despite Tate's insistence that Bridget stay and finish the work, Bridget wanted to quietly slip away and leave them alone. What was she supposed to do when Tate led him upstairs? Look away, hum a tune? Maybe they'd leave her with the dog. That would be all right.

As Kid replaced his barrel, Tate leaned down to the dog and passed him a bit of sweet roll. "Too cold for you to stay on the wagon?" She reached for a coffee pot sitting on a hot stone and poured cups for herself and Kid. "Hannah, you'll find a scrub pail and rag in the bathroom closet."

"All right."

At the bar, sitting side by side, the pair enjoyed their coffee and sweets with the ease of friends. Bridget left and returned with a bucket, finding them still there, discussing bits of local gossip, laughing. She wondered why they hadn't gone upstairs, but she was glad they hadn't. She loved Kid's voice and seeing Tate happy.

Scrubbing while sitting hurt less than kneeling on all fours, but each time she scooted forward, the dog's ears twitched and his eyes spied her. She ached to pet him, wrap her arms around his furry neck and hold on. When Kid chuckled at something Tate said—the two of them fully absorbed—Bridget used a single finger and tapped lightly on the floor. "Come," she mouthed.

The dog rose to his haunches, zeroed in on her, but refused to come.

You rascal.

Kid looked down at the dog and over his shoulder at Bridget. "He likes you."

"May I pet him?"

"Ah, you lucky boy." He snapped his fingers in Bridget's direction. "Go on."

The dog came, tail wagging, and Bridget grabbed him.

Kid watched. "You love dogs . . ."

Whatever he'd thought to say, he'd decided against doing so. Yes, she loved dogs, and she loved horses, and she loved a dear man lying in a cold box.

"I know where I've seen you." Kid chuckled. "You're the attic girl."

"Let me warm that up," Tate said. She cut Bridget a look and rose to pour Kid more coffee. "Our January beer sales are up," she told him. She had his attention again. "This stretch of cold has been good for business."

Tate didn't want her talking to the man and had pulled his attention away as deftly as if performing a card trick. The dog returned to his place beside the bar stool; Bridget finished scrubbing and took up her pail. In the bathroom, she poured out the dirty water and rinsed her rag.

"So long, Attic Girl." Kid walked by the door, pushing his wheelbarrow, his wool cap tucked under his arm again. "I'll see you tomorrow if you're still around. If not, happy travels."

"What's your dog's name?"

"Spot."

"Spot?" She couldn't resist. "That's very creative."

He stopped, considered. "Attic Girl is creative. Let me change that. I think you're more Br . . ."

Her heart banged. Had he read a description of her in the newspaper? Did *wanted* posters hang around the city?

"Britches," he finished.

Her breath eased. To a man, it was more striking to see a woman in farm britches than to see one standing idle at an attic window. "It's Hannah."

"Is it?"

Her heart nearly collapsed a second time. How much did he know?

"I won't keep you." He gave her a polite nod, his jaw firm, his hair looking windblown, and a wave just brushing the top of an ear. "Come on. Spot."

Relief washed over her when the back door shut and the hallway lay silent again. He'd surely thought her odd: unladylike in her britches, flannel shirts, and messy hair. At the same time, her appearance hadn't so disturbed him that he avoided speaking to her. She longed for company other than Tate, who was often cold. However, Kid's amiable personality likely meant he had a group of equally sociable friends. "Britches" would be a story he'd tell them over beers.

Even if he was one of the most handsome fellows she'd ever seen, if his daily deliveries and friendliness resulted in amiable, loose talk, he put her in jeopardy.

Thirteen

Tate slapped her ledger closed with such force the smack of the covers startled Bridget. After Kid left, Tate had resumed her bookkeeping with a smile playing on the edges of her lips, and Bridget had gone to the staircase where she dusted the iron balusters.

"No you don't," Tate yelled. She started across the room, an angry ear to the hallway where the tiny whisper of a door opening meant someone far less bold than Kid was trying to enter the back stairwell without being caught. "Get in here, June."

A girl near Bridget's age reached the entrance and stopped. Bridget's breath caught. The girl's battered face held deep bruising along the cheekbones, puffy eyes—one black and nearly swollen shut —a split lip.

Tate frowned and huffed and yanked a chair from one of the tables and slammed its back legs down. "Sit."

"She's hurt." Bridget frowned. *Have some compassion.*

June sank slowly, her narrow shoulders in a worn coat slumped forward, and she kept her eyes down on her trembling, gloveless hands. One fisted and loosened repeatedly over a large black velvet bow. Red with cold, the hands looked redder still because of the badly chewed nails.

Bridget hurried off the steps to squat at her side. Dr. Potter had schooled her on the treatment of accident victims. First a quick assessment of the most vital factors: airway obstruction, profuse bleeding, cardiac arrest. June had walked in on her own, was breathing ragged but able to draw deep breaths, and though she had dried blood in her hair and a split lip, she showed no signs of active bleeding. Nor was she moaning, indicating a possible broken rib.

Tate stood on the other side of the chair, using a wet towel to dab at June's puffiest eye. As she did so, June squirmed and sobbed quietly, sucking her bottom lip in an effort to keep from crying out.

"What happened?" Bridget immediately regretted the question. What happened wasn't the chief concern. She looked across June's lap to Tate. "Doc needs to examine her."

Tate stopped fretting with her towel. "Let's get her coat off."

June winced as they helped her, first one arm and then the other. Black and blue cuffs of bruising proved how hard she'd fought to get away.

"There might be internal injuries, bleeding," Bridget tried again.

"I'm not going out for Doc," Tate said, "and neither are you. He can look in on her tonight." Blood from a cut just below June's ear had followed her jaw down onto her chin. Tate rubbed as though it were a stain. "Tell Hannah who did this."

Bridget wanted to ask other questions. *How old are you? How did you end up in a brothel?*

"Tell her," Tate barked.

With her eyes still cast on the ruined bow in her hands, June whispered, "My husband."

"And tell her," Tate's words marched, "why you left the house on your night off and went to him."

"He's my husband," June cried. Her shoulders trembled as she sucked in a gulp of air and glared up at Tate. "I'm a fool. I wish he was dead."

"You don't," Bridget said. How much she wished she could crawl out from under having killed Cripe. "You don't wish that."

June turned on her. "Who are you? You don't know what I wish." Tears flowed over the swollen blue half-moons beneath her eyes. She pleaded to Tate. "I wish he was dead."

The words and June's tenor held such conviction, Bridget shivered. Was June telling Tate to see it done? *No, not that,* she thought again. *You don't really want a hand in that.*

"One of these times," Tate said, "he'll kill you."

"It's happened before?" Bridget asked. "Can't something be done?" She caught herself. "Something that doesn't end up with him dead."

Tate forced June's chin up. "I ought to throw you out. Refuse to deal with you another day. What would happen to you then? Without this house?"

"She didn't do this to herself," Bridget said. How could Tate judge the victim? There was right and wrong, definite as the two sides of a coin.

"He can't be fixed." Tate balled her towel and threw it on the table. "He simply can't be."

A knock on the front door made them all turn. Three women in large hats stood on the wide porch, their outlines visible through the stained-glass nudes. They faced each other as if refusing to acknowledge the images. Tate rolled her eyes. "Again?" She sighed heavily. "Take June to the chapel. I won't have her seen like this."

Bridget knew nothing of a chapel, but when June stood and started out, she followed readily. She'd already interacted with Kid—probably foolishly. Suppose the women saw her and were undercover detectives or reporters like Nellie Bly? At any rate, they looked like gossips, and she couldn't afford having them talking about the girl in farm clothes they'd seen at Plum Cake's. She thought again of the possibility that wanted posters could be hanging in post offices and other public places.

Only when she'd cleared the bar with June did Bridget hear Tate open the door. "Good morning."

Bridget tugged gently on June's arm, stopping her just out of the visitors' line of sight. "Can we stand here a minute?" she whispered. "I need to know who the women are." *And hopefully who they aren't.*

June slumped against the wall, compliant as a ragdoll. "He did this to me."

"You're safe now." No woman deserved a beating, ever. Just as no man deserved a wife who came and went willingly from a brothel. Ever.

"We will not step foot in a whore house." The words, shot from the porch, zinged across the bar and into the hall. Other comments, sharp as hatpins, didn't reach Bridget's ears whole. Instead, scattered phrases rained down like hail: "reporters," "papers across America," "your kind," "soiled reputations," "Easter march for the vote."

"Easter?" Tate bristled. "Nearly four months from now, and you're already at my door?"

"We are inviting representatives from the National Delegation. We need your word you'll stay away."

"Do you? I thought all women were welcome."

"This time our husbands will be watching, our pastors. People wanting reasons to discredit us."

Bridget relaxed. *Only suffragists and not interested in me.* She dared to peek around the corner. Tate faced the trio, her back to the bar, and her shoulders so erect she appeared three inches taller than normal.

The broad hats on the women made Bridget look closer. One brim held what looked like a serving platter of winter greenery, fir and red berries. The other two hats made her want to laugh, or weep for the poor birds who'd lost plumage, and weep harder still for the dead cardinal. A trophy kill to adorn a woman's hat, the bird had been pinned with its wings stretched out above its body. As though it had crashed there on the woman's head.

"We ask out of decency," Dead Cardinal Hat said. "Do not step foot in our parade."

"I'll close these doors myself," Tate said, her voice even and authoritative, "when you promise to feed these girls." Lips pursed, but

Tate went on. "How many will each of you take into your home? For how many nights can they sleep in your beds, on your sheets?"

"Trust in the Lord to provide for them."

Tate swept a hand to indicate the bar. "This seems to be the best He's willing to do."

Silence from the stoop but for a rustling of unsettled wool coats, mink collars, and feathers on flamboyant hats.

"Our concern," one spoke with a tight voice, "is getting the vote. You and others like you hinder our cause."

"Kindly," Tate's voice was equally strained, "remove your size twelve brogans from my stoop. When your husbands arrive, I'll tell them you said hello."

The slam of the door made the nudes dance.

Tate turned on her heels. "Society's perfect little women, Hannah. Following all the rules."

Bridget stepped out, surprised Tate knew she was there.

"Is that the world you're from?" Tate asked.

"I'm not your enemy." She pinched at the thighs of her britches, pulled them out in an exaggerated motion, and took a deep, formal bow. "You have to pity us pious ones, too."

"I do," Tate said with a slight hesitation. "Jezebels hang on one end of the stick, the sanctimonious on the other. Except that stick, Hannah?"

Bridget waited. Tate addressed her, but kept her eyes focused on June.

"Men hold that stick. When they twirl it, both ends spin at the same speed."

"Don't send me away," June begged.

Tate turned her back on them, returning to her books as if June hadn't spoken.

"She won't send you away," Bridget said. Hopefully, that was true.

She was familiar with the small window at each turn of the staircase, affording weak light, but with each step down, the light faded and the going required additional attention.

"You didn't light a candle," June said.

"We'll take our time." Reaching the bottom and with her eyes more adjusted, she looked back up. She'd taken the stairs from the bar to the attic a couple of times, but seeing the entire long stretch, basement to attic—a sweeping escape route—eased a bit of the knot in her stomach.

They'd taken only a few steps down the dark basement hallway when threads of streaming brightness caught Bridget's eye. To her right, the smallest shafts of daylight bled through the old slats of a trap door. She remembered the tugging, the painful dropping stair by stair. She felt certain she'd been dragged from the alley through that entrance. By Lily? By the woman who struggled even to climb three flights of stairs? Who was possibly Mum?

She shook away the idea of Mum and mapped the door's placement in her mind. It exited onto the alley, yards from the entrance Kid used. Police on a raid would come in through the front and backdoors of the brothel, see and use the grand staircase off the bar. In the minutes it took them to find the all-but-hidden back stairs, she could possibly rush down them to the basement and escape through the trap door.

June tugged at Bridget's arm with more urgency. "Stop. We need a candle." She nearly wept again. "I'm not going down there in the dark."

The passageway ahead grew darker the deeper it went. Shadowy depths turned pitch. "We have to go down there?" Bridget asked.

June struck a wood match. Half a dozen candles in brass holders lined a tiny shelf. Bridget had glanced over similar shelves, equally equipped, on each turn of the staircase and just outside her attic room. The first and second floors of the house had been electrified, but wiring the basement, like wiring the attic, must have seemed too newfangled and excessive.

"Ruby brings me down here," June whispered. Her hand shook as she touched her match to a candlewick. "She's not afraid."

"Afraid of what?" Bridget hushed her own voice, picked up a candle, and tipped its wick into June's flame. The brick walls smelled earthier than the walls in the attic, more like a crypt.

"Hurry," June's voice was raspy with tension. They'd come abreast of a closed door, and she pulled Bridget's arm. "Hurry," her fear increasing.

"Who's in there?"

"It's the Black Ghost. Tate says it's someone named Lily, but we aren't stupid."

Bridget's heart lagged. She'd known Lily was living in the basement, but she'd not considered the gloom. She'd not allowed herself to think *below ground*. "Why is she down here? Why doesn't she have a room upstairs?"

"No one wants to see her." June rushed on. "Never come down here alone."

Bridget moved from Lily's door and passing a second, caught a flicker of her candlelight reflecting off of a large brass lock. She looked back over her shoulder. "What do you know about Lily?"

"The Black Ghost? It looks like a snake. Ruby said the fire turned it into a monster. I don't know why Plum Cake keeps it, but Ruby said the door is always locked, and the Black Ghost can't get out."

The Black Ghost? A snake? The girls believed that? No lock dangled from Lily's door, and she made nightly treks to the attic and river. However, if June's fear, and the fears of others, were soothed by believing Lily was captive, so be it.

They reached the end of the hall, and Bridget caught herself slowing again. "What else does Ruby say?"

"She says the Black Ghost killed a man in the alley."

No. That was unfair to Lily, and Bridget vowed to talk the rumor over with Tate and see if it could be stopped. Without disclosing the truth. "Tate and Plum Cake care about Lily," Bridget said. "Burn injuries are terrible, but they don't turn humans into monsters or killers. Ruby, whoever she is, is a fool."

"I'm telling you, never go in there. Only Tate and Doc do."

"I suppose they carry garlic in their pockets?"

June's partially closed eye narrowed farther. "Would that help?"

"I was joking."

June whimpered. "Don't. The Black Ghost is real."

Mum, or a tortured woman who believed she was, lived with people harboring such fear they needed the smallness of labels to stave their panic. *How much longer,* Bridget asked herself, *can I live not knowing the truth?* "If Tate or Plum Cake visit—"

"Plum Cake doesn't visit." June pulled open a door. "She might not be real."

Fourteen

The place Tate referred to as the chapel held a row of small windows running just beneath the ceiling along the back wall. Too high to look through. From the outside, they were below ground but window wells afforded some natural light. Nearly a dozen claw-footed bathtubs sat in rows as evenly spaced as planted trees. Sheets of silk hanging over irregularly placed clotheslines reminded Bridget of bunting lining a parade route. The fabrics, though not placed strategically for privacy, shimmered with reflected light thrown from flickering candles. Three burned in front of a statue; three others burned in front of an occupied bathtub.

A woman with flame-red hair, who'd not bothered with a bathing slip, lay back, her breasts as exposed as those in the barroom painting. Another woman—or ought Bridget think *girls* of them both—sat tub side, fully dressed.

Bridget looked away, wanting to respect their privacy. Coming down the hall, she'd felt unsettled with pity for Lily and June's nervousness, but the chapel was peaceful, souled. The dim lighting and the mystery reminded her of the dense woods back home and visiting Old Mag just after sunset when the world was in transition and the nocturnal beginning to stir. The magical, changing hour.

"If you're done gawking," the accusation came from the woman sitting in the tub, "help June."

There was no need to answer, and Bridget didn't want to strike up a conversation with any more of the brothel's inhabitants. Too many already knew her story.

The one sitting in the chair wore a pale satin robe, lifted her fingers only, giving a half-disinterested wave. "I'm Hassie." To Bridget, she seemed no more spirited in sharing her name than she had been in sharing a wave. Her interest was on Bridget's clothes. Had she never ridden a horse or pitched down hay?

Following June to a tub, Bridget trailed a finger across a sheet of green, the silk stirring to life. *Healing.* The word came to mind, though she couldn't explain exactly how color and rich fabric healed.

June sank onto the chair next to a tub, her body going limp so quickly Bridget grabbed her shoulders to keep her from tipping onto the floor.

"Fill the fool a bath. Hot water is on the radiators."

The sharp order came from the woman with flaming red hair. Taking a second glance at her, Bridget decided she might be older than she first supposed. Possibly in her mid-twenties. Her hair, piled sloppily atop her head, proved she paid no more attention to her pins than did Bridget. The messy tresses seemed to boil in the candlelight. Slightly embarrassed for having stood stupidly, Bridget pushed in a rubber plug and turned on the spigot rising out of the brick floor. Keeping one eye on June, she hurried to the bank of radiators and carried back two pails of hot water.

As the tub filled, Hassie and Flame watched, their gazes keen on both her and June.

Flame broke the silence. "Help her undress."

Give me a dang minute, Bridget thought. Then, *Don't react. Smile and nod.* She helped June with her buttons, then with gingerly sliding the dress off her shoulders. "No," Bridget whispered, her breath clumping in her throat. Bruises spread like spilled wine over June's right side. How many punches were necessary to cause that? How many boot kicks?

"Doc needs to look at you."

Still holding the bow in one hand, June reached out with the other for assistance in stepping over the side of the tub. Like Flame, she demonstrated no shyness at being naked. So different from many of the women Dr. Potter treated, who went through contortions to avoid showing an inch more skin than necessary. June seemed not to be in her body at all, not to be aware of living there.

Bridget tugged at the velvet bow. "Shall I take that?"

Her gaze dropping, June looked a moment at the bow and reluctantly let it go. She melted limb by limb into the warm water, then sank back, and a fresh wash of tears ran down her face. "I wish he was dead."

Bridget wouldn't object again; she'd lunged at Cripe with a knife for what he'd done, and she'd wanted Mr. Fester to pay for harming his wife. June had a right to her feelings, but hopefully they wouldn't get her in even more horrible trouble.

As she sank deeper, June's knees rose, and her lips settled at water level.

Not on my watch, Bridget thought. *I'll pull the plug, drag you out.* Was the fear of drowning one of the reasons Tate had sent her along? That and because June so feared Lily she wouldn't likely have come alone?

Minutes passed as Bridget watched, wondering how a married woman had landed in the brothel. Her husband was wrong to beat her, though he likely felt her time in the house justified his actions. Couldn't he see the beatings weren't keeping her home?

Flame rose and stepped out of the tub, letting water sheet off her naked body and onto the floor. A glistening trail wound toward a drain. She pulled down emerald fabric. Wrapped in silk, she went with Hassie to the table with the statue and candles. They sat in front where four chairs were lined up, and though Bridget couldn't make out more than a few words, those sounded practiced and in unison, as if reciting a short prayer.

At the door and ready to leave, Flame stopped, came to June's tub, plunged in both hands and scooped handfuls onto June's face. "You damn fool!"

June's eyes opened with the shock of the water hitting her.

Bridget jumped to her feet. "Stop that."

"And you'll make me?"

Flame glared a moment longer at Bridget then said casually, "I'm Ruby."

You! The one telling others Lily's skin has turned into a snake's? Bridget needed a moment to swallow back anger. "I'm Hannah." Saying the name felt dishonest, but the name Ruby was likely just as much an alias. At Plum Cake's, women played at being other people and hid and disguised themselves even from themselves.

"You're new," Ruby said.

"I'm just passing through."

"Sure you are." Ruby headed back for the door. "We're all just passing through, aren't we, June?"

When Ruby and Hassie were gone and the hall quiet, Bridget soaped June's hair. The dried blood came away, revealing only a single, half-inch gash. The absence of swelling worried Bridget. Inward distension put pressure on the brain.

The water chilled and Bridget offered to fetch another pail of hot.

June shook her head. "I want to sleep. Bring me blue."

The fabric came off the line in a dance of unfurling hues. Bridget resisted rubbing the color against her own cheek, wrapped the fabric over June's shoulders, and followed her to the statue.

Gold silk lay over a small table and draped to the brick floor. On top, a large mirror reflected the burning candles and a plaster statue standing about two foot tall. The mirror made the figure appear twice its height. Feet to feet, the reflection was of a maiden with a beatific smile descending into a watery realm. A saint seemingly at peace in this world and the Otherworld. She wore a long white under tunic and a red knee-length cape trimmed in gold leaf. The burning candles and their reflections played light off her ebony hair and skin. With her left hand, she pressed two feathered arrows to her heart. Her right rested on a large anchor standing at her feet and reaching to her waist. Both objects spoke of Papa Henry's world and thus to Bridget. Arrows his people used to harvest buffalo and survive, and the anchor took her mind to the ark in the barn. The anchor, like an ark, was for waiting out a storm or season or simply a night in order to rest and restock the vessel.

"She's broken," Bridget said. The statue held several clear breaks with the pieces refitted and glued, but showed no attempts made to touch up the areas of flaked off paint. The statue was important to the house, given the prominence of a stage, silk, a mirror, and candles. Its presence turned the essence of an ordinary room into a chapel. Why leave it looking so broken? "Who is she?" Bridget asked.

"St. Philomena," June sniffled and pulled her sheet of silk tighter around herself. "Ruby says she didn't take shit from anyone."

Water gurgled from the tub June had used and a wagon rolled down the street in front of the house. Bridget tried unsuccessfully to let the sounds carry her away. The color of the statue's black paint didn't only say Negro; it also said Indian and all dark-skinned people. Seeing it standing there, broken yet honored, made her eyes sting.

June steepled her hands. "Our Mother, who art heaven . . ."

Bridget strained to hear.

". . . wholeness is thy name." June stopped.

Was she trying to remember the rest of the refashioned prayer? June rose, as if ending on the affirmation of wholeness *was* the complete prayer.

Fifteen

"I'll take June," Tate said. "Goose needs you in the kitchen."

They'd returned from the chapel, June still wrapped in blue, and Bridget watched as Tate helped her upstairs. *What now?* She wanted to call after them. She still wished Tate would send for Doc, but June did appear to be all right, bruising aside.

Half an hour later, a dozen peeled potatoes lay in the bottom of Bridget's kettle. Goose stood at a table, flour strewn across. He wore a conical paper hat he'd fashioned out of newsprint, and a white bed sheet pinned shoulder to shoulder reached to his feet. He looked clean and made Bridget think of a wall, prepped and waiting for a sign to be painted on it. Holding a ring from a mason jar, he punched along the sheet of dough he'd rolled across the table. His perfect circles neared two dozen and still he punched, cutting out more buns.

Tate appeared at Bridget's shoulder. "You'd better hurry up here or the girls won't be eating today."

"How's June?"

"Asleep the minute her head hit the pillow." Tate looked drawn. "You're settled in here?"

"Yes," Bridget answered, "though I can't stop thinking about Lily and the chapel with that statue."

Tate pulled out a chair, sank wearily. "Ah, the statue. Lily found it on one of her treks. Back then, we worried less about her leaving the house and trusted she could find her way home. The statue was behind St. Philomena's church. Do you know the place? Tall spiral," she glanced to the ceiling, "rising into the sky like the good people inside can be shot up through it. Peas through a shooter straight to the pearly gates. Lily saw the broken thing lying right along with its packaging. One look inside the crate and the priest must have chucked the whole thing out. Keep peeling. That's what struck Lily, a female symbol discarded so carelessly."

A shiver ran along the stitches on Bridget's stomach. It was sad to think of Mum or any woman walking alone, hiding from people, being so friendless and ashamed of her appearance she identified with a discarded statue. Picked up the pieces of the plaster and brought them home to a cellar room for others.

"You can imagine how coming upon the statue affected her," Tate said, as though nearly reading Bridget's mind. "A woman rejected for her appearance. Skin too dark for that holy place. The mail order house must have sent the wrong one."

"That's how Lily found me." Bridget took another potato from the musty-smelling burlap bag. "Broken in the alley."

"I guess that's true."

Bridget peeled, watched the brown rinds drop into her pile of waste.

"She glued the statue back together but refused to touch up the paint and pretend the brokenness wasn't there."

"It's a great symbol. What I've done makes me more broken than that. But for Lily—"

Tate grabbed Bridget's hand, stopped her from reaching for the next potato. "You don't still believe she's your mother? That's impossible."

The impossible happens every day.

"The color of the skin," Bridget paused, sighed. "The man who killed Papa Henry did so because of race. It's hard to imagine a Christian church so narrow minded when Jesus was black skinned."

"Why not? What's a church but a group of like-minded people, a club gathered together to chew over mutually agreed upon beliefs?"

"Your irreverence always makes me laugh. So tell me, Philomena was young and white, but what made her a saint?"

"Virginity." Tate nearly hooted the word. "She died 'pure as the driven snow.'"

Goose used a spatula, slapped dough rounds onto a baking sheet. His sweating face smiling. A discarded statue of St. Philomena having found a home in a brothel was obviously an old joke between them.

Tate took up a second knife, a potato, and began peeling. "St. Philomena was thirteen when she died, declared a saint for not having given up her virginity. Though I'll never know why churches are always in a tizzy over females' privates."

"Who declared her a virgin?" Bridget asked. "Who checked?"

Tate gave Bridget a wry look, her eyes laughing. "I do believe you've become corrupt under this roof."

Bridget swallowed. "My corruptness landed me here. Do the girls know Lily is responsible for bringing them the statue?"

"I'll ask around."

"Do you know what the arrows and anchor symbolize?"

"Survival. Archers tried to kill her, and the arrows turned and struck them. The king, whose favor she rejected, tried to drown her, but angels came to the rescue again."

"So she lived through it all."

"Mostly." Tate made a slicing motion across her neck. "I guess angels aren't as handy fending off an executioner's axe."

Bridget watched Tate's smile settle. Impertinence was a sport to her, an aid in surviving, but why had she really come into the kitchen? It wasn't just to tell an amusing story or even an inspiring one about a young girl who would not yield to a king. Had she come to be sure the murderous Hannah was indeed in the kitchen? Not sneaking back down to the basement and Lily's room? "Where was Lily living when the fire happened?"

Tate's knife slipped. She dropped it and the potato and sucked her finger. "Not serious," she said after a moment, examining what was no more than a scratch on her thumb. "You ask too many questions."

"I don't mean to, but I'm curious about her. What's her story? How did she get here?"

"The hospital sent word," Tate explained. "I was told another woman was about to deliver and had nowhere to go after. I visited her, told her she was welcome to recuperate here."

Bridget felt her mouth going slack. "You?" Tall, striking, obviously well fed, well housed, and well dressed. Did she approach girls in trouble as a savior or a recruiter? Grabbing up the knife and spud Tate had dropped, Bridget pushed them out of her reach. If Tate's story were true, Lily couldn't possibly be Mum. Unless Mum had been at the hospital having a second child. "Why send for you? Not someone looking like June with her battered face?"

"I never wanted her to stay permanently. I offered her a room downstairs for a few weeks."

"Why send girls here? Why not to a convent, a home? Anywhere else?"

"Options are rare. The city budget," Tate waved a hand toward the icy windows, "doesn't include housing for girls in that kind of trouble. The charity ward for delivery, but then they are sent off. Most families never welcome them back. If a family exists at all."

"And her baby?"

Tate sucked her finger again. "Lily had agreed to give the child to a Christian family, and then changed her mind, but the infant died." She pursed her lips at Bridget. "My proposal was a gift of time. I hoped Lily would use the weeks to locate someone to help her. An aunt, a cousin, a friend with a bit of compassion. The other girls, given time to heal and settle back on their feet, all found their way. Lily never tried."

"Why?"

"Do you ever stop? Who can say? The emotion associated with the child's death. No one to write to? It's been seven years." Tate stood. "Lily was the last. When she started seeing ghosts, I quit bringing other girls here. I'd failed."

She walked out of the kitchen, and Bridget realized she'd not answered the question about where Lily had been the day of the fire.

Sixteen

Day four. Bridget woke chilled despite her wool blankets. Even the heated bricks she'd carried up the evening before had gone cold. Had Lily visited in the night? Would another day pass without knowing the truth about her?

Bridget hurried into her clothes, looked longingly at the textbook and journal, and rushed downstairs to the bar where radiators covered in ornate brass filigree snapped and hissed out warmth.

"How is June this morning?" she asked Tate.

Tate fussed with the setting she'd arranged on the bar. Two china cups and saucers, two small plates. Napkins. The sight of two long chocolate pastries made Bridget's mouth water and her stomach growl. After Kid left, she might lick up the crumbs.

Before Tate thought to answer Bridget's question, the door at the end of the hall opened. Boots stomped to knock off any snow they carried, a wheelbarrow rolled. Tate smiled at the noise and gestured at Bridget with one perfectly manicured hand. "Don't mind us. Mind your cleaning."

Bridget gave Kid a polite smile and received one in return, but Tate had made it clear Bridget was to do her work, not join their conversation. She was happy to let the pair chatter on behind her, she didn't need to be a part of that. Kid hadn't brought Spot though, and she missed the Dalmatian. "To live without a four-legged brother or sister," Papa Henry had been fond of saying, "is to live poorly."

"Or a three-legged one," she liked to add.

She worked with two pails, dumping ashtrays into an empty one and washing the trays clean with water in the second pail. Somehow, she'd find a path back to land and animals. All land, all animals were sacred. She didn't need to live in Bleaksville. *But Papa Henry's land!*

"You okay over there?" Kid asked.

He and Tate both watched her. Had a sob escaped her throat? She did her best to smile. "Right as rain."

Kid finally pushed back his cup and stretched. Again, he and Tate had chatted companionably for an hour but not gone upstairs. What that meant, Bridget didn't know. Maybe Tate only allowed the house's services during open hours. Wanting to maintain an aura of integrity, not have men dropping in as they please, as though Plum Cake's was a common whorehouse. Not a high-end gentlemen's club.

Bridget grabbed her pail and walked out ahead of Kid, hoping to appear nonchalant, and far enough ahead of him that her going didn't appear planned. She hadn't stepped outside since her arrival and longed to breathe in fresh air. Standing over the lavatory's sink, fresh water running, she watched him start past the door. Cap tucked under his arm again, long strides, easily maneuvering his wheelbarrow. Did he know women lived vigilant, always aware of their surroundings, of unsafe locations, unsafe hours, leery as mice? While he was as safe in the world as a large cat? Going outside with him, she'd be safe too.

She followed him through the door, her breath quickening with the delicious cold rolling over her tongue and down her throat. It wasn't that he'd protect her from the police or Cripe's ghost, it was more that they wouldn't come in his presence. She turned her face to the sky. Despite the cold, the sun's rays glazed her cheeks and bloomed white behind her closed eyes.

She'd have only a minute before Kid was off, and she wouldn't squander it. Horses first. She ran a hand down each long nose, the flaring nostrils, the smooth swirls of fine hairs, and studied the deep, alert eyes. The animals were powerfully muscled, not built for speed like Smoke, but for pulling like Gus. What did they think of her? Not her person, but the scent and colors of her soul.

"Good boys," she said, knowing the modulation in her voice mattered more than her words.

"Hey." Kid worked alongside the wagon, lifting the empty barrel into place, watching her. "They like you."

"And I like them. I had a beautiful horse." Horses. Hadn't she lost them all? "A white stallion with large black markings was stolen and brought here to Omaha."

"I'm sorry. White with black markings?"

Had he seen Smoke? She couldn't make herself ask. The conversation was teetering down a dangerous road.

"You've gone to the police?"

She ached to tell him everything. Couldn't. "Are these horses yours?"

"Belong to the company."

"Do you own a horse?"

"I do. Board him a few blocks over. Spot's mine." A smile back in his voice. "At least for now."

"You wouldn't give away your dog?"

"Not everyone likes them. Spot's stubborn. He refuses to wipe his feet or quit shedding."

"You love him. You wouldn't get rid of him for being a dog." She kept herself from saying, "I'll take him." How could she? "Where is he?"

"Too cold, left him back at the stable."

"How many stables are there around here?"

He hesitated, his eyes glancing up to his right for a second. "Scattered around the city, I couldn't say. Downtown here, only a few."

"Where would the police take a horse if the owner," she hesitated, needed to think, "was say, struck by a trolley car and killed?"

He chuckled. "And the bloke's horse jumped clean out of the way and wasn't hurt? That horse?"

"Yeah."

"Keep it in their compound for a while." He shrugged. "Sell it, pocket the money."

Could he get a message to Cora, find out if she'd rescued Smoke? Could he be trusted with the task? Find out what the town was saying about her, of the farm, now that she'd disappeared? "Does Storz deliver to Bleaksville? Have you ever been there?"

"Can't say I have." He tugged gloves from a hip pocket, pulled them on, and lifted the wheelbarrow. "Someone there you need me to speak to? I could phone from the plant."

Bleaksville didn't yet have phones. Though the town would shortly. Agreements had been reached, money allocated. She couldn't tell him that; she shouldn't have mentioned the town at all. "I passed through it once," she waved her hand. "That was a long time ago."

With the wheelbarrow in place, he threaded a leather strap through its leg braces, and gave it a strong jerk. "Something in your craw? If there's anything I can do? Make a call, send a telegram?"

"Thanks, I'm fine. I didn't mean to hold you up."

He looked amused. "Why did you?"

"I needed a moment outside. Nothing more."

His expression changed. "You're not a prisoner here. Tate wouldn't do that."

She wished he could stay. They'd joke about dogs' names, unclaimed horses, anything that would keep him there. "I'm not a hostage. I've been sick is all, and Tate's helping me."

"You look well. Freezing, standing there shivering, but well enough. So why is Tate being secretive?"

"You've been asking about me?" His grin and raised brow made the nape of her neck flush. "You think I'm flirting with you, don't you?"

"No." A chuckle that said he lied. "You're different. You're not one of them."

"One of the working girls? How would you know?"

"If you're wondering, Tate and I are just friends. She could be buying her beer anywhere. She's a good customer." He glanced at Bridget's patched dungarees, the frayed cuffs of her shirt. "And I know you're not one of them because you look ready to wrestle a steer."

Wrestle a steer?

"If you think of anything." He touched the brim of his cap. "I'll be back in the morning."

"Maybe there is something . . ."

The brothel door opened, and Tate stood framed by the dark hallway behind her. Her face appeared pleasant enough but for the spate of tension her eyes couldn't quite hide. "Is everything all right?"

"I just needed a bit of fresh air," Bridget answered.

"I see." Tate remained in the doorway, holding it open despite the cold, wearing her prim lady's waist, smiling her pleasant smile. "Hannah, Goose needs your scullery help."

Bridget's throat tightened. She shoved her hands into her pockets. *Scullery? When I'm a doctor*, the oft-repeated mantra echoed hauntingly in her head. Back at the farm with Papa Henry, she'd been so sure of herself. Would she ever find that again?

Tate, still with a complacent face, pulled the door closed, but for a moment, she continued staring through the glass.

"You're freezing," Kid said again. "And I'd better keep moving. We'll stand around chatting out here in July."

She watched the back of the wagon and his receding figure on the high seat. *Ready to wrestle a steer?* Not only had he considered her clothes, he'd felt easy enough to tease her about them.

Turning back to the brothel, she stopped. No horses stood at the long rail where she'd last seen Smoke. No blood, either hers or Cripe's, soiled the snow. Her life was like that, appearing clean and smooth on the surface, but she'd fallen off a self-constructed pedestal and hadn't landed well.

Two girls stepped out of the kitchen as Bridget neared that doorway. Wearing bright robes that gaped at the necklines, their hair hanging around their shoulders, and their eyes dull as smoky glass, they paid her no attention. She thought to stop them and ask about June, but whether sleepy or drugged, they didn't look eager to talk.

"Left you a little something to eat right here," Goose said, tipping a kettle on the stove and letting it rattle down.

Bridget ate greedily, hardly noticing the stack of dirty plates and pans waiting for her. She'd not realized her hunger and the food, as always, was delicious. This time, potatoes, ham, and spices in a creamy sauce. She helped herself to a second serving, but it was the chocolate concoction she ate last that made her slow and hold the flavors in her mouth before each swallow. She sighed. "Goose, you saved one for me. This is marvelous."

He looked up from where he leaned over a table in his newsprint hat, his face just inches above a scrap of paper where he worked with a pencil.

"I've never tasted anything so delicious," she said.

He straightened. "You'd buy that in a bakery?"

She tried not to think about his clothes beneath the sheeting. His dedication to his job was admirable; the girls ate like royalty. "No wonder Kid sticks around for coffee and your sweets. You're a magician."

"Are you ready?" Tate stepped into the kitchen wearing a heavy navy coat and a matching cloche with a red silk rose pinned smartly on one side. "It's getting late."

She nodded at Bridget as Goose reached for a coat hanging on a peg, but she made no mention of the incident in the alley. *She's sorry,* Bridget thought. *She's caught too. Was it the fear of losing Kid?*

In the empty kitchen, left to her pot scrubbing, Bridget moved red bricks from the floor beside the stove to the top. She'd take a plate of food to the attic for later, another candle, and with warm bricks under her feet, she'd read.

She worked gingerly, sitting when she needed to rest her wound, stretching out her shoulder when it stiffened, and wondering about the girls upstairs. Had June come down to eat? How was she feeling this second day, and where were Ruby and Hassie? They must have eaten before she arrived in the kitchen and now had a couple of hours to prepare for the house's opening. How did a girl prepare for an evening of selling her body? How did she prepare the soul to survive?

With the last of the pans in the cupboards, Bridget used a towel and loaded the bricks, too hot to handle, onto a baking sheet. Only two flights of stairs and she could rest. She'd reverse her original plan for the afternoon, napping first, then her books. With her load, she started for the stairwell. A sound in the hall stopped her. A moan. Then louder, the name crying out from behind Plum Cake's door.

"Goose!"

Bridget had no idea when he and Tate would return. An hour? Two? She could walk away, pretend she didn't hear.

"Goo-oose!"

The name wept, desperate. Bridget set down the baking sheet, called through the door. "Plum Cake?" She'd been in the first room, going that far wasn't a breech. She opened the door and hurried through, but stopped at the drawn curtain. "It's Bri . . . Hannah. Are you all right?"

A ragged breath. "Get Goose."

"He's shopping."

A wail and the muffled sound of strangled weeping. "Get Tate."

"They've gone together." The sobbing was hardest to hear. "I can help."

"Goddamn! Goo . . . oose!"

"I'm coming in," Bridget said. "You need help, and I'm all you have." She paused for courage and parted the purple curtain.

A wall of stink hit her face. Then the sight of a huge, naked backside struck with equal force. A grossly overweight body—shoulders, back, buttocks, and legs. Guessing the weight was impossible. What did two large men squeezed into one skin weigh? Four hundred pounds?

Plum Cake hunched over the side of her bed, her hands planted on the mattress for support. She panted and trembled. Feces ran down the backs of her enormous legs, splattered over her wide blue heels and onto the floor.

Seventeen

Bridget gagged even as Plum Cake's agony, the guttural sobbing, raw and belly-deep, filled her with pity and sorrow. In bed with Wire the night after Papa Henry's murder, she'd cried as hard, biting on her blankets as anguish rolled over her in wave after wave.

Plum Cake's situation was bad, horrible, but her heaves of emotion seemed to come from an even more cavernous source. As though her helplessness unearthed myriad agonies from another time.

"It's all right." Bridget's eyes stung with pity. "We can fix this."

"I wish I was dead."

"I've seen worse," Bridget said. She hadn't. Never anything like this. She tucked her nose into the neckline of her shirt, took a breath there. "It's just illness. I've been around a lot of illness."

"Go away," Plum Cake moaned.

Bridget hadn't yet approached the bed, hadn't yet seen a face. Dr. Potter would be firm, matter-of-fact. "Your whole body is shaking. If you end up on the floor, we've got an even bigger problem."

Gasping, both hands still braced to hold up her weight, Plum Cake wailed louder.

"Hang on," Bridget said. *Why did I mention falling?* A yellow canary watched from behind bamboo bars, and a stack of newspapers sat on the floor beneath the cage. Bridget grabbed a wad and spread the papers on the bed next to Plum Cake. "Okay. We're going to just turn around and sit you on these." She tried to help by supporting the woman's elbow. "This direction, just a half turn, and you can sit."

Grimacing, Plum Cake inched her feet around, tracking the brown goo over a wider area on the carpet. She sank with a wet plop and smack onto the papers. A broad face with wide cheeks and blue eyes. The eyes held such intensity of color, a blue so translucent, so full of depth and light, Bridget thought of bluebirds with their sky-kissed pigment. Then of one of the silk sheets in the chapel. Still, however mysterious in their clarity, the eyes held tears that streamed down and around the hillocks of Plum Cake's cheeks. These were the tears of any helpless woman.

The size of the woman's body was not anything Bridget had seen before: breasts like thirty-pound infants and a stomach so large the girth extended nearly to Plum Cake's knees.

Plum Cake swiped her nose and upper lip with the back of a round hand.

"It's all right," Bridget said again. "Let's get you cleaned up."

Plum Cake sat silent, pressed her eyes closed. Her lips trembled.

The bed was a stack of lumber and reminded Bridget of barges she'd seen going down the Missouri River. A thick mattress cushioned the top. A nightstand held a bowl of butter and half a loaf of bread. Below, a blue and white enamelware washbasin held a bar of soap and a dry rag. "I'll be right back," she said.

She filled the pan with water from the bathroom sink across the hall. To avoid stepping in the mess, the floor needed dealt with first. She put the rag over the top and tried to slide her hands under the watery liquid and scoop. The smell was horrific, and she concentrated on breathing through her mouth rather than her nose. The human body, for all its incredible mystery and efficiency, was also at times terrible. Back in the lavatory, she poured her dirty water in the toilet and refilled the basin at the sink. More wiping of the floor and still more pans of water left the carpeting wet and stained, but as clean as scrubbing could do.

With each trip through the hall, Bridget looked both directions, hoping to see either Tate or Goose. The house would open in a couple of hours; Tate needed to be back in time to dress for that, but Plum Cake was so embarrassed, suggesting they wait for Goose would be cruel. Wiping and rinsing Plum Cake's legs, Bridget needed to force her rag between the thighs and calves, lifting and moving the rolls of flesh as she worked. Squatting in front, scrubbing Plum Cake's ankles and wide feet, she wondered about the woman's life. What pain had brought her to this? Bridget wanted to cry for them all: June beaten up, Lily so badly burned, Plum Cake in this condition.

Having dumped yet more reeking water, Bridget stood at the sink while fresh ran into her pan. She looked into the mirror. Whose eyes looked back, who was the stranger in her skin? She felt disembodied, no more alive than a machine.

With the cleaning, Plum Cake's breathing calmed, though she still sat without speaking.

Bridget finally took a step back. "That's the best I can do with you sitting. If you're ready to stand again, just for a minute, I'll hurry and clean your backside. Wash more between your legs."

Plum Cake's cheeks reddened, her blue eyes filled again. "I'm ashamed."

"Of course you are, but who isn't at times? Shame passes. We'll just get through this right here."

"You killed a man. That's worse, isn't it?"

Surprised, Bridget didn't answer.

Maneuvering Plum Cake onto her feet took hefting and encouragement. Ink from the newsprint had smeared across her wide bottom. Bridget could make out mercantile ads with drawings: a shoe, a corset. She decided against sharing the information. She scrubbed, running her rag between the great buttocks and wondering again what grief had sunk the woman to such a level. "There," she was finally able to say. She rolled up the newsprint. "All clean."

Plum Cake sat back down, rolled onto her side, and squirmed back into the center of the bed. She still had the mobility to get herself in and out. If she could do that, couldn't she waddle across the hall to the bathroom? The bedpan in the corner said she did her business there. With Goose's help? Had he martyred himself to a life of tending her?

"I'm ugly," Plum Cake said. "Of course no one would want to love me now." She lay panting with the effort of having worked herself onto her pillows and into the center of the bed. Beads of sweat, like the glass droplets hanging off her lampshades, ran along her forehead. She reached for a wadded bed sheet at her side and worked it down her middle with flapping arms. The outside swells of her breasts remained exposed, as did her bulging hips.

She lay half in the open, Bridget decided, not because the sheet was too small, but because covering only the essentials kept her body cooler.

Plum Cake studied Bridget, taking exaggerated moments to peer at the shirt and britches. Finally, she reached out, grabbed for Bridget's hand, and kissed it. "Bless you."

Two words, but with gratitude deep in her eyes. The scrubbing and gagging felt small in comparison to the gift. "You're welcome. Next time Goose goes out, you better have him send for me."

"What you must think."

Bridget patted the hand. "I don't think anything. It's a pleasure to meet you."

"You won't tell anyone," Plum Cake said. "That's an order."

"You have my word."

In the windowless room, Plum Cake's skin matched the pallid color of her sheet. How many years since she'd stepped outside and felt a ray of sunshine? Lily and now Plum Cake. How many ways did women allow, even orchestrate, their own invisibility? Something Bridget's own hiding in the brothel succeeded in doing.

"Don't hurt Lily," Plum Cake commanded. "Did she come to your room last night?"

Around the madam's blue-blue irises, the normally white sclera looked sore with the red of weeping. Her flesh, too, still moist with perspiration, flushed with embarrassment. If changing the subject and feeling jealousy were easier than admitting her mortification, Bridget would try to understand. "I don't think so."

"Did you upset her? Why didn't she come? It's too cold for her to be out wandering."

Bridget wanted to leave. She'd wash her hands thoroughly, though she felt certain the smell of feces had permeated her skin. She longed to go straight to the chapel and soak herself in a warm tub. Something her wound prevented her from doing. Thinking of the basement and Plum Cake's concern for Lily, Bridget remembered the large lock on the second basement door. "Why not have another lock installed on Lily's door?"

"I won't have it."

"Even if it's to protect her?"

"Have her live as confined as I am? Never." Plum Cake's lungs gave a great settling sigh as though the last remnant of her weeping were crawling out. "Let her die imagining her Hannah is back."

While helping Plum Cake, Bridget had been distracted from the ache in her stomach, but the longer she'd worked, and now with the crisis over, the wound throbbed. Carrying pans of water, getting up and down off her knees, the struggle to wipe clean the massive body. "I need to go now, or I'll be the one on the floor. Goose must be nearly back."

Plum Cake reached toward the dusty night table, brought the bread and butter to her lap. She pulled a chunk the size of a muffin off the loaf. "My heart won't last much longer. Then death . . . quiet." She used the bread like a spoon and scooped up butter. "Tick, tick and stop. Easy."

Bridget tried not to show her distaste as the madam shoved the whole of it into her mouth. She'd seen a man suck down a full glass of whiskey, then another, after his wife's death. Pain demanded feeding. What was Plum Cake's? "You're too young to be thinking about dying."

The madam swallowed, pulled off more bread. "Like a clock. Tick . . . tick. Quiet. Though not by my own hand." The blue eyes unrelenting. Eyes almost familiar. "Suicide brings damnation. God will decide my hour, my minute. It'll happen by His hand." She pulled off another chunk of bread. "I'm waiting on God's mercy."

Bridget looked away and to the bright canary. She yearned to touch the living thing and extended a finger slowly through the bars, but she couldn't reach to stroke a wing or the tiny head. Plum Cake meant to take herself to the edge of living, and she'd convinced herself doing so was all right. Because the moment of actually toppling over would be from God's hand. A small shove. Leaving her blameless.

"Tick, tick," Plum Cake said again.

In the attic, the new journal waited. Bridget's first entry would be to write about Plum Cake, a woman killing herself with food and a rationale that exonerated her.

Crumbs fell onto Plum Cake's chins. "Lily and I will die together." The crumbs rolled onto the sheeting over her breasts.

The bird flapped against the sides of its cage.

"Let Ollie out," Plum Cake said. "She'll come to me."

Bridget lifted the small cage door and the bird hopped to the front.

Plum Cake made a tiny whistling sound and opened her mouth wide. Yellow feathers fluttered as the bird, wobbly in the air, flew up the sheeting and landed on the madam's round bottom lip. With toes like golden stick bugs, Ollie clung, stretched her head in, and pecked wet bits of bread from Plum Cake's teeth.

"How long has she been like that?" Bridget asked Tate later.

"A couple of years at least. Her condition is the only reason she still tolerates me. The girls haven't seen her, and they imagine every sort of fantastical beast: three eyes, two heads. Plum Cake keeps me, I'm sure, because I'm no longer shocked, and she won't suffer the shame of fresh eyes on her. Only one thing holds more fear."

"What's that?"

"Being left alone for too long."

"Yet she doesn't go outside that room?"

"I think everyone of us could eat dictionaries and still not have the words to describe all the whys for what we do."

Eighteen

That evening, Bridget sat at the foot of Plum Cake's bed with a small knife trimming the madam's toenails. The smell of feces still lingered in the room, as did traces of capon with garlic cloves, freshly baked bread, and sweet pudding with vanilla flavoring—all of which Goose brought for the evening meal the three of them enjoyed. Plum Cake ate from a tray he'd made for her—a shelf of wood with two-foot-high legs. She'd even dressed for dinner. A flat purple dress front lay stretched over her. Lavender lace bordered the neckline and extended out an additional eighteen inches on both sides, long tails that tied around Plum Cake's neck. More lengths of lace at the ends of the sleeves knotted around the madam's wrists like bracelets. Bridget thought of paper dolls with their flat clothing and tabs. Purple buttons the size of plum halves dotted the front. Both decoration and distraction, Bridget supposed, an effort to misdirect the eye from the bulk of the body beneath.

Piano music, along with men laughing and shouting, vibrated through the wall separating Plum Cake's quarters from the bar. From the attic, Bridget had heard the same, but with a floor between, the noises had not felt so threatening.

"I'm glad you decided to come down," Plum Cake said.

Bridget glanced from the foot she tended into the next room where Goose sat on a stool. His face to the wall, his body hunkered like a schoolboy being disciplined, his glasses on the floor beside him, he peeked through a hole into the bar. "He said you *needed* me." She'd not imagined being asked to trim Plum Cake's toenails.

"I knew you'd enjoy spending the evening together."

"Thank you," Bridget managed. *Digging dirt out of your toenails is so much more fun than my journal.*

She looked again to Goose. His spying on the bar made her nervous. She'd not noticed anything unusual while cleaning there, no tiny, dark openings, no pictures without eyes. "Does Tate know you have a peephole?"

"I must have honesty," Plum Cake said. "I'm stranded. I need to know the girls are working. The truth is all I have, and I need to know Tate is telling it."

"I believe she's honest," Bridget said. "I don't think she'd keep anything from you."

"Is everyone working?" Plum Cake called to Goose.

Rather than shout back and have the sound go into the bar, Goose closed the small door and lumbered across the room to the curtain. "It's a good night."

"What is Ruby wearing?"

Goose shrugged.

Plum Cake flicked her wrist at him. "Go back. Tell me what my girls are wearing." She waited until he stepped away and whispered, "He has no imagination."

Bridget finished trimming the nails on one foot, poured a bit of oil into her hand, and began massaging the grease into Plum Cake's dry heel. She could scarcely bear the thought of touching the other foot. The job wasn't worse than cleaning up feces, but she couldn't unsee what she'd seen between the toes just that afternoon.

"I have imagination," she said. "And better eyes than him. I could tell you what the girls are wearing."

Plum Cake hesitated the length of one indrawn breath. "All right. You go to the Truth-Teller. See if my girls are pretty. See if they're admiring my picture."

"Oh, it's you." Bridget straightened. "Your picture in the bar. The eyes, of course. You have the most beautiful eyes." She hurried into the next room wanting to avoid any further discussion that compared the woman in the painting to the woman in the bed.

Plum Cake's questions about the girls' appearances and referring to them as "her" girls smacked of ownership, but Bridget tried not to form a judgment. There was too much she didn't yet understand, and Plum Cake was one of the most downtrodden women she'd ever met. Surely the madam wasn't actually thinking in terms of ownership, couldn't possibly be as arrogant as her words suggested.

Bridget tapped Goose's shoulder and waited as he shut the small door in front of him. Once closed, it disappeared, having the same flocked purple covering as the wall. She handed him the knife. "Have fun."

Sliding open the small door revealed a hole no larger than the tip of Bridget's thumb. She leaned forward. The room swelled magically with amber light. She'd dusted the large tawny globes of glass, but she'd not imagined how the room glowed at night when they were the only source of light. The staircase still left her in awe. The lazy, serpentine *S* allowed for a woman's gradual and very visible entrance: a stage on which women performed descents. Smoke from pipes, cigars, and cigarettes wound slowly upward into the chandelier and rolled along the embossed ceiling.

Gaiety. A large, festive party with two dozen or more men, including Doc, and several girls. Men in three-piece tailored suits, tweeds and pinstripes, threw down cards or rolled dice and cheered over the din at their luck. Or shouted just as loudly at the lack of it. Girls sat on their knees like children, leaned on their arms, carried them drinks. The girls wore low-cut, sleeveless tops and the sort of clothing Bridget had never seen in a store or a Sears and Roebuck catalogue. Tate stood behind the bar wearing more clothes than the others, though her sleeveless gown revealed a cleavage-deep plunge. Strings of pearls around her neck slid side to side over the tops of her breasts as she moved. The gems rested between her breasts when she stopped. Her hair, stacked higher than Bridget had seen, likely included a long switch braided in and, with the help of elaborate pins, crowned the crest of her head. The addition of a long, white feather outlined in gold added to her air of eloquence. The plume waved as she poured drinks into sparkling glasses.

Kid was not among those gathered. Her searching for him around every table and along the row of men at the bar, and the relief she felt at his absence, surprised her. She couldn't afford to care about him.

Ruby smoked a tiny cigar through an enameled holder. Her crimson lips worked the mouthpiece, parting and pressing. If the males watching thought of kissing or something else, Bridget thought of a fish. Her hair with its bright red henna looked even bolder than it had in the chapel. Moving among the men, her eyes rounded in kohl, she held a sultry pose. A lacy romper, a chemise also low across her breasts, thin straps dangling down her arms. Below a sash knotted tightly around her waist, her hips flared. Garters, clipped thigh-high, held up sheer stockings and invited eyes to gaze at her creamy, exposed skin. Heavy glass rings the size of grapes adorned her fingers. She clasped onto a man's hand and tugged him playfully toward the staircase.

Going up, she met Hassie coming down. Their hands touched. Fingertips dragged through the other's palm.

The longer Bridget watched, the more her stomach sank. The girls were more than sexual partners for the men. Bad enough, but they also pandered on levels of human servitude meant to demonstrate inferiority and vulnerability. Thin arms, scantily clothed bodies, and slippered feet were also part of the job. Satisfy male lust and inflate male egos: Make even the least attractive man feel superior to the girl he bedded. Build him up despite his attitude toward her.

She wanted to slam shut the tiny door. She wasn't sure what she'd expected, but not this. Not how the actions of the workers made her stomach roll and threatened to send her running to the bathroom to be sick. The girls were like the beggars she'd seen on trash heaps behind New York City restaurants. They hated the wealthy for how they discarded and wasted food, even as they were thankful for the scraps.

"Well?" Plum Cake called. "What do you see?"

Bridget slowly slid the door shut and dropped her head against it. If Lily were actually Mum, how bad had her life become for her to take up this work? And once begun, her soul carved out, who could blame her for not being able to escape. Bridget thought of the three suffragists who'd stood on the stoop the day before. Even women in secure relationships and secure financially, had to battle daily to keep open the doors of justice for themselves. The wounded woman, one without social standing, the hungry, the cold—how impossibly hard for her?

"Well?" Plum Cake's shout was louder this time. "Are my girls beautiful?"

"Yes," Bridget said, stepping past the curtain. Plum Cake wanted reassurances that everyone was happy. She wanted to believe the lie. Was she bedridden in part because she could no longer bear to witness the truth?

"Don't just stand there. Where's your imagination? What are they wearing?"

"Chemises, laces in bright colors." Just the telling made the queasiness in Bridget's stomach churn again. "Ruby's in yellow, straps sliding off her shoulders. That flame-red hair."

"Flame red?" Plum Cake's brows narrowed on Goose who held her foot. "You've never told me her hair was that red." Her eyes lifted again to Bridget. "Redder than your own hair? And Tate?" A hesitation. "What's she wearing? Is she keeping order?"

Bridget had meant to stay uninvolved in the lives of these women. She'd promised herself she'd care only about learning Lily's identity and keeping herself out of the law's hands. As soon as she'd healed and come up with a plan for how best to live the life she'd ruined, she'd leave. Now she was being asked to spy. Even on Tate. There was no other word for it. *What to say?* "She's striking. I hadn't seen her before in a low-cut dress or pearls."

Plum Cake nodded, but her eyes looked doubtful and full of more questions about Tate. She didn't ask them. "And the rest of my girls?"

"It's sad. They all look so young."

"Not a one had a childhood," Plum Cake said. "Tate tells me all their stories are different and all are the same. Nowhere to go, already trained to survive by selling their bodies, often from an even younger age. Living here is a big step up." She glanced around the room as though it, too, were a grand place. "A bed, food, money, living free of pimps."

"They're so vulnerable." The idea wouldn't leave Bridget. They dressed for men who purchased them for sex, but was that only half? Did they also dress for men who purchased them for their vulnerability, a posed inferiority, a striking contrast to assumed masculine sufficiency? Next to the women, the most enfeebled male could beat his chest.

Was it overly dramatic to think rape? The girls could leave. June walked out when she wanted, but how much volition did a girl really have when the alternative was huddled on a cold street? How much when a lifetime of belittling had convinced her she deserved nothing more than life in a brothel?

"What else?" Plum Cake asked. "Don't just stand there. What did you see?"

"That," Bridget pointed to the dark room she'd just left, "is the saddest thing I've ever seen."

Goose kept his face down, concentrated on Plum Cake's large foot.

"They all came needing," Plum Cake said. Accusation in her voice. Above the purple lace at her throat, the skin was beginning to turn pink. "Don't forget that. They are young, but not too young to be thrown out of homes. Or needing to run from them." The pink flushed red. "You suppose you're better than us?"

I murdered a man. "No, just luckier," Bridget said. Again, she felt anything but lucky. She needed away, time alone. "I've been on my feet all day. My stomach is throbbing, I'm going—"

"I used to watch Lily," Plum Cake stopped her. "She was the most beautiful one."

Bridget thought she'd never understand anyone at the house. "Mum? You loved her? Still, you paid her to take men upstairs?"

Plum Cake's chins rolled as she opened her mouth. "Lily never loved them."

Glancing to Goose, who still squinted over Plum Cake's feet, and back to the sheet-clad figure on the bed, Bridget felt she'd washed up on some impossible shore. Humans had the ability to justify whatever suited them. She started for the door but paused and turned back. "How long has Lily been here?"

"You don't listen." Plum Cake pulled her foot from Goose, flashed angry eyes at Bridget. "Seven years."

Tate had also said seven. If Lily were Mum, that meant she and Pappy must have faced almost instant deprivation in America. Had Pappy died as soon as the first year and Mum been pregnant? "Do you know where she came from?"

"Born and raised in Omaha." She pushed her foot, so that Goose lifted it again. "Are there any more questions, Inspector?"

"Maybe she only told you that to hide another life. Like making up a brothel name."

Voices and tinny music continued pulsating from the bar.

"Lily wouldn't lie to me," Plum Cake insisted. "And she doesn't owe me any name but Lily. I love her. Ouch!" She howled and jerked her foot.

"Sorry," Goose mumbled, as a drop of blood beaded where he'd pared too deep into her nail bed. Had he done so intentionally? Bridget wondered. Was he jealous of Lily?

"One more thing." Plum Cake lifted a fleshy hand and brushed at the front of her dress. The underside of her large arm waved. "Before you go, what was June wearing?"

The deliberate tone startled Bridget. Was this a test of her loyalty, or a test of Tate's? They were all mad. All expert at denial and flipping the course of a conversation as easily as flipping cards. "June's taking the night off."

"Is she ill?"

Since waking in the attic, Bridget had felt as though she struggled to keep a dozen circus balls in the air. Lies, half-truths, tests. She thought of Mrs. Fester, and of Dr. Potter's unwillingness to get more involved in the poor woman's life. Suppose Plum Cake's asking was honest concern, and she was the one person who could help June?

"She's pretty beaten up, inside and out." When Plum Cake's brows lifted in surprise, Bridget rushed on. "Her husband worked her over."

"What happened?"

"I don't know details. A fight with her husband, which I guess isn't new. And Tate doesn't want her on the floor looking so bruised up."

"She was seriously hurt?"

"No broken bones or anything like that. The bruising is bad though, and she has black eyes and a split lip."

"I wasn't told." She frowned at Goose. "Did Tate tell you?"

He put the tiny knife at the corner of another toenail and peeled as delicately as if he were skinning a grape. The rim of the nail began to lift and curl off. "She didn't tell me."

"And you didn't notice June was missing?"

Goose only glanced up through the thick glasses that made his eyes appear twice their normal size. The knife tight in his large hand, he lowered his face again.

"Hannah," Plum Cake said, "my decision to let you stay was the right one."

Ollie began to flap in her cage, and Bridget felt shutters slamming, a chill running up her back. *What had she done?*

Plum Cake scowled. "June is one of *my* girls. *I* need to be told what's happening to them." She looked at Goose, who kept his eyes on his work. "Maybe Tate has stayed too long."

"No," Bridget insisted. Minute by minute the aromas from the meal they'd eaten faded and the smell of feces grew stronger. "Tate works hard. She sees the place is kept clean, does the books, and she's out there now pouring drinks and keeping order."

"Thank you for stopping by," Plum Cake said. "I get lonely. Especially now." Her eyes moistened. "Lily hasn't been coming. Doc says she could go at any time."

"Because of old burns?" The question wouldn't leave Bridget.

Plum Cake's dark hair, in need of washing, lay heavily across her pillow. "Horrible burns. Internal organs have been damaged."

"Some blame her for the murder in the alley."

Plum Cake shrugged. "I guess that's good for you. It hardly matters to her."

What to say? Reason said Plum Cake was right. Why then did it feel so wrong?

In the hall, Bridget paused. At the end to her right, the bar's moody light and noise swelled. To her left was the exit Kid used, the alley, and away from the brothel. But the door also led onto night and the place where Cripe had died. Where would she run even if she could force herself out there again? She couldn't make it to Bleaksville on foot. Even if she could, what then?

In the stairwell, Bridget stopped. Climbing to the attic after what she'd seen, felt impossible. Like a crawl through a black wall, thick and solid as a tomb. She stood, shaky with the thought of how every inhabitant of the house was buried alive by something—class, gender, loss, handicaps of the heart. She felt along the edge of the wall and the small ledge, struck a match, and held it to a candle. Light extended over only the few nearest steps. She needed to lie down, but getting herself up to the cold attic and then facing that cold seemed impossible.

Suppose this was her last night at the brothel? If Tate sent her off for having confided in Plum Cake, how could she go without knowing for sure she wasn't leaving Mum? If Mum lived in the house, she couldn't die without knowing how much she was loved.

Bridget knew she increased the risk of being thrown out for what she was about to do, but not doing so was the bigger risk. "Nera, Nera," she whispered over the pounding of her heart. She took a step down. She'd steal the finger bone. Whatever the consequences.

Nineteen

The candle shaking in Bridget's hand sent a trembling reflection over the wall leading down. She went slowly, her nerves telling her to turn back even as her heart pushed her on. She'd ask Mum why they'd left her. Had it been the cost of another ticket, the uncertainty of finding housing? Had they not believed she'd have willingly gone hungry, slept on any floor, just to have stayed together? To have felt wanted.

She stopped at the bottom of the staircase, looking down the long, empty hall and taking a moment to gather her will. She would not give into childish fears.

Lily's door began to open. Bridget blew out her candle and watched in the dark as Lily stepped from her room, holding a lit candle of her own. She wore a floor-length cape, its hood drawn up, and her face veiled. The column of black made Bridget shiver. *Not an apparition from some sinister realm,* she promised herself. *Only a woman from this world.*

Lily turned, started for the shorter flight of stairs, the trap door, and the alley.

"Mum?"

Lily spun, standing mute and motionless.

"Please," Bridget said. "Don't run. It's me." She thought to say "Bridget," but if Mum feared having her real identity found out, the shock of discovery might be too much. "It's Hannah."

The candle Lily held threw a tall, shaking shadow up the wall behind her.

"You know me," Bridget said.

A slight nervous shuffle of her feet made Lily seem to stammer in place, undecided between staying and fleeing.

"Remember, you visit me in the attic." Dread hung in Lily's clothing—crept along the black warp and weft of the threads. "You're not afraid of me." *Only afraid of being found out by me.* "I was in the alley."

Another slight motion, this time along the bottom of the veil, proved Lily had given a small nod. She pushed her hood back, and though her face remained covered, a tendril of hair hung on the nape of her bare neck.

Red. Even in the dim candlelight, the color was unmistakable against the white skin. Not a match to Bridget's; not like two poppies on the same stalk. Lily's was darker, more auburn. Years had passed though, and time and age might explain the change. As might Lily's burns, affecting her hormones and chemistry in ways Bridget didn't understand.

Reason laughed at Bridget, said finding Mum was impossible, but Bridget fought back. She had her argument: Gus found Smoke.

"You're better now," Lily said. "Tate told me to stay away from you." A slight slurring of her words. "Stay, stay away. When it's time, she said you'd come."

"She told me the same."

"Forgive me."

The death space swelled around the edges of Lily's body. A smoky black rim, the maw waited. Bridget had known Lily lingered at death's door, but to see the death space, the grave of her leaving, struck fist-like.

"You've grown up." The veil swayed again with Lily's breath passing through.

Bridget thought of Cora's handkerchief with its wide lace covering Papa Henry's face. Another delicate mask over the solidly horrific. "Could we talk in your room?"

"Your dresses." Lily lisped on the *es*'s. "Come see your dresses."

"I'd like that." She wondered if Lily had taken too much of whatever Doc prescribed, or if she'd always struggled with speech.

In Lily's dark quarters, the air held the smells of medicine, loss, and longing. Deeper still the floral scent Bridget first caught on Lily in the attic. Here again, just as in Plum Cake's room, was a space where a woman had locked herself away.

Overhead voices and piano music combined with boot heels, sharp and heavy. The thunder danced the ceiling, buckled through the tin.

Lily lit a lantern, snuffed out her candle. She moved slowly, her walk stiff and unsteady. She'd found the energy days earlier to drag Bridget across the alley and down the steps, but could she now? She crossed the room to light a second lamp. Corners held onto their secrets, but the lamps threw better light on Lily, and for the first time Bridget could see the veil clearly. Over Lily's eyes the black fabric was only a gauze, however dark it rendered her world. The same fabric weight covered her mouth. A thick band nearly three inches wide of tatted funeral roses divided the two sections. The needlework there looked a quarter inch thick. Seeing through the thinner sections of the veiling proved hard. Seeing through the middle section proved impossible.

Bridget forced herself to look away, a gift to her own heart. The pattern on the worn scarlet rug brought back flashes of remembered pain, moving in and out of consciousness, lying on the floor with the red seeming to swirl. The exposed brick walls and the high windows matched those in the chapel, though these windows with their deep wells faced the alley rather than the street. Through them, if Lily were lucky, she'd see Spot's legs, and the shine of Kid's tall boots. Given the night, the panes were dark, and Bridget shuddered at the thought of Cripe's ghost prowling the alley and peering in.

Lily unfastened the cape from beneath her chin and hung the fur-lined cloak on a coat rack. Her shapeless black shroud floated around her ankles, seemed a dark, shadowy thing that climbed down her ruined spine. She watched Bridget as though still leery of having her there. Or maybe afraid she'd vanish.

"I doubted," she said. Apologetic, desperate, rushing. "Then you were there, needing me."

Bridget peered over the room, pretending only casual curiosity, but searching for some memento of herself. Some object from her long-ago life with Mum in the croft across the ocean. At the back of the room, a narrow bed with wrinkled blankets looked as though something small had nested in the center. A nightstand stood at the side, and closer to Bridget a sewing machine along with two tables like those she cleaned in the bar butted together to make a large workspace. Purple fabric, a couple yards wide and oddly shaped, lay over the tabletops and down the sides nearly to the floor. She needed a moment to understand it was another dress front.

"You sew for Plum Cake?"

"She's very ill. She doesn't want to be seen."

Scissors, a measuring stick, dressmakers' pins, and wooden spools of thread spilled across the purple. On the floor around the table, scattered fabric scraps. The edges savagely cut with a shaking, damaged hand scarcely able to hold scissors. In one corner, a rocking chair with a small attached cradle. Bridget had heard of a nanny rocker but had never seen one. A busy mother could put her infant into the attached cradle, sit in the rocker and rock her child while keeping both hands free to mend stockings or tend a second child in her lap. Who had slept in this tiny cradle?

"We're going to be all right now," Lily said. "We'll be together always."

"Mum." Bridget reached out one hand.

Lily took a clumsy step back. "No."

Bridget's eyes smarted. What did Lily fear? That touching would prove flesh and bones, not spirit? With deepening doubt, Bridget paced.

"I found you," Lily said. "Out there."

"Yes." Bridget studied the woman. Would it be right to say, "You saved my life"? When Lily thought her dead? What to say at all? She noticed the dresser and felt a shiver run down her arms. She crossed them. Where a mirror had been, a tiny white dress spread across unpainted pine. The dress stretched and pinned like a harvested butterfly. Ghostly, myth caught up in nightmare.

This was not Mum—no matter how Bridget had wished it. Everything about Lily was unfamiliar. A person would know their mother by more than a few strands of mismatched hair. In the presence of Mum, in whose body Bridget had lived for nine months, on whose breast she'd suckled, there would be a soul-deep connection.

Stupid, stupid to have ever let herself believe it possible. She'd wanted to know the truth, but she hadn't expected to feel this depth of hammering loss. She'd sought a replacement to fill the hole left by Papa Henry's death, but nothing and no one could do that.

"I saw him. You were bleeding. This time I saved you."

"You were walking? Did you see everything?"

"A bad man. A knife."

"Oh," Bridget couldn't keep the moan from her voice. "If only you'd picked up the knife." The knife was the single piece of evidence that would see her hang.

"I did wrong. I'm sorry."

"You don't need to be sorry. You couldn't have known it mattered."

Lily dropped into the rocker, the small knobs of thin shoulders and sharp kneecaps protruding. She was frail twigs, a body as void of flesh as the trees outside were void of leaves. "I was a child," she said. "A circus came to town. In a tent, pretty prizes lined across a table. Tiny dolls, cups with Queen Victoria's picture, toy guns. I reached for a painted jack-in-the-box, so small it could fit in my hand. Father stopped me. 'Prizes must be won.'

"A Negro child," Lily went on, her voice catching. "Four or five years old. They stood him on a stool behind sheeting. Pushed his face through a hole cut in the center, held out little bags of dry beans or rice. 'Step right up, hit the target, win a prize.'"

Bridget had never heard of the horrid carnival attraction.

"Father hit the child's face on the first try."

"My God!" Bridget hadn't meant to speak, but the grief rose unbidden from her gut. A crime against the Negro child and a crime against every white child who'd witnessed and consumed the poison. Who'd grow up and live with that poison in their blood. Act from it.

"The boy had eyes so sad I couldn't breathe," Lily said. "I screamed, another child screamed too. The tent full of adults laughed at us. You can't cage children. It's the worst sort of murder. The soul dies, but there is no quiet death."

Tate had said the skin color of the broken statue caught Lily's attention and emotions. Had Lily been remembering the little Negro boy?

Bridget's mouth was dry. If the Negro child were a man now, how had he survived the trauma? She felt shaky with grief. She wanted to sink into the chair at the sewing machine, run two fingers over the small brass plate: *Singer*. Trace the scrolling and pull herself back from an edge. This world, her fellow humans, were capable of unspeakable crimes.

"At night," Lily said, "the river sings. I go to listen."

"You shouldn't. It's too cold, too dangerous."

Lily tipped her veiled face up as the ceiling pounded, as if two men, unsteady on their feet, wove arm in arm down the hall and toward the alley. They'd finished their games, drinking, and lusting. Would they return home and creep into beds beside wives who feigned sleep?

"They are afraid of me."

The girls, the men? Lily's sadness felt thick as cloth. "Not everyone is afraid," Bridget said. "I'm not. Goose and Tate are not. Certainly not Plum Cake. She loves you."

"I've hurt her." Lily began to rock slowly, the wicker runners mourning on the brick flooring.

"Whatever happened," Bridget said, "she still loves you."

"I never gave her what she needed."

Bridget had suspected Plum Cake's love was more than sisterly. "She's not alone. She has Goose."

"I hope she hasn't done that to herself. She wouldn't like a man."

Lily's rocking slowed. The dress and veil she hid behind made Bridget think of a wounded animal hiding in a secluded place, waiting its death. Even the brick room was something of a dark, rock crevice into which Lily had crawled.

The two bumbling men were outside now, their voices coming in through the windows. The glass gray but for a tinge of red from the lanterns over the door.

Lily pointed. "Your dresses."

The room held so much, Bridget hadn't paid particular attention to the clothesline stretched along the wall behind her. "For Hannah?" *For your lost infant?*

Walking down the line of tiny dresses, all in whites, ivories, and creams, Bridget ran a finger over shoulder spans no more than a palm's width across. The dress lengths, however, were up to a yard long. Most astounding was the number. As many as fifty. She pulled one free and gaped at the extravagance. Enough tiers of ruffles and lace to suffocate an infant. She'd never seen a baby dressed in such excess.

"I never stopped believing," Lily said. "I knew you watched from heaven. You saw how much I missed you." The veil over her mouth sucked in against her lips. Released. "I knew you would come back to help me cross."

The piano music stopped, and in its sudden absence, the room felt hollowed out.

"You want me to help you cross . . . at death?" Did she think they'd ascend together with clasped hands? Like a drawing in some holy book? Lily pointed to the nightstand beside her bed. A dark book with gold embossed symbols on the cover: moons, stars, Ankhs, hexagrams.

"The day and month of your birth," Lily said, "and the letters in your name. They told me you'd be back this year. Now you're here." She let out a sudden loud sob. Her feet pushed against the floor, and the dry wicker chair bucked and squealed. "My baby."

Bridget went to her, knelt close though she avoided touching. "Please don't cry." How to change the direction of the conversation? "I love the dresses. They're beautiful."

Lily sobbed, and Bridget blinked back her own tears. Maybe blood didn't bind them in a family, but grief surely did. If Lily was so ill as to believe her Hannah had returned, Bridget vowed to play the role. Until she could find a way of safely escaping Omaha, she'd try to be the daughter Lily believed in. The daughter she'd failed to be for Papa Henry.

"Handsome." Lily lifted a shaking gloved hand, dragged it across her veil just above her ears. "Gray hair here. He makes me feel smart. I love his lies. He speaks like she is dead. She isn't dead, only bedridden."

Bridget's chest tightened. Had Lily's mind slipped away from 1905? Falling backwards to what year? *Time stacked on time,* Papa Henry used to say.

"He wants to bury his wife with the city pitying him. Pitying . . ." She struggled with repeating the word. "No one must know he's fathered a child."

"The man who fathered Hannah?"

Lily's rocking increased, one runner rubbing against a chair-side table, making a bottle on top sway. "Am I telling you the truth? I can't be sure any longer."

"You're fine," Bridget soothed. To lose one's mind had to be a frightening and sorrowful thing. To retain enough reason to recognize you were falling into madness had to compound both the fright and the sorrow.

The bottle toppled, but Bridget caught it before the glass struck the floor. The label stopped her: mercury. "Why is Doc giving you mercury? It's terribly toxic. I've never heard it being used for any reason other than to treat syphilis. And even then—"The air felt punched from her lungs. She'd never seen an actual case of syphilis. Only in books with graphic depictions of ugly gumma and the eaten-away flesh that left victims resembling lepers. She opened the bottle, poured a drop onto her finger, rubbed it. Not pure mercury. No doctor would leave that for a person, but Doc had refilled the bottle, had it in his possession, which meant he was buying and using mercury. What portions he used, she couldn't know.

"Terrible burns," Lily pleaded. "Tate says they are terrible burns."

"Tate started the rumors?"

"If they arrest me. Terrible burns."

Mercury and a veil. To hide disfigurement, possibly severe. Among the many attacks syphilis made on a body was the disintegration of cartilage. Lily likely had little or no nose.

"Tate says no one can know. She tells them my skin is a snake's."

Things made more sense. Tate and Plum Cake with their scheming didn't want anyone to know the truth about Lily's condition. Were they so worried about the house's reputation and clients choosing another establishment? Worried even the girls would run?

"With him," Lily said, "I was smart and beautiful." She rocked, continued to talk in the past tense. "His lies were the best things."

Female voices passed in the hall outside Lily's door. Workers headed to the chapel, having never seen Lily's face, having never seen what their work might eventually cost them.

"They said I wasn't fit to raise you," Lily sniffled. "They blamed you for my sin. Wanted to take you away. I couldn't let them take you." Her head lifted, and she looked up at the high windows as though something in the alley startled her. "That other one, dead. Mr. Stowe was dead."

She was Bridget, not Hannah. The dead man was Cripe not Stowe. The names, pulled from an imagined past or from a brain hammered by mercury poisoning, hardly mattered. If Lily could confuse a body covered in blood in a dark alley for the ghost of her dead daughter, she could certainly confuse the face of a dead man in that same darkness.

Lily's gloved fingers twisted in her lap. "My . . . mind? I struggle."

"You're fine. I understand what you're telling me."

The radiator hissed.

"I have a newspaper." Lily glanced at the nightstand next to her bed. "In the drawer. His throat is cut."

"Oh God." Bridget glanced over her shoulder. The book of numbers and a drawer beneath. She shivered at the thought of Cripe's dead and bloodied face looking back at her from a grainy photo. "I never want to see that."

"They come here, don't use their real names."

This was another possibility. With Cripe being sheriff of a town only some twenty miles away, suppose he preferred keeping his real name secret. Had he used Stowe as an alias? Even then, how would Lily know? Not from down in a basement room where a tiny white dress, pinned in a glassless mirror, appeared to fly.

Twenty

Day five. Or was it week five? Bridget's healing felt slow.

The wind wailed through the alley, the gusts funneling between the buildings. The coldest and fiercest-sounding since her arrival. To Bridget's ear, the noise was a combination of badger screams and wolf howls.

The light attested to a mid-morning hour, and though she still ached with fatigue, she reached for her clothes. A sharp pain hit her, making her wince and sit motionless until the stabbing ebbed away. She'd done too much yesterday, cleaning up the bar, working in the kitchen, all but bathing Plum Cake, and then not reaching her bed until three a.m. Today she'd suffer for the excess. She lifted her nightshirt and checked the bandaging. Only a single drop of blood had soaked through. She'd change the dressing later and inspect the stitches for signs of infection. If they healed well, they'd be out soon. She needed to be careful, making certain that happened. The police could find her at any time, and life on the run would be even more impossible with a wound.

On the table lay the beginning of a letter she'd started for Cora. *I'm all right.* The writing was so shaky with grief it might have been from Lily's hand. *I wish I could take back what I've done. I'd let Cripe live, let his own evilness destroy him. Now three are dead. Him, Papa Henry, and my life. You must sell the farm.*

That last line was all she'd managed. Tonight, she'd try to find the will and write more direction. What to say of Papa Henry's body and a burial she couldn't attend?

The stairway was little more than a seam between brick walls. Bridget rounded the second story landing and started down again. Stepping into the first-floor hallway, she saw Kid just outside in the alley, leaning into the gale, the wind buffeting. He started to open the door, leaving only one hand to steady his barrow. His cap flew off, he caught it mid-air, but his cargo tipped, and as he righted his load, the door banged shut.

She hurried to help, stepping out, bracing her feet and putting her full weight against the door.

The air smelled of winter. Last night's horse droppings dotted the alley, but frozen they no longer threw off odor.

"Thanks," Kid yelled over the wind and, with his hat tucked under his arm, started through.

A gust hurled down the alley, caught the broad door, and knocked Bridget forward over the barrel. "Ouch!"

Kid dropped his handles and helped her stand. "You okay?"

He didn't know about her stitches, and though she felt a sharp pinch as if one had torn, she bit her tongue against another moan. Snow blew into their faces, and they laughed at the struggle required to get his load through. She'd not laughed since Papa Henry's death, and the glee felt both wrong and right.

Inside, Kid used his cap and whacked snow off his shoulders and boots. "The devil's come to Nebraska."

Still amused, Bridget glanced back to the empty wagon seat. "Spot's not with you?"

"Oh hell!" Kid stepped close, bent to the glass with her. "He was on the seat, right there. I saw his ears lift in the wind, and I meant to grab him, but with the horses being sucked off the ground and—"

"Stop it!" She wanted to punch him just to touch surety again, someone healthy in their skin. "Your nose is very red. It's likely to fall off."

He held her gaze.

She needed a deflection or she'd sink into his arms. "Poor Spot. No dog likes spending the day inside."

"He's howling mad. Doesn't know I've done him a kindness." Kid smiled. "You feeling better today? Like I said, if there's anything I can do to help."

"Do you have a boat bound for Ireland?" *Would you come with me?*

The skin around his eyes hinted at the lines that would form there one day. For now, the flesh still spoke of a young man, albeit one who spent a lot of time outdoors.

"Slow horses," he said. "I could ask them if they swim."

They started forward. She understood why Tate took the time to sit with him in the mornings. Why when the coffee pot was empty, the tray of scones or cake slices gone, and the stool where Kid had sat vacant, Tate carried a lingering happiness.

"What happened?" Tate asked. She stood at the bar's rear entrance, her arms crossed over her chest.

Kid's voice lifted. "Good morning, Tate."

Tate's mouth had the set of a pleasant smile, but Bridget saw the unmistakable irritation and accusation in her eyes. How much of the upset related to Kid, and how much from her having visited Lily? With her stomach still tingling, Bridget gave Tate an exaggerated grin and took half a step closer to Kid. Matching his stride, they approached two abreast like a pair of doves.

Though Tate's arms remained crossed as two sticks, she smiled at Kid.

Looking through the Truth-Teller the night before, Bridget had seen Tate greet ghosts entering as though each were her favorite, the very one she'd hoped to see that night. Then she poured the man a drink and handed him to one of the girls. Her fondness for Kid was genuine.

"I nearly blew away," he said. At the bar, he slung a barrel onto his shoulder. "She saved my life."

Without acknowledging his comment, Tate pushed aside her receipts and poured him a cup of coffee, then one for herself. When he finished replacing the old and tapping the new barrel, he sat. Tate took the stool next to him. Sitting so close, the lace on her sleeve brushed the broadcloth of his. "Hannah's a good scullery maid, isn't she?"

Scullery maid? There it was again. Was the term to remind her of her place? Or to remind Kid? And the ill will? Tate had sat at Bridget's bedside, spent days helping her fight fever, and brought a book, a new journal. She was kind to Bridget in every way except when it came to Kid. Then winter rose between them. Tate-Many-Moods, Papa Henry would say of her.

Bridget headed to the closet in the hall. *I'll just get my scullery maid implements.*

"I love that restaurant," Tate was saying as Bridget returned.

"Aggie's favorite place." Kid reached for a sweet roll. "If something is going on, she wants to discuss it at Ed Maurer's restaurant. How about you, Britches, you ever been to Maurer's?" The small knot at the top of his nasal bone, half the size of a pea, was an imperfection by classical standards, but in his case, Bridget thought again, it adds to his perfection.

"What on Maurer's menu," Tate gently tapped the bar in front of her, pulling back Kid's attention, "does Agatha like best?"

"No question." Kid looked amused. "The German chocolate cake."

Bridget wiped tabletops, using a rag to sweep ashes into her pail.

"I love it." Tate glanced at the breakfast sweets she'd set on the bar. "Though I think the best baker in Omaha lives right under this roof."

As Bridget worked, moving from table to table, she watched the cold light mushrooming through the stained-glass nudes and sending a smeary wash of color across the floor. Like a mirage, the impression was beautiful and otherworldly. She longed for home where the Missouri River often reflected golds, reds, and greens from along its banks. The glide of baldheaded eagles overhead.

She finished the tables and began sweeping in the farthest corner. When Kid directed a comment to her, she answered as perfunctory as possible. She'd keep so busy and pay so little attention to their conversation, Tate would have no cause to think of her as a rival.

"Really?" Tate's shoulders drew back, and her coffee cup clattered on its saucer.

"The wedding will be late May, early June," Kid said. "'When the garden is in bloom'."

Tate stood from her stool, her movements a practiced grace as she walked around to the back of the bar. "So soon? Are you sure?"

"I think so . . ."

He's teasing, Bridget thought, but Tate wasn't smiling.

"That house, that garden," Tate managed.

"You know the place then?" Kid asked.

"Society pages."

"Her father's hiring a second gardener to get the grounds tiptop."

Tate picked up the tin coffee pot. Standing as straight as the glass bottles behind her, she topped off Kid's nearly full cup. "You've only been dating a year. Don't the two of you still quarrel on occasion?"

Kid considered. "Everyone spats now and again. That's healthy enough. Isn't it?"

"She isn't . . .?" Tate left the half question dangling in the air.

Bridget felt her own breath stalling, waiting for Kid's answer.

"No." Kid grinned. "She isn't. I haven't seen her more than a time or two without her shoes." He gave the pop of one chuckle. "I can confirm she has ten toes. Hopefully before the *I do*'s, I can confirm she has knees."

Bridget laughed and then quickly checked herself.

"What?" Kid lifted an amused brow in her direction. Then to Tate, "Marriage is the next step, isn't it? Find a nice girl, settle down, raise a dozen kids?"

"You'll keep this job?" Distracted, Tate banged the coffee pot against the bar edge before setting it back onto the hot stone. "You're not leaving?"

"I'll miss you guys." His glance included Bridget. "Some other bloke will be making the deliveries. I'll work for Aggie's old man at the bank."

Tate turned away, moved a bottle of whiskey on the shelf half an inch to the right, half an inch to the left. "Haven't Agatha and her family been pleased with your job at Storz? I don't see why you can't continue."

"Changing jobs?" Bridget asked. "You'll miss your horses. Spot will miss riding with you."

"You were out there." He nodded at the windows where just off the wide porch, two trees looked raked by the wind. "Twenty below, wrestling a couple of two-ton horses with their feet planted and no intention of leaving the warm stable."

"If you were paid more?" Tate asked. "Would you keep this job?"

"I'll earn three times what I'm making now," Kid said.

"Of course, but you already have a respectable job," Tate said. "I sense hesitation in you. You're not certain about all of this."

"I'm not hesitant." Kid pulled on his chin. "My folks weren't happy together, that's all."

"I'm sure your father is happy now. You're marrying a banker's daughter."

Kid's hand settled over the top of his cup, steam rising into his palm. The cup moved on its matching china saucer. An inch right and then an inch left as Tate had done with the bottle. "I'm not marrying a banker's daughter. I am marrying Aggie. And Pops is hotter than a poker. He's never forgiven me for not working full time with him in the smithy. Now I'll be doing that with Aggie's old man."

"Don't listen to him," Tate said.

Bridget imagined her saying, *Listen to me.*

"I don't fancy living crammed in a suit. Aggie and I'll make a good go at it, though. Her father is buying us a house, and I plan to repay every cent." He paused. "Hey listen, I haven't told my boss I'm quitting, and I don't want him knowing. I need to keep this job for a few more months."

"Once you're married," Tate asked, "will you still help your father on weekends?"

"He's my pops. He needs me on Sundays to help him catch up. I don't mind that and enjoy working with horses. The rest of blacksmithing is swinging a sweaty hammer in hell." He paused, looked hard at Tate, glanced back at Bridget, and resettled his attention on Tate. "What's gotten into you? We're talking about a fellow getting married, not buried."

"If you marry Agatha," Tate said, "you'll be spending Sundays in church. Sitting in the family pew, being seen, and listening to droning sermons about evil women like me."

"If your name comes up, I'll let you know. But I'll only hear it while passing the doors on my way to the smithy."

"The thought of losing our mornings together," Tate's eyes swam, "depresses me." She laid her hand on the top of Kid's and just as quickly drew it back and looked away. "A wedding. You're right. We should be celebrating."

Though Tate tried to put up a strong front, tension tightened the shirt across Kid's shoulders. He lifted a foot to the bottom rung of his stool, the toe of his shiny boot tapping the air. Was he only now realizing, Bridget wondered, how much he meant to Tate? How he validated something in her she desperately needed validated?

"I'm sure your wedding will be quite the affair," Tate said. "I'm sorry your mother isn't alive to witness the festivities. She'd be proud."

"She's been gone so many years," Kid said. "I don't remember much about her. Except being a sore disappointment. Maybe she had her heart set on a girl." He grinned. "Or I look too much like Pops. She didn't much like him, either."

"How could any mother not have loved you?"

"Pops would scold her now and again, say 'the kid ain't wronged you.'" He leaned over his cup, his eyes narrowed on Tate. "You all right? If you get this broken up over a wedding, what happens to you at funerals?"

She sniffed and gave a struggled smile. "That depends. Plenty of funerals make me celebrate the bastard is dead. As far as your wedding, I'm being foolish. I wish you happiness."

"Always thought I'd live by using these." Kid turned over his hands. "I suppose that's an old-timer's idea."

"Once you're married into such a respected family," Tate said, "you won't be stopping by a brothel to visit your old friend Tate. We can't meet even in public for a cup of coffee."

"I haven't thought about anything like that."

"I'm sure you want me at your wedding, and I would love to come." She started to top off Kid's cup again, blinked at seeing it full. "Please. Tell Agatha there's no need to send me an invitation. I couldn't possibly find the time."

Kid's knee bounced.

Tate turned, her eyes full, and she moved bottles on the top shelf and brought down a jar of dark glass. She pulled out a wad of bills and counted them slowly. "Three hundred and sixty-five." She pushed it forward. "There's more hidden—"

"Whoa." Kid's hands went up chest high. "I couldn't. Thank you, but I couldn't."

Bridget stood her broom against the wall and grabbed up the duster. She thought about running up the staircase, starting at the top, the farthest point away, but getting there would be a stupid climb. She settled on the first riser, still at the very outside edge of the bar.

"It's awful generous," Kid said, "but I don't need that." He swiped his hands against his muscular thighs as if he'd just that moment completed a task. "Thanks for letting me warm up." He stood. "I'd best get going before the wind carries off my horses and I'm the one pulling the wagon." He swung his coat on, took up the handles of his wheelbarrow, and paused. "I'm sorry, Tate. I do thank you for the offer." Passing through the door, he nodded at Bridget.

Tate stared down at the bills on the bar's glossy redwood surface, and then clenched her eyes closed, her face fighting for control. "He doesn't want my money."

"He's not thinking it's dirty money," Bridget answered. "He just wants you to keep it. For yourself." Was it the money that had upset Kid, or the look on Tate's face when, knowing she would never be invited to his wedding, she'd preempted a decline?

"He wants nothing to do with money from me."

"He's proud. Nothing else."

"He's willing to accept money from Agatha's family." She shoved the bills back into her jar. "Just do your work."

With each additional day at the brothel, Bridget felt as though she wound deeper into a labyrinth with ever tighter, more tangled pathways. "Last night I watched through the Truth-Teller."

"I suppose you were looking for Kid."

"So you know about the little door?"

"Did you think only Plum Cake's big chums knew?"

Before Bridget could respond, movement at the top of the stairs caught her eye. "June?"

Her face showed less swelling, but the purple bruising around her eyes remained, and the split lip had turned from red to black.

"I'll work tonight," she called down to Tate.

Tate frowned up at her. "Not looking like that."

"If I'm not working then—"

"Not looking like that," Tate repeated. "I won't have rumors started about abuse going on in this house. We're one of the finest establishments in the city, and we've already had a murder just outside the door. I'll not have any more idle talk."

"I need to work," June begged. She wiped at tears. "You didn't tell Plum Cake what happened? I know you wouldn't tell her."

"You'd best ask Hannah about that."

Bridget felt the jaws of a trap snap. She had told Plum Cake. Given details: bruises, split lip, black eyes, the sobbing. She'd even enjoyed doing so. She'd felt glad at having the important story. Plum Cake even complimented the forthrightness.

June's face fell farther. "You?" She studied Bridget as if she'd not seen her there. Or ever. "Who are you? What right did you have?"

"Plum Cake is not going to do anything," Bridget said. "She's not going to call the police, and she's not going to send you away."

"You bitch!" June's face crumbled.

Wind rattled the windows. Tate looked cold as the marble on the staircase.

"Plum Cake asked about everyone," Bridget struggled. That was true enough, but empty.

June rushed partway down. "What did you tell her?"

Two days earlier, Bridget had spent an hour with June in the chapel. She'd seen the full extent of June's injuries, imagined the two of them had forged something of a bond.

"Tell her you lied," June said. The cut on her lip, scabby and wide as a black bean, trembled. "Tell her you lied. Tell her I'm not ever going back to Chet." She sucked the dark lump, turned and started up the stairs, but stopped to look down at Bridget. "Tell her I wouldn't ever go back unless he promises never to hit me again. And promises to quit drinking so much."

Tate rolled her eyes. "Lord bless and keep us."

"I can't," Bridget said. "Plum Cake would never believe I lied the first time."

June took off, running back up the stairs. Her robe bounced behind her, but for all her bluster and guff, rushing stair after stair, she gained little height. She stopped yet again, glared over the banister. "I hate you. Mind your own fucking business."

"I'm sorry," Bridget said. She wouldn't try to assure June again that nothing would come of Plum Cake's knowing.

Tate returned to her stool. Beside her, steam still rose from Kid's abandoned cup.

June huffed and cussed up the stairs.

Bridget forgot her cleaning and started out. Let dust bury them all. She'd never understand. Mrs. Fester couldn't escape her abusive husband, had nowhere to go should she crawl away in the night. She had no means of supporting herself, and leaving her husband would mean losing little Timmy. The courts would place him with Mr. Fester. Where he'd live without his mother's protection. June, on the other hand, was safely away from her husband, inside a house where if Chet tried to pull her out against her will, he'd likely face a row of derringers yanked from red garters. June had no children to lose, and she had employment. However awful that labor was, she was already choosing to do the work. Not even beatings were making her stop. So, what poverty of soul convinced her to subject herself to the abusive man?

"Tell me, Hannah," Tate said. "How was Lily?"

Bridget tapped the duster against her pant leg, a gray puff appearing at her knee. "I kept her from leaving the house. She stayed in last night because I was there."

"You're clever," Tate said. She looked straight ahead as though memorizing bottle labels. "Be careful."

Bridget felt anything but clever. "Is Lily all right this morning? Maybe she doesn't even remember I was there."

Slowly, Tate turned. "Plum Cake will see you now."

Twenty-One

Bridget found Plum Cake just as she supposed she would: in her dimly lit room, propped on her pillows, a sheet down her middle.

"Are we circus attractions to you?" Plum Cake's eyes were narrowed, the irises slivers of bright sky. "You had to see the Fat Lady and then the Black Ghost. Your curiosity, never mind another's privacy."

"That isn't true." *I saved you.* "I'd never intentionally harm Lily." Though Plum Cake was right, visiting Lily had been about Bridget's need to know the truth. "How is she this morning? Have I ruined everything?"

"She wants to make you a dress."

"She came to see you? Told you?"

"Tate carried down her breakfast."

Bridget watched the madam. How could she simply lie there day after day, leeching the brothel news from others? She slept away a large portion, then she had the chores of her toilet, the bedpan, bathing with a rag, the excitement of each elaborate meal, the hours of imagining her girls through descriptions relayed from the Truth-Teller. She had the distraction of Ollie, Tate's obligatory visits, Goose's company, and now a supposed Hannah. It wasn't a life. Plum Cake knew it as well as anyone.

"Lily wants to make me a dress?" Bridget reined in her attention. "Frilly? White?"

"That's between the two of you."

Bridget didn't want a silly dress. She wouldn't wear it, and she didn't want to be standing there, told to report in, led around by the nose. *Go there, do that.* In exchange for what? Another day of safety? She felt frustrated, and her nerves frayed by the tension of not knowing hour by hour where she'd be in the next. On the street or in jail?

"These clothes suit me." She couldn't run down the alley with a skirt wrapping around her ankles. More than that, she'd worn britches living with Papa Henry; they felt like her last bit of self-identity.

"It's just a dress," Plum Cake said. "Sewing is the only thing Lily has. If she wishes, let her make you a hundred."

As much as Bridget resented being ordered about, she looked forward to seeing Lily again.

"Did your nosing around," Plum Cake asked, "result in discovering what you were looking for?"

"Lily is not Mum." She felt the loss again. "And I know she wasn't burned. That's really what you're asking, isn't it? Did I find out the truth?"

"She's still beautiful," Plum Cake said.

"You want her to claim burns rather than gumma? Mercury is prescribed to patients with syphilis. And old scars, no matter how disfiguring, don't bring on mental deterioration and early death."

Plum Cake clapped. "Oh my, a female doctor!"

"I'm not claiming that. I've seen pictures, heard of women hiding themselves."

"Can you help her?"

"There is no cure."

"Then what good are your books? Who have you told?"

"No one."

Lamps burned on either side of the bed, warmed the purple wallpaper behind them in a wide circle, but the room remained dim and somber as a funeral chamber. Windowless, the lighting always the same, the room never changed throughout the day or the season. Plum Cake never saw the dance of clouds, never saw rain, a sunrise or sunset.

"You know so much about medicine," Plum Cake said. "How much do you know about the law? Do you know what can happen to her?"

Bridget waited.

"Incarceration. In a woman's prison. A quarantine hospital. An evil place, it doesn't matter what name they tack on the front. The new 'American Plan.'"

"You have my word," Bridget said.

"Women sleeping on rags, starving. Fighting off rats. Pots in corners that are never emptied. Cruel testing, painful injections, no matter if the tests result in agonizing deaths."

Logs dropped in the front room's hearth, weighted thuds sinking into ashes.

"I've never heard of such a thing," Bridget said.

"Oh, it's a well-kept secret all right. The truth will get out someday. Women, even young girls, are arrested. Kept on suspicion only."

"The suspicion of carrying disease?"

"Arrest first, decide later if there is disease. Sometimes not for months later." She batted angrily at the air, flesh from her wrist to the elbow waving. "To think of Lily so . . ." Her eyes filled.

"That's immoral. It can't be legal."

"They've locked up thousands under the American Plan. Morality and legality aren't even cousins. Righteous men make laws to suit their fancies."

"Wouldn't Lily find sympathy? Wouldn't authorities know she isn't contagious to anyone?"

"She is a menace. Her presence threatens the lies they tell themselves about their White Kingdom." Plum Cake paused, looked beached on her wooden platform. "The girls, it's hard to know which ones are frightened enough of her to call the authorities."

"I don't talk to any of them. And I won't."

"Go to Lily. It's just a dress."

Spending an afternoon with Lily would be an easy afternoon. Especially after Tate's coldness, June's rage, and Plum Cake's accusations. Lily, hidden away, struggling mentally, was possibly the most honest of the house's inhabitants. Helping her, being a companion, would not make up for having killed, but it mattered. *I'm powerless*, Bridget thought, *to give back to the world in any other way*.

She opened Ollie's cage door, put her hand in, and ran a finger down one soft yellow wing. "If this American Plan is happening, then any time Lily leaves, it's not just the fear of her getting lost, but the fear of who finds her."

"From now on," Plum Cake said, blue eyes shining, "you'll spend the evenings here with me. After, you'll go to Lily's room."

"I can't measure you like that," Lily said. "Take off your clothes, dear."

Bridget was surprised. The previous evening, Lily had been afraid of touching. Now that was gone. Had Tate convinced her that Hannah was real enough to touch? That Pinocchio had become a boy?

She made a tiny murmuring sound when she saw Bridget's plain cotton chemise and bloomers. "You belong in fine things."

The silk and lace Lily pulled from deep in her wardrobe made Bridget smile. She slid the smooth fabric over her head and enjoyed the luxurious feel. The clothing smelled of cedar and long storage, not Lily's medicinal odor. Not the floral scent she used to try and mask the lesions rotting her flesh. When Bridget returned to the attic, she'd note in her journal: Lily no longer wears her nice lingerie. Was the gumma more painful with fabric, even silk, hugging the skin? Or would Lily rather her fine things disintegrate in a drawer than be used on so unworthy a body?

A basket on the floor held white and cream-colored fabrics, laces in the same angelic shades. A second basket contained yards of purples. Lavenders, plums, violets—they were all purple to Bridget.

She selected the darkest shade with the smallest flower print. "This one looks nice," she lied. "I'd like two pieces. A shirtwaist and pants." She'd insist at least on that, no matter what Plum Cake said.

Lily held one end of the fabric only to the height of her own waist, letting the rest drag and pool on the floor like a weighted thing. "Tate shops for me. She buys more than I can use."

"She's generous." Bridget thought of that generosity toward Kid too, and how he'd rejected her offer.

Lily's nearness and the window light afforded Bridget a better look through the sheer, top segment of the veiling. Eyes peered back, so sorrowful they made Bridget blink and look away.

Moving slowly, haltingly, Lily struggled. She lifted and let the fabric sag, draped and undraped the cotton over Bridget's shoulders and finally fastened one corner onto a chemise strap with dressmaker's pins. Her satin gloves made handling the slick pins difficult. When she dropped one onto the rug, she pulled another from her cushion. "Hold still," she scolded, "or I can't do this."

Bridget hadn't moved, but Lily's hands flitted as though she'd forgotten what to do next. "Is there a way I can help?" Bridget asked, though she had no idea how a seamstress measured and constructed a pattern.

Lily didn't answer. Her hands like small dark birds continued with their busyness. Securing pins only to pull them out again, dissatisfied with their placement.

When Bridget first entered the room, she'd found Lily crying. "I can't do it." She'd thrown down a ball of tangles: dangling threads and knotted purple lace that she'd been trying to gather into a ruffle. The long row of baby dresses, hanging futile as yesterday, proved she'd once been not only proficient in the art of ruffles and tiers but in pattern making.

"I'd like trousers," Bridget said again. What to do but chatter, pretend all was well?

"Like a man?" Lily stood behind Bridget now, pulling the fabric across Bridget's shoulders. Overhead, the first notes on a piano sent down plinking sound: Plum Cake's had opened for business. The footsteps of the first caller to enter from the alley crunched along the ceiling toward the bar. Bridget could understand Lily's aversion to the noise, the tromping overhead, the music, the ceaseless male voices ringing out. With the din, how could Lily forget her years on the floor and in the beds upstairs? How could she heal her spirit if there was never a night without the sounds firing through her?

A pin slid from Lily's fingers onto the floor. She took another from the cushion.

Bridget counted four dropped pins so far; she'd remember the number and later crawl over the floor until she'd retrieved them all. "Shall we sew another time? I won't leave. I'd love to stay and just talk." *I'd love nothing more.* Staying meant allowing Lily to repeat herself over and over. Bridget wouldn't care about that; she'd listen only to Lily's desire behind the chatter, her wish to connect with the daughter she'd lost.

At the end of the room, Lily's narrow bed with its dark coverlet and slightly wrinkled center looked as if she'd made it in the morning, but in the hours since, a child had napped there. The glassless mirror where the baby dress flew—winged and pinned—and the nightstand holding the newspaper with the photo of dead Sheriff Cripe made Bridget shiver. The night before, she'd inadvertently and regrettably made Lily feel bad for not picking up Papa Henry's knife. She hoped Lily wasn't still sorry for that. "Thank you for rescuing my hat. I'm happy I didn't lose it."

For all Lily's fussing, she'd done no more than pin one end of the fabric to the front of a chemise strap. "They sent me away."

Bridget swallowed against the tightness in her throat. Lily had also been rejected. Not by the distance of an ocean, but with that much distance of the heart.

More footsteps and a bang overhead startled Lily, made her grasp the fabric, pulling it away, the dressmaker's pin snapping off the strap, and the fabric landing on the floor.

The pin's scratch left a thin red line on Bridget's shoulder and filled with minute beads of blood. She covered the mark with an index finger and pressed hard, hoping when she brought her hand down the droplets would be gone.

"That nurse, that nun, was a cruel person," Lily said. "Watched all through my labor. A hawk perched on her wooden stool. As if I would run. I came asking for help. Where would I go?"

Bridget picked up the fabric, handed one end back to Lily. Since entering the house and finding out about Cripe's death, her own mind had at times run scattered and desperate, jumping from image to image. Here was Lily's mind too, her logic as disordered as the purple scraps under her table. "Please don't upset yourself. That was a long time ago."

More footsteps crunched across the ceiling.

With a shaking hand, Lily pulled another pin from her cushion, stabbed it dangerously close to Bridget's flesh, and back through cloth and strap.

"The nurse was sorry for my family. The shame I brought them." The pin dropped. Lily drew out another. "She frightened me, but I believed she'd make sure my baby boy went to a good family." She tried to shake the fabric into hanging straight but too much dangled on the floor. She shook it again. "Boys can survive."

Long minutes of lucidity, Bridget would write in her journal of Lily. *The sun periodically breaking through a dark and cloudy sky.*

Lily's fussing continued, pinning and smoothing. Then unpinning. She made chalk markings on the fabric, scrubbed them off with the heel of her hand and made others. "Oh . . ." she gasped, her palm flat against the bandaging on Bridget's stomach. Just as quickly, she drew back as if burned. "Pants? Like a man?"

Bridget had grown cold standing all but naked in the chilly basement room. Cold too, at listening to the heartbreaking memories of a dying woman. Lily wasn't Mum, but she had the same caring soul

"Shh," Lily scolded. She'd turned and faced the flying baby dress in the vanquished mirror. "Hannah has been gone so long." She let the fabric fall to the floor as if her hands had never held it. She started for the rocker.

Bridget changed out of the silk and back into her rough pants and flannel shirts, happy to feel the weight of real clothing. She returned the chemise to the drawer and began folding the purple fabric.

"The woman shouting." Lily rocked. "My mouth full of sheets, screaming still. Then the doctor poured something on a rag. I couldn't breathe."

"Please, don't upset yourself," Bridget said. She'd worry about the pins later and opened the book on numerology. "Show me how it works."

Lily ignored Bridget's question. "She said God was rebuking me." Her head rolled back, came around, and her chin dropped. "You were swinging. Around and around like the light in the ceiling."

"The doctor likely gave you chloroform. Waking up, you were probably dizzy, maybe hallucinating. I'm sure he didn't swing the ba . . . me that violently."

Lily reached out, and Bridget went to the chair, kneeling in front as she had the night before. Cupping Bridget's cheek, she let out a sudden sob. "A daughter! You were a daughter. I'd done that to you. Made you female."

"Is that what made you change your mind about adoption? Seeing a girl?"

"The nurse was angry. She said, 'they're waiting for a boy. They don't want this.' She meant to sell you."

"I'm sure she didn't mean to sell me." Bridget stopped. The line between selling and reaching out a hand to accept a large donation was thin.

"Boys are placed in the best homes. Girls are crowded into dirty orphanages and suffer. I didn't want her to have you."

Lily continued to hold Bridget's face. Did she blame the hospital for her infant's death? Bridget wondered. Did she believe they'd been careless, even negligent, given that the child was female? "That's why you refused an ambulance for me after the stabbing. You feared you'd never see me again."

The shine of tears in Lily's eyes, visible even through the black veil, dampened Bridget's.

"'Hannah,' I said your name." She slowed, her voice drifting. "I hadn't thought of a name. Hannah rose up like a secret I'd been keeping from myself. I wanted to hold you. We'd find a way, the two of us. I begged until they put you on my chest to quiet me."

Lily's hand on the side of Bridget's face slid slowly down, lingered on Bridget's jaw, and then slid farther to Bridget's neck. Clasped and held it.

There wasn't enough strength in Lily's hand even to cause discomfort, but the grasping fingers were unsettling. Bridget pulled away. "I'm here now. Nothing else matters."

"I didn't deserve you," Lily said. She pinched the black over her knees. "I deserve this. I'm glad we're leaving. It won't be long now. No one will be able to touch us again." She rocked for a bit then rose quickly from the chair. "Look what you've done." She walked to the table and picked up the fabric Bridget had folded. "Always things are torn apart, taken away, and I must sew them again."

Twenty-Two

"Not again," Bridget said later that night of the banging overhead. She'd folded the purple fabric, placed it back in the basket, and cleared the floor of every pin she could find. Now she sat at one of the worktables, copying the parts of the eye from her textbook into her notebook while Lily, swathed in her forever black, sat slumped in the rocker.

Only an hour earlier, Bridget had excused herself from Plum Cake, saying she was going to spend a few minutes with Lily. Unlike the madam's incessant talking, Lily often slept, and reading in a room with radiators made Bridget feel almost hopeful.

The pounding came again, harder, more impatient. Bridget put down her pen, settled against the back of her chair, hoping the noise would stop. She'd already spent three stints at the Truth-teller since the house's mid-afternoon opening. Several minutes each time, which was all she could bear in a single setting. Nothing changed between five p.m., ten p.m., and two a.m. The girls wore the same clothing, couples went up and down the stairs, men left, others came. Card games went on for hours.

Bridget stood. She'd asked Goose for a way Plum Cake might send a signal down into the basement. Had she expected a tiny fetching bell? He'd handed Plum Cake a stick of lumber. With it, the madam could make the ceiling quake. Her doing so now meant Goose was in the kitchen crafting some new confection. Leaving the tending of Plum Cake to Bridget.

"Mum?" she whispered.

Lily's head was still down, her hands limp in her lap, and the rocker immobile. No point in waking her.

Just outside the door, female voices drifted past on the way to the chapel. Tired and half-drunk, the girls had finished for the night, but they'd bathe and spend a moment with the broken statue before bed.

Crossing the first-floor hallway, Bridget craned to peek into the bar. Four men gripping cigars between their teeth sat with their fists full of cards. A pile of chips lay in the center of the table. A girl looking younger than Bridget sat beside a much older man, her sleepy head against his shoulder. Two girls chatted on stools at the bar. Bridget didn't know their names, and she couldn't bear knowing if they had husbands who beat them, or if they'd been deprived of childhoods, or whether they'd ever get out.

She hurried on. She meant to leave the house soon, but how could she leave a dying woman who needed her so badly? More than need, Lily trusted her. What was it to betray another so close to their death? Someone who believed in you?

"I'm dying," Plum Cake cried as Bridget stepped through the curtain. She clutched at her chest, her eyes swirls of fear. "My heart is booming."

"Take deep breaths." Bridget hurried to the bedside. Dr. Potter helped women keep calm in childbirth through steady breathing. "Blow out, slow." She knew nothing to do for a heart attack. "Breathe slow, one . . . two . . . three . . ." Ought she run for Goose in the kitchen? What could he do? Or Tate, who might be in any one of the rooms upstairs? Tate might at least know how to reach Doc. "Again, slow breaths, I'm going for help."

Plum Cake puffed twice through her plump lips. "I think I'm all right." Her white-knuckled grip on the stick of lumber loosened, and the fear in her eyes eased away.

Bridget placed the lumber on the floor. "Keep breathing slow," she said. "I need to go for help."

"No." Plum Cake grabbed her hand. "Stay with me. Listen to my heart."

Bridget laid a reluctant ear on Plum Cake's naked chest. She knew the physician who'd invented the stethoscope had done so to ease women's embarrassment at having a man press his ear to their bosoms. Plum Cake had no such qualms. Bridget tried to concentrate on the beats. The heart sounded fast but slowed even as Bridget listened. Had the racing simply been panic? Anger at being left alone for too long? Bridget didn't want to make the determination. "Goose may know how to reach Doc."

"I told you. I'm better. If you go, my heart will start again."

A rosy coloring had flushed back into Plum Cake's cheeks, and she'd stopped puffing with fear.

"You scared me," Bridget said. Plum Cake might be feeling fine, but Bridget's anger had her own heart beating faster than normal.

"You were with Lily. The two of you."

"For that you brought down the ceiling?" *For that you had a panic attack?*

"What was Lily saying about me?"

"Lily is sleeping," Bridget snapped. "It's hard to know what she's saying in her dreams."

"Did she make you a dress?"

"Lily wasn't up to sewing." Plum Cake allowed Bridget to use the house as a hideout. For that, Bridget owed the suffering woman civility. At least civility. "Lily is sorry," Bridget lied. "Sorry the two of you weren't meant to be together."

Plum Cake wiped her face with the corner of her sheet. "Sorry I'm not a man?"

"If she's not of those inclinations, you can't blame her."

"I'm all alone. I love her."

"And that's why you pounded for me. You got yourself all worked up feeling ignored and unloved? You've got to get out of that bed. Next time you get over-excited, you might really have a heart attack."

"Lily and I will die together."

Bridget toed the slab of lumber she'd put on the floor, pushing it out of reach. "That's nonsense. Why even say it? All that business about tick, tick and God deciding the minute. It's ridiculous. But you know that."

"You haven't lived my life."

Body odor rose from Plum Cake. For all the sponging, she still needed to be dropped in a cattle tank and soaked.

"I haven't lived your life," Bridget agreed, "and I suspect there's been a great deal of pain. Still, that happened in the past." She raised her hands, made a spreading motion of indicating Plum Cake's mass. "What you're doing right here to yourself is worse than what's been done to you. It's more cruel."

"How the hell would you know?"

"Because what was done to you didn't kill you. What you're doing to yourself now is." It was true of Bridget's own life. Papa Henry's death with all its pain hadn't killed her; if she hung, she was responsible. "We're both prisoners. The difference is I want to find a door out of this house. And not through death."

"Bully for you." Red blotched Plum Cake's neck. "The little farm girl who stabbed a man's throat wants to live. A little late, isn't it?" A slow blink and her eyes opened full of tears. "You can't leave this house. I won't let you."

The words should have sounded threatening, but they only sounded needy.

"What do you want?" Plum Cake asked. She sat up straighter, leaning back on an elbow. "I'll have Tate or Goose get it for you."

"There's nothing." Bridget paced alongside the bed, glad for shoes as she stepped on the carpet's stained ring. Maybe there was something. "June is scared you'll send her away, and if that happens, she may end up working off the street. Can I promise her you won't? She'll get things figured out, I'm sure."

"I won't send her away." Plum Cake sank back, relieved. "We have a deal."

We don't have a deal, Bridget all but moaned.

Plum Cake wiped her face again. "Don't be mad at me. I get scared. Being in here alone. If everyone walked out and the house was left empty . . ." Her breath quickened. "What if I didn't even know? If no one came when I called?"

Bridget sat on the side of the bed and took up Plum Cake's hand. The madam was a grown woman with over a dozen employees, yet her fears were those of a child. Weren't everyone's? "You're not dying tonight, and no matter what you say, you really don't want to. If you did, you wouldn't be hammering the floor with that stick of lumber. You've got to start eating better or no one can help you."

"What do you mean?" Plum Cake's eyes narrowed.

"Vegetables, fruit. Light soups."

"I don't eat those things." Her round face pinched. "I don't like them."

"I'll talk to Goose. I'm sure he can turn turnips into ambrosia."

"I'm not like this because of what I eat. Daddy eats like me and he's very thin." She struggled with fresh anger. "He loves me. He loves riding horses with me."

Your poor horse, Bridget didn't say. She saw no guile in Plum Cake's eyes; the woman honestly didn't believe food had fastened her to the bed. She thought the whole idea foolish.

The door in the outer room opened and closed. Goose came through the curtain, his arms stretched with a wide tray. What Lily did with tiers of fabric and lace, Goose accomplished with cake layers and frosting. This time, he'd sculpted a castle with a blue-icing moat, complete with two frothy turrets. A candle burned atop each like a miniature blazing flag.

"Happy birthday," he smiled. Both lens of his glasses held a bead of reflected flame.

"It's your birthday?" Bridget asked. That would help explain tonight's loneliness.

"When a cake turns out like this," Goose said, "we have a birthday party." He set the tray across her girth.

Plum Cake blew out the candles so fast Bridget nearly missed seeing her do it. She grabbed the knife beside the plates on the tray and in an instant sliced through what might have been King Arthur's fortress: turrets, bricks, and moat. A second deep cut and the castle vanished into a pile that matched Goose's suddenly dropped face.

"Hannah," Plum Cake said, "there was no need for you to rush up here." The slab of cake she lifted wobbled on the knife, and she caught it in her free hand. The palm disappearing beneath the bulk. She tipped that onto a plate and the chocolate wedge landed with the thud of a dead crow dropping from the sky. "Goose and I are going to have a little celebration. You should go to Lily."

You're helping kill her, Bridget wanted to tell Goose, who stood with his mouth hitched crookedly and his magnified eyes still alarmed. He wouldn't think he was killing her; he had his rationale—thick as two inches of butter frosting.

"Happy birthday," Bridget said on her way out.

More lights had been dimmed in the bar, but this time crossing the hall she didn't peer in. She was a puppet being passed from hand to hand, up and down, up and down. The girls still at work in the bar, still serving at the expense of themselves were also puppets, and she pitied them.

Opening Lily's door, her heart skipped. The room was empty, Lily's cape gone. How was that possible? She ran for the trap door. Settled, giving no hint of whether it had been opened five minutes ago or twenty-five. Bridget's winter clothes were in the attic, and the thought of the climb nearly brought tears to her eyes. She had no choice but to go looking; Lily might need her, but defeat wanted to sink her to her knees.

At the end of the hall, water ran in the chapel. She didn't know if Lily bathed there but checking to be sure only made sense. Few of the tubs held bathers. Burning candles showed heads lolled back and naked shoulders. Bridget knew instantly Lily would not be there, not bathing naked in front of others. Looking down the line, she was disappointed though not surprised by June's absence. She'd find her in the morning and share the news: Plum Cake promised not to send her away.

"It's you," Hassie called. "What do you want?"

"I was looking for Lily."

"Eww," a very blonde girl gasped. "The Black Ghost doesn't use our tubs."

Bridget's palms prickled. Even amongst those who considered themselves the lowest of the low, there was a hierarchy.

"Well," Hassie flung her arms out, water arcing in the candlelight, "I don't see her."

Bridget stepped back, too tired and worried to bother throwing a retort.

"We're trying to heal." Hassie's voice rang out. "We soak off a layer of skin. Refill the tub too hot. Promise ourselves the scalding means we're still alive."

"I'm sorry." Bridget would never forget them, but she had no answers. No trite lines of encouragement. She backed out, hurried for the stairs and the attic. Step by step, she prayed Lily sat in the dark, waiting there for her. At the door, slivered moonlight gave the room an eerie air of mystery and dread: Cold and gray, her empty bed, the table with her unfinished letter to Cora.

She wrestled with her fatigue, wanting to rest even for a minute or two. Lily always returned safely. The fatigue deep in Bridget's bones told her no. If she lay down, hours would pass before she opened her eyes again. Suppose Lily lost her way, wandered over street after street looking for her Hannah? Suppose she fell on a patch of ice and lacked the strength to stand, or a policeman found her and learned the truth of her illness? She'd be locked up.

Not this time, Bridget told herself. She'd let Papa Henry go alone, and she wouldn't make that mistake again.

Three flights down, peering out the alley door in her coat and Papa Henry's hat, she hesitated. She'd become nocturnal. Even inside the house, she moved alone through the bowels of the brothel like a rat while Plum Cake enjoyed her sweets with Goose and girls bathed in a sisterhood.

"I must steal the skeleton's finger bone," she whispered.

Two horses remained tethered in the cold reddish light. She kept her eyes fixed on the spot where Cripe had died. She didn't really believe she'd see him sitting there, knew if she did she'd be looking at a vision of her own guilt, and yet for a few yards she could only back away.

Lily had said the river sang to her at night. Bridget headed east, toward the Missouri. The cold nibbled at her face, turned her breath as white as the scrap of moon overhead. She finished the first two blocks keeping to the shadows. The absence of people, wagons, horses, even wind, allowed for quiet, eerie sounds that possibly indicated danger. At this hour, those who hid themselves during the day came out to thieve and prowl. Was the faint noise a man hiding in the next doorway? Was it chirring doves roosting on stone overhangs, changing positions, the coldest birds on the outside moving to the center? Was the motion up ahead an escaped convict or steam rising from gutters?

A sudden *swoosh* made her jump back, press herself flat against a building. A rat scurried across her shoes, and the noise that first alarmed her became the clap and rush of owl wings. The bird settled on a cornice across the street. Feeling defeated, she slumped against the building. This couldn't be her life now. She couldn't live in the night, hiding, running, slinking between buildings, her heart slamming.

She forced herself to stand straight again. She would not quit, would not die. Not tonight. She'd fight death just as she wanted Plum Cake to do. Her hands trembled, and she pulled at Papa Henry's hat to remind herself he was with her. She would learn new skills, reacquaint herself with courage, and face every red-eyed skeleton no matter the bones clabbering in pursuit. She didn't have to destroy every one of them, only stay a step ahead. She could do that.

She started again, huddling in her coat, her senses sharp.

At the end of the next block, she stopped, thinking at first that the owl was returning, flying close to the ground.

The flutter of a black cape, a limping run, a struggle on weak knees and dying legs came into focus. They called her the Black Ghost. Night possessed her, beckoned her out, and she answered. Night was her land.

In Lily's room with lamps burning, a sewing machine, a rocking chair—all decidedly human surroundings—Bridget wasn't afraid. On the dark streets, replete with threats, the black robe, and floating shadows changed everything.

Not daring to shout out, Bridget crouched. She felt struck again by Lily's haste. Lily wasn't a woman out for a casual stroll, enjoying the night's invisibility after a day of hiding. She ran, if the near-hobbled effort could be called running. She struggled as if chased, but no one rushed her heels. Bridget could see to the next streetlight, the dim open space threat-free. In the city, all things night spooked Bridget, but what so frightened Lily? Uncertainty kept Bridget quiet. So long as Lily continued to the brothel, she would only follow. They were safer traveling as individuals. Two voices, two sets of feet on the snowy stones, were more likely to draw attention.

The darkness held degrees and depths of pitch. The corner lamps illuminated circles and sank gaps into deeper abysses. She trailed behind. At times, Lily disappeared and Bridget's heart skipped until she saw shadow moving up ahead again.

Reaching the alley behind the brothel—the horses all gone now—Bridget watched Lily from the far end. Lily struggled to lift the trap door, steadied herself, wrestled the weight again, and worked herself under. The wooden planks, resting on Lily's back, slowly lowered.

Bridget used the rear door. The long hallway to the bar was dark, the amber lights inside off, and the house quiet. She couldn't face the long climb up, couldn't face the attic with its cold where without heated bricks she'd shiver in bed an hour before the sheets warmed.

Feeling along the wall and gripping the thin rail, she made her way down. She stood outside Lily's room, watched until the bar of light beneath the door quit, and then went on to the chapel. Inside the now-empty room, she stood before the broken statue and ran her fingers lightly over the cracks and wounds. She pulled down pieces of silk, wrapped herself in healing colors, and climbed into the tub she'd cushioned with her coat. Papa Henry's hat pillowed her head.

Twenty-Three

The canary's droppings smelled musty and added to the room's stuffiness. Reaching into Ollie's cage, Bridget folded in the corners of the soiled papers on the bottom. She'd woken that morning in the hard tub, her whole body stiff and exhausted. The basement dark and weighted. She counted the days she'd been hiding and healing at the brothel, though it felt only like working: seven. Even God rested after that long.

Plum Cake lay with her empty tray across her lap. Both plates bare. "Do you like them?" she asked. "They're awful."

"My pants?"

Waking in the tub and leaving the chapel earlier, Bridget first opened Lily's door a crack to see the room still dark and Lily in bed. Hurrying on to the attic to put away her coat and hat and change into her second shirt, she saw the fabric on her bed. A dark purple background and tiny pink flowers. She held it up, grinning: a pair of pants. Of a sort. Narrow legs and a waist tied with a drawstring. Hideous things Papa Henry and Kid would laugh at, but a gift sewn through the wee morning hours. A mother for her daughter. Believed-to-be daughter, but that didn't matter. Papa Henry had taught her love makes a family, not blood.

She'd pulled on the pants and tied the waist snug. Lily hadn't been able to take proper measurements, but with her head cleared or rested a bit, all she'd really needed was an approximate height. Looking down at herself, Bridget smiled. With her plaid flannel shirt, her outfit passed through clownish and went straight to hideous. She loved it.

"How is Lily today?" Using her fingers, Plum Cake parted her hair at the nape of her neck and drew the two fistfuls from behind and onto her great bosom. She brushed.

The madam, Bridget knew, had slept through the morning. After which, she'd waited on Goose to bring his tray with her first meal of the day. Now she sat before the empty plates, periodically casting looks down at them as if she might find a trace of something she'd missed. And brushing her hair, spending lavish attention there as if it were a full hygienic regimen.

"She's sleeping at the moment, probably dreaming of you." Plum Cake didn't really want to hear how Lily fared; she wanted to hear how Lily loved her. Which, given Plum Cake's suffering, Bridget understood the need.

"I'm much better," Plum Cake said. She held her brush and used a finger to wipe at a trace of mashed potato she'd spied on one of her plates.

Bridget had peeled the potatoes that forenoon, a never-ending, depressing job it seemed when standing over a burlap bag of spuds and considering how many in the house needed to eat. Peeling potatoes and washing pans were the main jobs Goose trusted she could execute to his satisfaction. However, this time the work was interrupted with a pleasant surprise: Kid and a perfectly thrown potato.

Just before his arrival, Tate sent her from the bar. "I think it would be best today if you went to Goose. He can always use an extra pair of hands." An hour later, as Kid walked past the kitchen door on his way out, he'd done the polite thing and stepped in. "Thanks, Goose. I may call off the wedding. Only a fool would walk away from your baking."

Standing over her peelings, Bridget realized that stopping to thank Goose was likely something Kid did every day. Breakfast scones or something sweeter always accompanied his coffee, and he'd not walk by the man responsible without saying thanks.

Kid saw her. "Hey, Britches." One brow lifted above his smiling eyes. "Nice britches."

Bridget pressed her lips to keep away the goofy smile threatening to embarrass her. "Someone very special made these beautiful pants for me. I will wear them proudly until they fall off."

He winked at Goose as if the two of them could see what she couldn't. Then back to her, a nod at the potato in her hand. "You got one of those for me?"

The potato she held was peeled and rinsed. Without taking a minute to consider, she threw it at him. A perfectly thrown pitch.

He caught it, nodded thanks, and took a large bite as though gnawing an apple. He went on with his barrow, his mouth full, and a grin on his face.

She wondered now what pleased her most, that surprised look on his face when the spud came flying through the air, or how perfectly she'd thrown the thing.

"I'm so much like Daddy," Plum Cake said.

Bridget left her reverie, glancing back at the woman stretched out on her barge.

"I suppose," Plum Cake went on, "that's why he loves me so. Riding together was the most fun. In the evenings, we saddled our horses and toured the farm, checking crops and fences. Just being together. He's never minded not having a son. He loves me so much."

She'd told something of the same story the evening before. It still rang false. A rosy childhood sounded too fabled. Only wagonloads of pain accounted for a woman becoming a madam and bedridden via her own feeding hand. What had she said of the girls? Not a childhood amongst them?

"Does he visit?" Bridget asked.

"No." Plum Cake looked back at the empty plates. Moved them a bit with her hairbrush and found a crumb beneath.

Bridget finished rolling the soiled paper and drew it out the small door while Ollie sat on her perch watching, and Plum Cake worried her tray. *Which one of you,* Bridget wondered, *is most caged? The most captured?*

"Is your mother still alive?" Bridget set the soiled paper on the floor by the curtain to be carried out when she left.

"Dead. Let Ollie out."

Bridget stroked the top of the bird's head and the yellow neck stretched like a kitten languishing touch. She stood back and watched as Ollie studied the open door.

Plum Cake made her customary tweeting noises with her tongue and front teeth that sounded more like moaning crickets than birds. She flinched as Ollie landed on her bottom lip, talons pinching tender flesh. Ollie dipped into Plum Cake's mouth and began pecking.

When I get out of here, Bridget thought, *Cora won't believe the stories.* Not even Kid would believe them, and he came six days a week.

"How's June?" Plum Cake asked around the bird.

"She's keeping to her room," Bridget said, careful not to say more.

"Ouch, you bugger!" With the explosive *bugger*, Ollie started, wings slapping Plum Cake's teeth. The madam fisted the bird, stared into the tiny ebony eyes. "It's my house. Tate works for me. She should have been the one to tell me."

"I'm sure she planned to." With an uneasy hand, Bridget flattened clean paper across the floor of the cage, trying not to catch any headlines about a murder or a picture of Cripe's dead face. Tate's main job, she increasingly realized, wasn't just to keep the books and manage the workers, but keep Plum Cake reassured that, even bedridden, she was still master of her domain.

"Tate's only an employee." Plum Cake stared into Ollie's eyes. "Hannah is as loyal as Goose."

Tucking the paper into the corners of Ollie's cage, Bridget

considered. Being needed was a tonic and a trap. If someone allowed herself to get as sick as Plum Cake, so that she needed constant care, were the people around her wrong for resenting having to play that caregiver role? Or for walking away from it? She felt compassion for Plum Cake, however, and for today, leaving the brothel would be a disastrous escape into nowhere.

"Tate's in love with her delivery boy," Plum Cake mused.

"Kid?" Bridget's face warmed, and she wondered if Plum Cake was probing and if Goose had relayed the flying potato incident. Had he said how perfectly thrown was the pitch? How much time did he spend mornings at the Truth-Teller while Kid sat at the bar with Tate? "He's getting married soon and someone else will take over the deliveries. He and Tate are just good friends. There's no harm in that. It's healthy."

"You're keeping Lily in at night?"

Was the woman a seer? Were there eyes everywhere? "You called me up here. I do my best."

"She got away from you?"

"She got away from us. Anyway, she's downstairs. Safe and sound." She wouldn't mention how Lily had scurried back to the house frightened. Maybe Plum Cake already knew that too.

"Be more careful."

"You won't let me nail down that door. I've even thought about taking Lily's shoes or cape, but suppose she wandered off without them?"

The cage was clean, but Ollie still worked on Plum Cake's teeth.

"It's hard to imagine Lily really believes I'm a ghost." Bridget said. The idea was as fascinating as a canary trained to pick food out of a person's teeth. "Ghosts don't bleed from stabbings. If Lily thought about it at all, she'd realize ghosts don't need to be sewn up, don't sleep in attic beds, or—"

Plum Cake grabbed Ollie off her lip. "Who doesn't believe?" she snapped. "We all believe the world is full of the dead watching over us. Saints, angels, our deceased, Gods." She flung a hand as if indicating a roomful of spirits. "All of them supposedly paying rapt attention to everything that happens to us." Her blue eyes narrowed. "All of them not concerned about anything else, just standing around waiting to be needed. As though the stupid problems of humans are more important than anything else a god could think to do."

A scream, followed by several crashing sounds, came through the wall from the bar. A second scream cut the air.

"That sounds like June," Bridget cried.

Plum Cake held out Ollie. "Put her back."

Grabbing the bird, Bridget felt the tiny heart pumping against her palm. She put the canary back inside the bamboo cage, dropped the latch, and started out of the room.

"No!" Plum Cake yelled. "Stay with me; I can't protect myself."

"It's June. I have to go." She rushed out though Plum Cake howled, demanded.

At the bar entrance, she stopped. Chairs were overturned, a planter lay on its side with soil strewn across the floor, a shattered glass lamp, the shards bright. June twisted against two policemen, one on each arm. Her face tragic.

"Stop!" Tate rushed down the stairs in a dressing gown, her feet bare. "Be careful with her. Whatever has happened?"

Bridget held back. She didn't want to expose herself to the police officers, and Tate was there now for June.

The two blondes Bridget had come to think of as the twins, along with Hassie, Ruby, and others, all dressed in some bit of lingerie, looked over the banister.

June continued struggling, screaming as she did. The piercing shrieks icing the room.

Tate, finished with the staircase, grabbed the sides of June's face, tried to make her focus. "What's happened?" When June only sobbed,

Tate turned on the men. "Will someone please tell me what's going on?"

"Her husband's body was found this morning down by the river. Throat slit."

Bridget slapped her hands over her mouth.

Tate searched June's face.

"You!" June screamed on catching sight of Bridget. "I hate you. He was my husband!"

A hive of murmuring passed along the overhead hallway.

Too stunned to move, Bridget watched the scene in disbelief.

June sagged suddenly, and the men, with their hats on their heads and their coat collars still up, hoisted her back to her feet. They watched the room, listened. Missed none of the accusations, took in gestures, nervous eyes.

"I hate you," June screamed again at Bridget. Then with more agony. "Plum Cake had him killed because you told her everything!"

She wouldn't, Bridget wanted to say, but what did she really know about Plum Cake? Plum Cake with her lies and emotional insecurities? Her constant, "my girls." As if they were her property. And last night's panic . . . was that related to this? Had she been aware of what was going on down by the river?

The taller of the two men spoke. "Who's Plum Cake?"

Tate moved the short distance, sank onto a barstool. She stared straight ahead, looking as stunned as Bridget felt. Did that mean she didn't know anything? Hadn't expected this outcome, or hadn't expected it so soon?

The taller man wrapped his arms across June's waist, freeing the second to pull a small notebook from his breast pocket. He started for Bridget. "She blames you. What's your name?"

Six inches shorter than his partner, Bridget thought of him as "Short."

"I asked you a question."

"My name is Hannah."

Goose marched past Bridget and Short and into the bar. He'd heard the screaming and crashing and come, not bothering to remove his newsprint hat or sheet apron. He looked even more the giant.

"Take her downstairs," Tate told him. She smiled at the police officers, "As you can see, she isn't able to answer questions at the moment, but I can help. Coffee? Or maybe something a bit stronger?"

Goose wrapped his arms around June, taking her from the arms that held her. Chest to chest, his glasses slipping down his nose, he started out with her screaming and trying to kick his knees.

Shivers ran up Bridget's spine. The brothel would open on schedule, it always did, and if June still screamed, her hands and feet would be bound. A gag put in her mouth. Tate had said to take her downstairs. That could only be the room next to Lily's with the lock. Was there a bed, a light? Was the place a cold cell with only a thin wall separating it from Lily's room? Being close to Lily terrified June.

As Goose passed Bridget in the doorway, she reached out, touched his arm. "Can you take her up to my room?" Her voice shook. "Tate, I'll take care of her in the attic."

"You'll pay," June sobbed, spittle hitting Bridget's face. "Dear, precious Hannah, you'll pay."

"Take her downstairs," Tate said again. "This is a high-class establishment," she smiled at the police officers, "as I'm sure you gentlemen know."

On the stairs going down, June still screamed, the sound receding. In the basement, that shrieking would be increasing. Scaring Lily.

The man Bridget now thought of as Tall pulled his own notebook from inside his coat. He crossed to Tate. "You think she did it?"

"No. She's too upset. Those emotions are genuine."

"You were all actresses before this, weren't you?" he asked.

"Lillian Russell could not have acted that scene."

Short still watched Bridget. "Tell me what you know."

"I don't know anything. I'm as surprised as everyone else."

"Chet Glastner . . ." He squinted at the name in his notes. "Knifed last night along the river. Omaha side."

Bridget didn't want to believe Plum Cake or Tate had ordered the hit. "Could it have been an accident," she asked. "Or . . . suicide? He must have been a troubled man. June hasn't been home to see him for a few days, which could have set him off. Made him afraid she'd left him."

"She looked worked over. What happened?"

"Hannah didn't leave the house last night," Tate spoke up, addressing Short, splitting her attention between the two men, answering their questions equally. "We have a severely burned woman and Hannah is her nurse."

Bridget shook her head, felt nearly mute. "She's right. I was with Lily. Terrible burns."

The officers glanced at each other. Their demeanors softening. They'd just informed a wife of her husband's murder, and now they were learning of a burn victim and her nurse.

"Why did," Short paused, checked his notes again for the name, "June accuse you of having a hand in this?"

Tate sat a pair of glasses on the bar, poured two fingers of whiskey in each. She pushed them forward and crossed the floor, her hands clapping almost musically at the girls looking down. "All right, ladies, time to make yourselves even lovelier. Hannah, please return to your patient. Gentlemen, enjoy a bit of pleasure on the house." She leaned toward the drinks, her silk robe sagging at the neck. "Only that for free," she teased, "but our doors open in an hour."

The men accepted the whiskey.

"I can assure you," Tate said, "I know nothing of the horrible incident that happened . . . where? Clear down by the river, did you say? Blocks from us? Let's enjoy our drinks and have a nice conversation. Tomorrow, if you'd like, I'd be happy to come to the station and sit down with a detective."

Street cops, not detectives, Bridget realized. Sent to deliver the news, they didn't have the rank to head up a full investigation. If anything more than an elementary probe was begun, men in suits would arrive. In the meantime, Tate made short work of the two in her bar.

Bridget felt sick as she headed for her room. She needed to be alone, not return to Plum Cake. Who called the girls hers. Who else would order the hit, if in fact that had happened? Though June, and likely all the girls who'd stood looking over the banister, darkness in their eyes, blamed her.

Twenty-Four

Across the barroom floor, the piano player banged his keys, filling the room with tinny ragtime. With her eye pressed close to the Truth-Teller, Bridget could see only the top of the man's bald head shining just above the sheet music. Tawny lights glowing, men slapping down cards, chips landing in the centers of tables. Others lined the bar. Doc, at the end, sucked on a glass. Hassie and Ruby circulated, young females like china dolls, painted, acting empty. Hardest to watch were the two youngest, even younger than herself, younger than June. Smiling, strutting, believing themselves grown up. They knew the mechanics of sex, enjoyed the money, even the attentions of older men. Did they know the long-term physical and emotional consequences of their actions? They reminded Bridget of a heavy drinker Dr. Potter watched and worried over. Weren't the girls also spending their lives by decades rather than years?

And Tate? She poured shots of whiskey, kept a radiant smile, made constant tallies on a sheet behind the bar. So effortless, quick little markings only a jot, an *x*, maybe initials, and then she turned back, hardly a moment lost. Pulled out another glass, greeted another face.

Bridget slid the Truth-Teller closed. The house felt terminal for every inhabitant. Death stalking, the secret kept hidden with tricks of noise, light, color, alcohol, girls purchased in thirty-minute intervals.

"Is the bar full?" Plum Cake called from her bed. "Is everyone working?"

"I can't," Bridget called just as loudly into the purple room. She'd arrived hardly a quarter hour earlier, and leaving Plum Cake so soon and in so desperate a state felt cruel, but she couldn't bear any more. "I'm going back downstairs," she shouted. What did it matter if her voice traveled into the bar?"

"My girls?"

The question never varied. Impending death kept the madam murderous company, and she lay, begging Bridget to stay.

Bridget started out. The lights were off in the first room so that no stream went through the Truth-Teller and into the bar, but enough illumination came from Plum Cake's bedroom to reveal shapes: Goose's empty bed, the broken-down sofa, scattered pieces of living, all looking strewn.

On arriving, she'd stared down at the madam, the echoes of the day before and the day before that drumming in an unchanging loop. The room a funeral space without windows, the massive woman with her pearly skin and sheet, a ghost of a life. Even prone, never a book, a bit of sewing, any distraction that might help nudge her back from her disastrous game.

"Why is June so upset?" Plum Cake had asked.

"You heard the screaming." Bridget tried to keep her voice steady. She'd spent the afternoon watching Lily sleep and listening to June's soft torment coming through the wall from the next room.

"You know her husband was murdered. I'm sure Goose told you everything." She wanted to demand honesty, but how could she believe anything Plum Cake said? Would a denial be the truth? And if by chance Plum Cake admitted she'd hired someone to do the deed? What then? Go to the police, a murderer herself? Run away, give up her sanctuary, sleep where?

"He beat her," Plum Cake said. "She must be happy he's gone."

"She's not happy."

"I don't hear her screaming now." The mystical eyes glistened. "Why are you so angry? Because June blames you? Because you feel falsely accused?"

Now, having closed the Truth-Teller and determined to leave, Bridget opened the hall door, hesitating to see if the corridor was clear.

"What about my girls?" Plum Cake yelled again.

Descending the stairs—was it the tenth time that day?—Bridget thought of the half-written letter she'd started to Cora. Torn up and then the scraps torn again and again, her own anger and frustration making her destroy the reference to a future. She would not write 'sell the farm,' even as she was a cliff face shearing off, crashing into the waves below.

In the basement corridor, light under Lily's door proved she was finally awake after more than twelve hours asleep. Seeing the light under June's, Bridget felt a knot in her chest easing. June wasn't huddled in a dark corner, too terrified to move. She'd lit a lantern, at least that, and was no longer crying.

Bridget approached June's door, standing close, just as she'd done nearly on the hour throughout the afternoon, listening to the weeping inside, and forcing herself to move away.

"June?" she whispered. Sleep was the best thing for her, and Bridget didn't want to wake her. "Are you all right? I'm sorry about Chet." How easy to say as much from behind a locked door.

A squeak of bed springs, the barely audible sound of feet shuffling across the floor. A suck of air and sniffling. Two soft slaps hit the door, and Bridget imagined June's hands lifting shoulder high and dropping against the barrier. Then the soft thud of her forehead.

Bridget lifted her own hands, matched them to the placement of where she'd heard June's landing. She dropped her forehead, the wood smooth.

"He wanted the best for us," June mumbled.

In what misguided world were Chet's beatings "wanting the best" for them?

"He was scared," June said. "He'd kill any man who hurt me."

June wasn't screaming again about how much she hated Bridget.

"Maybe there's another key to the room," Bridget said. "I could try and find it. Do you want to go to the chapel? Or the attic? Do you promise to stay quiet?"

Hands slid away; shoes shuffled off.

"June?"

Lily's door opened just wide enough for her to peek out. Her face with its customary black drape, the hood of her cape up. She looked sinister. On the street, that appearance would generate suspicion and hate. Attack.

"Hannah?" Lily said. Anxiety in her voice.

Bridget bit her bottom lip for the distraction of pain. No matter how sad, how tired, she could get through the night. Another day and another if she had to. She had to. "I'm right here. There's no need to go out."

"Is she there?" June's voice, frantic from deep inside the room. "Keep her away from me."

Bridget's own hands slid off the door. "Try to sleep."

"Keep her away from me."

"She's just a woman," Bridget whispered. "Like us."

"I thought I'd lost you again," Lily cried.

Stepping away to tend to Lily, Bridget's shoes had the added weight of stones. "I'm always somewhere in the house." The first rule of captivity, Papa Henry once said, is getting free as soon as possible. Time allowed for heavier ropes, stronger bars, the arrival of reinforcements.

"You won't leave me?" Lily asked.

Papa Henry hadn't mentioned emotional chains. "I won't leave you. I promise." It was a promise to herself as well. Given the speed of Lily's deterioration, she had only days, probably less than a week, though Bridget would have promised if it were a month or more.

"You were crying." Lily was nearly weeping with the thought.

Bridget led her back into the room, untied the cape strings at her throat. "I was upstairs with Plum Cake. You heard June in the next room." Was this the third or the fourth time she'd explained? "Her husband was killed."

Lily hugged her chest, not wanting to give up the cape. "The river talks to me."

"I know, but tonight we'll stay together." Bridget gently tugged the wool at Lily's shoulders and felt relief when her arms relaxed and the cape slid off. "We'll stay in together. Right here."

Throughout the afternoon, after learning of Chet's death, Lily's frightened fleeing the previous night had bothered Bridget. Lily had run down the dark and icy streets as if some phantom chased her. She didn't normally return traumatized at night. If sneaking off frightened her, she'd remain home.

"Last night?" Bridget hated asking. Doing so felt dishonest—the bully on the playground tricking the innocent into a confession. She hung the cape, as Lily moved to the rocker. Lily couldn't remember from hour to hour that her Hannah was in the house. How unlikely she'd remember a full day earlier. "Last night, did you walk all the way to the river?"

"I have a knife."

Bridget's breath caught. At times, speaking to a veiled face proved easy. At other times, she wanted to lift the lace and search the eyes beneath for clearer truth. Were those eyes haunted and full of fear?

"You carry a knife?" Bridget tried to sound as casual as asking about a handbag.

Lily's attention settled on the hanging cape.

"There? May I see?" Bridget pulled back one flap of the wool to the fur lining and the interior pocket trimmed with black silk.

"In the snow," Lily said.

"You found it in the snow?" Bridget pinched the crest of the hilt, eased the knife out. Traces of blood rimmed the blade where iron met an ivory handle. She nearly dropped it. She turned from Lily and spent a moment facing the brick wall June lay just behind.

Quiet now, probably sobbing into the bedding. Was the blood Chet Glastner's?

Impossible, Bridget swore to herself. Wasn't it? She was letting her own mind scatter like startled chickens. Scatter like Lily's syphilis-eaten brain. Lily had not killed Chet Glastner; Lily didn't have the strength to overpower a man; Lily had likely never even seen the fellow and wouldn't recognize him if she did. She'd found a knife and thought she needed to pick it up, make up for having left Papa Henry's knife behind. That was the only logical explanation. Yes, the timing was a terrible coincidence, but only that. The Missouri River ran along the entire eastern edge of Nebraska, along the entire border of Omaha. In winter, men trapped beaver and mink up and down its shores; they bore holes in the ice for their poles and gutted huge catfish along the banks. A knife could have dropped unnoticed from a man's gear or from any number of satchels.

If—and that was a tremendously large if—if Lily had come across the actual knife and brought it back, she was in danger. Suppose detectives arrived and ordered every room in the house searched. Suppose one night, entirely out of her mind, Lily walked into the full bar upstairs and dropped the knife onto a table? Even innocent of the killing, she'd still be taken and put in a quarantine hospital or worse.

"You told me," Lily struggled. "You said."

"It's all right." Bridget smiled, tried to shrug. Lily needed protection. "I'll keep this." She'd hide it in her room for now, possibly ask Kid to throw it in the river.

She pulled wine-colored fabric from the basket and wrapped the knife. *I'll protect her,* she swore. *Even if I'm charged.*

The thought struck her. Could she be charged? If they found her guilty of slitting Cripe's throat, why not charge her with Chet Glastner's? There was the slight connection between her and Glastner. Fabricating more would be easy, especially if police searched the attic and found the bloody knife.

Twenty-Five

At a long table in the kitchen, Bridget sat across from Doc and Tate. She'd been at Plum Cake's for eight days, and she still couldn't be in the room without thinking of the farmhouse kitchen. She and Papa Henry had shared not just meals over their small table, but hours of conversation and love while Wire slept at their feet. Now that room with its wood-burning stove would be ice cold. And Wire? He'd be with Cora if she could coax him away. More likely, he'd be in the barn with the animals he knew, lying sentinel beside Papa Henry's body.

Doc and Tate joined Bridget at the table. "An old bachelor," Doc said, "doesn't pass up a good meal." He pulled a flask from his coat pocket and set it beside his bowl.

Tate had been crying, and a faint scent of alcohol on her breath wafted across the table to Bridget. After Kid left, his morning delivery over and his cups of coffee drunk, Doc arrived. He and Tate visited Lily's room. Now Tate's eyes looked raw and her face scrubbed. Her world was coming apart, Bridget knew. The sinking ship took on more water every day. Tate likely carried some guilt for Chet Glastner's death, Lily's was imminent, Plum Cake was unhappy with her, and Kid—her last stronghold on a normal world—was leaving to join the ranks of men who scraped women like her off their shoe bottoms.

The two blondes entered the kitchen, Hassie on their heels. Ruby walked in beside June.

"She's out," Bridget breathed. "Thank God." June's hair was combed, and her black bow pinned above her ear.

"As long as she's quiet," Tate said.

The brothel's golden rule, Bridget thought. *Hide your pain. Make no noise.*

The girls served themselves from the pot on the stove and took the second of the two tables. Only Ruby looked over. Her cheeks were red from her nose to her ears, proving she'd just returned from a long walk in winter air.

Bridget thought to ask Tate where Ruby had been but decided against caring.

"Isn't she something?" The words shot from across the room. "Our little spy," Ruby finished. She sat on one side of June, Hassie the other.

Cold tracked along Bridget's shoulders. She wanted to dislike Ruby, but Ruby was likely the one who'd brushed June's hair, fitted the black bow over June's right ear. Ruby was a role model to the girls sorely in need of one. With her flame-red hair, her strut, even in her loud mouth, there was a message: "Do not break. Do not show shame."

June lifted glassy eyes in Bridget's direction but immediately dropped them. Still, she wasn't cursing and blaming.

Stirring cubes of beef around chunks of potato, Bridget had no appetite. June was out of lockup, but any imagined future for her remained dark.

Ruby mumbled something more, but the words—though they earned snickers at the table—didn't reach Bridget.

"Ignore them," Tate said. "Another two or three days and you'll be gone."

Letting her fork slip from her fingers, Bridget looked to Doc, though he'd lifted a paper. "That soon? Lily has only that long?"

The paper remained up. "Heart's quitting, organs losing oxygen."

"Then you're leaving," Tate said. "See to it."

"What about Plum Cake?" Bridget asked. "It's her house."

"I don't care what she wants."

This was about Kid. Bridget had no future with him, but neither did Tate. He was engaged to a young woman with an unblemished reputation from a wealthy family. Tate's love for him was as hopeless as Plum Cake's for Lily.

Ruby lobbed another remark Bridget didn't catch, but the laughter came across like a heat. Only June remained somber, looking at her meal with no more hunger than Bridget felt.

Tate watched Bridget as if reading her concerns. "We'll take care of June."

"That one," Doc said. His paper came down, and he scooped stew into his mouth. Another swig from his flask. "She informed me again this morning she's infected. I don't know how many times I need to tell her. She's got herself convinced."

"Could she be?" Bridget whispered, feigning interest in eating, spearing a potato with her fork.

"Nay." Doc returned to his reading, holding his paper up.

"She's addled," Tate said. "Too many drugs, too many blows to the head. Now Chet's death. She needs to believe an end is in sight."

"If she's addled," Bridget kept her voice low, "isn't it wrong to have her here?"

"Where should I send her?" Tate motioned to the kitchen's bank of windows as a gust of wind carried a sheet of snow across the view. "Another house? Out there? How long do you think she'd last?"

Bridget's gaze settled on June, then moved to the giggling blondes. That's why they were there, despite their age. Tate knew if she refused them, they'd only go to another house, perhaps had come from another house with poorer working conditions. Too soon, they were likely to end up on the street and trying to survive there.

Maybe there was no longer any hope for June, but Bridget couldn't accept there was no hope for any of them. Dr. Potter couldn't save everyone either, but he slept at night knowing he'd done all he could.

A tiny back page headline on Doc's paper caught Bridget's attention:

Kills Brother in a Quarrel
Isaac Chambers tonight stabbed to death his brother Joseph as
a result of a quarrel which began in a South Omaha saloon.
Both men were half-breed Indians.

Bridget felt she'd scream. "With Papa Henry's race," she sputtered, "it's always only the worst things that get reported."

Doc rattled the paper down, scowled at Bridget and then at the piece she'd read. "That? Redskins?"

"Brother kills brother," Bridget said. "Four short lines arranged like a stupid poem. The last line, like a wasp's stinger, half-breed Indians, half-human, half-animal, and therefore, not human at all."

The second table watched.

"You ain't that," Doc said. "Getting rid of them's necessary as getting rid of rattlesnakes."

"Bring people down, starve them, liquor them up, pick the lowest of those, and make them representations of the whole."

"Hannah?" Tate said. "Watch yourself."

Bridget wouldn't let them see tears. "Papa Henry was my father." Anger made her sink against the back of her chair. Could anyone understand the reverence in the word? "He was as honest, good, and fine as any man alive."

"Maybe they were good a hundred years ago." Doc sucked on his whiskey, licked a shiny bead off his bottom lip. "Now they ain't but savages."

"Hey!" The call came from the doorway. Kid stood there, looking sheepish.

"Kid?" Tate said. The skin around her eyes relaxed.

Ruby let out a loud whistle and the girls turned to look. He gave them a grin and lifted a "come hither" hand in the direction of Bridget's table.

Tate started to rise. "I'll see what he needs."

Kid shook his head and pointed at Bridget. "I need to talk with Britches."

Tate's glare at Bridget might have been an actual fired bullet.

"I can't imagine," Bridget said. If she ran to him, if she said, "Papa Henry was my father," he'd understand what that meant to her. She wanted to be alone with him, but Tate was jealous of their relationship, which threatened Bridget's welcome at the house. She'd promised Lily to stay with her until the end, and she'd do everything in her power to keep the promise. Even coddle Tate's fears. "You'd better come too," she said. She'd seen before how Tate's smile could look so perfect it might be printed on paper. All the while, her jaws strained.

Twenty-Six

"I've something to show you," Kid said as Bridget came from the kitchen and joined him. "When I saw, I circled back."

His urgency made her edgy, turned her legs dull. She glanced over her shoulder. Tate trailed behind, but she came on, not letting them out of her sight. They passed through the bar. Kid grabbed the handle of one of the wide front doors and held it open for Bridget to step out. "Down there," he said.

He felt warm, easy, but June's refusal to acknowledge her, Doc's news of Lily's impending death, and his vile words about Papa Henry's people, still cut her. She feared seeing what Kid wanted to share. She looked away, watched the two trees, quiet today, and spent a moment feeling the cold air on her face. Though not above freezing, the air felt dangerously close to that warmth. In summer, the businesses had bright awnings across their storefronts to shade windows from the heat, women walked with colorful parasols, men tipped bowlers, streetcars rumbled, and wagons were a non-stop annoyance. The awnings, too fragile for heavy snowfalls, were gone, leaving gray, stark buildings, and the streets were quiet but for the sounds of construction blocks over.

"You all right?" Kid asked.

Fifty years had passed since the Omaha tribe was forced to cede the land the city stood on, twenty since Standing Bear fought in an Omaha court to officially be recognized as a person, fifteen since George Smith, a black man, was lynched there for leering at a white woman. In all the passing years, had attitudes changed at all?

"Down there," Kid said.

She reached only to his chin, and he leaned close, nearly touching her cheek, sighting his eyes at the level of hers. "The middle of the next block."

She tensed again, wanting never to look, stalling her gaze on a shiny black automobile.

"That your horse?" Kid asked. "What's his name? He's stabled where I board mine."

Bridget's heart leapt. The porch swayed, and she grabbed Kid's arm to steady her wooziness. "Smoke!"

"I noticed him in the livery, wondered if he might be the horse you lost. Then seeing him on the street, I thought you could get a good look yourself."

Smoke's all right. Still in Omaha. She let go of Kid as her shock turned to anger. He was speaking, but she couldn't concentrate on his words. *Smoke in broad daylight. A stolen horse in broad daylight for the second time.* What did that mean? Leaving the kitchen, she'd felt gloomy and stressed. Now this. A sob gathered in her throat. How like finding Papa Henry's body all over again. She started for the porch steps. She'd get to Smoke, and this time she'd lead him away. Straight up the stairs and into the brothel if need be.

Kid caught her arm. She slapped his hands, tried to twist away, and ignored his efforts to talk her down. The more she fought, the tighter and the closer he held her. His body a wall, his arms pinning her. She fought tears, felt overwhelmed by a hundred losses.

"Hey, it's all right." He kept his arms around her, ushered her back from the porch edge and closer to the door. His coat was open, and she sank against his warmth. The strength in his arms added to her sense of loss. He meant to comfort her, but too many were gone, and soon he would be too. The world laughed at suffering.

"You can't go down there," Kid said. "They'll rip you to pieces. I'll go, see what I can find out."

He kept hold of her. He knew nothing about her losses, but did he sense that only his arms were keeping her together? When he did let go, she'd shatter again, plaster shards crumbling. How many times could a woman refashion herself back into some semblance of a shape, while still more bits of her were left on the floor? All the while fooling others into believing she was fine? Wasn't that the story of every girl under Plum Cake's roof?

"This is my fault," Kid said into her hair. "I don't know what I expected. Promise you'll let me look into this. You won't do a thing. Promise?"

She nodded because Kid wanted agreement, but a nod was not a promise. Seeing Smoke, realizing whoever had him felt no shame or fear in displaying a murdered man's horse, no shame or fear in being associated with the killing of a dark-skinned man—because doing so wasn't a crime—infuriated her.

Coatless and with the cold cutting through her flimsy pants, she shivered even in the shelter of Kid's arms. She wanted to ask his help in getting her horse, but she didn't trust what he might do. Suppose he went to the police? To him that would seem the sanest, safest action. She willed courage to settle her shoulders, brace her hips, and keep her knees strong. She stepped back and hugged herself. "That's not my horse."

She shivered, feeling the cold air between them stretch achingly wide. He lived in a world apart from hers and would soon marry someone from that world.

He pulled a red kerchief from a hip pocket and shook it open. A moment's hesitation stilled his hand as if he meant to wipe her tears. He handed it to her. She cleared her eyes and wiped her nose while breathing in the clean scent of his laundry soap and the bouquet of his body.

"I'm sorry," he said. "I didn't mean to upset you. Let's contact the cops."

He knows nothing about me, she thought again. Her tears made him feel guilty, and he wanted free of the burden. Only that.

"No police," she said. "Thank you, but that's not my horse." The more involved he became, the nearer he came to finding out the worst about her. "I don't need you to ride a white steed to the police. That horse," she repeated, unable to look over her shoulder again at Smoke, "isn't mine."

He took off his coat, wrapped the warmth around her. "Right. You were ready to charge off after a horse that wasn't yours."

Why was Smoke there? Her mind drifted back to the question. "What is that place?"

Kid raised a brow. "What do you care? It's not your horse."

"What stable do you use?"

"You think I'd tell you after that?"

She wanted to sink into his arms again. "Stay out of my business."

"Fine. I can see this was a big mistake. I'm behind now on my route."

"You've got plenty of time every morning for Tate." She turned for the door. It was easier to say the bitter words facing the brothel and not him.

"It's a faro house. And how I spend my time isn't your business."

She looked back at him. "A what?"

"A betting saloon. No females allowed."

She sniffed. "You loved adding that, didn't you?"

"Given the burr under your saddle, I did. Keep away from there." He shoved his cold hands into his trouser pockets. "I'm glad it's not your horse; you're crazy enough to get yourself killed."

She wiped her nose again. His kerchief was embarrassingly wet, too damp to hand back. "You won't need this." She balled it, keeping it out of his reach. "You'll have to use a white one in the bank. Wear only suits that come in three pieces."

Two tiny scores deepened between his eyes. Did he think she meant to insult him? *Never that.* "It's not Smoke."

"The man who rides that horse . . . the horse that isn't yours . . ." Kid paused again for emphasis, "sticks close to the ward boss. You don't want to deal with anyone in that gang."

Did this prove the rumors about Cripe were true, that he'd aligned with the local mob? Now that he was dead, had someone else in the group claimed Smoke?

"I don't need you looking out for me," Bridget said. Motion behind the nudes caught her eye: Tate jumping back. "Have you told Aggie about Tate?"

"What do you mean?"

"Have you told her there's a second woman? You know Tate's in love with you."

A blank look proved he'd never thought of Tate in romantic terms. "That's what you think of me? Some yahoo playing with her heart?"

"All I'm saying is she loves you. You hurt her by refusing her money and with your plans to walk out of her life."

"What am I supposed to do? I don't want her money."

"Dirty money?"

"I never said so. She's a nice lady. More than a nice lady. I enjoy her company, and I'll miss it. But I don't need charity."

"You sit with her every morning. You let her believe you love her."

"I've never used that word." He frowned hard. "It's not like that between us and you know it. She's a friend. A good friend, but just a friend."

Bridget reached for the door handle. "Tell that to Tate."

"She buys a lot of beer from us," Kid said. "Boss made it clear that if she wants to spend time with me, I've got the hour to spare."

"My God, it is about the money. Making sure she doesn't start buying from another distributer. Maybe one with a better-looking driver." She shamed herself. Fighting with him was a distraction and doing so was a child's attempt to mask her grief. Her brain knew it. Her heart screamed.

She'd opened the door only a few inches when his hand came over her shoulder, slammed it shut. He stood so close, he nearly pinned her. She could turn around, find his lips right there.

"What do you want from me?" he asked. "I enjoy a good cup of coffee, sit my ass down, and have a few laughs with a nice lady. She's happy, Boss is happy. Everybody's happy. You're the only one complaining. Frankly, Britches, it's none of your business."

It wasn't. Hadn't she already caused enough trouble by sticking her nose into places it didn't belong? "Tate loves you. That's all I'm going to say."

"Good." He pulled his hand back. "I'm sure Tate's had a hard life. If there was something I could do for her, I would. There's nothing, and I never asked her for a wad of cash."

Bridget wiped her eyes again. "I'm sorry. I'm obviously going mad living in this place. I'm unloading on you and that's wrong."

He sighed, nodded. "I wish I understood what was going on with you."

She stepped inside. "That's a white horse all right, but Smoke's spots are brown."

"You said 'black'."

"Brown."

He closed the door behind them. "A white and brown horse named Smoke?"

"I wanted to name him Cinnamon."

"What's going on between the two of you?" Tate asked. She'd hurried behind the bar to look busy, but her hands were empty.

"Her stolen horse," Kid said, "is not the one just down the street."

"How far away is the stable you use?" she asked again.

"Brown spots. Not your horse." He lifted his coat off her shoulders, pushed his arms into the sleeves and turned to Tate. "The fellow who rides that horse is hooked up with the mob boss. You need to explain to her what that means."

Tate's eyes widened. "You stay away from him."

"I intend to do just that," Kid said. "Stay away from him, his gang, and his new man."

Bridget kept Kid's kerchief balled in her hands. She squeezed. "That new man?" her voice shaky. "If he walks through that door, how will we know him?"

"Pompous fellow. Swaggers. Mustache wider than his ears. A leather vest tooled with broncos. Tassels swinging off his coat sleeves."

The shock of the description coursed through Bridget. They stared at her reaction, not understanding, waiting for her to speak.

Twenty-Seven

Bridget ran, reached the stairwell with her legs gone spongy, and took the steps down two at a time.

Was it possible the man Lily had called Stowe actually was a man named Stowe? Not Cripe? Had the world played a cruel joke? During Bridget's days of fever, when she'd hovered near death, had the world shuffled the cards, dealt them again in such a flash no one saw? Ace for a king. Stowe for a Cripe. Up the sleeve all along. She tried to remember her first conversation with Tate and couldn't remember Tate supply-ing a name.

Did I do that myself?

"Lily." She knocked. As she waited, her heart filled with new dread. "Lily," she tried again, found the door locked. "It's Hannah."

At last a slow rustling. She imagined Lily working herself from bed, possibly sliding her dark sack-dress over her head, then the veil. The black was dark enough to sink her out of sight, to hide her even from the person she believed was her daughter. Concealing herself from herself. Maybe needing that erasure most.

The lock slid open. "Hannah." Lily's veil askew, one droopy eye visible, the other covered by tatted roses black as onyx. "Here you are."

"I'm always here." She'd gladly reassure Lily a thousand times.

Satisfied, Lily faced the bed, her right foot struggling to correct the misstep of her left, and then the left in its turn.

Bridget grabbed her arm and steadied her. Was it pain making today so difficult, or the syphilis attacking muscle, taking balance now?

Lily collapsed just short of the bed, and Bridget caught her weight with frightful ease. She lowered Lily safely onto the mattress, swung the bony feet around, and pulled up the blankets.

"Hannah." Lily's voice was weak. "It's time for us."

The words tore at Bridget. Lily wanted free of her suffering, and yet her body clung to this world. "Soon," Bridget said. *Too soon.*

The nightstand drawer held the newspaper reporting Cripe's death and fought for Bridget's attention.

"Shh," Lily said into the silence. She struggled to lift onto her elbows but sank back with the effort. "They're whispering."

The corner where Lily focused was empty. "Rest now," Bridget said.

"Father and him. Whispers, whispers. Listen to them. A man can't go to the brothels."

Bridget tried to understand.

"Whore houses are full of disease."

"Hannah's father—I mean, my father? Whispering he couldn't go to brothels because of diseases?" She swallowed. And yet he'd used Lily as though she were nothing more than that? "Who was he telling?"

A hollow-sounding chirp of noise. A failed attempt to chuckle. "Father understands."

"Was there no one for you?" *Where were the world's mothers, aunts, sisters?*

Lily's eyes closed, and she sank into sleep.

Bridget paced. Growing up, Lily must have dreamed of a happy life, expected it for herself. Now she would die, never getting the chance to make those dreams come true. Never getting the chance to develop her talents, and the world never benefiting from them.

Bridget's pacing increased. Bed to the mirrorless dresser, the sewing machine, onto the baby dresses. Her nerves itching, her body needing to move. Back to the nightstand drawer. Empty but for a single newspaper with the headline: "Slaying at Notorious Gentleman's Resort."

She checked the date at the top, counted back the days to be sure they matched, read on to see *Plum Cake's*. This was the right paper, the right incident. A grainy photo and below that a clear picture of Papa Henry's knife. The photo showed a man, his throat looking stabbed. A stranger. Not Cripe.

"Mr. Stowe of Omaha . . ." Even half-prepared, shock rippled through Bridget. The article was short, the police asking for any information, noting the murder weapon pictured, no mention of it being from wigwam days. No mention of her name.

I'm innocent. The revelation sent her to the rocker, dropped her in. She'd not killed Cripe, and she'd not killed this man. She knew absolutely she had not. She'd never seen him before. Relief flooded over her in cresting waves, each as powerful and stunning as the last. She wanted to shake Lily awake, run screaming upstairs to Tate, search the streets for Kid. She could go home! She was innocent! She dropped her head back, closed her eyes, let the tears flow.

Innocent.

The pinned baby dress hung suspended, the line of tiny white gowns immobile, but the walls of the room began to creep. How could Cripe still be alive? She rose, hypnotically passed the sewing machine, her feet heavy over the rug's red swirls, to the brick wall. Back.

For eight days she'd carried stifling guilt. Accepted it readily. Had she hugged the lie to herself in punishment, to mask the guilt she felt for Papa Henry's death? Easier to accept the blame for Cripe's death than the blame for her father's?

Her mind ran loose, grabbing at one image and then another. She'd let Papa Henry go alone to the barn. Then after, when he'd been killed, she'd acted like some fanatical hero, grabbed a horse and his knife, and ridden to Omaha looking for a fight.

Covering the same track over the red rug, from one end of the room to the other, her breathing came faster. Boots stomped on her chest, wanted to break her body. The guilt she'd carried lingered, a stink that permeated her hair and the fibers of her clothing.

She was innocent, but that didn't solve her problems. She could be accused of Stowe's murder as easily as Cripe's. She'd carried the weapon into the alley, and the wound across her stomach proved she'd been in a knife fight. What more proof did a jury need? Doc, Goose, Tate, Plum Cake—they all believed she'd killed Stowe. Stowe must have been leaving the brothel, which meant Tate likely knew his name. Had Tate lied, letting her believe she'd killed a man she hadn't? Bridget's hands clenched, unclenched, clenched. Believing Tate guilty of that much ill will was impossible. Lifting out of fever that first morning, she'd opened eyes on a world so unbelievable it might have still been hallucination. Tate had not given the name of the deceased man, only referred to him as a ghost. Later, when Bridget was more alert, more able to question, the whole incident had been hushed up, dropped from conversation. She'd been glad, never wanting the topic broached again.

Her head spun. She needed a ledger just to line up the misunderstandings, or lies, and try to figure out what happened. And what it meant for tomorrow. She tried to remember every detail of the night she'd ridden into the alley: the bitter cold, seeing Smoke, hearing two men arguing, wanting Cripe dead, lunging with her knife, being knocked down, losing the blade.

Stowe must have been leaving when he heard Cripe shouting at her. He must have seen her fall and rushed back to her aid. By then, Cripe had picked up the knife, cut her, and must have spun at Stowe's interruption, catching the man's throat. With two victims on the ground—believing them both dead or dying—had he then seen Lily watching from shadows in her black garb? Had he then mounted Smoke and fled?

Bridget crossed to the radiator and turned the knob to let more hot water into the cast iron rads. She rubbed her nervous hands together in the heat and shivered with a new cold she feared would never leave. She was innocent of killing a bad man, but because of her riding off the farm and into trouble, an innocent one had died. She'd played a role in that, just as she had in Chet Glastner's death, just as she had in her father's.

And Cripe? He read the newspapers, and with only Stowe's body reported, he knew she'd lived. A witness who could testify against him. She'd feared arrest and a trial, but with Cripe still free, she might not live to see a day in court. He'd killed Papa Henry and Stowe. Why suppose he had only two killings to his name? There were likely others that, as sheriff, he'd labeled farm accidents or suicides. He was a desperate man, and he needed her dead.

She'd been right in her fear, but wrong in the number of people hunting her.

Twenty-Eight

Given the hour, Bridget expected the bar to be empty, everyone upstairs dressing for the house's opening. She'd wait there for Tate, tell her the incredible news. News that still felt as hard to grasp as clouds: She was innocent.

She pulled out a chair and laid the paper on the table. She'd read the article again. Slower this time.

"What are you doing here?" June's voice was full of vinegar. She'd stopped on the stairs at the sight of Bridget but came on again.

Dressed for work, Bridget thought. *Or undressed for work.* A pink chemise, flaring pink petticoats. That sort of outfit wasn't startling. The blood-red circle of rouge on each pale cheek, looking like a pair of gouges, was.

June went behind the bar, stood in front of a row of bottles. Going down the line, she tapped a finger on the labels, hesitating on each as though trying to read it before moving on to the next. She stopped, took a clear bottle from the shelf, poured two inches in a glass and grimaced at the taste. Starting and stopping, she forced the gin down.

It hadn't been a word, Bridget realized, that told June she had the right liquor, but the picture on the front: a friar in his brown robe. "Are you trying to get yourself thrown out?"

"What do you care?" June poured another two inches and came with her glass to sit across the table from Bridget.

She hadn't worked since her beating and despite her clothing, Bridget doubted she would again that night. She looked frail and suffering, anything but seductive.

"Reading the paper?" June rapped the sheet, her fingernails chewed raw and looking mauled. "Or you only acting high and mighty?"

Bridget didn't answer.

June tapped the column next to the picture of Mr. Stowe. "Read that."

The item, bordered with thick lines, hadn't caught Bridget's attention. "Greetings," she began, happy for the distraction from her own roiling emotions, "to the Christian men and women of Omaha . . ."

"Stop it."

"You don't want to hear anymore?" Had she thought Bridget's ability to read only some trick? She scanned the article. "He goes on, writing that women winning the vote would destroy Christian families and the Christian way of life across the country. And it's signed the faithful wife of the most Reverend Ernest Pritchurt."

"Stupid bitch," June said.

"That was not written by a woman." Bridget touched a finger to the salutation and read it again. "'The faithful wife of the Most Reverend Ernest Pritchurt.' The faithful wife? That's a line straight from the pulpit, telling women to submit. And the *most?* That word. Then his name in closing, standing at attention. A man so arrogant, he must take the final bow."

"Tate doesn't want women to vote." June sipped. "She thinks women are stupid."

"She's just afraid. She fears too many women believe in their own inferiority. They won't vote for their rights; they'll vote how they're told. For men's rights."

"I'd vote how Chet told me to. I loved him." June's face paled around the red circles on her cheeks. "Ruby says they will close the houses. What will happen to me?"

The picture of Stowe's dead face and his neck with its cut throat shrieked up from the paper. Was the sight of it, Bridget wondered, a death so like Chet's, raking shivers up and down June's spine?

June slapped down the paper Bridget tried to turn over. "Ruby says we won't have any protection unless we have pimps. He'll take our money, work us like whores. I already lived that!"

Everything needs to change at once, Bridget thought. The vote, fair wages, equal education, equal respect. *Impossible.*

The black velvet bow in June's hair tipped as she took another swallow of gin, the taste seemingly easier this time. "You go in the Black Ghost's room." She squared her eyes. "Maybe you're a ghost too. You could be dead. Hell's full of the dead. And this is hell."

"Please. That makes no sense. You know I'm alive."

"Ruby thinks you're here because Plum Cake and the Black Ghost are both monsters, and you are keeping them away from us."

Was the conversation another test? See how Hannah reacts to nonsense. "Neither Plum Cake nor Lily is a monster."

"I have syphilis. I can't ever get away." She leaned closer to Bridget, whispered. "You'll never get away either. You already been here too long."

I will, Bridget thought.

"Chet was ruined," June said. The defeat clouding her eyes felt worse to Bridget than had her hate. In the hate, there'd been fight. In the defeat, nothing.

"Tate was right." June looked down to her hands and their gnawed nails. "He smashed his hand at work. Two railroad cars. He couldn't do the job anymore."

Kid had lifted his hands, said, "I always thought I'd live by using these," and his doing so had revealed character. Bridget knew what it would take from him if he suddenly couldn't pay his own way.

"I tried to find work." June shook her head slowly. "I never been taught numbers, never had shoes or clothes for working in a store. We were so cold. Hungry all the time. If you can't live . . ." She sniffled. "If you can't. One day, we saw Tate on the street. Nice clothes. Fat . . ."

Bridget sighed. Anyone who thought Tate fat must have been skeletal.

"Our guts just screaming," June went on. "It started like silly talk, how I could do this work." She tipped her glass again, swallowed, and wiped a teary cheek. A red circle smeared across to her ear. "Roaches climbing the walls, rats at night. I started believing I really could save Chet. When I confessed I wanted to do it, he cried. He said he'd been thinking the same, how I could save us both. Just until he found a job for a one-handed man."

"I'm sorry."

"People say they would never. They don't know. Bones all crushed. When I came home the first time from here," she ran a wrist under her nose, "we bawled together. Our room stunk something awful. Chet waiting two weeks for me to sweep, wash his clothes. He didn't know how to do a woman's work. Even if he'd had two hands, wasn't living with pain, I wouldn't have wanted it. Him needing to be a man. I cleaned the place and had money to bring in food. I was proud of myself."

Water ran in a lavatory overhead, and from several areas, footsteps signaled girls moving around.

"We promised one more month," June panted. "He'd find work again. Maybe with my money we could save and open a shop. It weren't no month."

Bridget waited. June didn't need empty words, she needed to be listened to, heard. Maybe for the first time in a long time.

"Me being with other men." June lifted a hand to her mouth, her teeth finding a bit of cuticle, nibbling at the flesh. "He tried to husband me, the way a husband will do, but he started asking how it was with other men. Did I like it?"

Blood smeared across June's front teeth. She bit again. "This place ruined me, and it ruined him too. He quit looking for a job. He said I brung in enough money. I think he was ashamed of going out, being with men who might know me. Knowing what I was and thinking how it meant Chet wasn't a man." She paused, wiped tears that smeared more red. "When I'd come back here beat up, Tate wouldn't let me work. The liquor in Chet never believed that. He said my laziness cost him money."

With crimson spread across both of June's cheeks, Bridget rose and went behind the bar for a towel.

"It weren't just him." June bit and sucked the tip of a wounded finger. "It got so I didn't want to go home. Sometimes I lied. Said Tate wouldn't let me go. I couldn't stand Chet at the door waiting for my money, asking about the men, how it was. He wanted names." She had to stop and suck in air. "He called me a whore. Said I was dirty as them in the cribs."

"He was ill," Bridget said. "He didn't mean it."

"You don't know nothing. When he said the cribs, I knew." She wiped again at tears. "He was using my money to go out and whore himself."

Bridget took the chair closest to June and held out the towel.

"Hitting me," June said, paying no attention to the offered cloth, "it was all he had left. That was his way of still being a man."

"Abuse is abuse. There's nothing manly about it."

"I deserved it, what I do with men. God's going to do worse to me."

"That's not true."

"I wanted him to beat me," she cried. "Kill me. I didn't have no other way out. 'Just one more time,' I told myself, and I'd never go back. I never got beat worse than I deserved."

"June. Being beaten, that's what made you believe you deserved it."

June shook, growing more agitated. She slapped her hand down on Rev. Pritchurt's letter. The paper rattled. "I wish someone would tell that preacher. Tell him to say it in the pulpit, God doesn't curse me."

"Who cares what that man says? You're the only one who knows your story."

"When a man steps in the pulpit, that's God."

"When a man steps in the pulpit, that's a man. Some are good, and a whole lot of them are rotten. Not a one of them is God."

"Chet's family listens." She pulled back from Bridget's closeness. Carrying her glass, she walked unsteadily to the bar.

The pink petticoat and its swishing made Bridget look away. She slapped and brushed the purple, flowered material over her own thighs. Wasn't she dressed just as silly?

"The preacher said I didn't deserve to be at the funeral."

"Chet's?"

"This morning." June's eyes swam. "Ruby visited the coroner. She got him to say how the body was gone. The man said Chet's mother came with a preacher, had it taken away. I don't know when, or about any funeral. Maybe he's already buried."

"I'm sorry." Feeble words. How cruel to deny June a goodbye. Had she attended a service though, how would she have been treated? Would the preacher have singled her out, publicly condemned her, blamed her for the ruination of her marriage and Chet's death?

"You can read. Write a letter. Tell them to put it in the paper."

Bridget considered what a missive would mean to June. An act of rebellion, energizing and helping her heal? That was reason enough to write something.

June returned to the table. "Say we ain't evil. Chet's family will see it."

"Nothing I wrote would get printed. The owner of this paper won't allow it. Not something against his philosophy, risking his readership."

"You're scared."

"Plus the Comstock law," Bridget said. "Any material going through the mail that addresses women's reproduction, even references their sexuality, is considered obscene and illegal. The penalty is five years imprisonment."

"We aren't going to talk about those things."

"I know." She looked at the bottle, bright and solitary on the redwood bar, felt tempted to rise and pour for herself. "The law may be so broad though, so open to a judge's interpretation, that anything referencing brothels might be seen as violating the law."

"You're making up excuses," June slurred. "You won't do it for me."

"I'm telling you, it won't get published."

"You won't try."

"It's not that."

"We'll nail papers to posts."

"What posts? Metal light fixtures?" Bridget sighed. "It means that much to you?" The look in June's eyes said yes, it meant everything to her. "I suppose we could leave something on doorsteps."

"Okay."

Nera, Nera. Why had she spoken the thought aloud? "We would need to do so after dark, just to be safe."

"I don't hate you anymore."

Was it the alcohol softening June's anger, or was it the promise of a letter? Of having a voice, however briefly, however unlikely the squeak was to make any difference?

"What do you want me to write?"

"A woman's heart." June touched her breast, leaving a tiny red stain, half spittle, half blood. "A woman's heart, even living here, a woman's heart breaks."

"I'll write that."

June sipped, swallowed, and struggled a moment, her gaze finally resting on Stowe's picture. "Was there," she lifted her eyes, "one of Chet? At least his name? When I die, they won't print my name either."

"I'll sign your name on the letter. Just your first, of course. If word of the missive reaches Chet's family, they'll at least think of you."

June crossed her arms over her stomach, rocked.

"What's your real name?" Bridget asked. "Is it June?"

A small movement of June's lips, but no sound.

"It isn't June, is it?" *You can't speak your own name?* Bridget wondered. Had she been silenced so long? "June?"

"Can you say *your* name?"

The turn of the conversation made Bridget take a deeper breath, let it out so slowly June wouldn't notice. A girl unable to speak her name, asking of another if she had the courage to do so. "Bridget. My name is Bridget Wright-Leonard." It was the first she'd spoken her name since arriving. Doing so felt self-directed, and in the next moment, foolish. June was harmless though; she paid no real attention to Stowe's picture and had no idea Bridget was connected to it.

A door overhead opened and closed. Tate came into view at the top of the stairs. Behind her, other doors began to open, and girls dressed in their alluring work clothes greeted one another. Tate started down the long, *s*-shaped staircase.

"Ravenna," June said quickly. "It's his mother's name. She'll know I'm talking to her."

Tate floated around the first wide curve, descending in a pale blue, floor-length evening gown. Her three strands of pearls moved gently on her bosom, drawing attention to the low-cut dress and the tops of her rounded breasts. She was regal, and her eyes bore into them.

"Do you know Omaha?" Bridget kept her voice just above a whisper. "After I've finished writing something, do you know where we can have it printed?"

"There's a shop a block or two over." June pointed in a westerly direction. "It'll close at six. You write, and I'll go."

June knew the place and having the task, Bridget believed, would make her feel more a part of the adventure. More voiced and heard. "Okay," Bridget said. "Then tonight, let's say about midnight, we'll meet at the end of the alley and put sheets on doorsteps."

"It'll be fun."

Tate stepped off the last stair. "Ladies." She saw June's face and turned, looked instead to the paper with Stowe's picture. "Hannah, what's going on?"

If the newssheet being there on full display confused her, she held herself. Her composure said she'd already seen the picture, read the article, well knew the dead man was Stowe.

"We were talking about Comstock," Bridget said, uncertain why she felt the need to suddenly explain herself and lie about the response she'd write to Pritchurt's posting. She folded the paper and pulled it into her lap. "Birth control and such."

Having had a moment of distraction, Tate turned her attention to June's smeared face. "What's the meaning of this? Don't answer." She picked up June's glass and started for the bar. "I don't want to hear it."

"I know how to stop a baby from growing in me," June said.

Tate ignored her.

Others, wearing the colors of berries on their lips and cheeks, were finishing their descents. They too looked at June's riotous red and just as quickly looked away. Seeing the ground giving away under any one of them, trembled the soil beneath all of them.

"A penny." Ruby stepped off the bottom stair, her kitten heels hitting the polished floor. She stood beside June like a cross between a big sister and a harbinger. "Hammer it into a little cap. Let the copper turn green."

Not a pregnancy amongst them, Bridget thought. They likely knew more tricks than she and Dr. Potter combined.

"A nice dollop of Vaseline," Hassie said. She stood at June's other shoulder. "Those little buggers can't get through."

"Sponges, pessaries, condoms," Ruby said, as if firing off accusations.

Bridget struggled to keep her expression from showing either anger or weakness. Each item Ruby listed carried the barb of a sharp exclamation point, a "so there." Or a "go away. Get out of our lives." As for the methods, they sounded like remedies used by old fishermen's wives with their dozen children. The real reason the girls weren't walking around with bulging stomachs, Bridget suspected, was scarring due to infections acquired in the first week of working.

The hard look in Ruby's eyes hadn't changed. "What are the two of you up to?"

Bridget gave June a stern look. *Don't mention the letter.*

June rose, and for a moment she stood between Ruby and Hassie like a third pillar shutting Bridget out. But for the haunt in her eyes.

Light flooded the room as Tate turned on lamps, the chandelier blooming to twice its normal size, and a wash of golden red reflecting off the brass surfaces.

"Tate?" June's eyes pleaded. "Can I work tonight?"

What? Bridget thought. How did June plan to visit the print shop if she was working?

With a series of sighs, Tate's bosom rose and fell. She touched a strand of her pearls, wrapped them around a perfectly manicured finger. "Go wash your face. Ruby, get your powders. See if you can make her look alive. And find her some gloves."

Twenty-Nine

In the attic room, a blanket around her shoulders for warmth, Bridget wanted to forget she'd promised to write for June. She imagined June sitting with Ruby, Ruby plying her grease and powders, hounding June with questions.

Minutes passed as Bridget stared between a blank sheet of paper and her journal. June hadn't been able to say her name. *What of myself? What of my inability to speak my dreams even to paper?* She opened her journal, dipped her pen.

When she finished, she'd filled three pages with writing and drawings. A factory in the larger of Papa Henry's two barns. A place for women to earn a wage. She couldn't employ hundreds, but she could employ some. She would be a doctor in that way too, knowing the number she helped, however small, had to be enough. She closed the journal and brought her mind back to the letter she'd promised. She needed to write for them all: June, Lily, Plum Cake, Tate, and the rest.

She wanted to rant in what she wrote, let out all the rage boiling inside. Only men, however, were allowed to bellow and bang fists on tables.

To the fine men and women of Omaha,

We women of the night do not pursue our employment out of depravity. We derive no carnal pleasure from the debasing work. We come to the houses chiefly for two reasons: Society has taught us a painful self-loathing, convincing us we are no better than this work, or society has denied us any other means of support. Every one of God's creatures must eat.

A woman's heart, though she lives in the false luxury of the sporting district, breaks as readily as does the heart of your wives, your mothers, your daughters. Look to the city's leaders. Ask why the lowest are kept hostage. Ask why women are kept from having the vote on matters that determine their lives.

Ravenna and all the women of Omaha's lower ward.

Bridget put down her pen and waved the paper in the air to dry the ink. The letter, as written, would have to stand. Not enough and nothing new. However, nothing new was necessary. The truth was already blatantly obvious for anyone who cared to look.

She hurried down to the basement, afraid of finding Lily's room empty, or Lily sobbing at the thought of having lost her daughter.

Lily remained sleeping, the veil flat and undisturbed on her face.

"Mum.," Bridget laid a hand gently over Lily's. Skeletal. She'd promised to stay until the end, and keeping that vow would be the first solid step back into her own life.

A loud rap on the ceiling made her start. Plum Cake and her awful war club. There was nothing to do but hurry upstairs and take the club away before it disturbed Lily. Maybe she'd march it to Goose in the kitchen. Something for his oven.

"I'm here," Bridget said, stepping through the purple curtain.

"I want to dress for the evening. Goose is bringing dessert."

What shade of purple will you wear tonight? Bridget bit her tongue to keep from asking. She pulled a dress front from the wardrobe, not bothering to ask which, and flung it over Plum Cake. At the madam's feet, she pulled away the sheet that had been covering the woman, pubis to the tops of her breasts. On the night table, a bar of black soap floated in a basin of scummy-looking water. Bridget imagined Goose dipping his rag, squeezing out the excess water through his large furry fingers, and scrubbing Plum Cake's arm, lifting it, screwing the rag into the well of her hairy armpit. She blinked away the image.

Despite Goose's attempts, Bridget still wished she could douse the woman in a horse trough. Tomorrow, she and Goose would get Plum Cake standing on newspaper, and though the woman would complain the whole time, they'd scrub her and change the bedding.

"Did you spend the afternoon with Lily? Doc said it's her time."

Plum Cake hadn't banged on the ceiling because she was ready to dress for dinner. She was anxious about Lily, anxious about her own life, and the tick, tick of her heart.

"She's sleeping. She'll likely survive another day or two."

Plum Cake's eyes filled; her lips twisted. "Go to the Truth-Teller."

She needed to cry in private, but she also needed Bridget to stay close. "All right."

In the bar, the lights burned like feral eyes. Tate behind the bar faced a row of men on their stools. June still wore her ruffled petticoat, but she'd changed into a peasant blouse with a neckline so wide and loose it slid down her arms, leaving her shoulders bare. As she moved, the blouse dipped, varying degrees of cleavage flashing. She stumbled against the knee of a man who sat in his chair with his legs splayed a yard apart. He slapped down his cards and caught her. She settled onto his knee. Without a moment's hesitation, she picked up his drink and gulped it. His three companions looked over the tops of their cards. Leaning—her cleavage even more exposed—she helped herself to another man's drink. Then another.

"Tate," she yelled, swinging her pale arm to indicate the entire table. "You owe these gentlemen drinks." She kissed the man on whose knee she sat, worked to her feet, and staggered to the next table.

"Whoa there, filly." A man's raucous laughter.

"Here, girly," a glass raised in her direction, "come get it."

Bridget wanted to cry out. Like fire catching and spreading across a dry wheat field, laughter, hooting, and offers of drinks swelled on the instant. The piano player plinked on and the boozing men became a pack. Their energy feeding off one another, banding together in the enjoyment of seeing a woman degrade herself for their entertainment: the hilarity of a prostitute.

Voices rose. "Here" and "Over here." Drinks hoisted to see how quickly and how much they could get down her.

June knew they laughed at her, Bridget was certain, yet she acted more the buffoon, her smile open-mouthed, exaggerated. Without Chet to abuse her, did she need to find another source?

Not every man thought the situation humorous. A few stiffened in their chairs, held tight to their drinks, and frowned at their inferiors. A white-haired man in a starched linen collar rapped his walking stick against the floor, its tip covered in gold leaf. "Now, now. Order!"

Bridget wanted to spit in his eye as well. He would maintain the illusion that they were in a respectable establishment. What did that mean to him? That girls preferred to lie beneath his noble paunch? Enjoyed him taking his righteous pleasure as he took their souls?

Tate, with her gown and corseted waist, grabbed June's elbow, and the room went quiet. "It's time you went up for bed."

June spun away. "Don't touch me."

"June," Tate's voice hypnotic. She peeled a glass from June's fingers, set it back on the nearest table, and smiled at the men there, her brows lifting with an *oh-my-golly-isn't–this-something* look.

The piano player stopped, and Doc rose from his stool. The two men, one on each of June's arms, ushered her out of the room. Whether they escorted her to a room upstairs or the room downstairs would depend on how quickly she quieted once they reached the stairwell.

"Hannah?" Plum Cake called. "Is everything all right?"

Men picked up cards; Tate refilled drinks; Ruby and the others smiled, circulated, catered. The piano player returned alone and began to play. The evening resumed, June forgotten. As if the pain she'd shown had been no more important than cigar ash falling or a dropped card.

"Are my girls pretty?"

Bridget shut the small door and went to Plum Cake's bed. "Please don't bang on the ceiling with that stick. I'll check on Lily and come back to give you every detail," she lied.

Plum Cake dabbed at damp lashes, her hand shaking. "Will she die tonight?"

"I don't think so. Soon, though. You will not!"

Goose entered, his arms stretched with the tray he carried. He set it over Plum Cake's girth with the flair of delivering a gift. Two rows of pastries on each side of the tray looked like checkers lined up for a game. Huge checkers. Each pastry the size of a large, dark rose. Plum Cake went first, putting an entire chocolate in her mouth. She chewed, savored with much smacking, and finally swallowed.

As she relished the delicacy, Goose watched, his magnified eyes as large as his smile. When she finished with her first, he took a pastry from his side of the tray, and she watched him enjoy the chocolate. Watched him lick each pad of his fingertips clean.

Though Bridget had meant to leave, she stood transfixed, wanting to understand. Plum Cake picked up her second chocolate-covered teacake. Like watching June through the Truth-Teller, this act of self-destruction was hard to witness. Their knowing she watched added to Bridget's ache. What would she write in her journal? When survival seems hopeless, riding your horse off the cliff feels like an act of autonomy?

Tick-tick, she thought. "I'll just go and leave you two."

"Hurry back," Plum Cake said and filled her mouth with her second pastry.

Lily still slept.

Bridget considered waking her and helping her into the rocker, but she'd promised June. At the moment, that promise mattered more.

The men had laughed at her. Worse, June—a girl who could not speak her name—had seemed to not only accept the denigration, but seek it.

Back in the attic to retrieve the letter, Bridget pulled on her heavy dungarees over her flowered pants and picked up her outerwear. She stopped to run her hand down the cover of her journal, eager to relieve some of her tension by writing again. There wasn't time; June needed her words printed and the shop would close soon.

She hurried out and down the steps to the basement. Lifting the trap door only a few inches, she peeked out. Horses and buggies all faced west to avoid a snarl in case of a raid or shooting. Going that direction, she wouldn't meet Cripe or anyone entering the alley. If she heard a horse riding up behind her, she'd flatten herself into the shadows and hold her breath. If that horse were Smoke, she'd pray he didn't catch sight of her and whinny.

She stepped out. The sun had set only minutes earlier though the hour hadn't yet reached six. The sky in the west still held bleeds of reds and purples, but directly overhead clouds looked rough and dirty as a wagon-rutted, snowy street.

She would go to war for herself, fight against her own sinking away, the slow ebbing of her light and will into darkness. She thought of the girls in the beds upstairs, lying prone, crucified night after night, pounded on by men with hot skin smelling heavily of whiskey and pomade.

A bell over the print shop door jingled when she entered. The dingy cubby reeked of machine oil, ink, and disuse. Windows so grimy they looked covered in oilcloth. An old man who'd been sleeping on a stool behind a counter lifted his head to spy her with half-interested eyes.

"I need a letter printed," she said. "Fifty copies."

He glanced at the sheet in her hand, turned his gray chin, and peered at his old press. "One buck fifty."

The price seemed steep. "A dollar and a half?"

He squinted. "One buck fifty."

She had the money, and the copies mattered more than a bit of over paying.

He gave the old press another look and considered the clock on the wall. "Tomorrow."

The thought of leaving the protective walls of the brothel a second time and facing the possibility of meeting the police or Cripe made her pull in a deep breath. "I need them now," she said. "Two dollars if I can wait." She put the bills on the counter, watched his eyes as he studied them. He needed the money or he wouldn't have been sitting on his stool so late in the afternoon.

He accepted her letter, turned on a bulb hanging by a long cord over his worktable, and sat to his tray of type. He worked slow, picking up tiny letters from their bins with his right hand, then setting them in the tray he held in his left. Letter by letter, word by word. He stopped and looked over at her with an accusatory scowl. "This here could land me in the lockup."

Bridget saw only greed in his eyes. She pulled a half dollar from her coat pocket, snapped it down on the counter. "If anyone asks, I need you to say a man hired the printing. A gent you've never seen before."

The printer set back to work, looking down through spectacles even as he tried to keep his nose high enough to keep them from sliding off.

Returning to the house in the dark, the copies under her coat, Bridget felt better. She'd stepped out, faced the possibility of meeting Cripe, and returned safely.

Over the next hours, Bridget came and went from Plum Cake's bedside, to the Truth-Teller, to Lily. She felt like a single actor performing every role in a play. Dashing on and off stage to change costumes and return again.

June hadn't been escorted downstairs and into the adjoining room, but through the evening Bridget worried about her. When the midnight hour finally arrived, Bridget once again screwed up her courage to face the night. She promised herself the first successful venture out proved the second was just as likely to end well.

"Stay here," she said to Lily.

Lily was drooped in her chair, her sleep deep. A shapeless form in black, a cloth doll. Tonight, the doll's legs had no bones, could not lift the trap door.

Bridget hated to leave as far as the street, but the letter could be scattered over doorsteps in half an hour. Maybe even less time. Then in tomorrow's paper, there'd hopefully be four little lines on the back page about the surprise that had greeted shop owners. Speculation on who was behind the barrage.

Waiting in the shadows at the end of the alley, Bridget's courage waned. Night in the city birthed fears and suspicions she never felt in the country, and the joy she'd experienced that afternoon learning of her innocence felt long gone. It was a half innocence and a dire warning that Cripe needed her dead. The thought of him galloping up, riding high astride Smoke, jacket fringe swaying, made her wish she'd never promised June. Nearly seven hours had passed since the barroom scene, time enough for June to sleep off most drunkenness, though Bridget hoped she still lay passed out in her pink petticoats.

"Hannah," June shouted. She came on loud and rushing. "Did you make copies?"

Bridget wanted to scold her for the noise and for what she wore. She'd changed but still looked pathetically underdressed for winter. Her hat, a palm-sized cloche pinned just above the black bow over her right ear, looked as though it gave little, if any, warmth. Her short cape flared out, half open, its meager weight little better than a spring wrap. She'd pulled on a skirt, the thin fabric blowing against her legs and revealing their shape to the waist. "You must be freezing," Bridget said. "Why don't you go back? It's too cold."

"No. We'll hurry." June's breath puffed. "We have to go over one block to Farnam Street. There're more shops there."

Bridget pulled off her gloves. "Take these. My hat, too."

June accepted only the gloves. "I have a hat. Are you scared?"

June wasn't her normally shy self, and Bridget felt warmed by the difference. The letter, signed with the name of her mother-in-law, pleased June.

They walked. Gas lamps burned on the corners, but the only sounds Bridget heard were the striking of their heels on the frozen streets. The night was suddenly so quiet the silence felt eerie.

"Give me half of those." June held out her hand. "I'll cross, do over there." She hurried along her side of the street, her slight figure swinging up to storefronts, sticking her sheets under doors or tucking them into jambs.

Bridget tried to keep abreast, as minute by minute the night felt more wrong. The knife she'd taken from Lily weighed in her pocket, heavy and cold as a stone. She didn't know if the knife had anything to do with Chet's murder, but she didn't want June to see it. She wanted to find a gutter and drop it in.

They reached the corner. Bridget thought to holler at June to stop. The message was out. They'd left a dozen copies, and that was enough. With one eye trained on the shadows, her uneasiness growing, she saw a sewer grate, stepped onto it, and pulled out the knife.

A cry cut through the air. "Let me go!"

June! Bridget gripped the knife tighter. Two men held June. Even in the poor light, their navy uniforms were unmistakable. *Nera, Nera.* Bridget fought for calm and courage. The police officers couldn't be fought off with the knife as if they were hoodlums. Running across the street to help, she'd be nabbed too, but June couldn't be arrested alone.

"Stop right there!" A voice yelled at Bridget's shoulder.

One police officer grabbed and held her from behind, pinning her wrist to her lower back, wrenching the recently bruised shoulder, making her gasp in pain. Another uniformed man stood in front of her, used his billy club to lift her chin.

Despite the cold, Bridget's hand holding the knife felt suddenly slick with sweat. Her only hope was to let the knife go, praying it fell through the sewer grate and disappeared.

Metal clanged on metal.

"She's armed!"

Strong hands pulled away the flyers, snapped cuffs onto her wrists. "You're coming with us."

The men marched her down one side of the street, June on the other. Bridget cursed her nerves and memories of her arrested in New York at age eleven. There, she'd stolen apples, hoping to stave off starvation. No matter, theft was a crime. This arrest was different. This time the crime was daring to express her opinion. As though she had the same right to be heard as Rev. Pritchurt.

She counted the blocks, three east, three north to the police station. Even mounting the stairs to the building, officers kept June back and the two of them apart. Bridget tried to look over her shoulder and give a brave smile. June's earlier spate of energy and hope looked drained from her face. *Better than terror,* Bridget thought. And then wondered if that was true.

Thirty

Less than a dozen men worked at desks. Bridget supposed more officers worked the day shift, and most who worked the night shift were out on the streets walking their beat. One sat with a fat cigar in his mouth, his feet up, and his leering eyes on them.

The two officers who'd escorted June left off, but the one who'd taken the knife from Bridget stepped in to usher June across the narrow room. The officer who'd raised Bridget's chin remained with her. He pointed to a chair beside his desk. "Sit down."

She sat, but flinched when he swung a hand, flipping off Papa Henry's hat. She grabbed it from the floor and held the leather to her chest. He'd placed his own hat on his desk, the number 53 visible now on its silver plate.

"Who wrote that filth?" The question asked of June across the room.

"I can't write," June said. "She wrote it."

"That mean you can't read?"

"She reads doctor books."

Bridget's mind raced. Had June been in the attic? She seemed eager to supply answers. How many times had she been arrested? Did she know being forthcoming was the best course of action?

"Who decided to spread it over the streets?" The question asked again of June.

June still shivered with cold. Her knees pressed together tight, her whole body drawn up on itself. "Her." She pointed in Bridget's direction. "She said we needed to wait until after dark so no one saw us."

Officer 53 still hadn't asked anything of Bridget, leaving June's responses easy to hear. Pitting one against the other.

"She wrote it," June repeated. "She made copies."

"What else can you tell me about her?"

"She's hiding something," June's voice dropped. "I don't know what she did, but I know she ain't a lady's maid or a nurse. She never leaves for medicine, and the Black Ghost never had a nurse before."

The officer's face drew back, and he glanced over his shoulder to catch the eye of Cigar Man. "Hey Cap, sounds like the Black Ghost haunts Plum Cake's Resort."

Bridget listened in fascinated horror. She wanted to yell across the room and tell June to shut up, that she risked getting Lily in trouble. But the tumblers in Bridget's brain rolled and would not catch. How did the man know they were from Plum Cake's? How easily she'd fallen into a trap, allowed herself to be set up. How else to explain four cops being there, hiding in the dark, at just that hour? June's answers came without hesitation, without any natural hems and haws proving she was considering. Had she practiced under Ruby's coaching?

"She telling the truth?" 53 finally asked of Bridget. His bushy eyebrows hooded his piercing eyes and made his forehead appear sloped. He lifted the flyers and dropped them down on the desk. They fanned out. "You the one behind this filth?"

"I wrote it."

"Distributing illicit material. There's decency laws."

"You haven't read it. If you had, you'd know there's nothing . . ." She stopped at the bored expression on his face. This wasn't about illicit material; this was about teaching an uppity female a lesson. The arrests and sitting in the police station felt like a prank gone horribly bad. Had Hassie and Ruby cooked it up as a kind of goading or initiation into the house? Imagining there'd only be a couple of cops harassing them on the street? Had they giggled imagining how Hannah would run back with her tail between her legs? Had the man from the print shop called the authorities? He hadn't liked the letter. She hadn't told him anything though, or had she? She'd insisted she needed the printing done tonight—the number of copies could only mean they were to be distributed—and she'd told him she lived close. He could have followed her, clutching his money the whole way.

"Married?"

Bridget held her breath waiting for June's painful answer.

June's voice caught, her bow hanging over her ear. "No."

"Name?"

"I'm June. She says hers is Hannah. It's Bridget." Practiced. "Bridget . . . Wright . . . Leonard."

Hearing her name sent chills fluttering down Bridget's back. June thought she was being clever, maybe helpful to the police. She had no idea of the kind of danger she put Bridget in.

"Hannah,"53 said. He scribbled the letters as if legibility wasn't a concern.

How easily a name could be written, a person reduced to ink on paper, cut down with no more significance than a garden weed. "We were exercising our right to freedom of speech."

"Bridget Wright-Leonard? Where have I heard that before?"

She tried to smile. "I can't imagine. Do you spend a lot of time at Plum Cake's?"

He studied her, scowled. "I'm just booking," he said. "This ain't a court."

"It is. You're making up the charges right now, writing them down. You're creating everything I'll be left to face." She caught her breath, slowed. "It'll be my word against the written testimony of a policeman. What chance do I have?"

"Maybe it's a little late to be asking."

Bridget clutched Papa Henry's hat, tried to grip so hard number 53 wouldn't notice her shaking. Everything about the arrest was wrong, but she would not be cowed over by harassment. "Who told you we were out there?"

"Alias," he wrote beside the name Hannah. Then below, "Bridget Wright-Leonard." And below that, "Prostitute."

"I'm not a prostitute."

"Sure you aren't."

The two men who'd escorted June down the opposite side of the street, sat in the back of the room, their heads over paperwork. Bridget doubted they were doing anything more than listening. She wanted to scream at them, scream at 53, but she needed to keep hold of her anger or she'd only make things worse. *They are men, all of them,* she told herself. *Men, not sea monsters.* They saw the world from an altitude denied to women, but still they were men, of the same gentle sex as Dr. Potter, Papa Henry, and Kid.

"Age?"

"Eighteen."

The officer booking June pointed to a wall. "Over there." He pushed a slate into her hands, the name *June* chalked across the front and below that, *Prostitute.* She stood in front of heights marked on the wall behind her, her head reaching the five-foot-one mark. A camera clicked.

Bridget concentrated on pulling air deep into her lungs. "I need to send word to someone."

"That knife you pulled belong to you?"

"Please, do not write that I pulled a knife. I had it in my pocket. A woman can't walk the streets without some means of defense." She tried to soften her tone. "I'm nursing someone at the house. I need to send word."

He smirked. "I'll make a note."

"In here," the officer handling June ordered. She didn't move. "Come on," the man grabbed her arm, opened a door, jerked her through.

Only after the door closed behind them did Bridget see the black velvet bow on the waxed floor. "Where's he taking her?"

"Line up," 53 said.

Bridget stood in front of the height chart. Knowing a slate would be thrust into her hands, she put Papa Henry's hat at her feet. She wouldn't risk having it pulled away, possibly grabbed from her head and never seen again. She accepted the slate, *Bridget Wright-Leonard* chalked across the front. Below that, *Prostitute Hannah.*

The camera flashed.

The two officers who'd brought in June rose from their desks, stood shoulder-to-shoulder, talking. One a foot taller than the other. *Short and Tall.* They'd also brought June word of Chet's death, held her up when her knees gave out in anguish.

"Please," she called in their direction, "tell Tate where I am."

Neither nodded, though Tall glanced at the silent man with his feet still on his desk, the tip of his cigar a red, threatening eye.

"This way," Officer 53 said.

Bridget picked up her hat and June's bow and faced a long hallway. On her right, a brick wall. On her left, a long row of iron bars. The cells arranged so that captives couldn't see one another. 53 opened the first cell, and Bridget's heart fell. "Where's June? Put me in with her."

He pushed her forward. The door clanged shut.

"What's going to happen to us now?" She hated the pitch of fear, the tinny whine in her voice.

"Get some sleep."

"We can't spend the night here."

He turned to leave. "Likely to be longer than that."

"Please, I need to get word to someone."

"So you said." He turned out the lights. The door closed, leaving her in a darkness so thick it felt airless.

She grabbed hold of the cold bars to keep from sinking to her knees. "June?" she called. "Are you all right?"

"I can't stay here," June howled.

Bridget clung to the bars. "They can't keep us. Someone will come."

"Shut up!" The male voice came from a cell somewhere between them.

How many units ran down the row? Bridget wondered. How many criminals dwelled in the dark just feet away?

"Go to sleep," the man growled.

"June, I'm right here," Bridget said. The pity of such empty words. She had nothing else to offer. "I'm here."

In her panic and the pitch of darkness, Bridget feared turning around. Trusting the cell was empty took a confidence she'd lost with the clang of the knife blade on the metal grate. She'd seen a cot along the back wall, only that. No one sitting on it. No one lurking in a corner. Her first step felt dangerous, as though the floor an inch ahead might disappear, or a wall suddenly spring up. She stretched out her arms, shuffled forward until her shins bumped. She sat, pulling up her legs. The thin mattress smelled of odors she did not try to identify. She hugged Papa Henry's hat and June's bow to her chest. After a bit, she turned to the wall so she could press her knees and hands against the solid bricks. Brick like her attic room, like Lily's room in the basement with a red rug and warm radiators. Where Lily lay slowly dying.

Snoring rose from one of the cells between them, and as the minutes wore on, Bridget welcomed the sound for how it helped drown out the darkness. Though nothing kept her from hearing every time June sniffled or let out a sob.

The weight of their predicament wore on. She tried to sleep but couldn't. When a weak light stole in from the outer office, she jumped. Someone had entered the cell area. He avoided turning on the bright overhead lights by carrying a small lantern. She lay still, too frightened to turn. Footsteps grew louder, closer, stopped at her cell. A big man's breath, the rank smell of cigar smoke. Her heart thundered.

The footsteps resumed. Then the fumble of keys, the soft, slow squeak of an iron hinge, the light fading away.

Bridget flew from her cot, screaming. "June!" She smacked into the bars at a full run, her forehead whacking into the iron. She crumbled to the floor. "Get away from her, you monster." She worked to her knees, found the bars and gripped them to keep from falling dizzily over. "Leave her alone. She's sick. Full of disease."

"You clean?" the man asked June, and then answered his own question. "Working in that fancy resort, you'd be clean."

June didn't scream. Bridget heard no pleading cries or scuffling. Only a man's heavy breathing and grunting.

Minutes passed. Bridget returned to the cot. Footsteps, two people this time, leaving. June and the officer; June's face, distorted by the meager light, looked haunted and lifeless.

"June?" Bridget tried.

June turned, her stare so ghostly Bridget wished the two bright red circles still stained her cheeks. Her husband had beat her, been murdered only a few days earlier, and now she'd been arrested and raped. Did the soul have a safety mechanism where if sorrow built to a point, everything closed down?

The door leading to the outer office shut after them.

Making sense of what had happened felt impossible. Had June fought the man, she'd have been raped anyway. She'd likely be lying on the floor of her cell with severe injuries. Not fighting, though? What had that cost her?

Alone and not knowing if she was next, or what June would experience now—possibly murder, her body dumped—Bridget bit her knuckles and rocked. The dark, more hopeless than before, swelled around her, pressed in on all sides. She groped for Papa Henry's hat.

"Hey?" Another man's voice, deeper. "You're all right." A long, hesitant pause waiting for a response Bridget couldn't give. "I'm gonna hang," he said. The words heavy. "You ain't gonna hang. You hear me? They ain't going to do that to you."

Bridget touched the painful goose egg swelling on her forehead.

"You're gonna be all right there, miss," the man continued.

The darkness went on, humming long and thick. "Are you guilty?" she finally managed.

"Guilty as most."

The sound of the door opening again made her jump. *No, no.* It closed just as quickly. The breath of a man. No, more than one man. She slapped the pockets of her coat. Nothing, not even so much as a pencil or nail, to use as a weapon.

"I can't see a damn thing," one said.

Light flooded the room; the sudden glare of bare bulbs blinding.

"Good evening, gentlemen."

Bridget couldn't see the imprisoned fellow who spoke, but it was the same voice, belonging to the man scheduled to hang. By its location, she knew he'd risen from his cot and come to the front of his cell. Though he couldn't do anything to help her, her eyes stung at his kindness. He'd face the officers, make them look him in the eyes. At least that.

"Can't get any sleep in here," the inmate continued. "The other fellow, now the pair of you. A chap's likely to be so tired he sleeps through his own hanging."

The cops ignored him, stopped at Bridget's cell.

Tall and Short. Her heart kicked at seeing familiar faces. Men she wanted to believe could be trusted. Tall unlocked the cell while Short kept an eye on the office door.

"Come on." He motioned. "Let's get you out of here."

She didn't move.

"Hurry," Short urged. "Out the back way."

"We've got about thirty seconds," Tall said. "If you're smart, you'll use them."

She stood, wobbled a moment with dizziness but thought to grab Papa Henry's hat and June's bow. "Is June out there? I can't leave without her."

"She's gone. Come on through the back."

Passing the cells, she looked for her new friend. He stood at the bars, smiled a near-toothless grin, then suddenly threw back his shoulders and saluted her.

"I hope," she spoke around the lump in her throat, "you do sleep through it."

Thirty-One

Bridget stepped into the cold night, Tall and Short at her sides.

"Thank you." She choked out the words, needing away from them. "I know how to get back. I can make it on my own."

"This time of night," Tall answered. "Ain't safe."

Relaxing was impossible. Her mind straddled a ridge between trust and fearing what they might have in mind for her. Only as they'd walked two, then three blocks in the direction of the brothel, did her breathing slow. "Where's June?" she asked.

"I hope home," Tall said.

"You aren't sure?"

"We didn't follow." Short's words harsh. "Decided to save your hide. You out causing trouble, what did you expect was going to happen?"

"I thought if I didn't break any laws, then nothing."

She let them talk, her mind thrashing through what had happened. The police had her full name. A name acting-sheriff Thayer had surely supplied when he saw Papa Henry's knife in the paper. That account was filed away, dormant as a winter snake, waiting for a bit of warmth. When tonight's records went into their files, they'd find her name already there.

She had to leave the brothel, but where would she go? And how could she leave Lily?

"I read that writing." Tall's breath puffed moon-white. "I know women ain't got it easy. There's plenty of men want things better."

She believed him. She'd be wrong to assume one of the hundred-plus cops on the Omaha force represented the whole.

"It's something," Short said. He'd drawn his collar up against the back of his neck. "All the fuss women are stirring up these days. Going on about their rights and getting the vote."

He didn't sound judgmental, just surprised women were unhappy.

"Why," Bridget asked, "wouldn't women want a say in the laws they must live under? And why would anyone think they don't deserve that right?"

"When you put it like that," Short said, "I guess I'd let my wife vote."

They were passing under a streetlight, and the self-congratulations on his face made Bridget's teeth clench. "You wouldn't see it as her right, but as her husband you'd give your permission?"

"Sure I would. I'd tell her the best candidate—"

"Shut up," Tall said.

"It's men," Bridget said. "Not speaking up for their own mothers and daughters. Wives."

"Seven to feed." Tall's eyes scornful. "I can't risk losing this job."

The brothel's first and second floor lights were out, but a soft glow rose from the chapel's window wells. She was safely there, if only June was too.

"Thank you," she said again. She wanted them gone and a few minutes alone to steel her nerves before she faced the possibility of June not having made it back.

Neither man stepped away, and when she climbed onto the porch, they followed. Just that morning, it would be yesterday morning now, she'd stood in this very spot in Kid's arms. The door handle refused to turn. She pushed and rattled it again.

Keep moving, keep moving, she told herself. "I'll try the back." There was also the cellar door.

"Cap'll be redder than a pistol." Tall's thoughts had moved on. "He won't be wanting reports written."

"Reports?" Bridget cringed.

"Having to put on paper his reasons for taking disciplinary actions against us. Or us writing up reports with complaints about him. He'll want this all kept quiet. If there's any sort of reprisal, it'll be an *accident* happens to us."

"You've risked not just your jobs, but your lives?"

"We can take care of ourselves." Short stole a glance over his shoulder. "A cop's always watching his back. And you ladies, in and out of the slammer eight nights of the week. Ain't nobody paying any real attention, ain't nobody cares."

"Is it possible?" She hated asking. "Is there any way you can destroy the records taken on me tonight? I've done nothing wrong."

"The other one blamed you. In the Glastner murder. Ain't you that one?"

"I'm new at the house. June confused me with someone else; she no longer blames me."

They came around the side of the brothel and stepped into the alley. The red lights were out, horses along the rail gone, as were all wagons and buggies.

"Tampering, destroying evidence, ain't healthy," Tall said.

Short walked to the empty horse railing and looked over the trampled and snowy surface. "That fellow was killed right here. You heard anything about that? Any whore gossip?"

"It's all gossip," Bridget said. Her face burned.

"Learning something leads to an arrest," Short said, "that might help us smooth things over at the station. The women in there all been questioned. You too?"

She wanted to shout Cripe's name, tell them everything, but they'd march her right back to the station for further questioning. This time, she might never get out. Grabbing the door handle, she held her breath and pulled. Locked.

"You ain't answering my question," Short said. "You been asked about that murder?"

"I was no help. I didn't see anyone or hear gunshots."

"Wasn't guns fired." The statement so matter-of-fact, she wasn't sure what he believed of her.

A moan made them turn. A black lump lay on the cellar door. Bridget ran, bent to Lily, and helped her stand. "I'm here." Then louder, "You reek of booze."

"Jesus," Short grimaced. "Is that the Black Ghost?"

"She's my patient," Bridget said. "Drunk again."

Tall took a step forward. "You need help getting her in?"

"Stay back," Bridget warned. "She's likely to puke all over you. She usually loses a stomach full when she gets like this."

Tall remained in place. "She out every night? Always dressed like that? Always liquored up?"

"It's her burns," Bridget lied. "The pain is worse at night."

"I'll be damned," Short said, standing well back. "The Black Ghost."

Coaxing and supporting Lily, Bridget stooped to open the trap door. "This house contains only ghosts."

Two nights before, Lily had made it all the way to the river. Tonight, she could hardly walk. How far had she gotten before turning back? As far as the end of the alley?

In the basement, Bridget threw back the covers on the bed, and Lily seeped from her grasp as if bones and muscle had turned suddenly liquid. Looking down on her, the thickly tatted roses lying flat, cheekbone to cheekbone, Bridget's eyes smarted. Why was death sometimes long and cruel? At other times a quick snatch?

Bridget grabbed one of Doc's bottles from the nightstand. She wanted to drink every drop she could find, call up oblivion, and sleep until she woke into a better world. She couldn't. She had to hang on. She had to believe she could call up even more from herself. She could. She would. Starting with finding out the truth about June.

From the street, there'd been candlelight in the chapel. Someone still bathed or prayed, and maybe they'd seen June.

Three tubs held bathers. Naked shoulders, elbows on porcelain rims. June lolled in one, her eyes closed, her head back, her body so still she might have been passed out. The water in the tub looked as undisturbed as glass. Seeing her washed relief over Bridget. She wouldn't ask if June was all right. June was not. She *was* back in the house though and being watched over.

"Well, Hannah's come to join us," Ruby said. In the near darkness, she occupied the last tub. Four removed from Hassie and June. She still wore her lipstick, her eyes lined with shadow and kohl.

Bridget itched to rush the tub, hold her under water and watch the bubbles slowly rise. She doubted she had the strength. She placed June's bow on the chair beside her tub. June was alive, not wandering in the cold, not dead in a gutter. "June," Bridget spoke hardly above a whisper, "I'm sorry for what happened."

Ruby's drunken voice rang out. "Men take everything. Even birth. Claiming the race began with a man's rib, not a woman's womb."

Hassie kept her eyes on Bridget, answered Ruby out of the side of her mouth. "Women don't believe that one."

"A bit of burning at the stake, the tiny slice of a guillotine blade. Them'll make you a believer."

June remained still, feigning sleep. Begging in the only way she could, Bridget believed, to be left alone. She had her friends there, wanted and needed only them. Bridget turned to Hassie, thinking to thank her for minding June, but outsiders didn't thank family for caring for their own.

"You understand what I'm saying?" Ruby's words drunken, slurring. "They take everything. Even our imagination."

Seeing the threesome soaking together raised another troubling possibility. Had Hassie and Ruby gone to the police station for June? Had they paid a fine, or bribe—not knowing about June's rape—and seeking only June's release?

Bridget turned for the broken statue on its mirror. Inhabitant of two realms. A girl who until her dying breath honored her own principles.

"Where you going?" Ruby said. "You running away? You don't want to hear how we come down here and tell ourselves lies until our jaws ache. 'You'll be out of here soon, Ruby. Jesus has not forgotten you, Ruby.' We stand at that broken thing telling ourselves we ain't just pieces held together with spit."

"What do you want in here?" Hassie asked. "June doesn't care to talk to you. Leave your card with the butler, and he'll see she gets it."

"We're all painted clay . . ." Ruby's voice drifting. "White lips for mute wives, red for us."

Bridget noticed the wobble of Ruby's head. "I think you'd better get out. Get some sleep."

Managing only a weak grin, Ruby's lips went suddenly slack. Her head dropped forward, her chin touching the water.

Too bad, Bridget thought, *a couple of inches more and Ruby would have a snout full.* She stopped. Was there more to the darkness around Ruby than just her sitting in shadow? The death space? "Hassie," Bridget started for the tub. "We need to get her out."

In the poor lighting, Bridget wasn't at first certain what she saw. Then the blow of realization: Trails of crimson flowing up from Ruby's wrists, staining the bathwater. "Help me get her out!"

Hassie jumped, nearly toppling over the side of her tub. June too, suddenly alert, water splashing off her as she ran.

They grunted and struggled, Bridget and Hassie each under one arm, June lifting the feet. Bridget grabbed the first of Ruby's bleeding wrists, pressed the wounds hard with the heel of her hand. "Like this," she told Hassie, nodding at Ruby's other wrist. "Harder."

Lying on the brick floor, Ruby sobbed quietly, than began to shiver.

June brought their robes, and after they'd put them on and helped Ruby into hers, they wrapped additional warmth around her: silk sheets of green, gold, and red.

While they kept pressure on the wounds, Bridget considered. She'd seen the blood trickling out from Ruby's wrists through water still clear enough to do so. Ruby wasn't short of breath or particularly pale—both signs of severe blood loss. And Ruby sobbed, displaying emotion, an awareness of what she'd done, rather than a mind drifting and fading. "You're going to be all right," Bridget said.

With the bleeding stopped, they used the satin belts from their robes, and Ruby sniffled and cussed through the binding and knotting of her wrists. Bridget took one arm and Hassie the other, helping her up and walking her to a chair in front of the broken statue.

"Our Mother, who art in heaven," they chanted. The candles flickered. "Wholeness is thy name."

For several minutes, they repeated the prayer, waiting for all their emotions to quiet. The earth had trembled through the night, and now they'd not leave the numinous air of the chapel until the shaking settled.

Ruby reached out for June, drew her into her arms, and looked to Bridget. "You're only passing through. Remember that." She smiled, kohl from around her eyes streaking down her face. "I think you can make it."

Bridget couldn't manage a smile but hoped her face was pleasant enough. "I'm going to try."

Thirty-Two

Bridget opened her eyes to jabbing and blinked to find herself lying on the red rug.

Lily slouched in the rocker, holding the dressmaker's yardstick she'd used as a poker.

"I'm awake." Bridget sat up slowly and saw the bright light of midday through the windows. She couldn't see Lily's eyes as the stick slipped from Lily's hand, slid along the frame of the cradle, and dropped to the floor. Then Lily's hand, sliding off her lap, dangling.

Fighting back anguish at the sight, Bridget massaged her throbbing temples and checked her emotions. She had to stay strong, alert. After the previous evening's arrests, finding June home, and getting Ruby safely to bed, she'd sunk onto Lily's floor, believing that room safer than the attic. In the basement she had some hope of hearing police boots crunching overhead, magnified by the tin roof. Some hope of escaping into the alley.

Now that her name was on file, how long before officers knocked? Did she have hours, as much as a whole day?

An untouched bowl of oatmeal sat on the table, which meant Tate had brought Lily food.

So much, Bridget thought, *for counting on sound to wake me.* She rose, filled the teaspoon by only a quarter and held it close to Lily's face. "You have to eat something." Suppose she lifted Lily's black veil just off her mouth? "Even the smallest amount would help."

"You slept on my floor."

Did I? Bridget wondered. *Did I get any actual sleep?* She put the spoon back in the bowl, lifted Lily's hand, and set it back in her lap.

"What's your name?"

"I'm Hannah," she managed.

"He's gone."

By the amount of light in the room, Bridget knew the reference was to Kid. She'd missed him. She'd longed to tell him goodbye and find the name of the livery boarding Smoke.

"You love him." Lily's right hand slid off her lap again, and she slouched more against the right arm of the rocker.

Bridget tried not to panic at Lily's near collapse. "I don't love him. I hardly know him." That was a lie. They'd connected instantly. A friendship that would normally take months to establish might have been woven by the Fates working magic with their threads and spindles. "Maybe he isn't gone. I'll be right back. Then you'll eat at least a bite for me. Won't you, please?"

In the bar, Tate worked over a narrow checkbook with a fountain pen. "Pay day," she said on seeing Bridget, then closed the book. She nodded at a woman sweeping. "This is Sadie. She's back."

"Sadie," Bridget managed. "Your husband . . . ?"

"Resting in peace now."

"I'm sorry."

The woman with her hair in a rag smiled, then continued with her work. Bridget didn't blame her. Talking about the loss of a loved one was hard, especially with a stranger. Those who hadn't experienced the loss could not understand. For those who did understand, no words were necessary.

Bridget turned to Tate, not knowing how much Tate knew of the previous night: jail, June, Ruby. "I wanted to speak with Kid."

"And you supposed I'd wake you? You don't really believe the two of you have a future." Grief rode her face like physical pain. "Lily will likely die today. Isn't that enough for right now?"

It was. Nothing else was as large. Not Kid or knowing Smoke's location. "Did Doc visit her? Did I sleep through that?"

"Through his taking her pulse? Listening to her heart? We were hardly sounding trumpets. Where will you go after?" Both question and command.

"I didn't kill Mr. Stowe. If that's why you don't want me speaking to Kid."

Tate's mood softened. She stood and touched Bridget's forearm. "I wish you every blessing. I don't have a daughter, but if I did, I'd want her to be just like you. I know you didn't kill Stowe, but you're guilty of something. You're a fugitive, and I see the way Kid looks at you. I suspect you're entirely different from Agatha. Different from any girl he's known. You're strong, not simpering; you speak your mind. But a person on the run is dangerous." She gave a playful tug on Bridget's flannel cuff. "And you don't dress to win a husband. Leave him alone."

"He's engaged," Bridget said. "I could say the same of you. Surely, you don't believe the two of you have a future."

"You saved Ruby's life last night, and you've been good to Lily, even Plum Cake, which is heroic. I'm glad to have met you, glad you didn't die in the alley, but when Lily leaves us, so must you. Plum Cake has asked to see you, but if you don't want to go, that's your business. Just go back to Lily."

"The police know I'm here. They'll be coming to arrest me for Stowe's death."

"Chet Glastner's too?"

"You believe I killed him?"

Tate tugged at her own lacy cuffs. "I know you didn't, but if they arrest you, they're likely to make a nice package of it."

"That's what I can't risk." What had Short said? 'You ladies in and out of the slammer eight nights of the week. Ain't nobody paying any real attention, ain't nobody cares.' "Here, in Omaha," Bridget went on, "as far as the law is concerned, I'm a nobody."

Tate swallowed and lifted a hand to her heart. Her shoulders rose and sank. "Where will you go?"

"Home. Where I am known. I can't spend my life running, and the only chance I have is people who will vouch for me."

"You'll be arrested there."

"Yes, there, not here. The sheriff isn't the brightest thing, but I believe he'll at least hear my story. He'll know where I am. The whole town will, and I'll be able to employ a lawyer. If I'm arrested here, I'm likely to vanish." Thinking again of her encounter with the police and June's rape, she shuddered. Any number of things could happen to her if she were arrested. Including someone on the force, affiliated with the local mob, willing to hand her directly to Cripe.

Sinking back on her stool, Tate sighed. "I admire your courage. Hiding is no way to live, but all the same, at least you'd be alive."

"My name is Bridget Wright-Leonard."

Tate smiled. "Your friend Cora told me."

"More than the police are after me. The man who killed Stowe is named Cripe. If I survive him, all of this, you should come and work on the farm with me. There's plenty to do. Gardening, keeping the records. I have a house and I'm alone. I also want to start a factory. Nothing big, but something to employ girls." She looked deeply at Tate. "I could really use you."

"Thank you, but I have to stay in Omaha." She sighed again. "I'm sorry for everything."

"Don't be. We both know I can't stay forever. Take care of Papa Henry's journal."

"I'll think of you whenever I read it. And I'll remember the opportunity I passed up."

In the first of Plum Cake's two rooms, Goose lay on the too-small bed and snored. He'd not heard Bridget's knocking and did not hear her walking by. His apron and glasses were off, his mouth open. She imagined the kitchen full of dishes, but today he'd need to do them himself or rely on Sadie.

"Where were you last night?" Plum Cake demanded. "I banged for hours." She lifted a hand, turning over the palm and showing two blisters.

Keeping a civil tongue meant taking a deep breath and holding the stillness. "For hours?" Bridget asked. "Lily was forced to listen to you banging on her ceiling for hours?" Plum Cake's eyes darkened, but Bridget continued. "She must have prayed for the horror to stop. She might have imagined the racket was any number of demons."

"Where did you go?"

"If you got out of that bed," Bridget could scarcely keep her voice even, "you would know what goes on around here."

Plum Cake demanded of others the control she'd lost over herself. She needed someone always there to bring her food, stick a bedpan under her, or clean her up if they didn't reach her in time. Even someone with enough imagination to stimulate her banal existence: bring exotic desserts, sit in front of the Truth-Teller and describe the actions and clothing of girls she called hers.

Yet, she was physically able to get up. She'd stood while Bridget cleaned her. She'd likely stood for several minutes before Bridget heard the screaming. She chose to remain bedridden, which didn't make her situation any less real. Only sadder.

"How long," Bridget asked, "since you've walked into the bar? Have you ever been downstairs to Lily's room? Ever been to the chapel?"

"That place is a privy."

In the adjoining room, Goose drew in air with a loud snort, but settled back into sleep.

On the barge of her bed, Plum Cake scooted higher on her pillows, and then huffed as though she'd accomplished a real physical feat.

The once-healthy body, Bridget thought, now transformed by

inventions of guilt, doubt, and fear. In many ways, the madam felt mute to Bridget. The woman cussed and swore her explosive thorny words. Keeping her deeper emotions buried, unspoken or couched in lies about some wonderful childhood.

"Has Lily ever told you about the broken statue?" Bridget asked. "It's an inspiration to the girls. They say a prayer and are helped."

From a near-empty platter on the nightstand, Plum Cake reached for a cookie. "That privy hasn't helped anyone."

Given the size of the plate, Bridget imagined that when Goose carried it in, there'd been a stack of sweets. "The girls would be lost without the statue," she said. "Miracles happen down there."

Plum Cake chewed. "I don't believe you." The red on her neck blotched, crawled up to flame over her cheeks. She jabbed the bed. "This is my house." Cookie crumbs landed on the sheet. "I need you here at night tending the Truth-Teller. Here with me."

"I'm going home. Today, certainly tomorrow. When Lily—"

"I'll have Goose send for the police."

"Don't bother. They're on their way."

Plum Cake's eyes swam, her tears magnifying the brilliant blue. "You can't leave me here."

"I can't stay. You need to get up."

"Damn you."

"I can't help you any longer." Bridget stood beside the bed, took up the madam's free and blistered hand. "Be a warrior for yourself. Please. It's your only chance. Your only one. Get out of that bed."

"Damn you."

Bridget closed her eyes, held onto the darkness. The madam was one more in an endless line of hewn-down women. At what young age had her innocence been stolen? Had she experienced the grace of even one happy decade of childhood? How many times had she been shattered, until she no longer believed herself worthy of self-love?

Plum Cake swallowed the last of her cookie and pulled back her hand. "If I go out there, I'll be seen. Like this." Her round hands scooped at the air, indicating her bulk. "They'll see me."

"The girls are upstairs and the house doesn't open for a couple of hours. The only one out there is Tate."

"I want Ollie."

The little bird in her cage watched them.

"What do you fear most," Bridget asked. "Being seen, or dying alone in that bed?"

"I have Goose, and I can't climb down the stairs to your privy."

She was too large for the steps, Bridget agreed. Not too large though for walking into the adjoining room and into the hall. Just that, stepping out of her seclusion, might build her confidence. There, she could look right or left and see windows: natural light.

"Do miracles really happen down there?"

Bridget thought of the previous evening and saving Ruby's life. "Yes."

"That's true?"

Behind her ruinous physical state, Plum Cake still carried aspects of the beauty so prevalent in her barroom picture. Still the gorgeous eyes, pure as bluebird wings, still the translucent pastels resting in the folds and creases of her flesh, still the silent longing.

"I can't do it," Plum Cake blurted.

Bridget's emotions swung back and forth from love and concern to anger and frustration. "In the chapel you'll lose two hundred pounds instantly."

"You're lying."

Of course I'm lying. Anything to get you out of these rooms! "Your little tick-tick game. You won't have to play that any longer."

"I couldn't get back up," Plum Cake said. Her voice carried the ache of needing to believe the impossible.

Once you've seen the statue, you'll fly back up."

"You've seen someone fly?"

Bridget fought the urge to flee. Plum Cake wasn't so foolish as to deny all reason, the laws of cause and effect she'd lived all her life. She *was* that desperate. "Let's go into the hall and have a look at the stairs."

"Goose!"

Goose appeared in the doorway, winding the arms of his wire glasses around his ears. His thin hair stringy, the top of his union suit stretched over his girth.

"Tell her," Plum Cake said. "Tell her I can't go downstairs to the chapel."

Goose's bottom lip went slack. "You aren't able. You have to stay in bed where I can see you. I'm taking care of you."

"I'm right here," Plum Cake reached out, "so big you can see me." She faced Bridget. "I owe him."

"We don't owe people who are helping us die."

Plum Cake flinched. "He isn't."

"Just as you're helping him die."

Goose went still.

Plum Cake's face began to tremble. "What do you know about watching a man die?"

Bridget sat down on the opposite side of the bed from where Goose stood. She stretched out alongside Plum Cake and pillowed her head on the woman's large arm. "I haven't watched a man die," she said slowly. "I was too late. Papa Henry was gone when I reached the barn."

Thirty-Three

"I never dreamed this would be my life," Plum Cake said. From her bed and with Bridget still lying beside her, she looked around the room as though it, and not her body, was the limitation.

Bridget concentrated to keep from rolling off the narrow bit of space she occupied. "My great-grandmother always said, 'Fight death.' I think that means death comes to us bit by bit. Each thing we give up or quit on is a small death. How many of those do we get before the last one?"

"You're lucky," Plum Cake said. "A grandmother believed in you."

"And Papa Henry," Bridget said. "You had a loving father too. One who enjoyed spending time with you." Neither Goose nor Plum Cake answered, and after a few seconds, Bridget went on. "I think I need to add you and Tate as supporters. You too, Goose. You want the best for me, don't you?"

A sloppy-sounding suck burbled from Plum Cake's throat. "No one's ever called me a supporter."

Goose sat at the bottom of the bed, the platform not moving even under his tremendous size. His shoulders slumped forward, and he reminded Bridget of a haystack. "My gram told me I was a good-looking boy."

Bridget wondered at the comment. There in Goose's voice, riding below the deep bass, she'd detected a quake. Had his grandmother made him feel handsome, or had he felt lied to in an attempt to mask the truth? So that his grandmother's untruth burrowed straight into his little-boy heart? The lie of it cutting deeper each time?

Bridget would miss him too. Like everyone in the house, including herself, he was hungry for a bigger life. "Grown men don't need to be good looking. Mostly, you fellows aren't." *Kid was the exception.* She'd meant to lighten the mood, but Goose's expression remained gloomy.

"We're a mess," Bridget breathed into the quiet. "Our dreams too small or maybe so large we are afraid to believe in them."

"I have a dream," Goose said, that just-detectable shake returned. "I want to open a bakery. Plan to call it 'Bar-kery.'"

"Well, you son of a bitch!" Plum Cake slapped the bed. "You want to leave me." The bellows of her lungs sucked, expelled. "Bar-kery!" The word spat.

Goose pushed up his spectacles. "My name's Bar-tholomew. Bar-kery."

"You son of a bitch," she said again.

Bridget stood. With Plum Cake's slapping and moving around, it was stand or land on the floor. The woman's cheeks had skipped over red and jumped to the purple of dried wine dregs. The color of the residue left moldering overnight in the bottom of glasses.

"Help me up," Plum Cake commanded. "I'm going to your stupid chapel." Goose offered a hand, but she slapped it away. "Not you." She turned from him. "Get my dress, Hannah. I'm not going out there naked."

Bridget tried to help Plum Cake stand but wasn't much aid. Needing both hands to push herself off the bed, Plum Cake managed and stood while Bridget tied on the dress front. Plum Cake's great sagging back and buttocks were left in full view, but Bridget could only shrug. As she'd told the madam, at this hour, the girls were still in their rooms. Tate was in the bar, but Plum Cake's size wasn't news to her. Besides, Plum Cake was only going into the hall. That distance would be a milestone. Bridget planned to slam the door behind them, loud in Plum Cake's ears when she crossed that finish line. To suppose Plum

Cake could be coaxed all the way across the hall to the lavatory was fantastical. A future goal. One Bridget wouldn't be there to witness.

Plum Cake plodded, her fingers digging into Bridget's arm. Her feet scooted, her body rocked side-to-side, gaining little ground. With each step, she heaved theatrical breaths, hoping, Bridget suspected, to portray long-suffering. To punish them for their threats of leaving.

"You're doing great," Bridget said. She swung her free hand behind her back, curled her index finger in and out, beckoning Goose to stay on their heels.

They passed through the curtain into the front room, and Plum Cake stopped. "What the hell happened in here?" She turned her shoulders as if the mess was reason enough to quit and return to bed. The sight of Goose directly behind made her start forward again.

When they'd crossed the room of cluttered and broken things and passed through the door into the hallway, she turned on him. "I don't need you. Ladies only in the chapel."

Watching Goose's forlorn walk to the kitchen and his disappearance inside dropped Bridget's heart. "All right," she said, "let's head back. You did it."

"A goddamn Bar-kery."

Ruby stepped from the kitchen doorway as if Goose had shooed her out. She wore a robe similar to the one June had worn, bright with splashes of pink and yellow flowers. White gloves reached to her elbows. Her eyes bulged on seeing Plum Cake.

The madam froze for a moment, glanced back at her door, and caught herself. There was nowhere to run. "What are you looking at?"

Ruby's gaze darted from the madam to Bridget and back. Her face pinched, and she made no effort to hide her gawking. "You aren't . . .? You aren't . . . Plum Cake?"

"Who wants to know?"

"I'm Ruby."

"Ruby . . ." Plum Cake repeated the name slowly. "That hair. Out of my way, Ruby. I'm going to the chapel."

"You're not," Bridget said. "You've made your point. Trying that would be ridiculous."

Ruby made a show of once more gawking at the madam's size, even daring to tip her head right and left, eyeing the great wide hips, and seeing much of what the dress front did not hide. "It's not ridiculous," she sputtered at Plum Cake. "You need help. You're a barn."

Seeing Plum Cake stand there, not immediately screaming at being seen, or screaming for Ruby to get out of her house, surprised Bridget. She'd known the woman feared being alone, but hadn't realized that fear was larger even than her shame. How were her weight and fear tied together? And Ruby? She too fought for a place in the world. The gloves she wore were a stark reminder of how close she'd come to losing that fight.

"I can't stand here all day." Sweat rolled from Plum Cake's temples. "I'm going to the chapel."

"You can't make it," Bridget insisted.

"Because only you can? You're the only one who can survive a stabbing, escape a whore house?"

"You can do it." Ruby smiled at Plum Cake. "I believe in you."

Of course you do, Bridget thought. She pulled free of Plum Cake's bruising grip and began backing toward the bar. She didn't have time for this. The police might be coming down the street, and Lily needed her. There was nothing to do but get help. "Don't move. I'm getting Tate."

Ruby snickered. "Cover your eyes. She's probably playing in there with her delivery boy. Never mind." Her eyes widened as if she'd just remembered something. "Tate's been so long without it, I'm sure she's grown shut."

Bridget wouldn't let herself react, wouldn't give Ruby the satisfaction.

"I can't stand here," Plum Cake howled. She swayed and slapped a hand on Ruby's arm for support.

Ruby patted the hand. "I'll help you. We don't need Hannah or Tate. Tate's gone weak, lost her stomach for this business."

"Tate!" Bridget called as she rushed toward the bar. Seconds ticked, Plum Cake's knees and ankles were swelling, her heart likely pounding, and though Bridget imagined Ruby could smell advantage from a city away, this wasn't the time to fight with her. "Plum Cake and I need you."

Tate appeared in the doorway. Whatever she'd been doing, she'd stopped instantly and hurried for them. "What's going on?"

Bridget muscled back in to take Plum Cake's arm. "We've got this."

Ruby let go but hesitated. "I never wanted June to get hurt. But I had to do something." She turned, her colorful robe swaying at her heels.

"Did you call the police," Bridget asked, "out of a fear that we were developing a friendship?"

Ruby drew up. Turned around and gave Bridget a hard look as if saying, *you're too dumb for an explanation.* And went on.

"I'm going down," Plum Cake said.

"To prove what?" Tate scoffed.

They stood at the top of the stairwell, bunched together, Tate steadying Plum Cake on one arm, Bridget steadying her on the other. They stared down the steep drop. "This is a bad idea," Bridget said. Beads of sweat formed in her armpits, the centers of her palms dampened.

"A terrible idea," Tate said. The expression on her face was a mix of disbelief and nervous hilarity.

"Lily is dying," Plum Cake nearly wept. "Hannah is leaving me, and Goose wants a Bar-kery. He'll leave me too."

"Goose? That's just talk," Tate soothed. "Even he admits it."

Plum Cake stiffened. "You knew?"

"He won't actually do it," Tate said.

"All these years, lying to me." She wrested her arm from Tate, nearly pushing her down the steps.

"Goose?" Tate took a safe step back. "Or are you accusing me?"

At the bottom of the stairs, a black shape stumbled then slumped against the wall. "I heard you in the ceiling," Lily managed. "Sweetheart."

What have I done? Bridget thought. Plum Cake couldn't be convinced to turn back now.

Lily looked broken, huddling, absent in the black heap she made. Only death space now, like shadow in the bottom of a shallow grave. *I'll stay with you until the end,* Bridget promised herself. If the police came first, she'd become trickster, a ghost and hide under rugs, squat in planters, live on ceilings.

"She's completely lost her mind," Tate whispered.

"Hannah won't let you fall," Lily said.

It's Hannah, not Hercules, Bridget thought.

Plum Cake's knees were shaking. Ankles the size of whiskey jugs inched forward until her toes were off the edge of the landing.

Attempting the steps still felt horribly wrong to Bridget, but maybe also horribly right. Her mind was slowly shifting toward agreement. Plum Cake had accused Bridget of thinking she was the only one able to escape a brothel. That's what Plum Cake wanted, that escape. Powerful moments of change were rare. They rolled through lives like thunderstorms soaking parched fields and feeding rivers. They created openings that allowed stags to step through. Plum Cake stood at one such door, before one such storm. Her fear of being alone was a potent impetus. If she faced this portal and stepped through, she'd be changed.

Still, Bridget felt sick with worry. "Wait. Tate and I will go first. We'll keep just a step or two ahead. If you slip, we'll block the fall."

Tate's eyebrows lifted, sank, lifted. *If she falls,* the brows said, *we're all dead.*

Lily moaned.

"I'm coming," Plum Cake called down.

Bridget took a deep breath. "Ready?" she asked Tate.

Normally outspoken, albeit eloquently, Tate watched Lily with silent, anguished eyes.

"Tate?" Bridget tried again.

Keeping two abreast, Tate and Bridget filled the narrow stairwell and took the first steps down. Bridget glanced over her shoulder. Plum Cake kept one hand on the wall, the other gripping the railing so hard the wings of skin along the undersides of her arms swayed. For better balance, she leaned slightly back, her head and shoulders acting as counterweights against her massive stomach. She slid a foot out to the edge of the stair until her toes felt the air. Then farther, sliding the foot, the heel scraping down the front of the riser, keeping constant contact with the surface until the foot clunked, finding solid purchase. The wood squealed under the strain.

Step by step, Plum Cake huffed with effort and fear. Her size and lack of balance made turning around impossible, and each time Bridget looked back, the purple dress front bloomed with wider, wetter circles. Round splotches where purple clung to her sweaty stomach and breasts. Minutes, though it felt like hours, had already passed since she'd first risen from bed and most of the staircase remained to be navigated.

Plum Cake let out a half curse, half sob, and her trembling sent vibrations shuddering through the railing. The stair on which Bridget stood with Tate, two down from Plum Cake, vibrated. Should the stairs pull away from the wall, or even a riser break, Bridget knew Plum Cake would lose her tentative footing. They'd all drop, fracturing bones or worse. Lily, sitting helplessly at the base, was the most fragile.

"Mum," Bridget said, "are you able to go to your room and bring a chair?"

Lily's face beneath the black veil was impossible to read.

"Mum, we need a chair."

Lily worked herself to standing and moved off, no longer visible from the top of the stairs.

Safe, Bridget sighed.

Thirty-Four

Reaching the bottom of the stairs, they saw Lily had hauled her chair as far as her doorway but stopped there and collapsed over the back of it.

"Look!" Plum Cake shouted.

Bridget and Tate were already running. They helped Lily stand, but then Tate wrapped an arm around the slumped woman, forcing Bridget to step back. "I have her. You take Plum Cake." *Please*, her eyes added.

They'd left the door open at the top of the stairs and additional light came from the windows in Lily's room. Bridget carried the chair to the base of the staircase where Plum Cake still clung to the banister. "You did it," she said to Plum Cake, though she felt equally worn out and as deserving of congratulations.

At the doorway of her room, Lily lifted a hand, not wanting to go back inside despite Tate's coaxing. With Tate's help, she slid along the wall, her veiled eyes on Plum Cake. "What's your name?"

The question made Plum Cake wince.

Lily's hands lifted slowly in their satin gloves, cupped Plum Cake's cheeks, then wiped at sweat droplets. "Don't be afraid." She wheezed. "I've been burned." Another breath. "My skin is a snake's."

Her struggle to complete even short sentences struck Bridget. Death towed a squeaking wagon at Lily's side, waited for her to topple in.

"I stood there," Plum Cake pointed to the top of the stairs. "You begged for me. Your love."

Daring to come down, Bridget considered, they'd surrendered to the unexplainable. Now the waters rushed back. "Give her a moment," she whispered. "I'm sure she'll remember you."

Plum Cake fussed with the purple dress front, smoothed it over her stomach, pinched at the fabric covering her knees and settled it again. "You made my dress."

Lily gave no response.

"You made this," Plum Cake said. "Sewed it just for me. You remember that." She turned sharp eyes on Bridget. "I want her to show me the goddamn chapel. I want my miracle."

"It's at the end of the hall." Bridget walked beside Plum Cake, letting the madam hold onto one arm for support while Bridget slid the chair along with the other, allowing Plum Cake to sit and rest half way down the dark corridor. She'd have preferred walking with Lily.

"No, let Lily stay with me," Tate had said again. She kept an arm around Lily's waist, offering balance and encouragement. "I want to hold her."

Two feet inside the chapel, Plum Cake needed to sit once more. She stared at the spread of bathtubs and silk hangings shimmering in air currents generated by the door's opening and closing. She scowled at Tate. "You spent my money on this?"

Bridget dropped a comforting hand on the woman's shoulder. She doubted the money spent mattered to Plum Cake. Imagining the girls gathered there, where laughter and tears lingered in the walls, where they told the stories of their lives, and those stories were listened to, that did matter. Plum Cake felt the emptiness of being an outsider. She'd written herself out of her own better life, and accepting that was hard.

"It's a wonderful place," Tate said. "Isn't it?"

"I understand how you feel," Bridget told Plum Cake. "Come over the drain." The woman's continued sweating was a worry, and the thought of getting her back up the stairs an even bigger concern.

Bridget would willingly forego the bathing and the statue to have Plum Cake back in bed, but first the woman needed rest and cooling off. After that, Bridget decided, she'd go for Goose. Maybe he could fashion a travois as Papa Henry's people used, and Plum Cake could be pulled and pushed up. "A bath will make you feel better."

"I'm not bathing with you all looking at me." Though it was only Lily she watched.

Ignoring the comment, Bridget went behind Plum Cake and began untying the dress front. "It's all right. We see you every day." She thought to joke. "You're no longer all that interesting."

Plum Cake slapped at her.

"Hannah is right," Tate said, leaving Lily securely in a chair. "There isn't an inch of you we haven't already seen."

"You've all made a fool of me," Plum Cake sniffled. "Getting me down here. Go ahead, laugh." She narrowed her eyes on Bridget. "You lied to me. Lily doesn't bathe here."

Lily worked herself to her feet. "Plum Cake."

"She's remembering you now," Bridget whispered to the madam.

"I wash here." Lily began opening the buttons on her dress.

"There's no need for that." Bridget rushed to stop her. Lily had chosen to hide her body; no one had the right to challenge that, or shame her into doing otherwise. "Plum Cake didn't mean you needed to prove it."

"Leave her be," Tate's eyes swam. "Let her do what she must."

Bridget looked over the other three women. Each of them seemed to be experiencing something wildly different. "What's gotten into everyone?"

Lily freed two more buttons. Her sternum, a jutting knob of bone, appeared in the deepening vee of the bodice. She gave a slight shrug of one thin shoulder, then the other. The dress fell around her ankles.

Bridget's breath stopped.

A skeleton. Rib-thin. The flesh of her breasts consumed, bones held together by skin as thin as a wren hatchling's. Gumma sores the size of rose buds plagued her arms, legs, and chest. She pulled off the veil. Dark eyes, large in the starved face, copper-colored hair, thin and limp. The cartilage in her nose eaten away. A gaping cavity. Hideous to see.

Plum Cake's face pinched. She moaned.

Bridget steadied herself. This wasn't the time to faint or give in to her rolling stomach. She'd been expecting this. Plum Cake, too, must have known, but she'd not let herself fully imagine the extent of the disfigurement.

Tate's lips quivered, and tears she'd tried to hold back rolled down. She'd gone to the hospital and brought Lily to the house, Bridget remembered. Did she blame herself for Lily's condition?

"Christ!" Ruby gasped coming through the door. For a long moment, she studied Lily with unabashed curiosity. "Holy Christ!" She rubbed her wrists as if her wounds had begun to hurt again. After a long moment of blatant gaping she spun, shrugging, challenging. "What of it? We're all scarred." She picked at the fingertips of her gloves, pulled them off, and offered her bandaged wrists. "Which one of us ain't cut?"

Shrew, bobcat, angel, maybe all of them, Bridget thought. She hurried to help Lily pull up her dress and sit again. The lace veil lay on the floor like a plate-sized splattering of spilled ink, but she would not suggest Lily cover her face.

Tate, always staunch, who less than an hour earlier had told Bridget to leave the house, pulled a handkerchief from a pocket on her tailored skirt. She scrubbed her wet cheeks.

"I'm cut," Bridget said. There was the knife wound, but her wounding went deeper. "My father was murdered. Only days ago. I should have been there to help him." Making the admission, she felt more honest, though she'd say no more for fear of confusing and upsetting Lily. Let Lily believe in her Hannah.

No one appeared shocked by Bridget's news, only waited for her to tell more, their eyes shrugging as if to ask, *Is that all?* Compared to Plum Cake and Lily's disfigurements, and the knife tracks on Ruby's wrists, did a murdered father strike them as the stuff of every life? Bridget nearly smiled at their placid faces. She'd thought herself a leader in the depths of her suffering. In the contest for the hardest life, hadn't she been winning?

Plum Cake worked herself back onto her swollen ankles and over the drain. "Untie my dress."

Bridget loosened the neck straps while Ruby did the wrist ties. Tate tucked the kerchief back into her pocket and went to the radiators for pails of heated water.

"I was sixteen," Plum Cake said. She needed long moments to start talking, but as her body relaxed with the bathing, so did her tongue. "Father caught me in the barn with a woman. I'd heard the whispers, the talk about running her out of town. Maybe tying a stone around her waist and throwing her into the river. No one suspected that I watched her, carried the same wickedness in me." She glanced to where Lily sat. "If Father had caught me with a boy, he would have given me a simple whipping and seen us married. But a woman!"

Bridget ran a wet bar of soap up one of Plum Cake's arms, Tate up the other.

Plum Cake sniffled. "At the sight of us, Father doubled over in pain onto the dirty floor. A father's screams . . ." She stopped, sucked air. "A father's screams."

There it is again, Bridget thought. *Guilt.* We all blame and curse ourselves for perceived sins. Hadn't guilt sent her riding off with a knife hidden in the lining of her coat? Secretly wanting to destroy herself?

Lily stirred, held her stomach. "I had to." Her eyes were as rose-rimmed as the gumma. She stared at Bridget. "I couldn't let them."

They all stopped.

"I couldn't let them," Lily struggled. "The spinning, taking you." She rocked herself, one arm bending at the elbow as though she suddenly cradled an infant. She smiled down at the bundle only she saw, her face more hideous with the stretching of her lips, mucus running freely onto her top lip. Her free hand moved up, slow but deliberate, the fingers settling on a tiny, imaginary neck. Her jaw clenched, she bit her bottom lip with effort, her fingers closing. "I squeezed." Her hand dropped, sliding off her lap, her body sagged and tipped.

Bridget ran the few feet, caught her before she hit the floor, lifted her again onto the chair, and knelt alongside.

Lily raised her hand as she'd done a few days earlier, her fingers on Bridget's neck. "Your face," she slowed, seeing the past again, "turned a beautiful blue."

"Your infant?" Bridget asked. "You?" She searched the eyes full of such sorrow they made Bridget's stomach clench. "You did it?"

"I need my chair." Plum Cake's voice sharp, fearful. Ruby rushed to set it over the drain, and Plum Cake sank heavily onto it. "The next day, Father was so sick, he didn't leave his bed."

Tate's silence about Lily's confession, not adding any words of understanding, and Plum Cake's rushing back into her own story made Bridget's hands tremble with anger. She pulled her flannel shirttail free and wiped Lily's nose. Were they so unfeeling? Were they trying to hurry attention off the subject, distract Lily from her pain, and assure her they held no judgment?

"For a week," Plum Cake said, "Father kept to his bed. He'd never done that. Even the winter he broke an arm, he didn't miss a single morning or evening's chores. I prayed he'd get up, grab the leather strap, and tear my flesh. What I'd done was killing him. Then he . . ." With the hand Tate had been soaping, Plum Cake swiped under her nose, leaving a runner of soapsuds across her top lip. "God condemns suicide. If you do that, He'll condemn you to eternal flames."

"Oh please." Ruby lifted one of Plum Cake's breasts and worked her rag back and forth beneath. "Your man-made, all-seeing God. Supposedly keeping eyes on what we do, but never bothering with what's done to us."

Bridget let them squabble. Plum Cake wasn't winning the title of the most tragic life either. That went to Lily.

"You can hurry to the edge," Plum Cake insisted. "Who doesn't? That ain't wrong. It ain't stepping off. So long as God decides the day and the hour. A week after, Father screaming and shouting from his bed, he made Mother and my sister promise not to come to him. He made them get on their knees, swear on the Bible that they'd not bring him water or food. Made them tie him to a tree in the middle pasture. Use the horse to pull the knots tight."

The brick flooring burned Bridget's knees. She turned and sat, staying so close she could rest a cheek against Lily's thigh. Lily had made a painful admission, to which not even Tate was responding. By comparison, Plum Cake's story sounded false. "A healthy man," Bridget dared to say, "no matter how heartbroken, doesn't have himself roped to a tree."

"Father," Plum Cake went on, "expected God to come the first day, pluck him straight up, decide the minute. God worked slow, not quick like pulling a trigger. That August was so hot the sun didn't set even at night. Three days of him screaming for a sip of water. Help. Ma sat on the porch even through the nights, clutching her Bible, watching him out there across the field, skeeters covering her arms and face. Too scared to break her promise and carry him a cup. Too scared to come inside and him seeing her gone."

Water trickled down the drain. Soap bubbles popped.

Ruby balled her rag and threw it in her pail with a whoop. "That's the worst story I've ever heard." She turned to Lily. "But yours is worse."

"I could have snuck out at night," Plum Cake said. "Given him a sip. I hadn't promised. I waited to hear my name, but I was dead to him."

Bridget had heard Lily's story and now Plum Cake's. What had Plum Cake said just a couple of nights earlier? "Not a childhood among them." The brothel wasn't entirely responsible for taking the girls from innocence to brokenness; they brought their ashes with them. The house though, blocked roads out.

"When we knew he was dead—"

"Oh no!" Ruby cut Plum Cake off. "There's more?"

"I rode into town for the sheriff and the doctor. They loaded his body in a wagon. I heard the doctor say Father had come to him weeks earlier with pain eating his gut like a poison. I rode west, didn't wait even to get him in the ground. Spread my legs for any man interested. In a wagon, a saloon, behind a privy with his children playing in front and his wife at the window. My punishment. If Father watched, he'd know I was doing what our preacher preached. Submit to a man."

"Interesting," Ruby said. "I thought it was submit to your husband."

"What about your mum?" Bridget asked. "You've never gone back for her?"

"Can we all shut up now," Tate said. She poured soapy water down the drain and went to the radiators for a warm, clean pail.

Plum Cake ignored her. "Two months before Father took sick, Ma started keeping rat poison. Kept it right there in the kitchen cupboard. Her special silver spoon always shining next to the tin. She claimed it was for varmints, but we had a dozen cats in the yard, prowling day and night under the porch and all around the foundation. I never saw a rat, and I know they don't stay where there's the smell of cat piss."

"Wish I'd had your ma," Ruby said.

Plum Cake hoisted her stomach, drawing attention to her girth. "I don't need to worry. No man would have me now."

"There is no law mandating sex," Tate scoffed. "You can be a reed and say no."

It's herself Plum Cake doesn't want to be with, Bridget thought. The full-blown erotica of life, humming there in her body. It scares her, and she doesn't feel worthy of it. How deep was the fear that every hour since being caught in a barn and her father's death, she'd needed to force down the terror, feed it like a beast she could keep sated?

Hearing Lily's story and now Plum Cake's, it was easy for Bridget to feel their innocence. She couldn't live free though until she accepted her own. What had Dr. Potter said about illness? That it was self-inflicted? Life was self-inflicted. Still, Papa Henry had preached time's layered nature. He'd believed fixing today fixed the past and the future at the same time.

They'd finished with the bathing, and Tate pulled down the only silk close to purple: a dark eggplant color. "We'll need two, choose a second."

"Yellow," Plum Cake said.

Lily's head drooped, and Bridget remained chair side, watching as Ruby and Tate tied the two pieces together at the shoulders, giving Plum Cake color front and back. Watching them, she felt suddenly blessed. Right and wrong, black and white, like a cripple his cane, she'd needed that rigid moral structure to hold her up. But in these women, judged evil by the world, there was deep beauty and spirituality. What Papa Henry called holy. Their bodies were abused, yet their hearts shone through the latticework of their brokenness.

While Tate and Ruby took Plum Cake to the statue, Bridget took up Lily's hand. "Papa Henry and I often watched birds flying north in the spring, south in the fall. He remembered his mother's stories of massive buffalo herds, thundering the ground as they traveled, and living according to the seasons."

Lily's eyes, Bridget promised herself, were focused. She heard.

Bridget went on, "He saw death as only a migration."

"That?" Plum Cake stood at the broken statue, stared at the ebony figure. "Hannah," she called, waiting for Bridget to leave Lily and come to her side. "That?" she asked again when Bridget reached her. "That?" Fresh tears welled in her eyes. "You promised me." She lifted an arm. The shovel of one hand swung.

The statue hit the brick flooring, pieces popping and jumping a yard in all directions.

"My God!" Tate shrieked, gave Lily a desperate glance of grief, and faced Plum Cake. "How dare you? That was Lily's statue."

Ruby's mouth dropped open. "Whoa. Christ!"

Before Bridget saw her rise and limp over, Lily was folding to her knees before the broken pieces. Sobbing, she scooped chunks of plaster into her lap like gathering up a child.

"Is that why you did it?" Tate's anger flashed at Plum Cake. "To see her there on her knees because she rejected you?"

Bridget squatted beside Lily, opened her fingers and took out black, gold, and red shards. "Mum, it's all right. We'll fix her. She's not dead. We'll save her."

Plum Cake sputtered a muffled apology, but seeing Lily's ruined face seemed to deepen her sorrow. She stood in her silks, tears on her cheeks. "I wanted a miracle."

"I'm going for Goose," Bridget said as she helped Lily back to her chair. "We need him."

"I don't need that traitor," Plum Cake said. "I climbed down here. I can get myself back up. You just watch me."

"You can't." Bridget wanted to shake her, and at the same time, hold her.

Leaving the chapel, Bridget carried Plum Cake's chair, letting the madam once again periodically rest on the trek back down the hall. Tate helped Lily walk, though the motion was little more than a shuffle of feet and Tate half dragging a body. At the door to Lily's room, Bridget paused with Plum Cake to watch Tate ease Lily onto her bed, lift Lily's feet onto the mattress, then draw in Lily's flopped hands and fold them across her chest.

"She's bad," Tate whispered to Bridget when she'd stepped back into the hall. "I just don't know."

"Let's get Plum Cake upstairs," Bridget said. "Then I'll hurry back down."

Going up was both easier and harder. Not facing the drop, Plum Cake had less sense of losing her balance, but each stair required hefting her weight. They worked together, crying "Up!" and "Now!" Tate and Bridget helped to hoist the wide buttocks with each of Plum Cake's exertions, thankful for the silk barrier. From the front, Ruby sat with her knees wide and bent between them to reach under Plum Cake's stomach and help lift each heavy leg to the next riser.

Plum Cake huffed and cursed. On the fifth, she stopped. Sweat rolled off her, and the railing trembled under her grasp. "I can't make it."

"In the chapel," Bridget insisted, "you told your story. Now you weigh less."

Tate's lips moved. A half smile that too quickly sank into a full frown.

"Lift your gunboat," Ruby yelled at Plum Cake. "I ain't that strong."

The stairs shimmied and groaned. Her stomach pitching, Bridget peered over the thin rail and down. Looked at what seemed flimsy construction and the distance should the staircase collapse.

Plum Cake panted, fear nearly choking her. "I'm stuck."

"You're not stuck," Bridget persisted. "Take a deep breath. Just take two more steps. Then we'll rest again."

"Whatever brought you to us," Tate said to Bridget, "I'm glad we've met."

"Glad? Right now, while we're stuck in a stairwell?"

Plum Cake groaned. "You said we're not stuck."

"Concentrate," Tate scolded.

"I can't do it," Plum Cake swore again. A large wet spot had spread over each buttock. Sweaty silk also spanned her shoulders and clung down her spine. Her hand pressing against the brick wall was blanched, the wrist purple with blood pooling under the pressure.

Her hand on the banister shook as though she meant to rip the railing from its supports.

The stairs groaned louder the higher they climbed.

Plum Cake faltered. A knee banged. She swayed.

"Bones of a pig!" Ruby shrieked.

They all gripped tighter, waited for the staircase to settle. Bridget slid her hand a few inches farther up the railing, felt the slick of Plum Cake's sweat. What depth of humiliation was the madam feeling? "We're right here with you."

"Goose!" Plum Cake shouted.

"No," Bridget said. Plum Cake's weight was strain enough. The three of them added an additional three hundred pounds, and more, to stressed joints and wall anchors. "We can't call Goose. No more weight on the stairs. Plum Cake, you started up knowing you could. And you can."

"I can't."

Bridget's heart raced. The effort of each step was massive for Plum Cake. Even the pauses meant more time burning her ankles, weakening her knees, and straining her heart. Rests were not rests; the longer she took, the more likely she was to collapse.

"It's like having a baby," Bridget said. "The pain is always the worst right before birth. You're birthing you, and you can do it."

"That's stupid," Ruby said. "But Plum Cake, do it anyway."

"I can't."

"You can," Bridget said.

"How do you know?"

"Because you have to."

"You said I'd fly."

Tate whispered behind the wall of Plum Cake's back. "You said *fly?*"

"You just missed the flying," Ruby said, "by a couple hundred pounds."

Wood creaked and moaned.

"There's no way but up," Bridget shouted. "Quit wasting time. You saw Lily. She's suffering more than you. Climb! There's just a couple more."

"No, there's a lot," Ruby said. "Seven."

Plum Cake groaned and managed another.

"Ruby," Tate rolled her eyes, "how many steps now?"

"Six."

"I can't," Plum Cake sobbed.

From the top of the stairs, a chorus of voices began ringing out. "Make it five. Five, five."

Bridget looked around Plum Cake to see the brothel's ten remaining inhabitants huddled at the top. June stood in front, the only one not shouting, but looking down on them while behind her the others screamed, clapped, even stomped. Hassie had brought a chair, and she tipped it up on the back legs then gaveled the legs back to the floor. "Make it four. Four, four."

In the noise, and with more grunting and swearing, Plum Cake reached the top. She turned to sit, sinking as Hassie pushed the chair too quickly. With folding legs, Plum Cake nearly wobbled off the side, nearly tumbled back down the stairs.

Screams and a host of grabbing hands steadied her. She shuddered and panted.

Bridget stepped out of the stairwell with Tate. Goose had come from the kitchen but kept back at the girls' swarming. He watched only a minute, looking fragile as the spun sugar he sculpted on cake tops. He turned away, Plum Cake's triumph tragic on his face. The kitchen door closed behind him. Bridget imagined she heard the slide of an iron lock.

The girls, chattering and giddy, seeing Plum Cake for the first time, circled her chair like bees their queen. She smoothed the silk over her knees and lifted her eyes to them. "I did it."

Thirty-Five

Surrounded by so much fussing attention, Bridget knew Plum Cake no longer needed her. For the last two years at least, the madam had thought herself too ugly to be seen, had wanted her picture in the bar to remain the lie of her. The girls disagreed.

More than having made the trek up and down the stairs, more than seeing the broken statue, this community of swarming girls would help Plum Cake heal.

Bridget turned and hurried back to the basement.

Lily still lay stretched out on her bed, her legs straight, her hands positioned on her chest as if she'd been laid out for burial. The sight made Bridget grimace, but Lily was sleeping and the only thing to offer now was companionship. She carefully removed Lily's shoes and draped her cape over her, tucking the fur around her cold feet.

When Bridget next opened her eyes, a familiar hubbub rumbled overhead: footsteps drumming, tinny piano tunes pounding, gruff voices laughing, hooting. Given the dimensions of night, she'd slept in the rocker for as long as six hours or more. She didn't remember closing her eyes. She scarcely remembered covering Lily with the long black cape and moving to the chair.

The police hadn't come for her though nearly twenty-four hours had passed since giving her full name. Had Tall purposely misplaced the records? How long before Short stepped in?

Lily hadn't moved. She lay in the same eerily posed position.

"Mum?" Bridget lowered her head gently to Lily's chest. Crackling, the death rattle, lungs filling with fluid and allowing for only shallow breathing. A faint heartbeat. Chills splintered up Bridget's spine, backed her away from the bed. She'd known all week that death stalked Lily. Still, she wrestled long minutes with the signs. When she could, she turned and went upstairs.

Ruby, back in her long gloves, saw her standing just outside the barroom entrance and rushed out. "What are you doing here?"

"Tell Tate. It's time, Lily is dying." She waited only long enough to see Tate's face pale so quickly at the whispered news in her ear, Bridget feared the woman would faint. Not waiting to see it, she hurried back, knelt at Lily's bedside, and listened again to her chest.

Tate stepped into the room ashen faced, her eyes full of tears. "Doc's finishing his drink. I won't pour him another until he comes down."

"There's nothing he can do." Bridget's anger felt like that of a peevish child. Supposing she knew better than a doctor with schooling and years of practicing harkened on stupidity. She wanted someone to blame. She wanted life for Lily, not this death. She wanted a god to help, not a man who couldn't.

Tate stood twisting her ropes of pearls, the noose of beads turning her neck red.

Bridget's own sadness was heavy, tolling, but Tate's anguish felt more personal, cutting, tearing. "If you need to," Bridget said, "go back up." In her panic, she'd raced for Tate, but with the initial shock settling into grief and loss, she knew Lily would still be alive when the house closed. "I'll keep watch, come up again if she changes."

Tate nodded, touched Bridget's forearm, found no words.

With her gone, Bridget paced. After killing her own daughter, Lily hadn't left the maternity hospital in handcuffs; she'd been allowed to leave with Tate. What bargain had Tate made with the devil to keep the hospital from turning Lily over to the police? And now? Her rushing out hadn't been because she was needed back upstairs; Ruby was there. Nor was the fleeing an inability to sit with death. More likely it was Tate's inability to sit with guilt. Even though bringing Lily to the house likely saved her from the gallows.

The cavity on Lily's face seemed no less hideous with her lying prone, and Bridget lifted her gaze to the ceiling. "All this, there'd damn well better be a heaven."

She concentrated instead on the sleeping eyes and the relaxed set of Lily's lips. William Blake was said to have clapped with joy as he died. Lily wasn't clapping, but she looked at peace. "Mum," she leaned in close, her lips touching an ivory ear, "you're still beautiful."

Bridget swiped at tears, and unable to sit still, she paced again. Her hands trembled for purpose and the broken statue came to mind. The clay shards lay atop the mirror where the statue had stood, their reflected numbers looking impossible. She wrapped them in silk, sat them outside Lily's door, and headed up, slipping from the stairwell through the kitchen door so quickly she felt she'd done so invisibly.

Goose stood hatless, his backside leaning against the cold stove.

"You okay?" she asked.

In the kitchen, he never seemed the massive, unkempt creature of dirty clothes and broken furniture. He stared out over the empty room as if he didn't know what to do, or perhaps lacked the will to do anything at all.

"I came for glue," she said. Did he know what was happening? "Lily's dying."

He didn't answer. His language was sifting flour, cracking eggs, leveling off cups of sugar with the back of a knife. He pulled open a cupboard door and handed her the small enamel glue pot.

"How is Plum Cake?" Bridget asked.

A shrug.

"Has she been told about Lily?"

"Tate stopped, said telling her was mine."

"Are you worried about her heart? Whether or not it will stop ticking?"

She'd meant to lighten the moment, but his response was more a grunt. "She's strong as an ox."

"I'm sorry for my part in taking her downstairs. I had no right." She swallowed. "Only righteousness told me I did. She could have fallen, been seriously injured. Worse."

He nodded at Bridget's pants, her farm britches again, not the flimsy purple cotton. "Those your leaving clothes? Don't come back here. Fix your life."

"I'm going to try." He hadn't meant any mean-spiritedness. "Is Plum Cake still mad at you? She's going to be even more distressed when this is over. I suggest candy."

Back in Lily's room, the minutes both rushed and torpid, Bridget worked on the statue. The overhead din was constant. No wonder that after hours of the noise, Lily had nightly needed to sneak out and walk along the quiet river?

Doc pushed the door open. He leaned over Lily, used his stethoscope, and straightened. "Couple of hours. No more 'an that." He flipped the bottom of the cape back from Lily's feet, used a stiff finger and pushed on top of one foot then the other. He squeezed an ankle as if checking a piece of fruit for rot. "That blotchiness. Blood's pooling, the heart's quitting." He jutted his chin, importantly. "I'll give her morphine and let her go."

"You mean have her die? Push her over the edge?"

"She ain't going to live."

He'd hurry Lily out of her life, so he could get on with living his. He didn't know what Lily was experiencing. Even lying still as death, she might be lingering at some portal, watching from a bit of distance, waiting to step through at her own pace.

"If she's not in pain," Bridget said, "and she doesn't seem to be, then please don't."

"Might as well get it over."

"Let her decide when."

His face tightened. "Nonsense."

"You said it would only be a couple of hours. I'll wait with her."

"Suit you'self." He snapped his bag closed. "Women don't have the constitution to be doctors."

She nodded as pleasantly as she could. She didn't want an argument, only to be left alone with Lily. "I understand. It takes a man to do a man's job." She felt the hesitation in him. He wanted to agree, but he sensed she was laying a trap. She kept back the words, *because if a woman can do it, then the men who do are only human.*

"You know where to find me when you've had enough," he said.

With Doc gone, the odor of his cloying pomade and whiskey-thick breath lingering, Bridget tucked the fur back around Lily's feet. "Don't listen to him. I'm happy to wait. However long you need."

"Is it time?" A tiny breath on wings.

Bridget started with surprise. She took Lily's hand. Such a short life. Too short. "If you're ready," she managed.

"All right." Air only as deep as the back of her throat. "Let's go."

Four words. More than Lily had spoken in hours. But who was the 'us'? Did she mean herself and Hannah? Had the real Hannah already joined her?

"I'm right here," Bridget said. "Helping you cross." She was witness. "Papa Henry's there. He'll be looking for you." If she loved Lily, and she did, and all love was connected, which it had to be, then Papa Henry was there to show Lily her way. "Tell him not to worry. I'll be all right."

Motion at the door made Bridget jump. June peered through a four-inch slit. Her eyes fearful, her whole body hesitant.

"Come in." Despite June's fear, she'd come. For Lily, for herself.

June still needed a moment. Never having crossed the room's threshold, she poked her head in and peeked around as though she expected a host of monsters to be hiding in corners. She gathered her courage and stepped through. At the sight of Lily's face, she gasped and turned her back to the bed. Her shoulders rose and fell. Again. "Ruby said only the nose is gone." Taking a third deep breath, she faced Lily. "Eww . . ." she groaned.

"It's not so bad," Bridget said.

Ruby could have easily compared Lily's condition to leprosy, called her a snake, used any number of hideous descriptions, but she'd kept the rest of Lily's disfigurements a secret. She'd probably done so to try and win some favor with the girls and Plum Cake. If she convinced Plum Cake to give her Tate's job, where would Tate go? She was too proud to accept a room upstairs, especially if it meant working under Ruby, and too old to be offered one.

Keeping close to the wall, June stayed at the head of the bed. With her back against the bricks, she slid to the floor and pulled her knees up under her chin. From there, she could see only the side of Lily's face. Much less of the ravished cavity. "Ruby said I should come and see what it's like."

"Lily is only a woman who's suffered more than most." Bridget regretted saying so. June's husband had been murdered, and night after night she tucked her soul in some tiny tin box and lay down with ghosts. Her suffering was as great as any. "I'm sorry for last night."

"That man's sick now. He's going to die."

Was that why she'd not fought? Happy to infect the man? Or so she believed.

They sat, only whispering, Bridget occasionally fitting together clay pieces, only to put them down again, rarely using her glue. June remained in her spot on the floor.

Hours passed and when the noise upstairs finally quit, Tate

returned still in her evening gown and pearls. Her face struck with grief. "I only wanted to do the right thing."

At the table, the broken statue still looked hopeless to Bridget. She'd glued some of the larger bottom pieces together, but even there, small holes gaped and the section looked like a sieve. "Take this chair," she said to Tate. She rose to pull it bedside.

"No, no." Tate's voice trembled. "It's not my place to sit close." She moved to the nanny rocker. One hand balled in her lap, the other dropped into the attached, empty cradle. Her fingers open, soothing.

Bridget had never seen Lily make such an unconscious gesture. Lily had entered the hospital planning to give her infant up; she'd had no expectation of coming to the house. Who had needed a cradle?

The girls entered in twos and threes. Ruby had passed word. Few had seen more of Lily than a glimpse of a black robe vanishing into shadows or fleeing down an unlit hall. Now, their reactions varied. Some stared; others looked away. All made tiny sucking noises or lifted an alarmed hand to their hearts or mouths. All found places to sit on the floor and join the vigil. One of their own was dying.

Ruby entered last, and Bridget wondered if she'd just left Plum Cake's room. She smelled slightly of caramel, the sweet scent of browning sugar. Some confectionary Goose had made for Plum Cake, some treat to help mask her pain and put her in a stupor of sleep. He'd use the occasion to try to win back his place as enabler and savior.

Ruby had grabbed a robe, for warmth if not modesty, but like the others, she still wore her work makeup: rouge, mouth painted a fraction of an inch too wide to exaggerate her lips, eyes rimmed and shadowed and sultry. "At an Irish wake," her voice cut the quiet, "people tell stories about the dead." She picked up one of the pieces of the statue, turned it this and that way before reaching for the glue. "Has no one got a story? What about you, Hannah? You knew her for two minutes before she strangled your little neck."

Tate's reaction was fierce. "Shut up!"

"Please," Bridget said. "For Lily's sake. We can't do this now."

Silence hung until suddenly death thickened the air, stirred the space. The moment Lily left, Bridget felt it as painfully as if she'd been stabbed a second time.

For the next several minutes, girls sniffled and wiped tears. Then rubbed tired eyes and yawned.

"It must be five a.m.," Tate said. "Everyone to bed."

June and Ruby remained sitting as the others slipped silently from the room. Tate remained too, sitting in the rocker, pushing the floor with her heeled slipper, scrubbing at tears.

The depth of Tate's grief continued to surprise Bridget. She expected sadness, but Lily had suffered so much, and now that was over. Who couldn't be happy for her?

Ruby broke the silence, a near hiss at Bridget. "I killed the bastard." A crackle in the stilled air. "Chet Glastner deserved it."

"You're lying," Bridget said. June's face held the same flat stare it had on leaving the jail cell. Tate kept her gaze on Lily's body, not looking over. Bridget felt a wave of anger. She hated them down to their burned-out hearts. "You all knew? For how long?"

"I never wanted June to get hurt," Ruby had said that afternoon. "But I had to do something." She'd been referring to Chet Glastner, not June's rape.

"Ha!" Ruby said. A mirthless chuckle. "Your face, Hannah. You really should see your face."

"I never thought of you." Behind them, Lily lay dead. Bridget had believed Lily innocent. Hoped it for her. "How did you do it?"

"I sent him a note, told him to meet me by the river. I promised to bring June. I tested him with a kiss. A second. I knew then if it hadn't been for the ghastly cold, he would have taken me right there." She glanced at June and seemed to switch from storytelling to facts alone. "The cut wasn't clean—his coat collar, me standing too close. Not the quick swipe I wanted. He was bleeding pretty bad, but he struggled with me. I knew he'd get the knife away. I had to throw it. We wrestled and then he just dropped. I tried to find my knife but couldn't."

Ruby acted resolute, but the scars around her wrists proved internal agony. "We are sorry for him, aren't we, June?" she said. "But Chet had to be stopped." She looked at Tate, accusation in her eyes. "He was June's pimp. He would have killed her. You think I'd let that happen?"

"Lily saw it all," Bridget said. "She saw you throw your knife."

Ruby rose, offered a hand to June and helped her up. "Hannah," her voice was almost kind. "I know you won't go to the cops. And that makes you guilty too."

No, I won't, Bridget thought. What had June said in the bar when telling the story of her and Chet?

People say they wouldn't never. They don't know.

Thirty-Six

Banging on the alley door made Bridget lift her tired head. She'd slept slumped against Lily's iron bed frame. At the next knock, she jumped, suddenly remembering herself. *Police.* She scrambled up, grabbed her coat and Papa Henry's hat, and ran into the hall.

The door opening at the top of the staircase stopped her.

"Hannah?" Tate teetered there, still in last evening's low-cut, sleeveless dress, her eyes red and weepy. "It's the coroner and his assistant."

"Not the police?" Bridget asked. "You're sure?"

Tate nodded, swaying drunkenly close to the landing's edge. "I sent for them."

"You don't need to come down." *You don't look steady enough.* "I'll show them."

She hurried back to the room and stood beside Lily's body. The men would see only a wasted figure needing carted off. They were strangers who'd never known the woman. "Goodbye, Mum."

At the door, she motioned them in and stepped out. She didn't fear the men; they didn't care about her, but she couldn't be in the cold, clinical algebra of them carrying Lily's body away. Another parting as final as the death.

"Ahh. Will you look at that," one of the men said. "How many you suppose she infected?"

"Syphilis," the second man answered. "The Lord's smite upon a prostitute."

Bridget slapped her hands over her ears. Prostitute, only that. A life boxed and discarded. Not woman, mother, friend, dreamer, sufferer.

She waited until their footsteps quit on the stairs, then quit on the ceiling, and the house went quiet. Back in Lily's room, the small indent of her light weight remained on the mussed bed. Bridget straightened the blankets and hung the cape the men had flung on the floor. The half-glued plaster pieces of the broken statue caught her eye. She wanted to tuck at least a pebble-sized bit in her pocket, but she was leaving and had no right.

Taking spools of thread, she wound up the loose ends and put the wooden bobbins back in their tin. She pulled a strand of purple and another of white from needles and stuck the needles into Lily's cushion. Still unable to leave, she walked back and forth, found a pin on the floor, refolded the entire stack of purple fabrics, and tugged again at the blankets to tidy the bed. She freed the dress in the mirrorless frame and hung the tiny gown with the others.

The thick text that had predicted Hannah's return lay on the nightstand, and Bridget trailed a finger over the cover's embossing. In some realm of the unexplained, and unexplainable, Lily had experienced her daughter's return. Lily's truth, Lily's lived experience. As true as four stags carrying an omen to a kitchen window.

Standing in the doorway, she looked back at the tidied room. A chapter finished but for her own coat and hat on the worktables, ready for the grabbing when the hour arrived. Ten days had passed since she'd regained consciousness in the attic. Her cut had all but healed, and now she needed only two things before she walked out the door: the cover of nightfall and the name of the stable where she'd find Smoke. Armed with them, she'd go home. She'd leave Plum Cake's and all the house's inhabitants and throw herself on the goodwill of Bleaksville. She hadn't been able to go home when she'd thought herself guilty of murder; now that she knew she wasn't, she had no choice but to go. The truth and the community of Bleaksville were her only hope. She had no guarantees. Cripe had also lived in Bleaksville, had won an election there, and friends such as Thayer still believed him a good man.

At the same time, the thought of leaving the women who lived at Plum Cake's Resort made her want to weep. Just as she wanted to weep at the thought of never seeing Kid again. She loved him. He'd focus on Agatha and his new life as a banker. Forget Tate and the redheaded scullery maid he'd nicknamed Britches.

"Tate?" Bridget squinted into the barroom. "Are you all right?"

With its amber lights off and drapes drawn, the place looked eerie and sad, reflecting none of the gaiety Bridget witnessed through the Truth-Teller. Sadie had not yet arrived. Overflowing ashtrays, glasses stained with lipstick and tobacco, brass spittoons with trails of brown tobacco juice—all begged for attention. Tate sat at the ornate bar, tipped a near-empty bottle of whiskey, and poured it into a short crystal glass, its rim smeared with lipstick.

Bridget hesitated, wondering if she ought to leave and give Tate her privacy. Kid would be there soon, and given the gown and the faltering way Tate turned with red-rimmed eyes, she'd obviously spent the rest of the night there. She'd settled in at the bar and reached for whiskey. Leaving her alone so incapacitated was dangerous.

"Let me help you upstairs. You don't want Kid to see you like this."

Tate lifted her glass, tipped it back. Swallowed.

"Lily died peacefully," Bridget tried. "Her suffering is over. Maybe today should be a celebration." She didn't feel celebratory, and the comment was trite, but she didn't know what else to say. "Lily is finally with her Hannah."

Tate poured more whiskey, the bottle trembling in her hand. "Hannah—"

"Can we stop that now? My name is Bridget."

The liquid in Tate's glass sloshed. "Lily didn't kill Hannah."

Bridget felt pulled up. Lily wasn't there to defend her story, and Tate's contradiction rang cruel. "You're saying she lied?"

Tate teetered on her stool. "The nurse lied to her."

Bridget stepped close and into the sour, alcoholic haze of Tate's breath. She pushed the bottle across the redwood. "How would you know?"

"I saw the infant."

Lily's confession had been too rich with detail, Bridget believed, to have been a lie. She'd described the strength she'd felt in her hands, the force of her mother's love, Hannah's tiny, soft neck.

"You weren't at the birth," Bridget said. "You didn't see."

"You helped Lily." Her voice was drunkenly singsong. "You helped Plum Cake."

"You're changing the subject." Tate was such an emotional and sodden mess, suddenly weeping and struggling to catch her breath, that Bridget felt guilty for pressing on. "What do you know about Hannah?"

"I went for Lily at the hospital." Tate struggled, her voice soft and breathy, as if she trekked down a distant road. "The nurse called me to come."

Bridget shook her head in disbelief. "Someone from the woman's ward calls a brothel?" Days earlier, Tate had told Bridget as much, but the implications felt fresh each time Bridget considered them. A nun, a head nurse, or some leader of a religious organization made decisions that condemned young girls for life.

"Lily had nowhere to go," Tate cried. "No family. I offered her a bed, time." Tate turned droopy eyes to Bridget. "I gave her the gift of time. She could sleep safe, find help, and heal."

"You've told me all that. What about Hannah?"

Tate picked a handkerchief from her lap, sobbed into it.

The cotton and lace looked so wet Bridget stepped behind the bar for a hand towel. "Here."

"I need you to know it again." Tate grabbed at the towel. "How I meant to help. I hoped Lily would find a relative. A friend."

"Someone to help her, but she didn't try," Bridget repeated what Tate had told her before.

"I arrived early. The nurse at the end of the hall stood with a man and a woman—older, you know. Maybe in their forties. The woman held an infant. 'Bless you. Bless you.' She couldn't stop telling the nurse." Tate lifted her glass, held it. She lowered the drink. Her gaze dropped into it. "The couple was happy. The child wanted, loved."

Sitting still was hard, and Bridget thought of Ruby's expletive. *Bones of a pig!*

Tate balled the towel against her lips. "Loved." She fought to catch her breath. When she had, she tipped back her glass. "They came down the hall to leave. Their faces said they'd never believed they'd receive a child. The woman wept with joy." Tate bit on the towel, continued with muffled words. "The woman stopped." Tate looked at Bridget as if what she was about to say was especially important. "I was a stranger, but she wanted to share her joy. With me. Me."

The "me," sounded so pitiful, Bridget put her arm around Tate's shoulder. How much another woman's kindness had mattered to Tate was sad in itself.

"She didn't care about my silk dress or my lipstick," Tate said. "We were women. She showed me her baby. A beautiful, tiny creature. Eyes open, looking right at me. A tuft of golden-red hair. I knew it was Lily's infant."

Tate's sorrow was agonizing, but Bridget needed to hear everything. "Go on."

"The man was teary too, already in love with his new child. And the mother! I'd hoped for my son to have a mother's love. A woman who thought him the most precious thing in the world." She held the towel in one hand and twisted her pearls with the other.

Twisted until the pale beads pinched her neck, and Bridget winced at the skin turning scarlet and the bruising that would result.

"My heart broke," Tate said. "Life is ugly. Unfair. Why did this infant deserve more than my son?" The question was rhetorical. "The nurse took me down a corridor, nodded at a closed door. 'She's in there. Get her out of here. She tried to strangle the infant.'"

"Tried?" Bridget asked.

"I was in such pain," Tate went on. "I'd just seen my son walking down the street with his father. When that man saw me, he turned our son away and into a store. My boy was fifteen. I'd left them entirely alone all those years, only watching him grow up from afar. But that man wouldn't allow my son even to meet my gaze. Not even that."

Here was the story Tate hadn't shared in the chapel. It struck Bridget how one event, perhaps only moments long, could change the trajectory of a life.

"I didn't go after them," Tate said. "Afraid of hurting my boy, but my heart was broken. Feeling so sorry for my loss, I felt no sympathy for Lily. The nurse explained how she'd struck Lily so hard with a pan Lily was knocked clean out. The doctor had to save Hannah's life. Breathe into her."

"Hannah lived? My God." Bridget took a step back, remembering Lily crying, tears running down beneath her black veiling. "And you knew. You kept that from Lily."

Tate reached the bottle but needed both hands to steady it enough to pour.

"Lily was knocked out," Bridget worked with the news, "and when she woke, they told her the infant was dead."

"They always tell the girls the child died."

Bridget needed to move. Her body felt snared by this new information. She emptied three ashtrays into a fourth before she could face Tate again. "Lily became your friend, but you never told her the truth? How could you keep it from her?"

"I'd given my child to the man who'd wronged me. The man I despised most in the world." She let out a gravelly sob, sucked in a steadying breath, and gulped whiskey.

"I gave my son," Tate continued, "to the man I believed would treat him most like a son. Because the baby *was* his son. Doing so took everything from me. Everything!" She swiped at her tears as if they burned her cheeks. "I thought I'd sacrificed more than Lily. I wanted her hurt. I wanted her to hate herself."

"The way you hated yourself?"

"Yes."

"Lily was young, scared, alone, and half-drugged. And you let her carry that guilt to her death? Knowing it was killing her."

Tate's eyes drooped. She lifted her glass half an inch and set it back as if the effort were too much.

"Come on," Bridget returned to the bar, put an arm around Tate's shoulder. "Sadie will be here any minute. Kid too, and you don't want him to see you like this. I'll tell them you aren't feeling well."

"His wife was barren," Tate nearly screamed. "How could she not love an infant son?"

"The wife of the man who impregnated you? He was married?"

Tate nodded.

"Tell me everything on the way upstairs," Bridget said. She glanced at the sweep of marble, redwood, and carpeting going wide left and then wide right. There'd be plenty of time.

Despite Bridget's tugging, Tate refused to move. "Once I started showing, I lost my job and the bit of money I'd managed to save went quick. When I came home after his birth, my landlady had rented my room. 'I run a respectable place,' she said."

"Tate, if I don't get you upstairs right now, you're going to hate me."

"Two nights on the streets," Tate shrugged off Bridget's hands, "breastfeeding in dark alleys. Washed a diaper in a horse trough. Found a roach crawling in his swaddling."

"I can't carry you up. You have to help me."

"Cold. Winter coming. I couldn't let him die." She pushed at Bridget. "Die because I hated his father."

Moment by moment, Tate was more bleary-eyed. Bridget turned her on the stool, peeled her fingers from the pearls, and tugged her hands to get her on her feet.

"The man who'd wronged me . . ." Tate nearly stood but lost her balance and sank back down. "I had to give him my baby."

"I understand how hard that must have been," Bridget said. "You're not a monster. You suffered right along with Lily."

"Hating her kept me too distracted to hate myself." She sniffled. "But I fell in love with her." Tate flung her arms out. "She had a heart this big."

Bridget decided to let Tate rest a moment more before trying again to get her on her feet. She needed to keep her awake though, talking. "Even when you quit blaming Lily, when you became friends, you didn't tell her the truth?"

"She was already seeing ghosts. She couldn't raise a child. The couple in the hospital, they could. I owed them."

More than Lily? Bridget wondered. *Because they'd seen you? Without judgment?*

"They didn't deserve Lily pounding on their door. Wanting Hannah back."

Tate's head moved up and down, the motion more a bob than a nod. "I couldn't tell Lily. No court would ever give her Hannah. A fallen woman. Lily didn't deserve the pain of trying. She would have tried. And little Hannah? What did she deserve?"

Bridget lifted Tate's hands, tugged again.

"To be stolen off a playground swing?" Tate didn't budge. "To live running? Lily trying to keep herself and her baby alive the only way she knew? As I'd tried?"

At the moment, Bridget only wanted Tate upstairs. She didn't want to make a judgment about what was best for Hannah. Enough people had already done that.

Tate grabbed at her pearls. Twisted. "When Lily was herself, before her madness, she would have wanted Hannah safe. Loved. Letting her believe Hannah was dead . . .that was a gift. To Lily."

Listening to Tate's stumbling confession, right and wrong seemed moon-like: ever changing. How could Bridget decide Tate's guilt or innocence? Yet Hannah wasn't Tate's child, and so what right did Tate have—even if her intentions were good—to decide what was best? How was her decision different from the nurse's? They'd both decided Lily couldn't raise the infant.

"What were Hannah's parents told about Lily?" Bridget asked. "Should they be told now that she's dead?"

Tate's bottom lip shone with whiskey. "The charity ward tells everyone the same: 'Nothing is known of the father. Only that he was a clean, strapping boy. The mother was from a good, God-fearing, Catholic family.'"

"I suppose that's best," Bridget conceded. "Keeping away as much hint of shame as possible. Not having it follow the child her whole life."

"I don't want them to know Lily died in a whorehouse." She wobbled on her stool. "I don't want Hannah to know."

"Keep the secret for Lily?"

"Yes, for Lily."

"Hey, ladies."

Kid steered his wheelbarrow through the door, then stopped on taking in the scene.

Thirty-Seven

"Everything all right here?" Kid asked. Seeing Bridget back in her flannel shirts and farm dungarees, he added, "Britches."

Caught up in Tate's confessions, Bridget hadn't heard the wheelbarrow rolling down the hall.

Kid set the handles down. With Tate slumped over the bar, her bare shoulders turned from him, he looked again to Bridget, his eyes full of question.

"We're grieving," Bridget said. "We lost someone last night." He didn't need to know how Lily's death had also brought up grieving for lost children. She hurried for the lights. Too late, she realized illumination was a bad idea. Tate's low-cut dress, the exposed round tops of her breasts, the whiskey bottle, and the glass she clutched all stood out in stark clarity.

"I'm sorry to hear that," Kid said. He took the wool cap from beneath his arm and laid it at the end of the bar. "I'll hurry here and get out of your way."

With a trembling hand, Tate groped at her bare chest.

More like scratching, Bridget thought, a self-conscious, modest searching for dress fabric to pull closed over herself. Her hand found her pearls. She twisted. Her neck turned red once more.

"Son," Tate sobbed.

"Jesus," Kid said. He'd gone behind the bar and reached for the previous day's barrel. He stopped, turned, and touched Tate's hand on her glass. "You had a son? He died?"

Tate twisted her pearls. Tighter.

The skin on Bridget's shoulders prickled across her back in a hot scattering like shot. *There it is,* she thought. *Tate's secret.*

Bridget grabbed more ashtrays to empty. She hadn't seen the resemblance earlier: Their matching hair and eye color. The same curve around the mouth and something matching in their carriage. Both tall for their respective sexes.

She'd believed, as Kid did, that his mother was dead. He'd said so. She'd never let herself think in terms of similarities. She also saw striking dissimilarities. Kid's chiseled, shaven face, that nose with its tiny knot on the bridge, his muscled body. A stark contrast to Tate's smooth skin, delicate features, feminine lines.

Kid started, rushing around the bar before Bridget realized Tate was slowly tipping off her stool.

He caught her before her head struck the floor. On one knee, he held her in a sitting position. "Easy," he said. "Take a second to catch your breath."

Bridget dropped to Tate's other side, her gaze meeting Kid's. Would Tate want Kid to carry her upstairs? Would she want to stay and complete her confession?

Tate's eyes fluttered open. Her gaze met Kid's. "My son."

His Adam's apple rose and fell. "What?" he managed. Then to Bridget. "What's she going on about?"

Tate sank against his chest, grabbing hold of him. "I'm sorry. I'm so sorry."

He turned still as stone. He let her continue clutching, but his gaze was off, away.

What was it he tried to remember? A proof, a denial, some distant and half-remembered moment? Perhaps an overheard word in childhood, a whisper behind a door, the frown of a relative?

"Can you stand?" Bridget coaxed Tate. "I'll help you upstairs."

"I didn't mean to hurt you," Tate begged of Kid. She tilted her head to see his face. Her eyes pleaded, tear-filled, afraid.

He pulled her arms from around him and, unable as she was in finding her legs, all but lifted her back onto her stool. He stepped around the bar a second time and took down the previous night's barrel. Eyes straight ahead.

Tate's groping hands found her pearls again. Her already red and chafed neck turned purple with the cinching. "Please," she begged Kid. "I need you to understand."

His shoulders rigid beneath his coat, he kept his back to them. His hands white-knuckled on the barrel's wooden staves.

Making a fortress of his body, Bridget thought. As if to keep Tate's news from penetrating his heart.

He gave himself a long moment before coming back around. Focusing only on the bottle, he sat. Though he always sat to her immediate side, close enough for them to tip a shoulder and share a laugh, he left an empty stool between them.

A space Bridget wished she could fill for Tate. She wasn't the one Tate needed, and sitting there would only further separate mother and son. She took the stool on the other side, reached and coaxed the pearls from Tate's hand.

On the bar's redwood top, Kid's hands looked dropped. His gaze fixed on them as if they needed watching. He made a guttural sound, a cross between a chuckle and a curse. "I don't know what to ask. Except how the hell do you suddenly figure you're my mother?"

"I pursued your father," Tate whispered.

"Pops? You expect me to believe you and him . . ."

Tate reached across the space and touched his arm. At his flinch, she drew her hand back and grabbed up the towel. Balled it against her trembling lips.

He needs time, Bridget wanted to promise.

"You're telling me," Kid kept his eyes straight ahead, "Pops walked in this joint? That's crazy. He can't stand me delivering here. Calls this place Satan's den." He shook his head and faced Tate. "It wasn't him." He started to rise.

Bridget understood Kid's shock—she felt it herself. "Let her explain." Tate had a story and a right to tell that story. "Listen to her."

Kid sat heavily, eyes down again. When Tate didn't speak, he did. "First, you tried to make me take your money. Now this. What the hell do you want from me?"

"I wasn't working here then," Tate said. "Wasn't working anywhere. This," she looked around the bar, her face still crumbled with emotion, "came after."

Kid's thumbs began drumming the redwood.

Bridget wanted to reach and steady his hands. Feel their size and strength beneath her palms.

"Your father wasn't to blame," Tate said. "I pursued him. Relentlessly."

Bridget swallowed. She hadn't imagined Tate as the pursuer. Yet Tate had said so. Twice.

"My folks," Kid went on, his denial of her in the two, select words, "were married four years before I came along. You saying Pop's was married when the two of you . . .?"

"Yes."

"Did you know that?"

"Yes."

Kid's thumbs drummed harder. "And you went after him? To ruin his marriage?"

His supposed questions were clear accusations, and Bridget felt surprise over how quickly he'd passed through denial to arrive at blame.

Tate lifted her glass, hesitated, and set it back down. The glass scarcely touched the bar before Kid grabbed it. Pushed it the length of his reach away.

"I was young. A fool," Tate said. "Knowing he was married ..." She shook her head. "I don't know. I think that made it more fun. Part of the challenge."

"Challenge?" Anger plied Kid's face. "For two years, I been sitting here every morning. Now, you're giving me this shit? What have I been? Another of your challenges? Fool the fool's son?"

"I never meant to tell you."

"You couldn't wait."

They sat a moment, hearing only Tate's uneven breathing, the sniffling as she tried to bury her emotions in the towel.

Kid shook his head. "That's why this place is on my route? Why you buy from Storz?"

"You're my son." Tate's head lifted. Her face still wet, she looked directly at him. "A mother has a right to see her child."

"The boss tells me not to rush with you, gives me a shorter number of orders." He matched her look. "I asked. He gave me some bullshit about making sure you never switched distributors."

"He has no idea why I insist on you."

"But you made it clear. Me, or you buy elsewhere. Jesus, that makes it worse! I can imagine what he thinks is going on. The guys at the shop ... shit."

Bridget watched him. His mind circled the facts. Yet he hung back, discussing work, not breaching the deepest core. When he knew the whole story, the full truth within the box with its four corners of his pops, his deceased mother, Tate, and himself, the truth would change his heart forever. Mend it or crush it.

"I only wanted to spend time with you," Tate said. "Never to hurt you."

Kid rose so fast his stool toppled, hit the floor. He righted it, tucked his cap back under his arm, and took up his wheelbarrow handles. The rolling sound of his barrow faded down the hallway.

"I'll be right back," Bridget promised Tate.

Passing the kitchen door, she stuck her head in and called to Goose. "Tate needs coffee. Good and strong."

In the alley, she watched Kid hoist the empty barrel into an open slot on the wagon and give it an extra shove to be sure it was secure. He lifted the wheelbarrow to its place, fastened the leather straps through their buckles. She'd not offer him any syrupy platitudes either about how everything would work out. He didn't deserve having to hear them.

Finally, he faced her. "If you came to see Spot, he's not here. The damn dog rolled in horseshit."

"I came to see you."

They looked each other in the eyes and moved at the same moment. Bridget couldn't have said who stepped into the embrace first. He held her, and she dropped her head against his shoulder. She'd meant to ask him again for Smoke's location, but now her own concerns felt selfish.

Kid took a half step away, his hands sliding down to clutch her forearms. "Why you dressed in those britches again?"

He knew, but he'd have her say it. "I'm leaving."

"Bad timing. Tate needs you."

"No. Tate needs you."

He dropped his hands. "You finagle more hugs out of me than Aggie."

"It was just a hug."

"When did Tate tell you?" he asked.

"Just now. The same moment as you. You believe her, don't you?"

He pulled his gloves free, looked down at them. "It was a long time ago. Once in a while there'd be fighting, hushed silences when I entered the room. I was still in knickers; what does a kid know? Then Ma died. We don't see her family. I've always known there was something." He slapped the gloves against his empty palm. "Hell, I don't know what I believe."

The nearest horse snorted. The far horse shimmied in its traces.

Bridget waited.

"Ma . . . the woman I thought was Ma." He stopped, grabbed the rail on the wagon seat, and put one foot onto the runner. "I need to finish my route. I'll see you later."

"You won't."

His foot came off, his black boot catching light. "You're leaving right now?"

"I need to know where my horse is being stabled."

"You're planning on stealing it?"

"It's my horse."

"You can't waltz into a livery and take a horse."

"Please." She didn't want to argue. Couldn't carry the weight of cross words with him. She already felt bowed over with the heaviness of Lily's death, the burden of leaving new friends—especially him—and the terror of being hunted. "Cripe, the man who stole Smoke also killed my father. I can't let him get away with that and keep a horse Papa Henry loved."

"So why aren't you going to the law?"

"I can't."

"Why?"

"I can't."

He glanced back at the brothel door. "I need to go before she walks out here. We'll talk tomorrow."

"You're not listening." *Was it denial or just distraction?* "I don't have until tomorrow. I'm leaving."

"You think you're going to ride out of town on that horse, and no one's going to stop you?"

"Cripe can't go the police, either. Can't tell them the rightful owner took back the horse he stole. He'd be implicating himself in Papa Henry's murder. Not that anyone cares."

"Why is that? How does a man murder, ride a stolen horse, and no one comes after him?"

She hesitated. "Papa Henry was half Omaha Indian. They don't care."

He nodded. "Go on."

"He owned a farm in a white county."

"That made him an unpopular fellow? Owning land and living off a reservation?"

"He had plenty of friends. Only one enemy, but that can be too many."

"I'm sorry. Your pops being murdered, that's something to go through."

She wanted to weep, but doing so would convince Kid she was too emotional to break into a livery. "If I take Smoke, Cripe will come. He'll know where I am. He's too proud and stupid to walk away, and he wants me gone. When I reach Bleaksville, I'll see Thayer. If he's still the acting sheriff, I'll tell him everything."

"A greenhorn lawman?"

"I didn't say Thayer was green."

"You did."

"When Cripe shows up at the farm, that will be all the proof Thayer needs to arrest him. This will finally be over."

"Will it? You skipped over the part where you're likely shot before you reach Bleaksville. You all right with that?"

She ached to be back in his arms, but he was careful. He loved Aggie, and he'd just received the shock of his life. "I'm jailed here," she said. "Dead to my life. I must fight. Even if it's dangerous."

He climbed into the wagon and unwound the reins from around the brake handle. He looked ready to ride off and never return, but hesitated, looked back at her. "Go on, tell me again how you figure your little plan isn't going to be a big mistake? And why Thayer's going to believe you, but the law here won't."

Because here I'm wanted for Stowe's murder. Because here, Papa Henry's murder matters even less than it does in Bleaksville. "Cripe won't take being outsmarted by me. He hates me. Knowing I'm back in Bleaksville with my big mouth and Smoke, he'll want me shut up."

"When he doesn't show?"

"He has to."

"Say he doesn't—" Kid raised his hand as she opened her mouth. "Let me finish. Say he doesn't, and you've brought your horse back. Put it in your barn. What's to prove he ever stole it? Horse runs off, comes back. Suppose you're accused of hiding it for a few days, bringing it back. You're clearing him of the theft. Probably clearing him of your pops's murder."

Her eyes smarted. "You're making my point! No one here has any reason to believe me. The truth is less about provable facts and more about reputation. The police here won't help me. You said yourself that Cripe's thick with the ward boss." She shuddered remembering Cigar Man at the police station. "The cops have a picture of me with the word 'prostitute' scribbled under my name."

Kid shook his head, turned his face briefly to hide a grin of disbelief, and eyed her again. "You've been arrested? You are all kinds of trouble."

"I know what I'm doing."

He looked out over the horses with their heads up, eyes straight ahead, backs alert, anticipating the reins rippling along their spines. "You suppose you're some kind of Annie Oakley?" He began pulling on one of the gloves he'd been fisting. "You steal a horse and ride out of Omaha for twenty miles with a posse on your tail. You don't fit the part. Britches or not. If Cripe's a murderer, sooner or later, he'll meet the devil."

"If you don't tell me where Smoke is, I'll sneak into and search every livery in the city. I'm just asking you to save me some time."

"The sooner to get yourself killed?"

"So I can live. So I can bury Papa Henry, get back to tending the horses, his land, Wire."

Kid's brows narrowed. "How much wire you talking about?"

She wanted to cry. "Wire is a dog."

"A dog? And that's a better name than Spot?"

"Please."

"You're gambling your life on a maybe sheriff in a little town with a sorry name."

The freezing temperature and the cold of his refusal had her shivering doubly. She backed toward the door. "I don't need your help. As for Bleaksville? It's a little town or a huge family. Depends on how you see it."

A cloud moved across the sun, shading the alley. She shivered harder. "I have friends there who will believe me. If I tell them Cripe had Smoke, they will believe me. My friend Cora has come to Omaha twice. She'll fight with me."

"The two of you? Using hat pins or knitting needles?"

"She's not the only one. And Sheriff Thayer? He's not the brightest toad on the road, but he'll do the right thing. All I want is the name of the livery."

"I'm not giving you the name. You're likely to get yourself in a heap more trouble. You seem good at that." He sighed. "But I'll take you."

"You will? This isn't your fight; I don't want your help."

With steely resolve, he glanced again at the door leading to Tate. "We don't always get what we want."

She had no choice. Accept his help or spend days hunting up Smoke on her own. "Okay, we'll do it your way. Help me get Smoke."

He leaned forward, his elbows on his knees, the reins loose in his gloved hands. "You going to tell me why you're running from the law here?"

"I didn't say I was."

"Everything you're doing says it. You afraid of being accused of killing your pops?"

The question nearly crumpled her. "My God," she gasped. No one would ever believe that. Would they? But if she was found guilty of

Stowe's murder? Everyone knew the same weapon had killed Papa Henry. Her mind tracked down a list: The knife, her being at the farm when it happened, no witnesses to say otherwise, no one to vouch for her being asleep. And if she put Smoke back in the barn? "I loved him. Why would I do such a thing?"

"How about inheriting a farm, cattle, horses? How about a young woman wanting free of a mean old half-breed holding her hostage?"

"But none of that's true."

"You got proof?"

In her darkest nightmares, she'd never imagined being accused of Papa Henry's murder. A person's character, however, could be dismantled lie by lie. Drop a worm in the apple barrel. Another. Print the lies in the paper. Reprint them.

"Hey . . ." Kid dropped the reins, swung off the wagon in one smooth leap and grabbed her. "Not you too. No fainting."

She felt empty. So much had happened over the last string of days, and all of it was bit-by-bit sucking away her confidence. She steadied herself against him. She wouldn't lose faith. The deer had warned her she'd need courage. "I loved Papa Henry."

He sighed. "I know. I said I'd help, and I will. God help me, I don't know why I've agreed to horse thieving, but I said I'd help, and I will."

"Tonight?"

"Jesus!" He dropped his arms. "Does it have to be tonight?"

He'd just received unbelievable news that had him wrestling with his own life. It wasn't fair to push him, but she had no other option. "I'm out of time. Just help me get Smoke. I'll get myself home." He didn't know what she could do. "If I take Smoke tonight, I'll be home by morning. No one will know Smoke's gone before then. There won't be anyone riding on my tail."

He glanced again at the brothel door. "About midnight. Horses ought to be in for the night, everyone gone home. I'll meet you here."

"Down there, at the end," she pointed. "The alley's too dangerous."

"Why did I tell him?" Tate moaned.

Goose had brought two cups and the coffee pot Tate was wont to use in the mornings. Bridget poured for Tate, slid the china in front of her, and filled a cup for herself. "Kid had a right to know."

"He had a right," Tate snapped, "to happiness. I destroyed my son's life. I've lost him forever."

"You don't know that. He's shocked, but he's a good man. Give him time."

"I need to leave town. Get far away before I hurt him anymore."

"You're not a runner. Give yourself a chance at a relationship with him. Give him a chance."

Tate sipped coffee with the same urgency she'd sipped her glass of whiskey. "Plum Cake wants me gone. Ruby can have it!" Her eyes filled again. "Oh Bridget, I love that boy."

Bridget wrapped an arm around the woman's shoulder, felt her shuddering.

A knock on the front door made them jump. Through the stained-glass nudes, two cops in uniform and two in plain clothes waited on the porch. A sharper rap sounded on the back door. The hammer of a billy club.

"They're here." Bridget's heart banged. "They're here."

Thirty-Eight

With police officers at both doors, Bridget spent a half second hugging Tate and turned to run. There wasn't time to tell Plum Cake goodbye or spend a moment offering condolences at the loss of Lily. The trap door was her only hope, but the hall to the back staircase would put her too close to the men leering through the window of the alley door. She sprinted up the front staircase, taking the wide steps two at a time.

As she rose, she had a clearer view of the front porch. Not one of the men cupped the sides of his eyes to block the light and peer through the stained-glass bodies of women. They didn't see her.

Reaching the second floor, she raced down that hall toward the door to the stairwell.

Ruby stepped out of a room, white gauze bandaging her wrists and wearing only ankle-length silk bloomers. "What's all the noise?"

"The police," Bridget said.

At Ruby's side, June appeared in Ruby's silk robe with the bright flowers, her hair tousled and without its bow.

"I'm leaving." Bridget kept backing towards the stairs. "I may never see you two again."

Ruby nodded, smiled. She pulled the hair from around her shoulders forward over her bare breasts. "I hope you make it."

June's face grew paler with each bang from below.

"They're not here for you," Bridget said. She was thankful the two had each other. Whether they slept as lovers or sisters, she didn't care. She backed away faster. "Take care of each other."

"You won't tell them," Ruby called to Bridget's fleeing back, "about Chet?"

Bridget paused, her hand on the doorknob. "I'll take it to my grave."

"You whore." Ruby laughed.

"You would never again . . ." Bridget glanced at the bandages.

"Run," Ruby said. "Don't be a fool."

Bridget had raced up one flight and now had to race down two. On the first floor, she paused on the landing to listen. Men were in the bar.

In the basement, she rushed into Lily's room to retrieve her hat and coat. She grabbed the cape as well, remembering the cold ride into Omaha. On the street, with the cape covering her coat and britches, and the hood pulled over her red hair, not even Cripe would recognize her.

Crouched in the small stairwell to the trap door, she used a shoulder to lift it no more than an inch.

"Gentlemen," Tate's voice slurry and inviting, at the brothel's open back door, "won't you come in out of the cold."

She's a trickster, Bridget thought. Able to bring herself back from weeping over Kid, and with too much whiskey still affecting her brain, find the grit to act the seductress. To protect someone she cared about.

"Let me have a look at you," Tate teased. "Which of you fellows have I seen before? Though you might need out of those uniforms for me to be sure."

A man laughed. Short, without his partner, did not.

"Come on in here before I catch my death," Tate said. "I'm sure you big strong men can guard this door just as well from the inside."

When the backs of their navy-blue overcoats had stepped through, Bridget dared to lift the door an inch higher. The alley lay empty.

Walking fast, she pulled the black hood forward, over Papa Henry's hat and around the sides of her face. She followed the tracks of Kid's wagon out of the alley but lost them when she reached the street.

Several wagons and people moved about in the bright afternoon. She slowed to a less obvious gait.

Wrapped in Lily's cloak, the clothing of a woman so recently dead, she felt part shadow, part black ghost. She pulled winter air into her lungs, let it lift her shoulders. This wasn't the time to let her emotions give way to apathy. She'd done that before. When her parents left her behind in Ireland, she'd been only eight years old, and their going had been abandonment. They left in broad daylight, not sparing her the sight of their going, carrying sacks on their backs, parcels filling their hands—the sum of their belongings. She'd fallen to the ground, felt herself sinking away, her mouth filling with soil. Grandma Teegan had dropped to her knees and dug, rescuing what she could of Bridget.

Papa Henry's death, Lily's less than twenty-four hours earlier, and fleeing for her life had her sinking again. This time, she was the only one who could do the digging. She needed to keep air in her lungs. Albeit the grit on her tongue.

Kid wouldn't return for close to twelve hours. Until then, she had to hide in plain sight and trust that he would. She walked with one eye open for Cripe or Smoke. Horses stood at posts, harnessed to buggies, blew white puffs from their noses, and blinked sleepy eyes, but none were Smoke. Nor Gus. She worried most about him. Smoke was handsome, coveted. Though the thought of Cripe having him pained her, she knew he was safe. Gus was a workhorse, less attractive to people who didn't appreciate his strength and knowledge of plow, rake, and wagon. His dependability when a girl out of her mind with grief needed him.

She passed Ed Maurer's Restaurant and paused. Kid had mentioned the place, a favorite of his and Aggie's. Even Tate spoke favorably of the chocolate cake, which meant the establishment welcomed a well-dressed woman, regardless of her occupation. Likely had welcomed Lily before the ravages of syphilis sent her into hiding. Perhaps Lily and Plum Cake had come together. Before. Before everything changed for them.

Bridget went on, drifting in and out of shops to pass the hours and warm herself. Women did their shopping and rode cable cars home, but the shopkeepers were the same each time she entered. It was best not to stay long in any one place or visit a store more than once.

The pull of the Missouri River and its connection to home drew her east. She sat on the bank, her knees pulled up and the cape covering even her feet. Beneath the ice, fish lay quiet, waiting for winter to leave. Like herself. With no idea of how long her life would be cold and dormant. She needed the courage to wait, to maintain, to accept that for now maintenance was enough. When spring cycled back to her soul, and it would, she'd plant.

Her stomach growled. The sun was low in the west and sinking. She'd not eaten yet that day, and if she intended to spend the night riding, she needed to put food in her stomach. Then she'd rent a room and try to sleep for a couple of hours—though she doubted she could. If Kid didn't show, she'd have the key already in her pocket and a safe place for the night. This was her new life: Relying on herself. Always keeping one foot ahead of the skeleton's bones.

She turned from the river and started back west. Buildings and their wide cornices dropped brows over storefronts and threw shadowed patterns over the walks.

Kid would be finishing his workday, possibly loading his dray for tomorrow, tending the team. Then he'd go home, change his clothes, and confide in Spot. Would he go to Aggie next? Would he tell her about Tate?

And Tate? Had she sobered, opened Plum Cake's doors on time? Would she adhere to the scaffolding of routine to keep on her feet?

Before entering Ed Maurer's restaurant, Bridget removed Papa Henry's leather hat—sure it was obvious and odd-looking, bunched beneath the hood. She tucked it into her old coat pocket beneath the cape and pulled the hood back up to cover her hair. Inside, she lifted her eyes only enough to make a quick assessment of the nearest available tables. Voices and the clicking of dishes and forks came mostly from deeper inside, farther from the cold draft of people entering or exiting. She chose a table close to the front, but along the wall and out of the way. With her back to the other patrons and facing the large windows, she had a clear view of anyone approaching. If a man in uniform arrived, she'd know to keep her face down and leave.

A waiter approached. "Does this table suit you?"

"I'd like to start with a cup of coffee, please." Embarrassed, she realized she ought to have waited to be seated. Already she'd drawn attention to herself.

"I'll bring a menu."

She kept her hood up and allowed herself only sidelong glances. Plush walls, ornate chandeliers, gleaming candlesticks on white tablecloths. No wonder this was one of Aggie's favorite places.

The gray of deepening dusk caught her attention, made her think again of the long and miserable ride ahead. Coming into the city on Gus, the majority of the trip happened in daylight. Could she find her way when the entire trip home must be made in the dark? Riding Gus, she'd also carried the fire of revenge. Going home, she rode toward an empty house. Where creaking boards didn't mean Papa Henry rambled around the home, tending fires. The sigh of old wooden floors and foundations would now only echo those who'd lived there and were gone.

The waiter returned with coffee and a menu.

She'd yet to take a sip when she saw them approaching. A foursome. Two pair of matched sets. A middle-aged woman with her arm through a middle-aged man's. A lovely young woman with her arm through a young man's.

She'd heard about Aggie, had wrestled her into an abstraction easily kept at a distance. Seeing her on Kid's arm, that closeness, carved at

Bridget's heart. Threatened to slide her out of her chair and onto the floor.

She buried her face in her menu, felt it shaking as they entered and were seated at a table not six feet behind her. How foolish she must look, a single woman, unescorted, and hunkered in her wrap. She wished she'd thought to grab one of Lily's veils. She'd drop it over her face now.

Their nearness made it impossible for her to stand and leave without drawing attention. She could feel Kid's closeness directly behind her. They could turn, stretch, and touch fingertips. Thankfully, seated back-to-back, he wouldn't catch a glimpse of her boots or the cuffs of her britches.

The waiter returned, but she feared Kid would recognize her voice. She pointed at an item in the dessert section. German chocolate cake. Tried to smile as he nodded and left.

"As we agreed in my office," Aggie's father said.

Bridget's ears lit up.

"We'll see," the man went on, "that she's compensated enough to stay out of our lives."

"Sir," Kid spoke with a matching surety, "we did not agree on any course of action."

Given the time of day, Bridget supposed he'd left Storz before completing his route, changed clothes, and headed straight to Aggie's. There, he'd wasted no time telling the family his news. They'd sat in a stately study and listened to his story, discussed what to do but not reached a conclusion. Was it then that one of them, perhaps Aggie, suggested dinner? Had her parents agreed believing the rich atmosphere would remind Kid of the lifestyle they offered?

"This is a delicate matter," Aggie's father said. "I'll have my lawyers handle it."

"Tate is my mother."

"It's ghastly," Aggie said.

"And your father," Aggie's mother chimed in, "a married man."

Aggie, Bridget thought, *tell Kid none of this matters.*

"Father, can you keep this out of the papers? Will they still cover my wedding?"

"I'll need your word, son." Aggie's father clearly directed his comment to Kid.

"Tell him," Aggie whispered. "Promise Father. We don't want her coming around the house. Wanting inside. Or worse."

"What would be worse?" Kid's voice carried a keen edge.

Bridget felt the question rounding the table.

"Is worse," he asked, "her wanting to be a part of our lives?"

"We could pay her more." Aggie sounded close to tears. "Couldn't we, Father? She can't be seen coming to our house. What if she shows up at our wedding?"

"Don't worry." Aggie's mother. "I'm sure she hasn't a decent dress. Though I do worry if she recognizes a sensible comportment in matters like this."

Kid said nothing.

Let them go on undressing their souls, Bridget thought. She let steam rise from her coffee. The situation stood Kid on the crest of a ridge separating two disparate villages. Nothing was simple. One village offered a beautiful girl he loved, a chance to become a leader in Omaha, to make positive changes in people's lives. The other offered less wealth, less influence. A mother.

"Please," Aggie begged. "Let Father handle her. She could be our ruin. What will everyone think of us?"

The waiter approached their table and the conversation turned to ordering. Bridget fought an urge to use their distraction and peek over her shoulder.

With the waiter safely out of hearing again, Aggie's mother continued. "You can't put the family under that stain."

"You just can't," Aggie pleaded. "You can't ask it of me."

"If you'll excuse me," Kid said. "Turns out I'm not hungry." His chair pushed back so close to Bridget she felt the air move. "Good evening."

She kept her head down, peeked up only when he reached the door, his back still to her. She was too stunned to call his name. And if he stopped and turned back at her raised voice, he'd have to explain her. He had enough problems.

She waited until he'd passed the windows and she felt certain he wasn't going to change his mind and return. Very slowly, she looked over her shoulder. She'd hoped Aggie had a wart on her nose or protruding teeth, something Bridget had missed earlier.

Aggie was beautiful. She sat erect, her spine inches from the chair back. Her auburn hair swept stylishly up. Like her mother's. Like Tate's. Aggie's large hat was a sweep of winter plumes and netting and framed her face. She'd checked her coat but wore a fur muff wrapped around her white throat: a fox pelt. The animal appearing fastened by the act of biting its own tail. For all Aggie's distress, below her perfectly arched brows, her eyes were dry. A confidence there said Kid would come around and agree to their demands.

Bridget faced forward again, surprised to see a large piece of chocolate cake with a corner missing. A fork tipped on her plate, bearing traces of chocolate frosting. She ran her tongue over her teeth. Yes, she'd been the one to take a bite with no awareness of having done so. She took a second bite and glanced over her shoulder again. Had Aggie ever experienced unhappiness for more than a few minutes? Before someone catered to her wishes? Before today, had she even realized Omaha had brothels? She'd sounded offended by the mere idea of a woman such as Tate. As though even knowing such things bruised her sensitive nature. If she had heard of brothels, had she believed they were inhabited by half-women? Never mothers who loved and lost sons.

None of which made Aggie bad. She had what every parent wished for their child: a life of sweet oblivion. Though she looked as fragile as a clay statue.

"Horrid." Aggie's mother rose from her chair. "Take me home, Howard."

The three left as the waiter, approaching their table with a tray of drinks, stopped to stare after them.

Bridget ate cake, drank cooling coffee. She knew she'd not picked this restaurant by accident. She'd known exactly what she was doing. She'd hoped to find Kid there. And she had.

Thirty-Nine

Standing in shadow at the end of the alley, Bridget shifted her weight from foot to foot to warm her toes. Midnight had come and the hour was gone. Kid promised to meet her, but as the minutes wore on, she realized the promise had meant more to her than him. She considered the scrap of conversation she'd overheard at the restaurant and tried to imagine where he'd gone after leaving. She supposed he'd let off steam, pounded iron in his father's smithy, maybe scrubbed Spot. Scrubbed the poor dog again. With his anger cooler, he'd likely gone back to Aggie and her parents and renegotiated the terms. He'd been put over a barrel, but he had to weigh the options with his future and Aggie's in mind. Make rational decisions.

What then? Had the foursome settled around a warm fire, a maid carried in celebratory sherry and imported chocolates on fine china? Had Aggie smiled over house plans her father rolled out? Breaking into a stable to help reclaim a horse would not be even at the bottom of Kid's list of priorities. That sort of behavior was inappropriate for a respectable man.

She took a step out of the darkest shadow and glanced to her right. Midway down the alley, Plum Cake's red lights still burned and over a dozen horses stood in the cold. Ragtime music and laughter spilled out each time the door swung open. The thought of sneaking through the trap door and sleeping in the warmth and familiarity of Lily's room made Bridget sigh with longing.

The risk was too great. She turned and started for the room she'd rented.

"Britches? That you?"

She'd been listening for a horse, but Kid came on foot. She wanted to run to him, but his approach was casual. He'd changed clothes again and wore riding boots, a sturdier coat, a thick leather hat. Well-worn, comfortably fitting. Not the hat of a banker. The brim wasn't as floppy as Papa Henry's, but worn soft, wide enough to shield his eyes from the sun and keep rain and snow off the back of his neck.

She smiled. "I thought you'd changed your mind."

"I gave my word." The answer easy. A man relaxed. "I had to wait until Cripe brought your horse in."

"Did he see you?"

"Give me some credit. Then had to wait for Betz to close up and go home."

"Betz?"

"The bloke who owns the stable. It's this way."

They walked. Had Aggie's father doubled his payoff to get Tate out of town? Doubled what Kid would earn at the bank? Bridget couldn't know the terms they'd agreed on, but judging by Kid's mood, he was happy with the decisions made.

Not breaking stride, he glanced over and studied her long cape. "That's quite the wrap. Fur-lined? Goes well with your britches and hat. You milk cows dressed in fur?"

"Milking wasn't my job." Did he remember the cape from Maurer's Restaurant? The huddled figure with a menu to her face like Goose reading a cookbook? How could he have missed it? "I fed the horses. Anyway, it's not mine." Though it was now.

The night was quieter than the night she'd found Lily rushing back to Plum Cake's, the knife that had killed Chet Glastner hidden inside the cape. She cringed, thinking about blood that might still be there. She hurried to change the topic. "Is there also a gray horse at Betz's?"

"Haven't looked. Cripe stole a pair?"

"Gus, the gray, is the workhorse I rode to Omaha."

Snow crunched under their feet and the cold worked Bridget's face. That afternoon with the sun shining, albeit in a cold sky, the thought of riding back to Bleaksville hadn't scared her. In the dark, with the temperature dropped even further, the thought made her hands tremble. If in the long ride home she lost Smoke, she wouldn't just be losing evidence. She'd be losing everything.

"Twenty miles?" Kid asked. "You rode a mule that far? Why didn't you take the train?"

"Too many would have tried to stop me. And I couldn't wait all day for the evening run."

They'd covered two blocks and gone to the middle of a third. Kid stepped off the sidewalk. "We'll cut through here. You're saying, in the dead of winter, you rode a plow horse twenty miles?"

"I rode Gus. Where are you taking me?"

"It's just up ahead. That Cripe's a real cowboy, ain't he? He's liquored up good."

"Then he'll be hung over tomorrow. He won't know Smoke's gone until the afternoon. I'll already be home for hours."

"Betz will know before the sun's up. Soon as he gets there to start watering, he'll send a runner to notify Cripe."

Bridget peered around them, kept her eyes open for any strange movement. Kid walked boldly, not bothering to keep them in the shadows. At over six foot, a part-time smithy and a full-time barrel slinger, he didn't worry about being accosted.

"What's it like?" she asked. "Not having to keep one eye open over your shoulder? Not being constantly afraid of some man jumping you?"

Kid slowed, looked down at her. "You been jumped?" His brows furrowed just beneath the brim of his hat. "Worse?"

Policemen stepping out of the night, nabbing her and June. Was that worse? They started again, and she thought of those she'd left.

She'd write letters, keep in touch with everyone at Plum Cake's. When she took the train in with Cora, they'd stop by and visit.

"Hey, you still with me?" Kid asked. He'd gotten a yard ahead. "Keep up."

"You'll leave as soon as you show me where Smoke is, right? Just show me the place."

"Why are you so worried about me?"

"If we get arrested, the newspapers will write a feature story about it every day for a week." She lifted her hands, made quotation marks in the air. "Fiancé of prominent Omaha debutante arrested in the company of a known prostitute." She took a deep breath and quick steps to keep close to him. "Aggie's family will be mortified, and you'll be in big trouble. Again."

"How do you know I was in trouble?"

"I don't." She swallowed. "I imagine you were, though."

"I thought that cape looked familiar. You best worry about yourself and quit spying on me."

"You think I'm that interested in you? And you don't need to worry about me either."

Amusement touched his face. "I'm sure you can take care of yourself, just not right now. Your little horse-thieving plan is a bucket full of holes."

A light shown in an upper window of an office building, but at street level only the corner lamps burned. "You said it wasn't much farther. That was six blocks ago."

"It's just ahead."

"Another six blocks?"

"Give or take a few."

She walked so close to him she could slip her arm through his. He might like that; he enjoyed her company. They were pals, real chums. Clap-on-the-shoulder friends. She wanted to plant a kiss on his lips, say, "There, stupid. I'm a female."

She wouldn't. She didn't need added complications to her leaving.

"Let's go over this again," he said. "We steal your horse, and if we aren't *shot*, we ride clean out of Omaha. Then you're betting on Cripe high-tailing after you, and his doing so is going to prove to the whole town that he killed your pops? Right? That's how we're doing this?"

She ran, getting a couple of steps ahead and stopped dead in front of him. He pulled up just short of knocking into her. "First of all," she looked up at him, "there is no *we*. Secondly, we covered all this already. Cripe will be too galled to resist coming." Kid could pick her up like a chess piece and set her aside, but his eyes said, *I see you. I know you're hurting.*

"Cripe is so riddled with self-importance," she went on, "he doesn't consider murder enough. He couldn't leave without trying to inflict one last insult. He cut off Papa Henry's braids. Probably for trophies."

"I'm sorry."

"I told you his mother was Omaha Indian. He pronounced it Oh-ma-ha. He was proud of her."

"Lucky him." Kid pulled his coat collar higher on his neck. "A mother he was proud of."

Bridget started forward again. "Keep up."

Buildings helped shelter them from the wind, but as they entered another block, ice crystals blown from rooftops and cornices peppered Bridget's face. "He adopted me," she said. "Legal papers signed by a white judge, filed in a white court of law. 'The white man's way,' Papa Henry called it. He'd already adopted me his Indian way by speaking it so. But with papers filed in a white court, he believed my inheriting the farm could not be contested." She stepped around patches of ice. "We never expected it would be a few years instead of decades."

"Losing a parent is hard. I never thought gaining one would be. I think children grow up quick so they can raise their parents."

As they crossed a wide intersection, the north wind caught the front flop of Papa Henry's hat. Bridget pulled up the hood of the cape and felt the fur brush her cheeks. "We're visible from four directions," she whispered.

"Always Papa Henry?" Kid's strides long. "Never just Papa?"

"In Ireland, I had my pappy, but he took Mum to America. I never saw them again." Her eyes felt dry, but she heard the sob in her throat. "Papa is too close to Pappy."

"Damn, you're hard."

"He didn't keep her safe. He took her away though she fought to stay. Keeping her safe . . . he owed her at least that."

"Do you know the circumstances? If there was nothing he could—"

"She's dead."

"All right, I hear that." He pointed at a large, long wooden building. "Betz Brothers Stable. We'll go around back."

The wool cape with its heavy lining felt suddenly too constricting. The weight gathered and bunched around her ankles, needed kicked out with each step. If they had to run, she'd peel it off, drop it in the snow, and hope she could retrieve it later.

Behind the building, they stood alongside the door with their backs pressed to the exterior wall. With no illumination from a streetlight and cloud cover shutting out the stars and moon, the darkness was deep, felt colder.

Kid held his hat and put an ear to the livery wall. Listened. After a moment, he put his hat back on, pulled it low in the front. "Ready?"

"This is where you leave," Bridget said. "You've done enough. Go back to your life."

"Britches," his voice emphatic, "you don't know your way around in there. You think you're going to give a little whistle and your horse comes dancing?"

She was thankful to have him there. She could get her own horse, but he proved the world remained full of good and honest men.

"Hey," he said. "No tears. This is the fun part. You ever stole anything big as a horse?"

"I'm not crying." She sniffled. "My nose is just cold. And I'm not stealing. You ever broken into a place big as a stable?"

"I'm not breaking in."

"You are, and I'm scared."

"Me too."

"I can't carry the weight of you getting shot. Even arrested."

His hand was on the latch. "There you go again. Maybe someday you'll explain why my getting in trouble would be yours to carry."

"It just would. Open the door and leave. I can lead Smoke out."

"Yeah." He pushed down the rusty latch and rolled the door three feet back on its equally rusty rollers.

"Really?" she whispered. "That wasn't locked. With a bunch of horses inside?" She followed him, stepping where he stepped, the darkness so thick she kept one hand on his back. "You messed with the lock."

"Could be."

The smell of manure and horses was welcome. She couldn't tell the stable's size though, and wished she'd taken more time outside and gotten a better measure of the building's depth. If it were small, only eight or ten stalls, they would likely have already met a night watchman. If the stable went much deeper, a man could still be rising from a sleeping cot in the back and reaching for his gun. "I could never have found Smoke in here."

"You admitting I was right?"

"Could be." Again his glad mood twisted her heart. That he had the space for teasing spoke to his future with Aggie. "Smoke? Are you here?"

No horse nickered in response or stomped a foot.

"Don't move," Kid said.

He stepped away from her touch, his boots sounding on the dirt floor, crushing bits of straw. Soft flutters of noise came from several areas. Horses, alert to them, swished tails over rough winter hides, shuffled hard hoofs.

Kid struck a match, lit a lantern, and held it high.

"How'd you know where to find that?" Bridget asked.

"My lucky night, ain't it? The lock on the door didn't catch for Betz and some fool left a lantern right there behind the first support."

She was too nervous for joking. Suppose Smoke wasn't there after all? Or suppose he'd forgotten her and balked when she tried to ride him. And Gus? If only he could be there too.

Kid hung the lantern. "Hurry." He nodded to the left. "Get your horse. I don't want to keep this lit any longer than necessary. I'll get mine."

"Kid, no. Please. You can't come with me."

"If a fellow wants to take a night ride on his own goddamn horse, there's no law against it."

"I don't know what I ever liked in you."

He started right without replying.

Stall gates ran along both sides of a center aisle. As Bridget walked down, her heart fell with each stall holding a horse other than Smoke or Gus. "Maybe Cripe tricked us. Came back and took Smoke."

Kid clicked his tongue. Then the sound of a gate opening, his hand patting a horse's neck, the swish of a saddle blanket coming off a railing, a leather saddle landing with a thud across a broad back. "Keep going."

"I wish you'd leave."

"This is hog-killing time. You ain't having fun yet?"

She wasn't. With every stall she passed and every set of eyes that belonged to a strange horse, she felt the walls closing in tighter. She passed two more gates, two more horses with sleepy eyes that did not recognize her.

"Smoke!" He stood at the back of a deep stall, his head high, a giant of a horse, his white coat looking like winter breath, his black spots blending into the semi-darkness. Wide-eyed, he tossed his regal head. "Kid, he's here." She lifted the rope loop off the post and opened the gate. "Good boy. Come."

Smoke hesitated.

"Come boy."

The horse started forward, his hoofs landing loud in the near quiet. She fell against his neck.

"He's gone," she whispered. "Did you know? We've lost Papa Henry."

Forty

Bridget and Kid reached the far end of Bleaksville with the sky growing brighter in the east. She felt brittle with cold despite the added cape. Her mind droned with exhaustion. When she pulled up Smoke, Kid did the same with his mare. "Home," she said looking down the quiet street.

It was too early for the shops to open, though lights burned behind still-drawn shades. The dirt street, small homes with smoke rising from chimneys, a single bank, single hotel, single post office, and mercantile—it might have been paradise. Or only Bleaksville. She'd been away for an eon and for only days. She'd changed in that time, but the town hadn't. A shift of such tectonic proportions as Papa Henry's death ought to have altered everything. One of Bleaksville's citizens, who'd lived there over seventy years, breathing himself into the fiber of the village, was gone. Where were the weeping women, the sashes of black bunting, and the men saluting in his memory? Still, this was home. She could collapse over Smoke's shoulders, and he'd get them to the farm.

"Hey," Kid said. Morning stubble darkened his jaw. "You're not planning to fall off that horse, are you?" His own was tired and restless. His saddle creaked as he checked the mare. "You need to ride with me?"

She glanced at the inviting space between his straddled legs and the saddle horn. For miles she could have been all but sitting in his lap, sleeping against his chest, his arms around her. "Now?" she asked, hoping he didn't realize how close she was to tipping off. "I think I've got it from here."

"Miles back," Kid said, as though he read her mind, "you didn't look so tuckered out."

She clucked her tongue, urged Smoke on again. "Try and keep up." They rode down the street.

"Busy place," Kid said. "No telephone lines."

"There's the telegraph office and plans for a switch board."

"Automobiles?"

"No petro station." She could feel Smoke's muscles relaxing under her legs. "Dr. Potter thinks automobiles are a wicked fad. He believes racing down roads at fifteen miles an hour is nothing but a speedy way to die. And he can't understand why young people are always in such a 'goddamn hurry.'"

"Pops agrees." Kid held his reins loose, giving his horse her head. "He doesn't believe me that automobiles have taken over cities east. I sure wouldn't mind streets without piles of shit everywhere." He reached down and gave his horse two firm pats on her neck. "Sorry, girl."

"What would Spot do without horseshit to roll in?"

"Cows'll likely still be around for a while."

Riding past the mercantile, Bridget saw the glow of a low light burning in the back. She could slide off Smoke and bang on the door until Cora answered, but telling Cora everything that happened would be hard and take time. Thayer needed seeing first and the horses rested and watered. "The sheriff's office is just down there."

They rode on in silence. In front of the office, Kid stepped out of the stirrup sure-legged and came around the back of his horse.

For Bridget, drawing her leg over Smoke took effort. Her knees buckled under her weight the moment her feet touched ground.

Kid caught her, his arm around her waist. "Steady now."

During the ten days she lived at Plum Cake's she'd scarcely had enough sleep to keep functioning. Now that she was home, she'd sleep for hours, even if the only safe place to do so were deep in a haystack. She pointed across the street to the town's hotel. "You can get a room there. Sleep a couple of hours before the Omaha-bound train arrives." He knew enough about horses that he wouldn't put his through the return trek without a few days' rest. He'd put her in a cattle car and let her ride too.

"I'll tag along."

"When you don't show up this morning"—the blood was returning to Bridget's legs—"Tate's going to be worried sick. She'll think you hate her."

"She'd be wrong."

"She'll suspect we're together. Blame me."

He took Smoke's reins from Bridget's hands and wrapped them around the hitch railing. "Why would she think that?"

Bridget glanced again at the sign across the street: Hank's Hotel. "I'll bet he's got coffee brewing."

"You want coffee?"

"After Thayer, I'm going to visit my friends Cora and Dr. Potter."

"Fine. I'm anxious to meet them."

"You're stubborn."

They took the two steps up.

Thayer had just opened. Fresh logs in the sooty fireplace had yet to catch hold, but even the small fire had the office warm in comparison to the winter air outside. Thayer sat at his desk, looked up when they entered, and blew air through the gap in his teeth. "Well, I'll be pistol-shot clean through."

For the seven years Bridget had known him, he'd had an unkempt beard, always with a thin rat's tail of tobacco stain running from his lower lip down into the bush on his chin. The morning after Papa Henry's murder was the first she'd seen him with his struggling, Cripe-ish mustache. There hadn't been much growth since. But his hair was combed, his shirt clean, and his badge shiny.

Bridget pushed back the fur-lined hood, removed even Papa Henry's hat so that Thayer got a good look into her eyes. "Sheriff." She hoped he'd forgotten their last encounter when she'd accused him of not caring. "It's good to see you sitting there."

"Where the hell you been? Whole town gave up on you." He looked hard at Kid then leaned to look around them and out the window. His brows scrunched. "Where'd you get that horse?"

"Cripe had him," Bridget said. "Just as I thought."

"That so?" He eyed Kid up and down. Again. "Who are you?"

"This is Kid," Bridget said.

"Ain't no kid," Thayer grumbled under his breath. He stood to his full height, his chest out. "You're a stranger to my town."

"Sir." Kid removed his hat and stretched out a hand. "The name's Dan. I came to be sure Britches made it home safe."

Dan? Bridget didn't say. She didn't insist she could have returned safely without him.

Thayer refused Kid's hand. He glanced down to his desk and two gold pieces glinting in the lamplight.

"I came to tell you everything," Bridget said.

"You turning yourself in?"

"I haven't committed a crime."

"I ought to lock you up straight off."

Kid stepped back from the desk, but Bridget saw the way his gaze went to Thayer's gunless hips, then slowly over the room, missing nothing: The two bolt-action rifles racked on the wall behind the desk, the pair of empty jail cells, and even the door in the back. She waited for him to cross the floor, open it, check for a back room or back alley, and the possibility of someone entering unannounced. He didn't, but he looked through the front windows, checked the street they'd just left. She wanted to tell him to relax. Bleaksville might look like a Wild West town—more like a ghost town—to someone from the city, but the people were civil, good folks. Even without telephones and motor cars.

"You're wanted for the murder of Mr. Benjamin Stowe," Thayer said. "And that fellow there," he pointed with his nose, "looks like he'd put you up to the murdering."

Though Kid didn't twitch a nerve, she felt surprise catch him. She hadn't mentioned she was wanted for murder, but she hadn't asked him to come. It wasn't as though she owed him an explanation. "I didn't kill anyone."

"Stowe's throat was slit with your knife. Ain't no bigger proof." Thayer's lips parted, his snagged tooth flashed wet. His gaze sank again on the two gold pieces, then lifted over to a newspaper clipping nailed to the wall: His picture and a column of copy. The article looked cut from a paper with the tip of a knife and a drunken hand. There it hung for anyone who came through the door to see. Just as Plum Cake's picture hung in her bar. As if to stave off an ache of otherwise unimportance and stake a claim on a single moment in which they'd felt seen.

"Cripe killed Stowe."

"How you explain your knife doing the slitting?"

Suppose Cripe had sent Thayer a telegram, or the police in Omaha had, instructing him to arrest her and escort her back?

Thayer's eyes twitched again in Kid's direction. "What you looking at?"

"Not causing any trouble here," Kid said. "Just listening to my friend explain things."

Thayer motioned at two straight-backed chairs along the wall. "Why don't the both of you have a seat?" When they didn't move, he sat himself, pointed again to the chairs. "Sit down right over there. I don't want no sit-u-ashun here."

Bridget dragged one of the chairs close, sat directly in front of the desk, and let Lily's cape fall over the chair back.

"As far as that feller, Stowe," Thayer said, "I saw Chief's knife."

Saw it when? The morning of Papa Henry's death? Or was he referring to the newspaper write up, the picture of Stowe with his slit neck and Papa Henry's knife below?

Thayer sucked spittle through his teeth again, a wet sound, and narrowed his eyes on Kid. "Now I told you, nice as you please, sit down." He was eight inches shorter than Kid, but the one with the badge.

Kid grabbed the arm of the second chair, carried it in one hand across the worn floor, and planted it directly in front of the door. He sat, blocking the entrance, took off his hat, and hooked the Stetson on one knee.

"I came home," Bridget said to Thayer, "knowing I could trust you, trust this town. I was afraid that in Omaha I'd be put away so quickly and silently, no one here would know I needed help. Might never know what became of me." Thayer could still have her locked up and delivered back to Omaha without anyone in Bleaksville knowing she'd ridden in. But for Kid, sitting behind her, watching.

"So talk," Thayer said. "Evidence points to you. Your knife, you riding off all wild-like, wanting to pick a fight 'cause you thought Chief's death wronged you."

Bridget fought to stay civil. "I was there when Stowe was killed. The three of us. I dropped my knife and Cripe grabbed it. He killed Stowe for trying to save me. He knows I can testify against him. He's killed twice for certain. There have probably been others, and he'll do it again."

Thayer rapped a thick finger beside the gold pieces. They shivered on the desk. "Weren't but two days ago Cripe dropped them Judas coins."

Bridget's mouth went dry. "You believe me then?"

"He's been a buddy of mine since he first rode into town. Deputized me every time he needed a week in Omaha to sow some wild oats."

Sow some wild oats. Bridget moaned. *A stupid euphemism to make boys using girls sound innocent.*

"I ain't keen on calling a friend of mine a liar," Thayer said. He leaned back in his chair, rocked forward again, and dropped his forearms on his desk. "It do appear likely the man who took that goddamn Injun's horse is the man who killed that goddamn Injun."

The fire caught and crackled with higher flames.

"His name was Henry Leonard," Bridget said.

"I looked into the law, and if it ain't just like I said," Thayer cleared his throat. "What happens to redskins ain't in my jurisdiction. And there ain't no mistaking that knife. A skinner's from wigwam days. Horn handle, eight-inch blade."

Yet again. Thayer declaring the knife was all the proof he needed.

"I saw that there picture," he stopped, drew the paper from a drawer in his desk, and dropped it on top.

Reverend Pritchurt's letter, Papa Henry's knife, and Stowe's grainy photo. A man who'd died saving her life.

"Seeing that there, that right there," Thayer knocked on the photo of the knife. "I rode the train straightaway. Even showed the police that note you left Cora. Gave them your name, said you were about yea high." He slid one hand off his desk, held it out as though demonstrating a six-year-old's height. "Red hair. They told me a gal with hair the color of damnation whored right there at the house where Stowe was felled." He caught his breath. "Where you been hiding?"

"With friends."

"Police said the whore claimed she didn't know a thing. She'd entertained men all night and fellows could vouch for her. Said she never did raise a sore word against a man."

Another day Bridget might have laughed. Ruby may have acted to the police like St. Philomena herself, but she'd carried a shiny knife—probably did again—and she'd used it.

"You want to run it by me again," Thayer said. "The three of you.

Cripe kills Stowe and the two of you walk away? Leave Stowe dead? You and Cripe shake hands?"

"I believe Cripe thought I was dead."

"This is damn informal," Kid said, still sitting by the door. "Shouldn't you be writing down her statement?"

"I ain't all that convinced she's telling me the truth."

"Britches." Kid's voice was low, even. "I'm tired, and this here is a waste of time."

"You there." Thayer pointed at him. "Maybe we don't do things the way you slick city boys do, maybe we got our own way of handling what needs done." His gaze slithered off Kid and returned to Bridget. "Law in Omaha asked me plenty of questions about you. I told ever'thing I knew. You riding a train full of unwanted waifs all the way from east."

"What does that have to do with any of this?"

"Well now, Cripe writ to the law. Seems you have a record there for thieving." He pointed to a wooden file cabinet. "You had family too, New York City said, but weren't any of them interested in keeping you no more. Cripe tightened up all them screws."

"Cripe started a file on me?" Bridget had never imagined. "Because he hated Papa Henry so much? I was eleven. I stole apples. My grandmother was starving." She couldn't bear to turn and meet Kid's eyes. In the half hour they'd been in Bleaksville, he'd already learned too much about her.

"I told them," Thayer went on, "how you thought you'd study doctoring. Right there in Omaha under their noses. I believe they was going to visit that school and see what else they could find out. See you was there."

Bridget blinked back tears. She'd feared all along that she'd lost her probationary status, now she knew for sure. Papa Henry was devastated too.

"Britches? You all right there?" Kid asked.

Thayer stabbed one coin with a thick finger, pushed it around to the other side of the second coin, like moving walnut shells in a shill game. "While you been hiding, the town had a special election. Seems Chief's murder set them thinking how there's a need for a permanent sheriff."

"Let me guess," Kid said. "You were elected."

Behind his desk, Thayer shifted. "I ain't just *acting* sheriff no more. Whole town marked ballots. Cripe never counted on nothing like that. Hell, I woulda never believed it myself. Now I'm the law in this town."

"Cripe must have told you he was never returning for his job," Bridget said. She turned Papa Henry's hat in her lap. She'd been struggling with a question she both needed to ask and feared asking. "Has anything been done with Papa Henry's body?"

"Cora hired boys to carry the stiff to the icehouse. That box's so deep in blocks, burning in hell ain't ever going to thaw him out."

She glanced at Kid, saw disbelief and understanding in his eyes. Imagined him saying again, *this here is a waste of time.*

"Don't tell Cora that I'm back. I don't want her to see me like this." She'd told Kid seeing Cora was next, but she'd said that minutes ago, maybe days ago. Before she heard the news about the police visiting the medical school. "I need to get home." Even sitting, her body was giving out. The longer Thayer talked, the more she felt as if he were climbing her back. His weight dragging up her spine. She needed to walk through rooms where two generations of Leonards had lived, talk things out with Wire.

"Him too?" Thayer asked. "You taking him out there? The two of you alone?"

Kid said nothing. His hat still propped on one knee, but Bridget saw a new look deep in his eyes: Amusement. He waited for her answer to Thayer.

"You won't be seeing Cora and old Doc today," Thayer said before

Bridget could respond. "Doc stopped to tell me he was riding out, a family supposedly dying. I didn't ask no particulars as doctoring ain't in my jurisdiction. Cora went to help."

"You've no idea when they'll be back?" Bridget asked.

"Well now, my crystal ball ain't said." The gold pieces on the desk looked like a pair of eyes gone blind. "Stowe killed back of that fancy whore house," Thayer went on, "with your knife. And you saying Cripe done it. But that there, Plum Cake's, I know that was one of his favorites. He swore to me a man pays a pretty price there, but he can count on clean whores."

Kid gripped his hat, pushed it on his head, and stood. "We're done here." He walked forward, planted his hands on Thayer's desk. Leaned down to meet him at eye level. "It's been a real pleasure meeting you."

"I ain't said we are done."

"You know where to find us. The two of us." He straightened, looked down his nose on Thayer. "Out there alone."

They stepped back into the cold. Bridget sank against Smoke's long neck, threaded her tired hands in his mane.

Kid mounted his horse. "How'd you say that went in there?"

She couldn't face him. "Terrible."

He leaned down, wrapped an arm around her waist, and swung her up into the saddle in front of him. He turned his horse a step and reached down to pull Smoke's reins free. "That's something," he said. "You and I agreeing."

Forty-One

The moment Kid opened the side door on the old barn, Wire bounded out and jumped at Bridget. She dropped to her knees in the snow, blinked back tears, clutched for minutes until he quit squirming and softened in her arms.

"Hey boy," Kid said. He squatted beside them, gave the dog's cowl an affectionate tug and rub. "Looks like you missed her."

Bridget knew Kid loved dogs, and in his reaching instinctively for Wire, he built another bond with her. *I'm here*, his action said. *I'm witnessing your sorrow.*

She led Smoke inside and on seeing Gus cried out. "You're back. I didn't get you killed." She fell against the horse's neck and hugged him. His being there was a gift of hope. With all she'd lost, and despite all the recent blizzards of grief, seeing him was a ray of hope breaking through, urging her to hang on.

Holding the bridle on his mare, Kid walked her back and forth at the other end of the barn, testing the reactions of Papa Henry's team to having a strange horse in their midst.

"Coming that far," Bridget said of Gus, "not knowing the way. In the dead of winter. It's more than great. It's nature acting different than it does." She looked into the horse's large eyes, watched the sweep of his long lashes. "You're a miracle."

"Or could it be the police found him?" Kid asked. He unfastened the belly straps on his saddle, slid it off, and carried it to the nearest gate. "Once he was identified, that friend of yours, Cora, even Thayer, likely had him shipped back in a cattle car."

She watched Kid slide Smoke's harness over the horse's ears and down, then gently tug the bit from Smoke's mouth. They were both tall, handsome, lean, and muscular. More than that, they were fitted to their worlds. *I need that,* she thought. *I need to work and work until I find the confidence to open a door and not be afraid a wolf stands just there.*

"You okay?" Kid asked. "You're staring."

Bridget brought her attention back. "Thayer wouldn't pay to have Gus shipped. Not without a guarantee of being reimbursed. Cora would."

All the horses in the barn needed attention and a show of affection. She went to Luna-Blue and took up a curry brush, patting and stroking the horse's flank. She'd avoid the place where Papa Henry's body had lain, gather strength first. When she could no longer refuse the inevitable, she left the stall, slowly closed the gate, and went to stand on the spot. The bloodstains were gone. "Do you feel it?" she asked Kid. "What's happened here." She lifted her arms, closed her eyes, and turned in a slow circle. "Papa Henry said sites have memory. Places like Sand Creek and Wounded Knee. The sorrow lives on. Rocks remember things, trees where there's been a lynching. The soil. It's all alive and remembers." She felt weightless in her turning, as if she were cottonwood drift suspended in the air. Suspended over a past that would forever be there.

"Christ, that's sad," Kid said. He was looking over the place, even up to the haymow where a row of half-feral cats peered over the edge. "There isn't an inch of land on this Earth where something bad hasn't happened. Maybe land remembers, maybe it doesn't. People can heal spaces if they set their minds to it."

She let him talk. Watched him hang bits, reins, and move into Luna-Blue's stall.

"The sun rises, spring comes around," he said. He ran a slow hand over the mare's swollen belly as if taking measurements and calculating how far she was in gestation. "Horses drop foals."

"But this here." Bridget knew she sounded pitiful, Plum Cake-pitiful, but Kid had shoulders strong enough to hear her out and not think she expected him to fix matters. "This here is my inch, where I have my life."

"I'll finish watering," he said. "Then let's get some sleep."

There's something he does with his eyes, Bridget decided. They say he's smiling, even when he's not using his lips. "You think I'm just tired?"

"Look at us. We're both asleep on our feet."

She wasn't helping with the work. Though she'd been in the barn a few times every day for the last six years, Kid was the one who'd looked around and acted: found a bucket, the water pump, and oats in the bin. Her mind said the chores were hers to do, but Kid was right; she struggled just to keep upright.

"Enough," she said. "They are okay for now. We can come back later." She started for the house.

Kid caught up before she reached the kitchen door. "Britches, find a good farmhand. Don't settle on the first bloke that staggers in here wanting a job."

She wasn't sure she even nodded in response. Opening the kitchen door, the air hit her with a slap, colder and deeper than the air outside. Dead air, as though something had been leached away, and something heavier moved in. She fought her way through the wall of it, lifting one heavy foot over the threshold. Then the other.

Kid's voice was somewhere near, but her head pounded too loud, and she labored to breathe.

She woke with dusk descending and the light in the room gloomy. She needed a moment to understand her surroundings. The room was warm, there the stove pipe running up from the kitchen, there her dresser with red calico hanging alongside the mirror. She lay in her own bed. She was home. Though being there felt like a dream she dared not trust. She might wake again and find this waking hadn't been real.

Wire stirred at her side, rose, and stood on the bed looking down at her. His tail wagged.

The smells of frying onions and bacon rose from the kitchen. "You want to eat, don't you, boy?" She wrapped her arms around his neck. "But it isn't Papa Henry cooking."

Kid stood over the stove, smiled when she entered. "She lives."

"What time is it?"

He pulled a watch from his pocket. "Almost five."

She swallowed a knot in the back of her throat. "The train arrives in two hours."

He set plates on the table, put crisp slices of bacon on each, and turned to the stove. "I'm not moving until half the food in this pan is in my stomach."

"I don't remember anything." She glanced at the back door, the last place she did remember being. "You must have carried me up to bed. Did you sleep?"

"Like a bear in winter."

The warmth in the house proved the rooms had been heating for hours. Which meant after getting her upstairs and before sleeping himself, he'd started the stove in the kitchen. A few short logs, cut to fit the firebox, remained by the back door, but to build a fire in the main hearth he'd had to go out, find the woodpile, and carry in. After only a couple of hours, he must have pulled himself from sleep, re-fed the fires, found the root cellar and the smoke house, and prepared a meal. He even had eggs sitting in a bowl, and since he'd not fried a couple, she presumed he meant them for breakfast. All while she slept.

"Thank you," she said. He'd brought life back into the house. Given her a many-layered gift. "You've done more than you know."

He turned potatoes and onions with a spatula. "Pops and I had to cook for ourselves." He tossed the kitchen utensil in the air, watched it spin end over end, and caught it by the handle.

"Goose would be impressed."

As Kid filled her plate, she looked out onto the empty lane stretching to the county road. "Has Thayer come? Anyone to do the chores?"

He shrugged. "Word must be out you're back, able to water your own stock."

She agreed: Word was out. Thayer had likely told half the town she'd returned. They'd told the other half. And yet no one had shown a face to welcome her back or offer condolences for the loss of Papa Henry. Would they ever? If they'd been told she'd murdered a man in Omaha? Was living in a brothel. With those lies, could they also believe she'd murdered Papa Henry?

"They're giving me time," she tried to sound confident, "baking goods to bring, planning to come tomorrow." When Kid turned his back, she slipped a slice of bacon as deftly as she could from her plate and held it under the table for Wire. "We should hide the horses. In case there's trouble when Cripe arrives. They've already witnessed Cripe killing Papa Henry. I don't want them having to lay eyes on him again."

"First you need to eat," Kid said. He sat down across from her. "That dog weighs plenty. You're lighter than an empty beer barrel." He picked up his fork. "I'm thinking we hide right along with the horses." He chewed, paying no attention to Bridget's objections to his staying. He swallowed and continued. "If Thayer doesn't arrest Cripe at the depot in town, and Cripe shows up here, that's all we need for today. We still don't know everything. Suppose Cripe bought Smoke from someone, didn't have a hand in any wrongdoing?"

"How likely is that? If he shows up, and he will, he's the right man."

"We can stay on this," Kid said, "see justice is done. We don't need to ride in roughshod and die trying to make it happen tonight."

"There's only two ways this can go. Thayer arrests Cripe or he arrests me."

"How the hell did you get yourself in this mess?"

"I woke one morning and found myself in a nightmare. I don't know from there."

Kid looked at her a moment, then dropped his eyes back to his plate.

"Thayer knows me," Bridget said. "And he knows Cripe. He'll do the right thing, even if he hates it."

"You keep saying."

"He didn't arrest us. He has doubts or we'd be behind bars."

"You saw the two gold pieces. Judas coins, he called them."

"This isn't your fight."

Kid stabbed with his fork, filling the tines with potato. "It's all right to accept help when you need it. Isn't that why there's so many of us? Quit trying to prove you're so damned independent."

His remarks stung for their truthfulness. "Aren't you here trying to prove something? You're mad at Tate and the world, and you're here because you need a dragon to slay."

"I'll see this through."

"I know you will. To stop you, I'd have to tie you to a post. I don't think I can." She stabbed her food as well, her fork punching through slices of potato and clicking against her plate. "What about your work? You missed today, and you're going to miss tomorrow. You could be fired."

"Already quit."

She stared at him. "You quit your job?" Was he going to start immediately at the bank? She couldn't ask. "Tate's going to be sick and sorry."

"You've said so. We're all sick and sorry, aren't we?" He sighed. Then a sudden eagerness brightened his eyes. "I have other plans."

"Of course, the bank." There was no use arguing. She'd met her match in terms of stubbornness. Something she wouldn't admit to him.

He picked up a slice of bacon. "I'm glad I came. Dragons or not. Seeing you with your horses, with Wire, not on your knees scrubbing floors. Being in this house where you lived with your pops, I understand your needing to get home."

She said no more until they'd finished eating and were putting their winter gear back on. "Before we get the horses away, there's something else I want to show you."

"Holy hell." Kid pushed back his hat. "What an incredible ship."

They'd left Wire curled under the table, walked through the dark, and stepped into the larger of the two barns.

"Officially, it's an ark." Bridget held the single lantern she'd lit, watched him walk slowly down the length, his gaze running along the ark's long side until he reached the far end. "I helped Papa Henry with the building," she went on, "which is kind of a lie. He was ninety-five percent done."

"You should learn to straight-up lie. Don't tell me you're doing it. I want to think you built this whole goddamn thing."

"I can hit a nail every time, keep a saw from binding, and measure a stick of lumber to within an eighth-inch accuracy."

He started back, slim-hipped, his coat open, one gloved hand trailing over the wood. "I figured you for that. An eighth-inch accuracy."

Bridget bit her tongue. *I will not ask how Aggie is with a wood chisel.*

"An ark, like Noah's?" He stopped, looked up at the height. "Did your pops plan on pulling down the barn, launching it on the river?"

"Arks aren't for launching. They're for staying right where you are and weathering the storm." She closed her eyes, took a deep settling breath, and reopened them. "He lost his son, and his people were victims of genocide. Smallpox delivered in nicely folded blankets. The ark helped consume his attention, challenge him physically and mentally. Fill night hours when he couldn't sleep." She hoped Kid didn't hear the small squeak in the back of her throat. "I guess all of that amounts to challenging himself spiritually."

Kid patted a strong hand on the oak the same way he'd done with his mare. "Holy hell," he said again. "How?"

"He first had to teach himself to read ship-building plans." She stepped to a nearby table and unrolled a thick scroll of pages. "Even teach himself how to rig pulleys and get them attached."

They both looked up, but the three-story-high ceiling was dark, hiding the brackets and hooks.

"Can I see inside?" He stood at the ladder leaning against the stern, his hands already on the side rails. He started up.

"I'm having it dismantled," Bridget said. "I'm going to build my own ark. I need the wood and this barn to do it."

He'd reached the top and leaned over the rim, looking inside. "Tell me that's another lie. You can't just take this thing apart. I've never seen anything this amazing."

"Everyone has to build their own ark. Papa Henry will be pleased." *He would.* "I'm turning the barn into a factory. Using this wood for walls and tables. Papa Henry's spirit will always dwell here."

"What kind of factory, and how exactly do you plan on accomplishing that?"

"The kind where a woman can earn a wage. And bit by bit. The way he taught me." She tapped a finger on the plans. "Not worrying ahead. Letting each step reveal the next. First is taking that down, saving the wood. I know of one sewing machine sitting idle."

"You'd need more than one man to disassemble this." He perched high above her on the oak rim of the ark, one leg stretched out along the ridge, the other hanging free, dangling in the air.

She couldn't look. Humpty Dumpty had sat more securely and things hadn't worked out for him. She set the lantern down on the table with the yellowing sheets of plans, each larger than a full spread of the Omaha Bee Newspaper. "Can you envision this place as a factory?"

"Britches, from scrubbing floors to dismantling a ship . . . ark, excuse me, to running a factory?"

"That would be a no, you can't imagine it. Papa Henry imagined and built this ark. I've lived in awe of it all the years we've been together. He wanted it to be an inspiration to me, just as it was for him. In comparison, building a factory will be small."

"Yeah, but—"

"But he was a man? I'm only talking about the first step right now. Imagining. That's only a mental act. Not a physical one. It's not climbing a mountain. Just a little push in the head. Looking at a spotted dog and not automatically naming him Spot."

Kid swung his free leg back, toes finding a ladder rung, and he seemed to hover a moment in the thin air as the other leg came off the ark and around.

Careful, she managed not to shout. She didn't speak until both his feet were securely back on the barn floor. "What time is it?"

He drew out his watch. "A little after six."

"You think I'm talking through my hat about the factory, don't you?"

"Didn't say so. But Thayer said you're also planning on medical school."

"I'm sure I've lost my seat in that class. It was probationary from the beginning." She shrugged, even as she felt a twinge of sorrow lift from her heart to her bottom lip. "The future is a long time. I'll try

other states, other schools. I hadn't wanted to go far from Papa Henry."
She shuddered. "It's too hard to think about right now. What time is
it?"

"A little after six, plus two minutes." Teasing, but not annoyed over
how she'd just asked.

"How many workers, sewing stations, do you think the place could
hold?"

He shrugged, as if to chide her from the impossible dream.

"If you can't even take an imaginary trip, you're the one in trouble."
Her nerves were frayed: being back in the presence of the ark, Kid's
high-wire act, Cripe's impending approach.

"Okay. I'll play along."

"At Plum Cake's, I thought about turning this barn into a place to
help women, but I couldn't write it down. My hand refused. What if
Tate saw and thought my idea stupid? Or someone else who'd laugh.
But there's a girl there, June, who can't speak her own name, and there
I was, unable to speak my dream even to paper."

He studied her, no longer interested in the ark.

"Doesn't a dream deserve as much ownership as a name?" she
asked. "If I couldn't write mine, wasn't I living as crippled as June?"
She laughed at his expression. "So I'm way ahead of you. I've written
out the plans a hundred times."

He started forward, counting off yards in long steps, down the
side of the ark into the deepening dark to the far wall. "Forty feet. To
within an eighth of an inch."

"I need space for cutting tables."

He came back. "You're going to do surgeries here too?"

"Worktables for sewing. I think I'll create a line of women's
britches." She swung a hand in the direction of the ark. "There's lots of
wood right here." He stood so close she detected the same scent she
detected on his kerchief. "You're looking at me as if I've gone mad."

"Not that," he said. "But I am looking at you."

"Yes, you are."

"Yes, I am." His gaze bore into her eyes, settled on her lips. He lowered his head, kissed her, then wrapped her in his arms. "Imagine this," he said. "We concentrate on figuring out how to stay clear of Cripe's crosshairs."

She nodded, hoping he saw only agreement, concern for the horses, not disappointment and longing. He'd kissed her but ended the passion quick, pulling her into a hug instead. Brothers hugged sisters; sons hugged mothers. Hugging expressed affection, but it didn't necessarily say *I love you.* Sometimes it only said *I like you a lot.*

Forty-Two

Standing inside the open gate of Luna-Blue's stall, Bridget watched Kid with side-eyed glances as he put the workhorses in reins. He'd taken off his gloves and, one by one, he removed an iron bit from the tack wall, rubbed the cold metal in his palms, held it close to his mouth and blew warm air over it as he approached the targeted horse. His efforts didn't warm the iron through but made the immediate touch to a warm mouth more agreeable. Even Gus accepted a bit like parting his lips for apple slices.

She tried to lift the rope harness she held, but her arms were stiff and heavy. The hour had nearly arrived. She'd rested, eaten, and shown Kid the ark. Now she faced her fate. Did Thayer believe her, or had he tucked the Judas coins in his pocket? She raised the rope again and Luna-Blue tossed her head in refusal, her white mane lifting in the air and settling back over her neck like silken angel wings.

"She's gone wild," Bridget said. "She's going to need a lot of attention." The thought carried hope. Tomorrow promised work, purpose.

Trying once more to slip the harness over the soft white muzzle, Bridget stopped. Her failure had nothing to do with the horse. Fear had turned her arms to noodles. "I can't stop shaking."

Kid stood behind her, reaching his arms around her, and covering her hands with his. "Here, it's all right." Speaking close to her ear. "Shaking doesn't matter."

That was true. It was only shaking. A business of the body, not of the will. It didn't speak to what she could accomplish over time.

"I'll get so good at handling horses I can join the rodeo."

He guided her hands, sliding the coarse lead over the tip of Luna-Blue's nose, up her long face, and over her ears. "Right now," he said, "it's a horse, that's all. And just to be clear, you're one of the bravest people I know."

Her heart shuddered. *Am I brave enough to live through losing you?*

He took his hands off hers. "Ready?"

"I'm scared of Cripe," she admitted, bringing Luna-Blue out of the stall. "But being here in the barn," she glanced at where Papa Henry had lain, "maybe I'm more scared I can't hold onto the farm. Maybe being afraid of letting Papa Henry down is the real reason I ran to Omaha. Not towards revenge, but away from the terror of failing."

Kid nodded. "All that's for another time." He looked over the barn. "Let's leave both lanterns burning. No surprises hiding in the dark on our return."

She pulled her coat collar higher and the hat she was beginning to think of as her own lower. They ushered the horses through the narrower side door and into the paddock outside.

"You know someone who can fix that door for you?"

"Papa Henry was waiting for a nicer day. Not spring. Just a nicer day." She took Smoke's reins in one hand and Luna-Blue's in the other. "I'll find someone."

Kid held two lines in each hand, bringing the team behind her. A click of his tongue now and then kept his mare following the procession.

Going down the lane, the cold moon overhead threw shadows across the snow and lit their way. The wind, like a great soul's breath, inhaled and exhaled gently, occasionally lifting wisps of snow that performed pirouettes and fell back. Bridget knew winter nights on the farm, welcomed the cold, the dark, the stars, and imagined the frozen ground waking under their feet. There was no rumble of wagon wheels, no jingle of traces, but the commanding noise of twenty-eight hoofs, lifting, scuffing, pounding, clopping. A wall of powerful shoulders advancing.

At the end of the lane, she led them away from Bleaksville and anyone who might be coming from that direction. Half a mile farther, they reached a path, little more than a break in the trees.

"It looks steep." Kid squinted into the dark drop. "You're sure about this?"

"There're no holes. It's narrow, but not too steep. Smoke's been down with me many times. I'll take him first." She held out Luna-Blue's lead. "You bring her. She'll be skittish but all right following him. We'll come back for the others."

"Yes, ma'am."

Trees on both sides of the cut had laced their roots together and rain and snow had washed away topsoil. A ramp remained, exposed ropey vines that formed thatching, and kept hoofs from too much slipping. At the bottom, they tied the reins of the two horses to low tree branches and climbed back to the road for a second pair, once again coaxing the horses down single file. "We'll leave Gus for last," she said. "He won't run off, and until we've got them all down, he'll see no one else does either."

When all the horses were safely down, Bridget lifted her arms, turned completely around. "This is Old Mag's clearing." The night's uncertainty still perched like a specter, but the land, the trees, and the river held only peace.

Kid took in the area, his gaze catching the silver line of the frozen river only a good stone's throw away. "This is a nice little shelter. It'd be a great summer place to picnic. Old Mag doesn't mind you coming here?"

"She loves company. Don't you, Mag?" Bridget patted the trunk of the downed oak. "Aggie would like it here. You could bring a blanket and pack a lunch."

His face looked even more chiseled in the soft, grey light, his jaw dark with a thirty-six hour stubble. He'd pulled his hat low on his forehead and the eyebrow he raised nearly touched the Stetson's brim. "She hates ants."

"You can't hate ants." Bridget brushed snow from Old Mag's table-wide girth. She sat and swept off a spot for Kid to join her.

He walked around a bit, found a fir bough, pulled it from the snow, and shook it clean. Dropping the thick mat on the ground beside Old Mag, he lowered himself and sat. His shoulders only a foot from Bridget's knees, his legs stretched out, his booted ankles crossed. He leaned back, resting against Old Mag and pulling his hat completely over his eyes.

She told herself he simply thought using the trunk for support would be more comfortable than sitting on top. Maybe he was right, but she couldn't exactly invite herself to share his seat. Besides, the space between his shoulders and her knees was still companionably close. He wasn't avoiding her. He'd held her twice before. Or was it three times?

"My God," she said, "I'm counting the times. How pitiful."

"I suppose."

"You suppose what?"

"Whatever you're supposing I should suppose."

She slapped his shoulder. "Don't suppose anything."

He tipped his hat off one eye and looked up at her.

"Never mind," she said. *Sitting on your little throne, your ass is still going to get wet.*

"You had no idea about Tate?"

"That she was your mother? She certainly acted it every morning, making sure her boy had his breakfast. But no, I had absolutely no idea."

"I'd gone to Ma's funeral, tossed dirt onto her coffin. You never imagine there's a second."

She thought of Lily. Sometimes a person does imagine there's a second. "Do you resent being lied to?"

He sat up straight, resettled his hat, and braced an arm on Old Mag so that he faced Bridget. "Damn right I do. I know they did what they believed best, but at the moment, that's not helping much. Worse is thinking I might never have learned the truth. Believe me, I'm not having any part of hustling Tate . . . my mother," he corrected, "out of town. I'm not sending her off to live the rest of her life alone."

"The only thing she wants is your happiness. She'd leave if you asked."

"All this time, I thought I knew her. But I didn't know a damn thing."

"She tried to keep you. She even hid with you a couple of nights in an alley, but she feared you'd die in the cold. She gave you up to save your life."

"King Solomon." The name given slowly, as if Kid couldn't decide between irritation and amusement. "The true mother giving up the child to save its life."

Bridget watched the horses, Luna-Blue at Smoke's hip and then a minute later Smoke smelling her neck. Even when they stepped apart, they never separated more than a few feet. "Papa Henry should still be alive."

"You angry at him for getting killed?"

"I'm angry at him for being dead." Her throat muscles felt caught. "I wish he had taken a gun and been prepared to defend himself."

"If he'd shot Cripe, even in self-defense, you don't think they'd hang a red man for killing a white sheriff?"

"He ended up dead anyway. Didn't he?"

"He left you with a life. If he'd killed Cripe, who knows what might have happened to you. You wouldn't be the most popular person in the county. I wouldn't blame your pops for what happened."

Bridget remembered lying in her warm bed, Papa Henry at her door, saying there was trouble in the barn. "It's not him I blame."

The frozen river made grinding, sighing, and snapping noises as though the ice shuffled. Trees were quiet around the clearing though along their tops, crests swayed.

"The engagement's off," Kid said.

"Really?" Disbelief threatened to knock Bridget from her perch. What was the proper response? A whoop of celebration or a lie? "I'm sorry." *A lie.*

"Don't be. Not for me. Or Aggie. She'll be engaged again within the year. Her folks will see that happens, and she'll be better off."

"She loves you."

"In her way. She'll be happy again soon enough. Because when Mommy and Daddy are happy, she's happy. Mommy and Daddy's friends will be happy, her whole social circle will be happy. No one has left the pen, and just as important, no mongrel has gotten in."

Bridget couldn't suppress her laugh. "Mongrel?" His seriousness made the comment even funnier. "How *did* you get in?"

His brows scrunched again as if surprised she'd need to ask. "My looks."

"Well, I don't see it, but at any rate, your looks couldn't have changed all that much. One disagreement with Aggie shouldn't matter."

"Every day I sat with her, listened to her stories, heard her opinions on mine, I was changing."

"Aggie has stories? I've misjudged her."

"Tate. Sitting and listening to Tate. I was a ham in a smoke house. Going from raw to cured. Not changing so much as I could see it, but over time." He bent a twig on his fir mat and broke it off. "I wouldn't have made Aggie happy. She wants, and she deserves to keep, the kind of life she's always known. But that life would fit me about as comfortably as these." He lifted Bridget's heel off the ground, looked from the size of her boot to his. "But I've no right to take that life away from her."

"You knew who she was."

"I didn't know the bank got rid of people through their lawyers. Or that Aggie would agree to those sorts of dealings."

An owl hooted in the distance, the sound mournful, harkening loss to Bridget. "Tate will be heartbroken. Maybe you and Aggie can still find a way to—"

"Not interested. A man lives with others, but he lives first with himself. I don't want to live with a bastard who'd sell off his own mother. I'm damned lucky I found this out today. I don't think Aggie and I would have made it to the altar, but I'm damn glad it's over sooner rather than later. It's Pops that has me worried. What you heard in the restaurant with Aggie's father was nothing compared to what happened with my old man. He's so angry at Tate for telling me, his heart's a lit fuse."

"Did he know you were spending mornings together?"

"He knew I delivered to Plum Cake's. He hated it. Still, he never imagined I was having coffee, making friends with Ma. He thought I slipped through a back door, met some bloke uglier than Goose, exchanged barrels, and was on to the next delivery."

"I suppose it's understandable he wouldn't want you to know the truth about her."

"It's the truth about him he never wanted me to know." He snapped the twig in two. "He believes Tate confessed to punish him."

"Ridiculous. She's your mother. Why do men think everything is about them?"

"You know all about men, do you?"

"I lived in a brothel."

"Scrubbing floors?" His eyes were laughing. "I can see how that would make you an expert." He went on, "Pops lied at first, claimed he'd never heard of Tate. When he came clean, he said he didn't know why I gave a plug nickel what woman carried his seed. He thinks I'm making a hullabaloo over nothing."

Bridget needed a moment. "Hullabaloo?"

"He didn't stop there." Kid lowered his voice. "Said, 'She whelped you, so what? Dogs do it, pigs do it. Men build skyscrapers, bridges, telegraphs.'"

She considered. His fighting with his father had him more upset than his broken engagement. "How did you answer him?"

"Easy. Skyscrapers, bridges, telegraph lines—ain't a one of them has a soul."

"Grandma Teegan would love you. You're amazing."

"Listen, don't tell Tate what he said. She doesn't need to hear his craziness. He believes his old-timer's nonsense, but geezers like him are sliding into their graves. Their nonsense will go with them."

"But you'll miss him when his time comes?"

"I'll miss him something fierce. I'm not saying he's a devil or a saint. Just that he's a damn fool."

"I suppose we all are."

"Ain't that the rub."

A coyote howled, then a second began yipping. The noise sounded close but Bridget supposed it came from as far as a half mile away and traveled unobstructed down the frozen river. The horses remained milling, even napping on their feet, heads down, necks drooping, eyes closed. All but Kid's mare, whose ears pricked at the sound.

"City horse," Bridget said. "She doesn't like ants either."

Kid flashed a smile, but had no quick retort.

She screwed up her courage. "You've quit your job and broken off your engagement. You could stay here and help me farm."

"I don't know the first thing about managing a spread like yours."

"You know more than I do. You know how to harness a team and . . ." she struggled to think what else he might know, ". . . things.

Papa Henry wrote it all down in a mountain of ledgers. Following his instructions will be easy. You're only a one-hour train ride from your father and Tate. She could spend as much time here as she likes. She's talked about a love of gardening and there'll be the factory too."

"You proposing to me?"

"Heavens no! I need help, and you said hire a good man. If I don't end up in jail, or dead, I still hope maybe there will be a medical school willing to give me a chance. A house needs people living there to keep out mice, fix windows, and keep doors tight." She looked up at the horses. "You're good with them."

"You plan on medical school, starting a factory, and running a farm all at the same time?"

"Living at Plum Cake's taught me something. You can run a business from bed if you hire the right people. I wouldn't desert you. I'd take the train home any weekend I could and help with the planting and calving."

"I can't." He lifted a hand to stop her. "I haven't talked to Tate yet, but she's got a right to a clean slate, a life where no one has ever heard of Plum Cake's. She needs to leave Omaha."

"But you opposed Aggie's parents when they wanted to send her away."

"They weren't suggesting I go too."

Bridget reached down, pulled her own twig from the snow and started snapping off tiny, attached shoots. How ironic that Tate and Kid would end up together and far from Kid's father.

"Tate needs more distance from Omaha than an hour's train ride," Kid said. "Reputations travel like wildfire. In your small town, there'd be no hiding." He paused. "You looking to see more of the world?"

"You just proposed, right?" She didn't give him the time to answer. The hole in her heart couldn't bear being stretched any wider. "I can't."

Every day she'd spent at the brothel, she'd considered running as far away as possible, leaving Nebraska, even America. Becoming someone new. And to go with Kid? What miracle? She looked over at the horses, especially Luna-Blue, Smoke, and Gus. She couldn't go. She belonged there on the farm, tending the land and animals. She wouldn't walk away from that, and she wouldn't walk away from the dream of being Bleaksville's doctor. If she left with Kid, too soon she'd hate herself for giving up. Too soon that self-hate would sour their relationship. She was home now, where she'd live surrounded by honest folks who knew her name and whose names she knew. The religion of community, belonging, and living on land, souled by Papa Henry's ancestors.

"I need to stay here," she said.

"And I need to do the right thing. Being with Tate . . . Ma, makes me happy. Don't say it; I hear how that sounds like Aggie. I can't let Ma stay in that place, though. Being able to give her a new life, in a city the size of Chicago or Denver," he nodded, "that would swell me up like a tic ready to burst."

"She wants out, and Plum Cake wants her gone. Tate's the problem. She won't want you changing your life to rescue her."

"It's not a rescue. It's a privilege."

"Maybe you and Aggie can work things out. She might want to move with you."

"Back to that," he groaned. "Even if Aggie claimed she would accept Ma, I'd know what she was thinking. I don't want to live with a wife biting back how she really feels. Begrudging me from day one. You can't hide that kind of animosity."

"You must have loved her."

"Thought I did. I mean, look at her. But that isn't everything. I want a woman in my bed at night that I'll look forward to waking up against in the morning. Someone strong and honest enough to challenge me. Someone beautiful who . . ." His lips pressed. He turned back, face to the clearing, and crossed his long legs again at the ankles.

The sound of the train whistle on the other side of the river made them both start.

Forty-Three

With the horses secure in the woods, Bridget led the way again. Rather than taking the road with its extra distance, then following the bend around and coming up the long lane, they climbed a fence along the back of the pasture and cut through. Cows huddled around haystacks, turned silent eyes in their direction. Reaching the paddock, they climbed a second fence and crouched behind the water tank.

The broken barn door lay open, the buttress kicked aside, the whole hanging wide and gaping by a single hinge. In the swollen circle of light just outside the door, traces of snow floated in the air like dust motes. A horse with dragging reins stood still and tense.

"That wasn't the horse in front of Thayer's office," Kid whispered. "I think Cripe's here."

"Thayer let us down?" Bridget could scarcely bear the thought. Her mind raked back over the conversation with him that morning. If he'd really thought her guilty and not Cripe, wouldn't he have arrested her?

Kid touched her back. "Stay here. I'm going to peek in. Make sure we're right. Cripe, not Thayer. I'll be right back."

"Then what?"

"One thing at a time." He looked around the tank at the barn and back at her. "Hey." He lifted her chin, touched her trembling bottom lip with his thumb. "You're the bravest person I've ever met."

"Well, if it ain't the Injun lover."

They jumped at Cripe's voice and spun. He stepped out of the dark ten yards away, the tassels on his coat moving with his approach.

"Inside." He jabbed his gun barrel in the direction of the barn. "I need my horse."

They obeyed Cripe's orders while he kept his pistol pointed at their backs. Entering the barn, the space felt changed to Bridget, the unnatural quiet like a presence. Even without the summer noises of flies buzzing and swallows in rafters, usually there were the constant sounds of horses snorting, pawing, milling, scratching on posts, cats in the loft chasing and tumbling one over the other.

They reached the first empty stall and Bridget slowed. The flickering lanterns turned stanchions into shadowboxes, posts and barn supports into dark barriers.

"Keep going," Kid whispered at her shoulder.

"There's no back door." He couldn't walk them out a rear wall and onto the frozen river. Even if he wished he could.

"Stop," Cripe barked. "That's far enough. Where's my horse?"

"You bastard." Bridget faced him. "I'll never tell you where Smoke is."

She'd not gotten a good look at him in the Omaha alley. Now she could see that since his leaving Bleaksville his face had grown meaner. Ruddier, tighter. He looked as though he never drank water. Took his whiskey with a glass of beer.

"Put the gun down." Kid's palms in the air urged calm. "I'll show you. But Britches stays."

"Well, if you ain't a real hero. You know what we call heroes around here?" He paused, as though the answer deserved consideration. "Dead."

"Coward," Bridget said. "You could have just taken Smoke, not shot Papa Henry in the back."

"That redskin?" Cripe sneered. "I wouldn't waste the bullet."

She tried to lunge, but Kid grabbed her wrist, held her fast. "You killed Stowe too," she said.

She and Kid were out of the coldest drafts, but Cripe remained nearer the front, his breath visible, his dull eyes tracking from them to out beyond the hanging door and back. "There ain't a court can prove it was me and not you."

"You'll hang." She'd not let him see her fear.

Kid kept her at his side. "Threatening him right now?" he said out of the corner of his mouth. "Really?"

"You." Cripe's gun jabbed the air at Bridget. "Someone needs to teach you a lesson." He unbuttoned his coat, the front of his vest visible, complete with rearing broncos. He looked out the door, checked the lane again. "I'll ask one more time. Where's my horse?"

Who was he expecting, and was he drunk? Bridget wondered. That would explain his flushing.

"I hid him," Kid said. "She doesn't know where. You and I'll go. But only if she stays."

Kid's grip on Bridget's wrist felt bruising. She tried to pry open his fingers with her free hand. "He's lying. I hid Smoke. City boy can't find his way at night. He'll lead you both straight through a hole in the ice." *Just as I will.* "Why Smoke?" she asked. "Why kill Papa Henry over a horse?"

"Stay behind me." Kid tugged.

"He could have *bought* a horse just as striking." Bridget's eyes stung. "I just don't understand."

The sound of clopping neared the barn. Cripe cocked his ear toward the gaping night, his dry lips beneath the dung-colored mustache sneered.

A figure stepped from the dark and into the pool of weak light. Thayer. His pistol rose.

"You came." Bridget sighed, relief racing through her. She grinned at Kid, "I told you."

Cripe seemed equally pleased on seeing Thayer.

"I'll take 'em from here," Thayer said. Beneath the brim of his hat, his gaze shifted from Kid to Bridget. "The pair of you is under arrest."

"What?" Bridget's heart dropped. Kid tugged again, putting himself nearly in front, but she struggled against his efforts. "Thayer! I trusted you!"

"Took your time getting here," Cripe said.

Giving Cripe a snag-toothed smile, Thayer moved his gun, sloppily, like a careless child not understanding the weapon's deadly power, paying no attention to how he handled it, swung it, no attention to where he pointed.

Kid tensed before Bridget realized what had happened. Thayer's aim had landed, the barrel of his gun sighted squarely on Cripe.

"What the hell you doing?" Cripe sputtered with disbelief and anger. "I was just explaining them the facts, how I come for my horse." As he spoke, he raised one hand as if conceding, catering to Thayer. "Tell them how free and clear you brung me that horse."

The revelation banged through Bridget. She needed no more confirmation than the malice of Cripe's voice and the look on Thayer's face. She felt as though she were back in Lily's room, Ruby making her confession, neither Tate nor June showing the slightest reaction. Once again, she'd let herself be too easily blinded. The morning she'd found Papa Henry's body, Thayer had stood in the kitchen. *A feisty horse*, he'd said, *will run off given half a chance. A barn door left open.* How had he known about the open door when she and Cora had already hefted it back up, worked a stone in beneath, and put their weights against the buttress?

"You killed him."

Thayer sniffed. His flimsy mustache twitched higher on the right. Then on the left. He'd also been drinking. "Weren't never the plan to kill him." He sounded almost apologetic, his eyes pleading with Bridget. "Him looking at me. That old redskin oughta stayed in his bed, minded his own business." His eyes widened at the sight of Cripe's gun pointed at him.

The barn shivered, rafters threatened to shake loose and fall around them. Grabbing hold of Kid for stability, Bridget thought to say sites do remember, but Papa Henry's entering, time flashing back, the confluence of two realities, left her mute. She saw the sorrow on Papa Henry's face as he stepped cautiously through the kicked-open barn door, knife drawn, Wire at his side. The sorrow at seeing Thayer, the man he'd known since the man was a boy, who'd played with Papa Henry's own son. The fear in Thayer's eyes, a man whose options instantly cleaved down to a pair: kill the Injun who could identify him, or flee Bleaksville and never return. Papa Henry realizing the futility of the blade he held against the gun Thayer had pulled. No way out, the bridge had gaps at both ends. Papa Henry glancing over his barn, Wire, his horses, understanding he would die there, but praying Thayer would not go to the house, to the daughter in her bed. Then his decision, warrior-wisdom, turn his back, make Thayer shoot him there. Reduce Thayer to the coward, haunt his spirit with his own cowardly act so long as the man lived. Papa Henry feeling the white-hot heat of the bullet entering, the drop to the floor, the swish of spirit leaving. No awareness of the knife being taken away, the cutting of his braids, Thayer sticking the blade through coat, flannel shirt, and skin, as if simply returning the weapon to a sheath.

Kid held her.

A piece of straw floated off the edge of the hayloft. She watched it drifting slowly down, felt uncertain as to which world it inhabited. This one, with Kid keeping her upright? This one with Thayer and Cripe pointing guns at each other?

The chaff catching light, golden as silk reflecting candlelight in a chapel, settled into an empty bucket. Something to be thrown. She couldn't reach it, but what might she reach if Kid let her go? The tack wall, ropes, an iron rasp, nippers. Closest was a pitchfork. At which man would she throw it? Could she hurl it far enough, and with enough accuracy? No and no.

"So you gave him the horse?" Kid asked Thayer.

"I owed him." Thayer tipped his head in Cripe's direction. "I settled our poker bet."

"Usually," Kid said, "a man bets his own horse."

"That weren't no man." Cripe kept his gun pointed at Thayer even as he tried to coddle and wheedle their friendship. "Redskins ain't us."

"Us?" Bridget cried. The pair agreed on their inferiors. Was the whole of their association based solely on hatred of the same people?

Kid kept hold of her, and she wanted to cuss at him too. *Do something.* But what?

"Since you been gone," Thayer said to Bridget, "ain't a lawman questioned me about Chief."

"That's right." Cripe's neck blanched in spots, burned in others. "We ain't got a problem here. Put your gun down. Ain't a man in a hundred miles cares about redskins."

"Thayer," Kid's deep voice held no accusation, only inquiry, "you're saying you killed her pops, took Cripe the horse?"

"Chief weren't no kin to her."

"Easy." Kid's freehand rose again, flattened in the air. "Just trying to get all the facts before you two muskrats shoot each other."

"Who the fuck are you?" Cripe asked.

"And you," Kid looked to Cripe, "weren't afraid of riding that horse wherever you pleased because you had an alibi the night of the killing. You were in Omaha when Thayer liquored up the courage to ride out here. You probably made sure to play faro in a room full of witnesses until the crack of dawn. Then a day later, you meet Britches, things go bad, and you kill Stowe."

"That bastard," Cripe's curse boomed, "ought've minded his own business too."

Bridget quit struggling. She and Kid had been all but wrestling, her trying to pull away, him holding her tight. He wanted to protect her, but he couldn't. If he took the first bullet, that only delayed her taking the next by a couple of seconds.

"I love you," she said to him. What else to say in their final moments? She tried to turn, make the cowards shoot her in the back.

He jerked again on her wrist, pulled her hand behind him. "I know. You can't help yourself."

With his remark, he meant to spur fight back in her, but she didn't understand the need for his roughness. He pushed her hand again into the small of his back and onto a hard object. She needed only a second: a gun tucked into his belt. In appearing to wrestle her, he'd gotten his hand to where he wanted it. He moved hers to just above the pistol, pressed it again as if to say, *keep it there*. She didn't dare look. She knew he'd eased his hand onto the firearm.

"The fuck you two doing?" Cripe asked.

"You don't want this hell cat loose."

"We can't let 'em take over our country." Thayer wasn't keeping up with the conversation. He eyed Cripe like a brother philosopher. "Redskins in braids farming white man's land, keeping white girls under their roofs. Hell, that weren't even Christian."

"Where are his braids?" Bridget demanded. It made no sense to care at that moment, but she cared deeply.

Cripe's reply was oily. "Hanging on my wall with the rest of my trophies."

Bridget wanted to weep not just for herself and Kid but for the horses waiting in the trees, the trees themselves, Wire, and every living thing. Papa Henry's killing wasn't about a bet; the real force had been hate.

"This's gone on long enough," Cripe said. He grinned too widely at Thayer. "I'm gonna put my gun down." His barrel dipped slightly, but his hand still clutched. "I'm gonna leave this here with you."

Bridget inched her fingers down, felt Kid's large hand solidly gripping the stock of his gun, inched them back up.

"This is white man's country." Thayer worried his justifications again. "White man's law."

Papa Henry had been right, Thayer carried the stink of guilt and it made him nervous. The longer the standoff continued, the more unsettled both men grew. Thayer nearly panting, Cripe sweating despite the cold rolling in and trembling the tassels on his sleeves. Kid sensed it too. His body hummed. His knees loose, ready to spring in any direction. *Do it!* She tried to dig a finger through his coat.

Thayer sucked air in between the gap in his teeth. "See here, the thing is," he said to Cripe, "why'd you'd come back? I coulda finished these two, brought the goddamn horse along again."

Cripe's gun rose a quarter inch, a half inch. He spat to the side. "Thought to spare you the trip."

"Ain't that a kindness." Thayer chuckled. A second sounded even less natural. "My taking a redskin ain't no count. Now we got ourselves this Stowe. A white feller kilt. These two here claiming they's witnesses."

Looking into Cripe's eyes, Bridget saw a man stalled by indecision. He'd wanted Thayer to kill them; Thayer to be standing over the bodies in the barn. Instead, he faced a stand off.

"You work for me," Cripe said to Thayer. "Don't go worrying facts. They ain't important. All you need to remember is I always take care of you."

"How you figure it goes with these two dead?" Thayer asked. "Me still alive?"

"He sends a bullet whizzing right between your eyes," Kid sneered. "He thinks you're dumb as a toad. Is that the word you used, Britches?"

"He didn't come for Smoke." Bridget spoke as much to herself as to Kid. "He came for Thayer."

"Shut your trap," Cripe hollered. And to Thayer, "You're the law now. Sheriff Thayer. I figured wrong. I don't need you dead. You tell any story you like. Say you saw someone snooping around in here. How was you to know the Injun lover was back. And that fellow there, you never seen him in your life. He looks like a killer to me. A jury won't have no cause to doubt you."

Thayer nodded and stretched his lips, his gun still aimed, his eyes watching the barrel of Cripe's.

"Won't nobody care," Cripe went on. "Accidents happen every day. A person gets shot, and all you got to say is you feared for your life. The whole town'll be clapping your shoulder and buying you a beef steak so big it'll take two men to carry." His mustache, like a smile cut into his face, lifted. "Lawman's got to have the stomach for killing."

Thayer tapped a temple with his free hand, nearly knocking his hat off. "I think they're right. I think you come for me."

"You're my pal," Cripe said. "I came to pay you. Those two gold pieces, they're just the beginning. I'll testify how they come at you." The tassels on his sleeves went from swaying to jittering. "By the way, congratulations on the election. Never figured you for it."

"Nice and easy, put your gun all the way down," Thayer said.

"Well, goddamn. You a real sheriff now."

Bridget's breath sucked in as she felt the muscles on Kid's back harden. Whatever would happen, it would happen now.

"Put the gun all the way down," Thayer said again. "I ain't killed a white yet, and I ain't figuring to drop them and catch a slug from you."

"Bastard!" Cripe yelled.

The barn exploded in a barrage of light and noise, guns firing from every direction. Bridget felt herself being spun, hitting the floor, Kid's weight dropping over her, the air knocked from her lungs.

At the edge of the loft, Mr. Fester looked down, the gun he'd fired hanging at his side. Six or seven pistols and rifles had all detonated at once and as many as a dozen men stood with him: Cora's husband, Mr. Graf, Dr. Potter, and men whose families she'd helped nurse.

Kid rolled off, tucking the gun he'd not fired back into his belt. He scoured her face as if to read there if she'd been hit anywhere. Satisfied, he stood and helped her to her feet.

On the floor, Cripe stared, sightless. Blood ran from a jaw gruesomely half blown away. Bridget covered her mouth and moaned. Thayer lay clutching his chest, his face twisting with agony. She ran for him. Pulling open his coat, she winced. Blood covered the front of his shirt, drowning his badge in red. His hands fell away, his head lolled to the side. She used the heels of her palms, leaned, and put pressure on the wound next to his heart. Crimson oozed, bubbled through her fingers and up the backs of her wrists.

Kid crouched at her side. She met his gaze, then looked past to Dr. Potter on the steep stairs, working his way down out of the haymow on his old hips, poking his cane, carrying his bag.

"Hurry," she called. Thayer was no longer conscious. She threw a leg over him, straddled his body for a better position, and put her weight onto the heels of her hands. She wasn't certain if that was the right thing to do, so close to his heart, but she couldn't stop. Thinking only, *too much blood.* "Fight death," she screamed at him. Screamed at Plum Cake, screamed at Ruby, screamed at herself. "You have to fight death!"

Dr. Potter reached her, but another long moment passed while he placed a hand on Kid's shoulder for support and lowered himself to the floor. He pressed two fingers to the side of Thayer's neck.

The flow of blood over Bridget's hands was quitting. She'd flung open Thayer's coat, knelt on the lining, her britches soaking up his blood. *Too much blood,* she thought again. "What else?" she begged of Dr. Potter. "He's dying. We need to do something."

Dr. Potter pulled his fingers back from Thayer's neck. "Son," he acknowledged Kid as he rose, using the shoulder again to help hoist himself back up. He looked at Bridget. "It's over."

"Isn't there anything?" She kept the pressure on Thayer's chest.

Dr. Potter gave a small shake of his chin.

Too much death. She couldn't form thoughts about who was to blame, only that there was too much death. A disease of death.

Kid took her hands, Thayer's blood running onto his. "Here. Can you stand?" He drew her up. "Step off."

She trembled and slouched against him. Blood soaked her cuffs, her knees, even the crotch of her pants—as if she'd bled there, helped to deliver death into the world.

The men were down, formed circles around the bodies. "A three-holer," she heard a man say of Cripe's wounds.

"Bridget!" Cora rushed into the barn, her cheeks red, her wool coat reaching to her ankles. She paled at the sight of the bodies. "Dear God in heaven." Turned her attention back to Bridget. "Dear God in heaven," she said again.

Bridget hurried for her. "I'm all right. It's not my blood." They'd reached each other and locked in an embrace before Bridget thought to say, "Don't touch me, you'll ruin your clothes."

Tate stepped through on Cora's heels, her eyes searching the crowd, settling. She kept back on seeing Kid, her uncertain hands straining in the folds of her coat. "Son."

"How the hell?" He walked toward her.

Tate made a tiny motion, pointing at the gaping door. "I took the train." She tried to smile and ended up biting her lip. "You won't believe this part; I rode a horse."

"What are you doing here?"

"I knew the town name. Cora and I met—"

He stopped her. "But what the hell are you doing here?"

Her face crumbled.

"Ma." He took her in his arms. "It's all right."

Forty-Four

Men muttered, discussing what they'd heard from the barn loft: Cripe's confession about a murder in Omaha; Thayer's concerning Henry. Adrenaline and the sight of the two bodies on the floor kept them milling, even after two had hoisted the broken barn door into place and braced it, shutting out the wind.

Dr. Potter used his cane, pointed to horse blankets. "Someone cover these men. And get a wagon down here."

Bridget sat on the bottom loft stair next to Cora, hardly hearing the condolences for Papa Henry, offers of future help, and generous "welcome homes." It was Cora who nodded thanks, and Kid who, after wiping his hand on his trousers, put it out and expressed gratitude for their coming, for lying low in the cold barn and helping to see justice done.

"Everyone to the house," Cora said. "It's freezing in here. Tate and I will start coffee."

Kid took Cora's place beside Bridget. "It's over." He wrapped an arm around her. "Now the healing starts. Slow bastard that it is."

Dr. Potter leaned down to Bridget, his thin black tie swinging away from his white shirt—the front still spotless beneath his overcoat. "There was no way to save him. The bullet entered the left ventricle . . ."

The dance of oxygenated blood, stopping there, pooling, clogging, quitting. Feeling dizzy and disorientated, she nodded, forced out an audible, "Yes." After everything, that it should end like this. "How do you do it?" she asked. "When does death get easier?"

"Never." He laid a hand on her shoulder. "And if that day did arrive, that'd be the day a decent doctor retired." He nodded at Kid. "Take her on up to the house. See she gets out of those clothes."

At the kitchen stoop, Bridget stopped them. A wagon rolled toward the barn, men led their horses from out of the orchard and from behind the house. Inside, other men talked loudly, all vying to be heard.

"Listen to that," Bridget said.

"Wait until one of them recognizes Ma."

"Don't worry. I suspect the only two from Bleaksville who'd recognize her are lying dead in the barn. The fellows in there are staring at her beauty."

"What the hell is she doing here?"

"Being a mother."

"Coming was dangerous."

"You don't think she can handle herself on a one-hour train ride?"

He looked down at Bridget. "I know, I know. Relax." He reached and opened the door. "But she's my mother."

"Someone needs to go for wood." Tate's voice, clear and harmonious, rose over the hum inside. "The fires are low."

Two men, both coatless and hatless, hurried through the door, nearly knocking into Kid and Bridget.

Just inside the kitchen, Cora grabbed Bridget's arm. "Let's get you cleaned up."

They passed through men waiting for coffee in the kitchen and others smoking in the main room beside Papa Henry's desk. Cripe and Thayer seemed the only topic of conversation. Men had gotten over their surprise, and now heads shook saying they'd suspected the truth all along. Bridget grinned inwardly at their perfect hindsight. Except, maybe they had suspected. Wasn't that what brought them out to the farm to hide in the dark with guns and find out the truth?

She let Cora carry up a warm pail of water and coax her out of her clothes.

"What happened?" Cora grimaced at the ugly black stitches. "Shall I call Dr. Potter to come?"

"Tomorrow is soon enough. I can't bear anything else tonight. Was it you who rounded up everyone?"

"See this here." Cora leaned close to the mirror, fiddled a bit at her temple, and plucked out a gray hair. "This is your fault. You had me worried sick."

"Look at that. You're first. You'll look like Gus in no time. How can I make it up to you?"

"By promising you'll never do anything so foolish again."

"You had Gus shipped home?"

"Well, I wasn't fool enough to try and ride him back."

"How did tonight happen? Kid and I were only gone about an hour."

"Thayer came into the mercantile this morning, awful nervous about something. Mr. Graf asked questions but didn't get straight answers. Early this afternoon, a telegram arrived from Tate, asking if you and Kid were here. Mr. Graf rode out and saw smoke rising from your chimney."

"All afternoon people were rallying?"

Cora rolled Bridget's bloody clothing into a ball. "They rode out but found the place empty. Mr. Fester suggested they hide and lie low for a spell. I was told to stay in town, but when Tate arrived at my door, there was no keeping her away."

"What about the sick family you were helping Dr. Potter nurse?"

"Rotten meat. Shitting for two days. Thought they were dying of a plague. By the time we got word they were so sick, they were getting better. The chamber pots in that house. Lord! When Mr. Graf arrived with the telegram, we were never so happy."

Bridget wrapped herself in a towel. "Cripe was elected, yet the town rallied because of doubts?"

"After Henry was killed and you turned up missing, there was quite the town meeting. More a shouting match. Some wanted a sheriff sworn in that night, said they couldn't sleep without one. If that's what you call an election. Most of us had walked out. He ran unopposed and received ten votes. However, that was the majority of those who'd stuck around. Maybe it was all of them."

"That wasn't a real election."

"It was legal according to the village charter. Those of us who walked out knew there'd be a vote, and still we chose to leave. I won't say I'm glad he's dead. I'm not, but I'm glad what he stood for is gone."

Bridget pulled open a dresser drawer for clean dungarees and stopped on seeing the red calico sway alongside her mirror. Was Grandma Teegan's braid hanging there so different from a ghostly baby dress pinned in flight?

"Bridget, why not wear that skirt you bought? I'll fix your hair. Like a lady, not a nest."

As Bridget came down the stairs, she saw Kid standing in the main room, the hearth roaring again, and a cup of coffee in his washed hands. He grinned at her skirt and white waist. "Britches," he said, "sit here." Mr. Fester occupied the chair Kid indicated, and Kid clapped a hand on the man's shoulder, all but pushing him out.

"Take the chair," Cora said at Bridget's protest. "I'll see about helping Tate in the kitchen."

She sat and Mr. Fester gave her a companionable nod. He didn't speak, but the nod and the look in his eyes said he was glad to see her back home and in one piece.

The conversation in the room was no longer on Cripe and Thayer. Had moved on to questions about beer. Men asked Kid about Storz's brewing practices and about the massive complex the company had built. No man appeared eager to face the cold again, but relished instead in the hour of community.

There's grace in this room, Bridget thought. She imagined Papa Henry behind his desk, nodding and smiling.

Forty-Five

Those who'd ridden out from Bleaksville, even Cora and her husband finally left. Tate still puttered in the kitchen, washing coffee cups and waiting for Kid. She needed to keep busy while Kid brought the horses back to the barn. Something he'd sworn to Bridget "City Boy" could do on his own. "Need be," he teased, "I'll tie their tails together. You get some sleep. It's been a day."

How could she sleep? She sat watching the fire in the living room, Wire sleeping at her side, crowding her in the chair, his front legs and chest in her lap. She ought to go upstairs and leave Tate and Kid their privacy, but going upstairs only meant she'd have to hang over the banister to hear.

Just as importantly, she'd yet to show Kid and Tate to their rooms and make sure they had enough blankets. She'd sleep in Papa Henry's bed, Tate would take hers, and Kid the spare room. Even then, knowing her guests were comfortable, how could she sleep after all that had happened?

Kid startled her, stepping into the kitchen, shutting the back door, and stomping his boots on the rug. "Jesus it's cold."

"There's coffee," Tate said. "Unfortunately not much else. I miss Goose."

"I could fry a couple of eggs, add a bit of bacon."

"Could you?" she asked.

"Won't take a sec."

"You need to know the truth," Tate said. "The affair with your father was my doing."

"Ma, that was so long ago."

"It's right now for me. Please, son."

Bridget imagined Kid's eyes searching his mother's. And Tate? How did her eyes plead? She'd missed nursing the baby, steadying the toddler, and encouraging the boy. Now she needed to explain to the man.

"I've cursed and questioned myself a thousand times," the rattle of a trembling cup placed on a saucer, "asking myself why I pursued a married man. The answers are always different. Was it just to see if I had the power to win him over? Did I want to destroy him?" There was a long pause. "Or did I secretly want to destroy myself?"

"You don't need to do this," Kid tried again. "You were young. Pops was ten, fifteen years older."

"I was old enough. I knew what I was doing."

"He should have done better by you."

"I thought so for years. Standing here with you, my grown son, I think I was wrong. He did the best by me. He gave me my greatest wish. He raised you to be an honorable man." She hesitated. "I did imagine his wife, unable to have a child, would cherish you, thrilled to have a beautiful infant. But the origin of that infant was too much; I underestimated the pain I brought her, and I'm sorry for that too."

The talking stopped, and Bridget tried to identify the sounds coming from the kitchen. A pan sliding on the iron stove, the crack of an egg, Kid using busyness to give himself time to consider.

"We sat and talked mornings for nearly two years," he said. "You never dropped a hint. I wonder now if maybe I knew. Didn't know what I knew, but knew."

"I've spent my life protecting you. I don't want Agatha to ever know about me."

"You're a bit late."

"Oh no. You didn't?"

"Ma." The word was slow. "I'm not ashamed of you, and I don't give a rat's ass what Aggie, or her family, thinks. You and I'll leave Omaha, get a fresh start somewhere."

"You're going to be married." Her voice desperate.

"Was."

A log settled in the hearth, sparks rose, popped and quit again.

"You're a good man. Live your life."

"I plan on it. We'll go together, but I'll get you your own place if you want. If one roof sounds crowded."

"Why ever did you tell Agatha? You have to fix matters with her."

In the ensuing quiet, Bridget knew they stared at one another.

"Kid," Tate took her time. "I named you Dan. May I call you that? Your father . . . you didn't tell him I confessed the truth?"

Wire still snored softly.

"You did," Tate sighed. A swish back and forth of skirt fabric, a fast but light tread on the wood floor as she paced. "What did he say?"

"Not much." The slide of iron on iron at the stove, Kid pulling off his pan, abandoning the cooking. "He only grumbled something about being sorry for how things worked out."

So, Bridget thought, looking across to Papa Henry's desk and imagining him nodding, *if Kid's parents can keep secrets, so can he.*

"We should go west, see the mountains," Kid said. "We owe each other that. I deserve to feel I'm doing right by you."

"I've shamed you terribly."

Boot strikes on the floor, Tate's muffled sob, and Bridget knew Kid had taken his mother in his arms. "You didn't shame me. Maybe you woke me up some, only that."

"I never wanted this, and what about the next time you meet a young woman and fall in love?"

"I couldn't love any gal who thought she had the right to judge you."

Oh, to be a fly on the wall, Bridget thought. The conversation was easy to follow, but now there was another long pause. She wanted to leap up, gather her skirt, and run in the room after them. Were they facing each other or looking away?

"If you aren't marrying Agatha," Tate spoke slowly, as if unwrapping a whole new line of thought, "and you want to be in my life, then I've no cause to run and hide."

Kid didn't answer.

"Lily," Tate went on, "spent the last years of her life hiding behind a veil. Plum Cake, you know, hid in her room, hardly leaving her bed. I won't live hiding in fear of someone finding out my past."

"What are you saying?"

"I won't live hiding, locked away from myself. I know everything I've done. Every right thing and every wrong thing. It's in here. I carry it. What others think about me has no weight in comparison. I've already heard every slur, suffered it all. I've spent too many years on my back. Now I will stand."

Bridget imagined their faces. Tate not giving up control, Kid studying her in his considered way.

"I'd rather face the judgments," Tate said. "I was afraid you would never accept me, but you have. A mother's wish granted. The worst anyone can do now is inflict the truth of me onto me. Cut me with my own self-hatred. I stood in front of a mirror long ago and faced myself. Had to. I needed the brutal, honest truth about myself in order to keep away, allow you your childhood. No one can harm me beyond my beliefs about myself. I won't go back to the brothel. It's no longer the only way I have of seeing you. Bridget has offered me a job here. I want to at least try."

"In Bleaksville?"

"Folks here are kind; they came to help her." A sniffle, a second. "There's your father. He's raised a fine son. I owe him for that. I can't take you from him. I can't take him from you. I know you love him. You must, it's your nature. If we go off somewhere, guilt will begin to fester in you. I don't want my mistakes to infect your life any more than they already have. Living here, I'll just be an hour away. Such a slight distance; we can see each other as much as we want."

"Whoa . . ." Kid said with an easy but long stream of breath.

"We can't know the future," Tate said, "but I'm not afraid to try."

"I quit Storz." A moment of silence followed. "From here I could keep tabs on Pops easy enough. Help at the livery a day or two a week . . . if he's struggling. If he wants. Britches is going to need help running this place."

Bridget slapped her hands over Wire's ears. "Really?" she screamed. "That's a yes?"

She wondered though, as she heard them laugh at her outburst, could they be happy in Bleaksville? Kid would have plenty of hard work to feed him. But Tate? Would she ever feel she belonged? Could she ever put down her past enough to feel truly welcomed?

Forty-Six

A row of five men sat along the backside of a long table. Men who did not suffer cheap cigarettes, Bridget noted. These men bought their tobacco in shiny tins and sucked on pipes with long shanks and bowls of carved rosewood. Their sweet-smelling smoke drifted into the air, swirled ceiling-high.

She'd been home six weeks. Papa Henry was buried, and for three days they'd kept a fire burning in his honor. Three days of tending, smoke rising, time for his soul to rise to the red road in the traditional way of his mother's people. Now, with the arrival of March, trees were still stark, but spring was on its way. Within a couple of weeks, red and brown buds and tiny, lacy green leaves would cover the branches like an emerald mist. Robins would sing.

The president of the medical school's admissions board sat in the center chair. He lifted a sheaf of papers, held them in the air. "Miss Leonard, a significant number of facts have recently come to our attention." With a stern voice, he tried to mask what Bridget knew was glee.

She sat on a chair placed for her some six feet back from them, not invited to the table, not welcome to sit too close to the distinguished superiors. She'd lost her probationary status, she knew that, but they had summoned her to the masquerade for the pleasure of telling her face-to-face. It pleased her. Had a simple letter arrived with the news, she would have written back, pleading for an audience.

"Miss Leonard." The president adjusted the spectacles sliding down his bulbous nose. "Your acceptance to this medical establishment was granted on a probationary basis." He cleared his throat and read from the top sheet of his papers. "Since then, new disclosures have arrived."

He'd already said as much.

"You were a thief in New York, arrested under the name of Bridget ... Wright."

Dragging out the name as if the discrepancy were of vital importance. More. A devious and intentional deception on Bridget's part. His white brows lifting, suggesting she'd tried to commit crimes under an alias and only steely detective work had uncovered the truth.

"Wright was my name. My father's name, my mother's name, God rest their souls. I go by Bridget Wright-Leonard now. That's my legal name, the one I used in applying for admission. Your records must show that."

He puffed, undeterred. "A half-orphan known for previous vagrancy."

Always the half-orphan. She sighed. To those without the imagination to see individuals, only the gloss of categories, a half-orphan meant living relatives who didn't want, and chose not to support, the child. Freeloaders who bred and then inflicted their wormy discards on society.

The man turned over the sheet he'd read from and lifted another. "Miss Leonard, you were a recent suspect in the murder investigation of a Mr. Stowe of Omaha."

"Sir," she protested, though she'd always feel partly responsible for Stowe's death. "I was cleared of all charges in that case."

He tapped on the first sheet he'd reviewed as if questioning the need to remind her again of the New York charges. "A suspect all the same. For which there must have been due cause." He peered at the two men on his right. Turned his head to nod at the two men on his left. They nodded in return. "January of this year," he faced her, "you and a known prostitute were arrested for loitering on the streets at a prohibitive hour of night."

She didn't answer. Did all the sheets hold the grand proclamation of only a single sentence? The more to lift into the air, rustle, and then lay back down with the gavel of his hand smacking the table.

"The charges include vagrancy, solicitation, and distributing illicit materials."

"It was a letter in support of women getting the vote, and an appeal to help the women who are forced to make their living in the most dangerous, unhealthy way." Their faces remained stoic. No eye suggested understanding. "You are all willing to admit a woman to your college, but you don't support her having the vote? Let her be learned but keep her powerless?"

"The records show you spent significant time at a well-known brothel."

"Plum Cake's, by name, sir."

One of the men gave a nervous sniff. Then tried to hide that with a forced clearing of his throat. They weren't doctors but wealthy business-men whose philanthropy supported the school and earned them positions on the board. "Our institution does not admit prostitutes."

The word said it all; their minds had all the flexibility and com-passion of stone. "The good women living there saved my life."

"I'm sure they did," he answered. Another sheet, another grand gesture of waving it above the table. "There is also the recurring lack of morality of your living the last six years unchaperoned with a male Indian. Many years your senior."

They hadn't liked the idea of her living with Papa Henry when they gave their probational acceptance, but they'd swallowed their distaste because of the weight of her qualifications. And their determination to have a token number of female presences in the class.

Bridget stood, her skirt brushing her ankles. She'd had two weeks since receiving the summons and knowing there was only one explanation for it. She'd gone to Old Mag, let a few tears run, and then gone to the barn to talk about the future with Kid.

She nodded at the paper held out in front of her. "That single charge is the reason I decided to subject myself to your little gathering. When I first sat before you, I didn't defend my father, and that sorry act has troubled me ever since. Put on another sheet of paper that Henry Leonard was the most respectable man I've ever met." She trailed her gaze down the table, met each pair of rheumy eyes. "Henry Leonard was a man of honor and principle. I don't know how you live with your daughters, why the idea of a father and daughter under the same roof disturbs you. And I dare not consider it."

Faces jerked in surprise. Teeth clamped on ivory pipe tips.

"Honorable Henry Leonard," Bridget went on, "did not sheepishly follow and obey the opinions of supposed superiors. To his death."

They puffed. They lifted chins to pull sagging skin from too-tight collars.

She'd come to clear her own conscience and speak for Papa Henry. She had. "Thank you for your time." She turned to leave.

"Should you request admission to any other medical school," the man's voice struck her back, "they will be served the file."

She turned around, faced them.

The groups' spokesman took a deep, angry breath. "There's not a medical school in the country that will have you. Schools have their reputations to protect, the reputations of their graduates, and the reputations of their donors."

There it was. Their reputations. She emulated Tate, tried to stand tall but not threatening. They feared her—at least what she represented. Which was a future where their ideas no longer held sway. Frightened as wet hens, they feared being left behind. She looked down the line again. Gray and grizzled, they were the past, a time of counted days and old men. The world changed rapidly around them, and they would shortly be replaced. They knew women would one day get the vote and fill governments, businesses, and medical schools. With their moldy ideas and decomposing hearts, they were fighting to stay relevant in a world that waited—more impatiently every day—for them to move on.

She pitied them. What was it to see the only world you've known passing away? That fear had to carry pain.

"Gentlemen," she said. "Good day."

She'd sit in the courtyard for a few minutes, feel the sun on her face, listen to the winter birds, and then walk on and visit her friends at Plum Cake's. She'd continue her rounds with Dr. Potter for as long as he was willing and able to climb in and out of his buggy. Though he'd yet to receive any response, he'd posted ads in papers asking for doctors interested in a rural practice with a "qualified assistant." Whether that doctor ever arrived or not, she'd continue studying. That row of men, despite their assumptions, did not speak for admission boards across the country. And even if they were correct, midwifery did not require a license. There was no law against setting broken bones, cleaning out wounds, even suturing. She'd be a healer one way or another.

Back in Bleaksville, Bridget stepped off the depot platform and accepted Kid's hand up into the wagon. Wire and Spot climbed over each other to be the one to sit in her lap.

"Ma has dinner waiting," Kid said. He shook the reins. "Step on there, Gus."

They rolled down the street where Cora stopped sweeping the walk in front of the mercantile to shout out a greeting.

"Good evening," Bridget shouted back.

They crossed Nettle Creek and faced the road leading back to the farm before Kid snapped his fingers at Spot and Wire. "That's enough, you two. In the back, it's my turn."

She leaned against him and felt the welcome pressure of his arm around her shoulder.

"Bastards," he said.

He hadn't had to ask. "I'm all right." She smiled. "The future is a wide-open place full of medical schools. This year, next year."

"And by God, I know you'll find one."

Forty-Seven
Bridget

This journal Tate bought me is nearly full. I'm ready to finish it and close the cover.

The calamity of losing two citizens in a gunfight has shaken Bleaksville and made the Omaha papers: **Lawmen Killed in Shootout.** From there, the story became a wildfire, sweeping through papers across the country. That's prompted the town board to do what they can to refashion the town's reputation. For starters, they plan to change the name Bleaksville to something less gloomy. Nettle Creek is the current favorite. They also need a new sheriff. Kid's name is on the ballot, though it took impossible effort from Tate and me to talk him into running. For decades before Thayer and Cripe, Bleaksville hadn't had a murder. Kid's counting on Nettle Creek never having one. If he wins the election, he's confident he can continue his work on the farm and still help his pa on occasion at the smithy. He doesn't want to do anymore sheriffing than being seen walking up and down main street a time or two a week.

He doesn't say so, but I wonder if he's thinking being sheriff will stop any chatter over Tate living just outside town. An ex-woman-of-the-night. Stop any bloke supposing he'll take a late-night ride out.

Mr. Fester works with Kid. He was the first man hired. Kid works him hard. They're taking the ark down and building tables. I don't know how long Mr. Fester's good behavior will hold. Having a job, a paycheck, something to feel pride in—so far he's clinging to those and going through the work of building himself back into a man. I think of Chet Glastner and how things might have been if he'd not smashed his hand. How might things have been for Mr. Fester if it had rained that awful summer and the tornado that ripped apart his house and barn had touched down just a quarter mile east or west of his place? I think of him with his misfortunes as a broken statue, and his last tragedy as Plum Cake's wide hand sweeping St. Philomena to the floor yet again. Humans aren't meant to live poorer than the mice in their walls. Abject poverty strikes them blind. Sightless, they thrash, and their fists hit those standing closest.

I like knowing where Mr. Fester is and seeing sweat roll off his face. I like seeing him and Kid grinning and discussing how best to change an ark into rooms. If Cora can forgive me for running off, Kid forgive Tate and his pops, June forgive Ruby for slitting Chet's throat, and if I can live without judging the girls who work the upstairs rooms at Plum Cake's, then I can try and forgive Mr. Fester.

I can't solve every social problem. No man or god since the beginning of time has been able to accomplish the feat. The best I can do is become a country doctor, or healer, helping and earning the community's trust.

I hope some of Plum Cake's workers will come when the factory opens. Especially June and the two youngest girls. Hassie has said she will not. She oversees the brothel now, and she's convinced Plum Cake to let June have Lily's room. June is working with Sadie, serving as part-time housekeeper and part-time cook helping Goose. He hasn't opened his dream shop, The Bar-kery, but he bakes in Plum Cake's big kitchen and carts his cakes, candies, and tortes to restaurants interested in buying them. Word is out, and orders come in for special cakes.

Plum Cake is up and wearing dresses with both a front and back. She's dressed from noon to the last ghost's departure. She wanders through the bar, poses by her picture, though she mostly sits in the kitchen, whipping or chopping for Goose, talking to the girls as they come and go throughout the day. Ruby left Omaha. A few days after June moved downstairs, Ruby boarded a train, leaving behind everything she owned. Even her story. What more telltale sign? I believe she left intent on finishing what she'd tried in the chapel. This time, she got a room far away. Some place where her body couldn't be identified, and she'd go into an unmarked grave. A clean disappearance. Not even a stone from this world hounding her sleep.

Kid and I tease each other about getting married. He says he'll never ask because I'll turn him down just to be stubborn. He'll wait until I do. I will. In time. Right now, we both know it's too soon.

I've sat along the river many days waiting for the deer to return. Hoping for the messengers to serve as bookends. A sign as striking as the biblical rainbow, promising the world will never again be destroyed by floods. But the world shifts. Shifts again and refuses to stand still. Grief blows doors off hinges, but we survive by planting our feet amongst our families and friends, and by braiding our souls into one iron chain.

Closing this journal, I dip my pen and end with those who are gone and very much still with me: *Ruby, Lily, Papa Henry.*

About the Author

Margaret Lukas taught writing for several years at the University of Nebraska. Her award-winning short story, "The Yellow Bird," was made into a short by Smiling Toad Productions in Canada and premiered at the Cannes Film Festival. Lukas has writings in anthologies, magazines, and online. Her debut novel, *Farthest House*, received a Nebraska Arts Council Fellowship Award. *River People*, her second novel, won a High Plains Book Award, and is the first book in her River Women historical women's fiction series. She lives in Omaha with her husband.

Other Books by Margaret Lukas

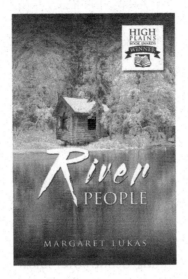

Book 1 in the River Women series

River People is a powerful novel with unforgettable characters.

In Nebraska in the late 1890s, seventeen-year-old Effie and eleven-year-old Bridget must struggle to endure at a time when women and children have few rights and society looks upon domestic abuse as a private, family matter.

The story is told through the eyes of the girls as they learn to survive under grueling circumstances. *River People* is a novel of inspiration, love, loss, and renewal.

"Wonderfully redemptive, *River People* brings alive a surprising group of underdogs, their life in the backwaters, and a scoundrel or two who care more for propriety than taking care of their own. A spirited tale of early Omaha you will want to share with your friends."

– Theodore Wheeler,
author of *Kings of Broken Things*

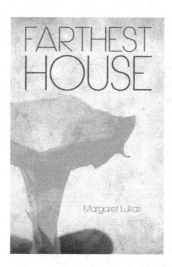

When Willow is born and her mother dies moments later, only the narrator of this spellbinding debut novel knows the death isn't from complications of childbirth. Amelie-Anais, buried on the Nebraska hilltop where the family home resides, tells the story of deceit, survival, and love from beyond the grave. Following Willow's life and Willow's incredible passion to paint despite loneliness, a physical handicap, and being raised by a father plagued with secrets, Amelie-Anais weaves together the lives of four enigmatic generations.